I0550184

RAIN FUND

Marc Brem

Fons Sapientiae Publishing

ISBN 978-0-9569907-9-2

Published in the United Kingdom by Fons Sapientiae Publishing, Cambridge, United Kingdom

To Oliver Maximilian and the miracle of new life

Foreword

This is a work of fiction, but highly plausible. The facts on which it is based have been verified. Computer hardware viruses are technically trivial; they do exist and are virtually impossible to find out. The numerous bits and pieces of a computer are manufactured by an intricate network of subcontractors, generally located in Asia. They cannot be all tested, and even so, their testing would be difficult and prohibitively expensive. The imbedding of hardware viruses into sensitive computers by criminal or intelligence organizations is therefore far from far-fetched.

The mathematical prowess of some autistic savants has been widely documented. Their ability to discern patterns in numbers is a fact, and their potential use in the financial industry is a no-brainer.

In the same vein, Latvia has really been dubbed "a Mafia State" by its own Prime Minister, and the Turks and Caicos Islands are a fiscal paradise living off tax evasion.

But, as mentioned, this is a work of fiction. The events, institutions and characters described are entirely made up. Any resemblance to actual persons, living or dead, is entirely coincidental.

Prologue

Three years ago.

Sin Kiang Army base, Alashan plateau, Gobi Desert, Northern China

Today was to be a fateful day for the Sin Kiang base: A great day for China that nobody should know about; a bad day for China's enemies and a very bad day for a few dozen Chinese citizens.

Sin Kiang army base looked just like any other remote army outpost for training infantry recruits of the glorious People's Liberation Army: A few corrugated roof-barracks and training grounds, everything swept continuously by grit-bearing desert winds. The strange patterns the different sand concentrations were creating were the only entertainment for miles. Nights were cold. Days were hot and dry. It was a bleak place where visibility was often reduced by sand storms, and that was probably one of the reasons it had been chosen for the "project". Not that in any case would have satellite imagery detected anything other than basic soldiery training and normal troop movements, but one can never be too careful. This was, in fact, a special base: Below the innocuous-looking surface, was where the real work was being done. Engineers and programmers were working arduously in well-lit underground air-conditioned rooms. They were dressed in regular unadorned army fatigues, and it was made sure that their behavior, in the little free time that they had, would look like that of any regular soldier. China is one of the few countries were total secrecy is achievable, a tribute to the efficiency of a right mixture of discipline and repression. And China being the largest standing army in the world with more than three million members, who would be interested in a remote base where a few hundred grunts were training to jump ditches and fences?

In charge of this facility, over- and under-ground, was General Wong Zhuang Wei, in the Chinese name order requiring family name first. No insignia was showing his rank, and for good reason: What would such a high-grade officer be doing in such an unimportant forsaken place? The base was, uncharacteristically, not dependent of the Lanzhou Military Region command: It was a self-standing special military project, reporting directly to Beijing.

A knock on the door caused General Wong to lift his eyes from the document he was reading.

'Come in'. He quickly removed his reading glasses and threw them on the large desk, as if he did not need them. He looked up at his aide standing to attention.

General Wong was old and felt so. He was thin and wiry. At 75, his eyes, bones, joints, and everything else ached. But, regardless of his small stature and age, he was intense and sustained by his life-long ideology of old-school hard communism. He had been raised by fanatical communist parents, being constantly reminded that he was born in a soldier camp during Mao Zedong's famous Long March. It was therefore no wonder that he despised the new generation of free-enterprise geeks running Beijing nowadays. He was part of the nucleus of old-timers making sure in the Politburo that this state of things did not get worse. He was thankful that, at least, the army was still controlled by both the state and the Party through two different, but equally weighted committees. His office was an image of his personality: Windowless and Spartan. A huge desk covered every inch with documents and no computer, which was ironic in the context of the "project". A map of the world. And an old-fashioned picture of Mao. General Wong's uniform was unadorned, but his rank and power were seeping through. It was easy to underestimate him, but General Wong was very bright, spoke five languages and was extremely familiar with the ways of the Western world.

By a slight widening of the eyes, he signaled the standing Colonel Jeung that he was free to speak. Jeung was tall for a Chinese, and only 40 years old. In spite of being a career soldier, he was also wearing an insigne-less uniform. He had been General Wong's aide for over three difficult years.

'Project *Peng* roll-down has been completed to the last detail and all traces and documentation have been erased, as planned'

'Then you know what you have to do, Colonel. The last part of the project close: The removal of all witnesses', Wong cut in a sandpaper voice. 'And no hesitation. This is a matter of National security'.

Jeung blanched. He was still standing at attention and sweat was visible on his forehead. He was about to say something.

'You are a good soldier, Colonel Jeung. But you are young and have grown soft in too comfortable times. I have the perspective of history that you have not: China has to take its rightful place in the world, and if the price is the life of 183 of its citizens, then so be it. What they have achieved is going to save a thousand times more lives in the future. But secrecy is paramount. They have to be eliminated and this facility has to be destroyed without any traces. You know it, and you have known it for a long time'.

The fact that China was destined to be the most prominent nation in the world was polyglot Wong's favorite subject. And his life's goal. He quoted to Jeung, for the millionth time: '*Quand la Chine s'eveillera, le monde tremblera*', his favorite aphorism from the French Intellectual Alain Peyrefitte who wrote already in 1973 a book so titled. Fanatic General Wong's was an intelligent man: he had doctorates in philosophy and in political science. His being both fanatical and educated made him even more frightening.

Jeung flinched but he had to hold his ground one more time. He was a decent man. General Wong was not someone to cross, but this was simply mass-murder. 'But, General. These people are talented and brilliant patriots, who can still do great things for our cause!'. They had had this discussion before, and it was hopeless.

Wong slammed his desk with his fist. 'Enough! We have been over this countless times. And now is hour zero. You have your orders, Colonel'.

Wong grimaced as he felt he had hurt his wrist. 'After all workers have been eliminated and disposed of, report here for the start of the military evacuation and base destruction protocols'.

A discomfited Jeung saluted briskly and turned around. As he opened the door, Wong called after him: 'Colonel!'

'Yes, general'

'Remember what a great American revolutionary once said', Wong said slowly with emphasis on the "American",' Three may keep a secret, if two of them are dead'.

'Yes, General'. Without turning back, he closed the door behind him. He had heard this Benjamin Franklin quote a thousand times.

Wong reclined in his chair sighing and massaging his wrist. He was wondering how was his revolution to be won with sissies like Jeung?

After closing the door behind him, Jeung stopped to take a deep breath. His hands were shaking, and he was covered in sweat despite the air-conditioning. He steeled himself and followed the neon-lighted narrow corridor towards the holding cells where the workers of the base had been placed earlier, uncomprehending. The damp and bare concrete hallway was weighing even more on the dread overcoming him. Jeung was wondering if he could go through with it. Placing the barrel of his handgun to the back of the head of a kneeling man he knew and appreciated? Pull the trigger? He imagined feeling the detonation, the tremor in his shooting arm and the warmth of the viscous gore. He suddenly felt sick. He stopped, turned around and ran to the toilets he had passed at the start of the corridor. He rushed into the first stall, falling on his knees to vomit into the bowl. After a few minutes retching and crying, he went to the stainless steel sinks to rinse his mouth and freshen up. The mirror reflected an ashen broken man. Steeling himself, he started rationalizing as he exited the toilets, thankful they had been unoccupied. What could he do? Refusing his orders would do no good but add him to the list of today's victims. And this project was really important. While he was treading towards the most difficult moment of his life, he tried to remember the lectures about *Raison d'Etat* at the Beijing National Defense University, the Chinese equivalent to Military Academy. And he was not the one who will have to pull the trigger anyway, just order it… He remembered his heated discussions with General Wong about the 'how': The innocent scientists could be poisoned, gassed or simply buried alive. He remembered the callousness of these conversations, made easier by the fact that they were relevant to events still far in the future. Jeung had argued against murder: Why not at least keep them prisoners in a special facility and make use of their talents. He had argued to no avail.

Jeung reached the steel door of the first set of holding cells. He wiped his eyes with a still-trembling hand, cursed Wong one more time, took a deep breath and pushed the door open.

A few minutes later, the first detonations were heard.

Chapter 1

e4 e5

Marriot Hotel, Copenhagen, Denmark

Jack Zimmerman, psychiatrist and autism specialist, was a good man. He was a regular Joe, like you and me: a working professional with a family, a few friends, no enemies. He was a happy man right now. He should have known better.

The Marriot Hotel in Copenhagen, on Kalvebod Brygge and close to the Christianborg Palace, was a fantastic venue for a conference. With calming river views, sea air smells, European quaintness, fantastic Scandinavian food and typically clean Nordic interior design, it was an ideal location for professionals to take some time off their busy schedule and ponder the big picture. That is where the Autism Society of America had chosen to hold its international conference, this year with HFA, High Functioning Autism, as its main topic. With autism being nowadays recognized as a condition affecting a few individuals per thousand, this was a crowded and active three-day conference. There were panels on many subjects, chaired by the leading specialists in the field, educators, psychiatrists, psychotherapists, and research physicians.

Dr. Jack Zimmerman was a paunchy middle-aged suburban family man set in his habits. He had come only half-heartedly to this conference. He did not enjoy far-away business trips and preferred his comfortable routine: Home after work, an occasional drink with friends, a good restaurant with the wife, a Sunday barbeque. Jet-lag and hotel rooms were not his cup of tea. He was also weary of the inane conference arguments on whether Einstein, Newton, Tesla, George Orwell, and other celebrities had been or had not been mildly autistic. And the heated controversy on whether autism should be considered a disease to be cured or just a difference to be accepted bored him by its lack of practicality. But this meeting had proved something special. The rumor of an appearance by famous high-functioning autist Temple Grandin had not been fulfilled, but his own presentation about "Numeracy and pattern recognition by Asperger's syndrome-diagnosed children" had been extremely well received by his peers. He had enjoyed the respect of his colleagues and their questions implying he was some kind of authority. And he probably was, he did think, at least in his specific numerical applied specialty. Apart from the routine question about some autists' real mathematical talents and circus-like demonstrations, it was an interesting and challenging dialogue.

And then, there was Alyssa.

Jack was basically a faithful family man. He loved his wife and two children, and in 17 years of marriage, never had he succumbed to temptation. There had been opportunities here and there, but to Jack it was not worth the risk to his marriage or to his self-esteem. He had had enough girlfriends before his engagement, enjoyed life and done all that interested him. But Dr. Alyssa Orlov, whom he had met at this conference, was something else. She was one of the most beautiful women he had ever met, Slavic blond and statuesque, and she had the poise of a supermodel. She was also classy, intelligent and literate, speaking perfect English with a hint of Russian accent that made her even more attractive. She had asked him pointed questions after his speech, and asked to continue their discussion over a cup of coffee. Unlike his wife, she was really interested in his work. She was irresistible, laughing at his *bon mots* while touching him lightly. Her classic dress code was so sexy by what it suggested that it was maddening. Coffee led to cocktails. She told him about her practice for autistic children in Germany and about her divorce, and then again how interested she was in his work. She was a pure enchantress and there was no way he could have resisted her charms. Very few men could have. She had invited herself to his stately room for a night cap without making it sound crass, and she had caused his heart to beat like a love-smitten teen-ager when he opened his stately room door.

And now here she was, sitting demurely on the king size bed. The lighting was soft. She had taken her jacket off and, so Jack thought, probably popped open one more button of her shirt. Never had Jack been with such a beautiful woman, and male hormones were clearly fogging his brain. He was watching her perfect figure and pretty face, in a state of disbelief. She was magazine-cover material. He felt on the top of the world, with only a smudge of guilt which alcohol was keeping in check. What happens in Copenhagen, stays in Copenhagen, doesn't it? It would not hurt anyone: Caroline would never know.

Alyssa patted the bed cover beside her: 'Come and sit near me, Jack. Do not be shy'. Jack's heart started beating fast, and there was a rush of blood towards his nether parts, typical of the male expecting sex. It was still very much unlike him, and he sat shyly on the bed, not too close. He was unsure on how to proceed. She handed him the glass of Grey Goose he had poured her from the minibar: 'Have a drink. Relax'. Jack gulped half of the glass down in a desperate try to bolster up his courage.

Dr. Alyssa Orlov took back her glass and stood up to place it back on the dresser. She looked at Jack with half a thin smile on her lips. 'I want to freshen up a little, please do not go anywhere', and she headed for the bathroom. As if Jack was going anywhere! Watching thin, athletic and so womanly Alyssa walking to the bathroom had extinguished any remnants of guilt, probably with help from the vodka.

After a minute or two, Jack felt tired, so tired he wanted to lie down. He resisted falling asleep with all his might, but his mind was slowing as he watched Alyssa come towards him. She pushed him back on the bed, and sat on his lap, all clothed. In Jack's clouding mind, it looked like a sex game, but he was not enjoying it. He was dimming and did not even feel the prick of the needle to the side of his neck. It felt good to let go, but he suddenly felt very bad. Blood was rushing to his head, his heart was beating fast, too fast, and his throat felt constricted. A sharp pain tore through his left shoulder. 'A heart attack!' was the thought popping in his mind. He tried to shout but nothing came out. She would surely see he was in trouble! It took all his energy to open his eyes, and, through his panic, he was surprised to see Alyssa's blank expression as she was looking down on him. He felt as if she was weighing on him and constricting him between her knees to keep him immobile. And it looked like she had something like an automatic syringe in her hand. 'How strange' he was wondering as he was fading away. He understood he was dying. "Why?'. He shuddered powerfully, nearly throwing her off, took a last gulp of air. His last thought was for his wife, Caroline, with regret.

Dr. Jack Zimmerman had been a good man. Decent.

Dr. Alyssa Orlov, or whatever her name really was, clinically checked his pulse at the carotid, making sure he was dead. Her personally developed mixture of barbiturate, muscle relaxant and heart-stopper had worked like a charm, again. Injection after having her victims ingurgitate Rohypnol-lined drinks eliminated the need to fight them or actually sleep with them. And there was no reason to order a full-fledged criminal autopsy: Nobody would suspect anything more than the heart attack of an overweight middle-aged sedentary male. She climbed down, placed the small injector back in her handbag and went to thoroughly wash herself in the shower cubicle. After a few minutes, she took a wet towel and took the pains of cleaning Jack's hands. This was definitely an innocent heart attack, after too much food and drink, but no need to leave too much traces of DNA around. She took another wet towel to wipe every surface she remembered having touched. Nobody would check, but in this business, you never are careful enough. Alyssa went to empty a few mini bottles of spirits into the sink, and then placed the empty containers on the bed table. After rinsing and drying her own glass, she finally got dressed and made a last check of the room.

Putting on her sunglasses and a kerchief on her hair, she opened the heavy door carefully, hung the "Do not disturb" sign, and checked that the thickly-carpeted hallway was empty before leaving the room with a natural walk. She still made sure to lower her head when in the field of the hallway security cameras.

Jack's speech having been delivered meant his body would not be found until the next afternoon. By then, she would be richer and far away. In fact, in an hour, she would already be far from the hotel with her hair dyed black and dressed like a Russian backpacker. Dr. Alyssa Orlov would disappear, forever: There never had been one, and never should be one again. She had no idea why this sweet and harmless family man had to die. Pity. But she did not really care; she was a professional, after all.

Chapter 2

Nf3 f5

Inside Business Weekly, Issue 683, September 2012

Is today's most successful hedge fund running on exploited mentally-challenged?

By Nathalie Zini

The financial industry should be heavily regulated and thoroughly scrutinized.

This has long been this reporter position, reinforced by nearly weekly scandals. The purpose of a financial system should be to support society as a whole by easing the access to capital for the country's economic activity. Instead, it has become an impenetrable industry based on naked greed and incomprehensible products creating money from thin air... until the bill is due; bill that the tax payers will foot. Or their children and grandchildren. Shall I remind the reader of Bernard Madoff, the more recent Allen Stanford Ponzi schemer, Lehman Brothers, Bear Stearns, the mortgage crisis, the Euro crisis, the Global Financial crisis from 2007 and which effects are still felt today?

And did I mention rogue traders, high-speed electronic trading and tax evasion? I could go on, but the point is staring everybody in the face: Transparency is what we need. Transparency and accountability.

Wall Street insiders often tout the "Rain" hedge fund as today's most successful. The name is not widely known to the general public, as Rain is a private company and no official numbers are available of its profit or performance. Did I mention transparency? Like other successful funds, "Rain" will only handle big money from clients that have been referred or recommended, and it is said that they refuse more clients than they accept. Sources confirm that even applying to become a client, without any guarantee of becoming one, requires signing a whole pile of NDA's. This will remind some of shady operations like those of the infamous Bernard Madoff, and the alleged fantastic performance that made him a person to be sought after, and not having to court potential clients. Disclaimer: This reporter in no way tries to compare the Rain fund to a Ponzi scheme or anything illegal, but just shows the marketing parallel that exceptional performance allows for. In fact, other sources confirm that a recent SEC audit has come out clean for the fund, and nothing surfaced out of the ordinary. What is then the fund's secret? What do they know that others don't? Why the secrecy? And why such a careful expansion of their clientele?

What little is known is that the Rain fund was founded in 2006 by Olivier Van Dijk, a London-educated ex-trader of "strategy-based-exotic derivatives" from Barlow Capital ,who took a few clients away with him. Coming from outside the financial dynasties and old-boy networks, his fund was cold-shouldered at its humble beginnings. Van Dijk lacked the Jr. or Roman numbers to his patronym, and the fund was reportedly struggling until he took in a partner in 2009. Alex Prilutski, reportedly an old college friend of his, injected money from an unnamed group of investors into the fund and took the CEO's job he is holding to date. Both men, definitely upstart Wall Street outsiders, are actively running the fund. The limited amount of employees is extremely secretive about the 'how', the 'what' and the 'who'. None was ready to talk to us, reportedly as a result of extremely draconian contracts.

Uncharacteristically the fund is also mum about the methods it uses to invest its funds: They describe it as "all options opened and based upon a sophisticated analysis of trends in all areas of Finance". Very useful information…

A small tidbit of real information appeared through in the mountains of data uncovered in the Wikileaks affair in 2010. One cable linked to international money movements, referred to the Rain Fund as using persons affected with autistic symptoms to chart trends as a basis for investments. Could that be true? Could it work? Would it not be a glaring breach of these people's human rights? Handicapped people at the service of greed? Could children be involved? To all these questions, the fund refuses to comment, and will not reveal anything about its "trade secrets".

We contacted a leading authority in the field of Autism, Dr. Rashid Jubran of the NYU School of Psychiatry. According to Dr. Jubran, the likelihood of having autistic persons with those kinds of mathematical talents and working in an established fund environment are infinitesimal. He added though, that autism is an umbrella word for all kinds of disorders covering a whole range of conditions and seriousness, and basically, everything is possible. Dr. Jubran adds that a layman's definition of autism spectrum disorders could be a qualitative impairment of social interactions, together with restricted and repetitive activities and interests. But, he continues, individual symptoms do occur in the general population, without a sharp border between pathological severity and simple idiosyncratic traits. He cites the famous Dr. Treffert, leading researcher of what is called "savant syndrome", who estimates that fewer than fifty or so such individuals are believed to be alive in the world today and that most are gifted artists rather than mathematicians. Having such people working together in a social environment would be near to impossible, in his opinion.

Is the Rain Fund really the most successful today? Are they using people with behavioral disorders? And if they do, is it legal or even moral? How big is the fund and is there no fear of a domino effect if it crumbles? More questions than answers. The company is tight-

lipped and would not even answer my simple query on the source of the name "Rain Fund".

Raining money?

Chapter 3

Nxe5 Qf6

Prometheus Foundation Estate, Washington County, New York State

Tim was a nineteen years old deeply autistic young man. It had been very difficult for his parents to cope with him, emotionally and financially. He was now working for "Rain Fund".

He looked like everybody else of that age, maybe just a bit nerdier, until you tried to interact with him. He was sitting in front of his computer in the huge room where they had him work. There was a man behind him, the orderly caring for his needs, and he had seen that there were another two people some distance away in the room, working at other computer stations. But who cared? Tim was oblivious of other people and other people's needs. He did not understand the concepts of empathy, society, care or respect. He was clicking away on his computer; looking at rows of numbers and graphs both his screens were fed. To the orderly behind him, it just looked like lines and columns of numbers and symbols; to Tim, it was translating into beautifully colored patterns, moving in unison and building images that were logical in their progression. Tim liked the familiarity of these patterns; he liked the security of knowing how it would look and progress. He was clicking in his own numbers in order to create his own interpretation of how these images should look like. He understood that what he typed interested the people around him, that it had a mathematical significance they cherished in some way. But he did not care: He was fed, cared for and entertained; most of his wishes were taken care of. He just wanted to play with colors and shapes that other people did not understand. His parents had hated that he wanted to know the whole Amtrak time table by heart, and repeat it *ad nauseam*. They had looked scared that he wanted to make up words only he could understand. He could not understand why. It is the outside world that looked strange to him, not the other way around.

Suddenly a dark spot appeared in the lower right corner of the pattern he was extrapolating. It was menacing, the kind of black an astronomical black hole was probably made of: sucking in all around it. The black spot started to grow, slowly, but inexorably. It was lurking like a beast, destroying the bright colors around it, as if eating them. Tim was frozen in place: He was scared, but could not tear his eyes off the black thing that was trying to take over his patterns. There was something in the computer trying to take over his patterns: That was highly disturbing. Tim was getting mad and scared at the same time. This was his pattern, his images and he did not want anything to interfere. But he was losing control of what was happening on the screen. It was like a black beast, eating up his beautiful images, and destroying everything. A black Beast. A Beast! Tim started shouting uncontrollably, eyes fixed on the screen.

And he fell from his wheelchair in a frightening fit.

***

Rain Fund Offices, Manhattan, New York City

My day had started as usual: I had sent my moves to the six anonymous chess masters from around the world I was currently playing with electronically. I was feeling good about these matches and good about myself. People would have you believe that premonition and a sense of doom will always precede bad news. It was obviously not the case.

I angrily threw the magazine on to my desk. The desk was bare but for my two feet, my empty espresso cup, my iPad and now the "Inside Business Weekly" magazine. I am somewhat compulsive and like a virgin desk.

My name is Olivier Van Dijk, pronounced "Van Deyk", and I am the founder and chairman of the "Rain Fund". Olivier was spelled the French way, thanks to my Belgian heritage. Of course, the Chinese genes I inherited from my mother made me look a rather exotic European. I have always felt like a citizen of the world: Belgian father, Chinese mother, educated in the United Kingdom, well-travelled, and living in the USA, you do not get more cosmopolitan than that. I sat up and lowered my feet to the ground. Sighing, I let my eyes roam onto the magnificent view of Central Park which I had chosen our offices for. We had the full 33rd floor, but this was the pearl: the full-windows corner office with Park view. My large office, decorated by a leading interior designer in a clean Asian naked style had only one painting, an original Vladimir Volegov I loved. The fresh flowers vase I insisted was always replenished soothed me and gave my office a natural smell. It was a very little piece of Mother Nature in a compacted Metro environment. Wealth definitely had its perks, but I prided myself of middle class roots and wanted to believe that I was not interested in the pursuit of money for its own sake. I avoided ostentatious displays of luxury, reinvested my money in the company and took the time to enjoy my simple life passions, mainly extreme sports. Of course making money came with an endless stream of worries.

I sighed again. At least Ms. Zini had my name spelled right, but I hated her kind of publicity. I had founded the Rain fund on a great idea, and the less people knew about it, the less problems and the less competition I would have. Why do all these journalists have to poke their nose and make everything look un-politically correct? *Fouille merde*, -shit-stirrers-, the French call them, and rightly so I would add.

I checked my 1954 vintage Rolex Submariner watch, a rare indulgence for which I had outbid a fellow hedge fund manager. 10:08. Alex was again fashionably late, on purpose of course. I grimaced at the shoulder muscle I pulled this morning in *Parkour* training. I am still very fit for 39 years, but I should become more careful with age. It was getting easier to get hurt, and took longer to recover. I have loved extreme sports since adolescence, and with the success of the fund, I have had the time to indulge. This morning, I did easy *Parkour* exercises at the gym with my instructor, jumping over stationary vaults and falling down into rolls. I should have stopped there, but chose to go free-running in Central park. I pulled a shoulder muscle by trying a *'saut de chat'* over a low wall in the park. This cat jump is a forward dive over an obstacle with the body horizontal, a push off with the hands while tucking the legs, to bring the body back to a landing vertical position. Nevertheless, it would take more than a pulled muscle to convince me to slow down.

The door of my office opened, without a knock. Alex came in, smiling.

'Hi Olivier! Sorry I am late'

Alex was a small man, with dark good looks, always dressed to kill in designer suits and expensive loafers. Today it was a grey Armani suit on a pink shirt. A big contrast to my casual jeans and Polo shirt. Alex Prilutski was very bright, but always managed to look like a shady overdressed Mafioso.

'You are not sorry. You are late and on purpose. I do not feel like B.S. today'. I had known Alex since we were students at the London School of Economics and he dressed normally. I knew him like the palm of my hand and I was getting less and less patient with his little games. We were like an old couple and his flaws seemed to become bigger and bigger with time. Divorce was looming below the horizon.

'Sorry', he kept smiling. What he was really telling me is that he'd rather meet me on neutral ground than in my office.

'I am still the founder and Chairman of the board of this company, and I want our monthly coordination meeting to be in my office, on time'

Alex was still smiling, toying with me. 'Of course, no problem. But let us not forget how the fund was faring before I brought in my investors and took over the day-to-day management. Now, clients are lining out the door, and we are the most successful fund. Ever! You probably are upset about the piece in the Business Weekly', he points at the magazine on my glass desk,' but I think it is great for business. Relax my friend'. He brushed his trousers as he sat down in one of the chairs in front of the desk, showing off his golden cufflink.

Alex was pushing my buttons, of course. I knew it, but it still worked, especially because he was right. God, I started to hate him. Before I could retort, he cut: 'I know, I know. It was your fund, your great idea! I heard it a million times. I was with you when you saw "Rain man" with Hoffman and Cruise in the London *Cinematheque*, and then dreamed of having a retarded idiot genius doing your charting! And this fucking journalist thinks Rain is for raining money! Funny'. He was smiling mischievously.

'These people are not idiots! And yes it was my idea'. I raised my voice. He was so good at getting me mad: he knew I hated it when he called autistics "idiots". And I continued: 'Of course, it took time to get to understand how to work with these people. And of course, you are a great salesman and nitty-gritty manager. And you brought in money, that I am not sure is totally clean. Still, I am the visionary and soul behind Rain. Stop those silly games'.

It was not totally true I had had the idea behind the fund after seeing the 1988 Oscar winning movie "Rain Man". It had come to me a little later, after reading about the real-life character that inspired the screenplay: Kim Peek and his eidetic memory. Of course, history will never say either that it came to me after having got seriously drunk.

'OK. Sorry, Olivier. You know me, no harm meant'. He was still grinning, irritatingly. 'And remember, that the best thing we have going for this business is this deniable hint of our very special charting system. Just like Israeli nuclear policy: Everybody knows they have a boatload of nukes, but they keep denying it with a wink. People suspect we use idiot-geniuses to make money, we reinforce it by "no-comments", and they flock to give us their monies'.

I had heard that many times and I hated both Alex's crass style and his Israeli-based comparisons. Alex was Jewish, and probably ideologically Zionist, which I thought hypocritical if you lived and breathed everywhere in the world but in Israel. On the other hand, I had to admit he was right: Since the *Wikileak* story, business had been picking up, and we had been denying regularly. And the more we denied, the more people came around!

'OK, truce Olivier. Let us get down to business'

Since I had taken Alex as a 50% partner, we had divided the work as per our respective strengths. I had kept chairmanship by contract, but I was now owner of only half the company. It was true that the business had been faltering: It had been difficult to achieve a working system with our autistic employees, and I was not very good at salesmanship. I had had only few clients and the results had been in line with what other funds did on average. Alex, on the other hand, was the consummate salesman, the executive officer, the micromanager, in his dodgy second-hand car salesman-style. He was working 20 hours a day and I had to admit he was brilliant. I was not ashamed of my role as the visionary entrepreneur resting on his laurels and enjoying his hobbies. I was much more interested in the execution of my original idea: Using, guiding and interpreting mathematical prodigies to define money market trends. So, I saw my job as keeping a loose supervision on the work of our in-house psychiatrist in charge, and as trying to improve the system. That left me with plenty of time to enjoy life.

Alex took out a few papers from his dossier; he was a pen-and-paper guy, not trustful of electronic notes. He crossed his legs, showing off the perfect crease of his pants. I took out my iPad, although I rarely used it for notes. Another of my hobbies was the full use of my brain. I was a fan of the famed USM,-Ultimate Study Method-, and regularly trained my memory, my speed-reading skills and mental math. I prided myself of never having to take notes at meetings.

Alex started right away: 'First order of the day: The increase of the IT budget. As you saw in the memo, Olivier, we are getting bigger fast and Ofer needs more hardware for computing power. An increase of 50% is in his opinion the bare minimum for the projected needs until the end of next year. It is a lot of money, but peanuts compared to the tons we are doing, so should not be a problem. It is a must, Olivier, unlike the private jet I wanted and that you vetoed like the Scrooge you are'.

I opined, ignoring the side comment. 'I don't object, Alex. But please check it up again. I made a simple comparison of our computing expenses versus the Industry average, and we are already around double. It is more of your area so take it up with Ofer again. Even if we have money, we do not need to throw it away. And he should know we are not a rubber stamp for gadgetry buying sprees'.

Ofer Dobry is our IT guy, with the title of Vice-President and a huge seven-figure salary. Alex brought him in when he invested, and the geek is a real genius. Again an Israeli connection, he is supposed to have been working in AMRAM, the ultra-secret Israeli Army computer unit allegedly responsible for the Suxnet virus which crippled the Iranian nuclear program. This army unit is considered the best software school in the world, and if it is true, hiring Ofer was a masterstroke. He was very young, still shy of 30, and he really looked very strange: Thick glasses, unkempt hair, shifty eyes and questionable hygiene habits. He spent most of his time in his office, eating greasy take-out, and leaving half-empty containers to rot around. He was also muttering to himself in Russian all the time, a language he was using to talk to Alex, even in front of me, in spite of his accented but excellent English.

'OK. But you know IT is part of our success, and Ofer knows what he is doing. There are also cyber-security aspects not to be overlooked. As you have just read, people are getting interested in us'. Alex ticked something in his file. 'Next point, the new lady doctor Jack wants in. This is more of your area, but I say again: Go! Things are going fine, so let us keep expanding'.

Jack was Doctor Zimmerman, the psychiatrist I had worked together with since the Fund's inception. He was selecting, taking care and managing our autistic savants. Jack was also a true friend that, unlike Alex, I would trust with my life. He definitely had a full plate, and if he wanted help, he would get it. And as much as I needed to restrict the number of people who knew the details of our operation, I could easily understand why we needed the extra staff.

'I understand this lady doctor he brought has been vetted by Jan and has signed all the secrecy agreements. So, I will just meet her for a final interview before we go ahead'.

Jan was Jan Thompson, our head of Security. He is an old tough-looking South African, ex-Recces, the famed South African Special Forces Brigade, also brought in by Alex. When I thought about it, Alex had now a much stronger power base than me in the company. I did not like Jan, who looked and behaved like a bully, but the total secrecy and control over our employees required us to use people like him. And we have had no leaks or other problems ever; so no complaints.

'Have you met her, Alex?'

'Yes, briefly. She's a hottie, but I do not care for educated women, and especially shrinks. You decide', he answers in his usual macho style.

I ignored him and continued: 'I'll talk to Jack and get him to set up the meeting as soon as he comes back from his conference. I'll close this thing with him ASAP. In fact, he was quite frantic looking for me just before he left. He wanted an urgent meeting, but I was at this Kung Fu retreat in California. Have you seen his last memo about the problems with Patient Three?

Alex just nodded.

'It looks like he has had more psychotic episodes about the "Beast" lurking in the machines. I suppose that is what Jack wanted to talk about! This is worrying because 3 is our most successful subject'. We referred to our autistic patients/employees by numbers. I did not mean that as disrespect but it was easier for working purposes. And we called them patients since we were also treating them and helping them fully integrate into society. Some of the patients had had bouts of hysteria while working the computers and we did not know what the cause was.

Alex dismissed me with a hand flick: 'Not the first time. Before, it was the "Black Thing"…This is your thing, Olivier, but I would cut Patient 3 loose and look for a replacement, you know. Trying to fix him will cost money and resources'.

It always irritated me when Alex was so cavalier with the whole operation, as if he did not understand where the success of our fund came from. But I controlled myself: 'First of all, we are contractually bound to give him the best care possible. And it is not as if we can replace him like that, especially him. It will take years, while years of investments in him go down the drain! Let us not forget that these people make us the money. And also remember that he is not the first one having the same delusions; this is something we need to solve'.

Alex looked doubtful. 'OK, OK. Your thing. But keep me out of this "Beast" bullshit. And now to the next item'.

I did like to show off my memory tricks, so I cut in: 'You mean the SEC audit. I understand it went fine?'

'Right, it did. But I am still rattled as to why we were audited. According to Jan, it was not routine, and I trust his gut instinct. I have asked him to re-check everybody and re-evaluate our policies and procedures'.

'Why? Do you think we…

I was interrupted by a knock. The door opened even before I could answer, and the head of my assistant, Myla, leaned into the room: 'Sorry, Olivier'. Myla has been my faithful and indispensable assistant since the foundation of the Fund. She was an overweight but zealous and totally reliable woman in her fifties, and it was not like her to burst into a meeting.

I looked at her sternly, but she looked pale and shaken.

'What's wrong?'

She answered in broken sentences: 'It is Jack, Olivier. He had a heart attack. He is dead. His wife just called. He died in Denmark yesterday'. Her voice broke and she stifled a sob.

I must admit, shamefully, that my first thought was: 'What am I going to do with the program? '. I checked myself. Have I become a heartless banker bastard? And then the reality sank in, stabbing my heart: my best friend in the world was no more.

Chapter 4

d4 d6

Private studio, Elite Gym, Manhattan, New York City

I was on my back, my arm was hyper-extended, and I was struggling to move my body to relieve the pain. I was hurting and it felt like my elbow was going to pop out, but I could not reposition myself to get out of the arm-lock. I arched my back to try to create an opening, but my attacker shifted his weight accordingly. I tried to twist away and pull my arm in to no avail. I tapped the floor to surrender, and Rui released me. We just stayed on our backs on the floor, panting for a few minutes. Rui was my Brazilian Ju-Jitsu instructor, and we had finished our bi-weekly work-out with a training fight. I was so distracted that he creamed me much more easily than he usually did. Jack's sudden death had me rattled and worried about my own mortality, as if contagious.

Since the great success of the fund, I had pursued my early-life interest in extreme and combat sports, at the expense of the intensive work I used to be investing before. Unlike Alex, I did not believe in the pursuit of money as a quest in itself, but as a mean to be able to do what you were really interested in. And Jack's death reminded me that time was running out for life's enjoyments. Selfish, but true.

Rui Monteiro, breathing heavily beside me, was more than my personal trainer; he was a friend and a confidante, and maybe even my down-to-earth shrink. Very muscular, hairy and dark skinned, he was a very simple young man with a healthy and wide outlook on life. I could talk to him about anything, and he would dissect it into simple tenets towards logical conclusions. He had grown up in squalor in Rio's *favellas* and had had to fend off for himself and his single mother, helping to raise his two brothers and his sister. He had taken up the combat sports Capoeira and Ju-Jitsu at a young age to be able to protect himself and loved ones in this unforgiving environment. He had survived to become a successful professional fighter, which ultimately turned out to be his ticket out of the slums. He was now a famed fighter and trainer in Mixed Martial Arts organizations, married to a beautiful American-born Brazilian girl, and supporting his family back home. Rui had been around very nasty people and had done things he was not proud of, but only for survival. He had only told me a little part of it, and it was scary stuff. All in all, that had given him a good perspective on the intricacies of life and a clear understanding of the border between right and wrong. He was naturally intelligent and had come to understand the world from the ground up, way below the ivory towers.

Rui said with his thick Brazilian accent: '*Assim é a vida…* Life must go on, Olivier. You'll have to get over it'. He knew what was bothering me, of course. 'I have lost many friends in my previous life, and there is not much more to do than honor them by keeping on. Life is for the living, and it is to be enjoyed every single day. You never know when the Lord will want you with Him'. He was crossing himself as the devout Catholic as he was.

'Thanks Rui. I am trying to get over it. It has been already five days, but I cannot get over it'. I was still out of breath and did not want to talk about it. 'It will not be easy. And I gotta run. See you next week'. I usually liked to talk things over with him but not Jack, at least not right now. I knew he could respect that.

I left the studio for a long warm shower to release the new small aches and pains. Pity I did not have time for a sauna, but I had an important meeting Upstate. I had to interview the lady Jack wanted as an aide, but who now probably would end up as his replacement. As if anyone could replace Jack?

I checked myself in the mirror, before starting to shave. Still athletic, and good-looking, even if I said so myself! Only a hint grey hair and of love handles at 39. It was called eligible bachelor or something…

There is nothing like grooming to get your mind off things, and when I got into the underground garage below the Exclusive NY Elite Gym, I felt better. I climbed into my 4 year-old Toyota Land Cruiser V8. Unlike Alex, I was not into flashy cars. I preferred big and comfortable. I checked my Rolex. 10:19. Now, I would have to hurry.

Driving a truck in New York City requires paying attention to traffic, and it kept my mind off things, but as soon as I cleared upstate, my mind drifted again to poor Jack. Yesterday's funeral had been heart-breaking: his devastated wife Caroline and her two teen-aged boys trying to look strong and fight back their tears. I was all teared-up myself and, after two attempts, I had to let Alex read the eulogy I wrote, my throat getting constricted as soon as I attempted speaking. Never take life for granted! I had known Jack for over 6 years, and although he was technically working for me, we were more like partners in the Rain Fund endeavor and we had become best friends fast. This was one of those natural friendships, with different but completing personalities, that click in as if ordained from above. Jack was reliable, good-natured and easy, and an exceptional family man. I met him in a long line of psychiatrists I was interviewing when I founded the Rain Fund. After seeing a few experienced and overdressed, but boring, autism specialists, he was a breath of fresh air: young-spirited and not pompous, bright but not complicated, casually dressed and immediately receptive to my ideas. His only experience with autism had been his thesis, and he was therefore not set in axiomatic patterns: He was still curious and challenging old ideas. We clicked immediately. I think he really saw my project as a life endeavor, just like me, and threw himself in it with passion. I took a gamble when choosing Jack over experts who looked much better on paper, but it really paid off. And in retrospect, it was probably the only way we could have succeeded the way we did. I remember the crooked smile he sported when I offered him the job on the spot and asked him to shamefully send home the remaining candidates sitting outside the office.

I kept day-dreaming while driving on the quiet roads of Upstate New York, reminiscing the good times, the Sunday barbeques with Jack's family, his frank laughter. With my being single, he used to forcefully invite me to events like Thanksgiving or Passover. Jack and Caroline were always thoughtful, and oblivious to the fact that singles have sometimes much more fun than married people. Or so the story goes. In fact, I think they were right and maybe, it was me who was envying Jack.

I chuckled while checking the rear-view mirror. These thickly woods-lined Washington County small country roads are often deserted, which makes driving quite relaxing. There was a silver Audi behind me, and it struck me that I had seen it in the City, in screeching braking behind me. Probably a coincidence.

Back to my thoughts. I now wondered how Jack's life work could be just turned over to a new coming stranger. How could Jack's shoes be filled? How big a problem would it be for the fund?

Deep in thought, I nearly missed the turn to Greenwich, and had to brake strongly to avoid missing it totally. Luckily, there was no car close behind. As I stopped a few yards after the side road, I saw the Audi braking suddenly, although it was still quite far behind. This was now very strange! I backed up the few yards to negotiate the intersection, and the Audi stopped, as if watching me. Of course, it could be lost travelers looking for their way, but it was strange indeed. Who would be following me and why? On the side road, I used all the power in my V8 engine to make some distance between me and the potential follower. You could never be too careful. I knew the area well and, after a mile, I checked that the Audi was not yet behind me, before doing a sharp turn right into a very small path between the trees. I was going too fast and the big car slipped and started to roll. Thanks God, and maybe thanks to some Toyota electronic system with an acronymic denomination, it straightened and came to a halt. My heart was beating fast. Was I becoming paranoid? I did a three point turn-around and edged forward to look intently at the road. In fact, when I thought about it, my destination *was* a company secret. Could that be industrial espionage? Nothing like that had ever happened to the best of my knowledge.

And suddenly, the silver Audi roamed in front of the clearing I was in, speeding, probably to catch me back. I was quite deep into the clearing, in order to avoid being noticed. But I could not see the driver either. What should I do? Follow the car? Confront the driver? I decided that I had better get to my meeting discreetly, and be more careful about tails in the future. The location of the Prometheus Foundation should be kept secret. I waited for two minutes on the dashboard clock before I climbed back on the road, turning left and away from my follower. I pushed the engine to its maximum in order to clear the road fast, in case my tail doubled back. I knew the area well and could get to my destination by other country roads.

But this had rattled me, with the good side effect of diverting my thoughts from Jack. I pressed 5 on the speed-dial of the car phone. After three rings, a deep voice with a thick South African accent answered: 'Yes, Oliver'. Jan never called me Olivier, only Oliver and I suspected it was on purpose, to unnerve me.

'Hi Jan. It's *Olivier*. Look, I have kind of a situation here. I am driving to Prometheus, and I think I was followed. I managed to shake my tail, but I was already on the road to Greenwich. It was a silver Audi, an A6 I think.

'Did you get the number?' Did you see the driver? Was he alone? Was he aggressive? Was he trying to hide the fact he was tailing you, or was he blatant about it? Any distinctive marks on the car, accidents, color, equipment?' Jan was spitting questions like a machine gun.

Wow! As I said, this guy was a professional. It sounded like he had some experience in tailing people!

'I think he was trying not to be noticed, but it is not easy on those empty roads. I also think it was a woman, but I am not sure, I only caught a glance'

'Plate number?' he repeated tersely, like he was angry with me for not being more helpful.

'Sorry! Did not get it, it went too fast and I was not ready'

'Any idea who could it be? Anything else you remember?'

'No, not really. I am driving to the compound by the long route and I'll keep my eyes open'

'I'd rather you would cancel the compound and come back to the City, Oliver. Better be sure whoever that was does not make the connection'

'It's *Olivier*, and you are still working for me and not the other way around. I am going to the compound. And you Jan, you do your job to keep everything safe'

I really did not like this guy.

There were a few seconds of silence, and then: 'OK. Just want to be as safe as possible. I am on it and I'll tighten security'. Jan did not sound apologetic at all. I cut him off.

The detour took me another twenty minutes, driving with one eye on the rear-view mirror, and I finally could see the entrance of the compound. The Prometheus Foundation compound is a walled 100 acres property, isolated in the Washington County countryside. Each time I catch its view from the distance, it makes me feel good. The Foundation, from its access road, looked like an early Twentieth Century English Manor in green rolling hills. In the light of the late morning, you really felt like going back in time, to a period when things were slower. It was a big building but looked proportionate in the grand grounds around it. You could see from the road the long driveway leading to an impressive stone stairs entrance, and could not help looking for the butler waiting for you there. It was a very quaint and special place, close to my heart. It was also the part of our operation that we were trying to keep secret. As I came closer to the gate, one guard came out of the guard house. I saw a white 4x4 near the gate with somebody in the driver seat, and another guard in the guard house. It looked like security had already been beefed up. Jan was a dick, pardon my French, but an efficient one. I stopped by the big sign "Private Property. Keep Out! Armed Response". And a smaller: "Beware of the dogs". I chuckled: the sign always reminded me of Latin class and Pompei's *"Cave canem"*. Already in Rome, two thousand years ago, were properties guarded by canines. The world did not change much in essence.

The brick wall around the property looked innocuous but I knew it was covered with cameras and other sensing devices. This place was really secure. I should know: I paid for everything!

The mustached guard came to the window: 'Good morning, Mr. Van Dijk. We were expecting you'

'Hi Dan'. His name was catalogued in my USM-trained memory. I did not know the other two watching me from the car and the guard house. 'Is my interviewee already here? '

'Yes, she is, Sir. She has been processed, and she is waiting for you inside'. He looked slightly embarrassed. 'Mr. Van Dijk, Mr. Thompson has asked us to do a bug sweep of the car before you come in. It will just take a minute'.

My Head of Security was really beginning to piss me off. 'Open the gate, Dan. If I am bugged, they already know where I am. I'll park in, and then you can check what you want. Go now'

Dan hesitated for a second or two; and he even casted a glance over my shoulder. I turned to see his colleague getting out of the SUV with a device in his hand that looked like a metal detector. But Dan pressed the remote with an embarrassed look and the barrier lifted up. I accelerated in, throwing gravel around. I was annoyed; I had this inexplicable feeling that I was losing control over my own company. I would have to do something about that, maybe be less nice to everybody, or talk it over with Alex. I made a mental note to take some action.

I parked in my reserved spot, near the grand entrance of the magnificent building. And I noticed a lonely little grey Honda in the Visitors section. Certainly my interviewee, as visitors were usually not welcome here. I checked my watch: I am ten minutes late, thanks to the detour.

***

Manhattan, New York City

Special Agent in Charge John Reilly stepped out of the elevator on to the deep carpeted hallway. It definitely looked the part of the penthouse floor at twenty fifth level of the posh Manhattan building. There were only two apartments on this floor and they must be huge. And there was no doubt which of the two was his destination. The hallway on the right side of the elevator doors was bustling with activity and a police tape was restricting access. The soft background music from the building's speakers was slowly becoming inaudible as Reilly got close. A young uniformed policeman was standing near the 'Do not cross' yellow tape with a clipboard in hand; and he was already moving to block his path. Reilly extracted his badge from his trench coat pocket and flipped it open.

'FBI. Need to go in'

The young policeman was taken aback, at loss at what to do.

'You need to take down my name and shield number, and the time of my entering the scene. Then you let know the guy in charge that I am coming in. Probably Lou Masco'

The policeman blushed a little and did as told. He was probably a fresh rookie on his first scene-securing assignment. A bit shy for a cop, John thought. After taking John's details, he went a few steps to the door of the apartment down the hall and hesitated getting in. John saw him signal someone inside, and heard a loud grumble from inside: 'What?'. That was Masco all right, and his head popped out of the door frame. 'Reilly? Come in', he bellowed while signaling him with a large hand gesture. Reilly went under the police line and walked to the scene. As he passed the young policeman going back to his post, he resisted the impulse of a childish head fake just to startle him. Children doing a man's job, he thought. Nowadays a cop is first and foremost a box-ticker, in triplicate.

He shook hands at the door with Lou Masco, and resisted the powerful urge to discretely wipe his hand on his coat. Lou had sweaty palms, hairy fingers and a wimpy handshake, and he always managed to look crumpled and far from immaculate. Lou was a small wide-shouldered man, wrestler-style, going bald and trying to cover it up by spreading around much too long greasy hair. It was easy to underestimate Masco, but John knew he was a top-notch detective, hard-working and with a nose for ferretting criminals. It had made him the number one homicide detective of New York City finest. He always caused John to think of Inspector Columbo, of Peter Falk fame.

'Thanks for the heads-up, Lou. I appreciate'

'Yep. You should. Do not mess up my scene'. Lou was a man of few words.

'You know we'll have to make this federal, Lou'

'Not sure. I suppose some time. Come on in, have a look'

'I'll let you do the work, but if it is as you said, there is no doubt it is our serial'. He followed Lou inside. 'Number Four. Minimum. One in Connecticut, previous one here in NYC, one in New Jersey, and now this'.

Lou mumbled something akin to 'Yeah, yeah, yeah'

'Who found him?'

'Housekeeper'

They went through a living room twice the size of John's apartment, with an impregnable view of NYC skyline; there were two scene investigators around, in white coveralls, dusting around and taking pictures. As they entered the burgundy carpeted bedroom, the unmistakable stench of death irritated John's nostrils: a mixture of tinny blood smell and excrement. No matter how blasé you thought you were, death has the effect of reminding you of your own mortality.

The victim was on the bed, with a medical examiner checking him up. John knew him from past encounters as a serious professional: Tom Lin. Tom looked up at John, and nodded, lifting tweezers holding a crumpled playing card. 'Just extracted from the vic's mouth'. He straightened it with his gloved hands. It was a Two of Hearts.

John said: 'A red card. I told you, Lou. Always red'

'You don't know that. It's only the fourth in a row. Could be a coincidence'

'I bet you it is not. Something in this twisted perp's mind'.

The medical examiner was still bent over the corpse. He was extracting crumpled pieces of paper from the corpse's mouth. It was gross. The dead man had a puffed appearance, with blown out lips, bulging eyes and an engorged tongue sticking out. Tom Lin straightened out one of the four crumples he had taken out: It was a one-hundred dollar bill. 'And there are more' he said.

John sighed. 'Definitely our guy. What was the victim doing? Professionally, I mean'

'Dunno yet. His name is… was Lindwood Parker, III. The third, can you believe that?'

John did not answer; he was already googling on his smartphone. 'Cause of death?'

Tom replied while extracting more crumpled dollar bills from the victim's mouth: 'Garroted. Metal traces on the strangulation line. I would think a piano wire, but will need to check'

'That's what was expected. Same M.O. Wow!...', Reilly was reading from his phone. 'This guy had been in the news. He beat heavy insider trading charges last year. Big scandal'

Lou swiped his crumpled hair: 'The last guy in New Jersey was also famous. His company was lending money at outrageous rates to credit-poor wrecks who could not get it anywhere else. Or were too stupid. Another slime-ball. He was also very much in the news about a lawsuit or something'

John ignored the political incorrectness and sighed: 'We have us a serial killer on the prowl for New York bankers. Bankers, Lou. Think of the political fall-out'.

Chapter 5

Nc4 fxe4

Outskirts of Riga, Latvia

Latvia is a very small country on the Baltic Sea, ensconced between Lithuania and Estonia, with a population of only about two million people. Many would be surprised that Latvia, once part of the Soviet Union, has been a member of the European Union and of NATO since 2004. But the country is far from the European average standards of living: Years of Soviet Socialism have made it a grey and poor place for years to come. The ingrained Bolshevik bureaucracy and the socialist education system have conditioned several generations, and it will take time to reverse their negative effects. On top of that, the global financial crisis of the last decennia has hit Latvia particularly hard.

Such an environment is unfortunately a fertile soil for the development of organized crime, just like it was in post-perestroika Russia. Few would also believe that the president of a country would actually call it a "mafia state". But this really had happened: In May 2011, President Valsis Zatlers moved to dissolve the Parliament, the Saiema, after the legislature rejected a request by

Latvia's Anti-corruption Office to search the house of a parliament deputy and businessman suspected of corrupt deals. He proceeded to say on National Television: "We need to be honest before ourselves - Latvia is considered a small mafia state, and this is not the best reputation for a country".

It is in a sumptuous villa in the rich suburbs of the capital Riga, that Aivars Bartulis lived. He would not disagree with his ex-President. Aivars had started as a foot soldier for the infamous Ivan Haritonov gang in the late 1980s. This "king of the racket," ruled the streets, murdering, kidnapping and extorting the citizens of Latvia. In the early 1990s Haritonov and his gang even tried to control the shipment of oil products in and out of Latvia and reportedly used their dirty money to start a bank. They were so powerful that when they were brought to trial in 1994, none of the 10 witnesses showed up. Aivars Bartulis had climbed the gang hierarchy gradually but surely, because he combined, unlike most of his criminal colleagues, strategic thinking with ruthless street smarts. When the Haritonov gang was finally dismantled, Aivars was already up-coming with his own organization, more tuned in with the times. Few knew that he was now the head of the leading crime family in Latvia. He had had the vision of expanding his personal flavor of crime brand abroad with the numerous Latvian emigrants, especially to the United Kingdom and the United States.

Aivars, once a nimble street-fighter, was nowadays obese, as he liked good food and had relegated physical activity to his subordinates. He was sitting in his office, decorated like the backroom of a Museum, with a clutter of sculptures, paintings and extravagant trinkets. The word popping to mind when coming into the room, was "kitsch". Coming from a modest background, Aivars had the need to show off his wealth in the most quantitative but totally tasteless way. The centerpiece of the design in his office was a huge Venitian Murano glass chess set, blue and translucent, on a marble table. Aivars had started playing chess when spending time in Soviet prisons, and had become an avid and gifted player. He had learned to play both sides in his head when he was, sadly too often, thrown into solitary confinement. He now had a valuable collection of antique chess sets all over his villa to entertain his obsession, and he was playing electronically with chess masters all over the world. He had just sent his moves to his seven current adversaries and felt good about them.

Aivars was sitting behind an antique marquetry desk, inlaid with mother-of-pearl and ivory, covered with golden pen holders and ivory letter openers, and even a decorative Faberge egg in its protective glass container. He was now talking on a special top-of the-line satellite scrambling phone. Nowadays, criminals had far better equipment than their police counterparts who had to fight for dwindling budgets. This conversation, in Russian, was definitely private. Only thirty per cent of Latvia's population was ethnically Russian, but nearly all Latvians spoke the language. For those born before the 1990s, it was their first language, as ordered by the czars of the Soviet Empire. For the new generation, if not of Russian colons descent, it was a second language.

The conversation had started with no greetings. Aivars had barked: 'Report!'
'No problems. Nobody suspected a thing and there was no autopsy requested. Not that there would have been anything to find'
'Is the problem now contained?'

'Yes. We do not expect more. The replacement will take months or years to become proficient, and by then we shall have tightened our control. We'll have to get rid of the Belgian guy soon too'

'Remember that this is now our biggest money maker, by far. Make sure there are no more incidents. The fund has to keep working and grow, at all costs'

'I will. Everything is under control now. The SEC was in and found nothing'

'Have you checked whether any information had been passed on to them?

'Our contact said no. He was supposed to bring in the data he was compiling, but we contained the problem before the hand-over'

'Do you know where is this data?'

'Eh, eh...'. Aivars's interlocutor had a hesitation.

'Check it and retrieve anything problematic. Now! Why do I have to think of everything?'

'I am on it. Now. Sorry'

'I understand all other operations are running 7% over plan. You'll be contacted tomorrow for the next batch of laundry'

'OK'

'Now that everything went fine, you can pay the other half to the lady as agreed'

'Will do'

'That's it then. Go back to work'

 'Dasvidania'

Click

Chapter 6

Nc3 Qg6

The Prometheus Foundation, Washington County, New York State

I left my car open with the keys in the ignition for the Security bozos and jogged. I was late for a meeting that, I did not know yet, would be one of the most important ones of my life.

I hated to be late; money and power had not changed that for me. I climbed the stairs of the grand entrance two by two. The building was a renovated luxurious estate built in the beginning of the last Century by a New York City industrialist. He was in paper if I remembered correctly. I bought it, relatively on the cheap, from an estate attorney, during the last big housing collapse. The size of the House, the isolation and the huge landscaped grounds made it perfect for its purpose.

In the high ceiling foyer, under the watchful eye of the receptionist, and a few security cameras, sat the lady doctor I was to interview. She was sitting under the huge chandelier and looking at the grand original hunting-scene tapestry hanging on the wall. Not really my thing: But it looked the part and had come with the house.

'I am terribly sorry for letting you wait, but I had unexpected trouble on the way', which was true. I made it sound like car trouble, which in fact was also technically correct. 'You are Doctor Wheelan, I assume'.

She stood up from the leather couch and extended her hand. I had a brief bout of hesitation while stepping in her direction. God, she *was* gorgeous. Alex was right. And I could not avoid noticing she was obviously Eurasian, like me. What were the odds? When you had a mathematical brain and had juggled numbers all your life, that's the kind of things you wonder; I would have to calculate the exact probability. Doctor Wheelan had blue eyes, but almond shaped. Together with her high cheekbones and silky Oriental black hair, the effect was mesmerizing. I remembered she was in her mid-thirties, but she looked even younger, as Asians often do.

I never believed in what the French call "*coup de foudre*"; thunder strike with the meaning of love at first sight. But something happened, there and then. Maybe not love, but some special connection, premonitory maybe. I never had felt like that before, though I was enjoying my celibate status with plenty of sexual activity; mainly with brainless but extremely beautiful young women.

'Laura Wheelan. No problem, I was enjoying the architecture. This place is of another time. You are Mr. Van Dijk?'. Her hand shake was firm and frank, and she immediately struck me as a no-nonsense person. She was dressed elegantly in a conservative business suit that could not hide her beautiful figure. And high heels, my weakness. Her eyes twinkled a bit, and I wondered if she had noticed my look-over. A bit embarrassing, but I was a man and this was probably simple chemistry. I was dressed in jeans, polo shirt, and moccasins, and I suddenly felt self-conscious about it. Which chemical reaction was responsible for that? I was the potential boss, was I not?

'Yes, Olivier Van Dijk. They do not build places like this anymore, and I was lucky to get it. Please come with me Dr. Wheelan, let us go to my office. She already wore a pinned badge of orange color. Flashy orange was for visitors. I did not need a badge, but I was sure

Jan Thompson was currently thinking about how to make me wear one.

She followed me up the fantastic double marble staircase. There was a lift at the back, hidden between two huge stone columns, but I always choose the stairs if possible. The first floor was closed by glass walls and doors on both sides, a concession to modernity and security. We took the right and I swiped my pass in the reader, before punching in my code. This was my office away from Manhattan, generally empty these last months. The door closed behind us and we went through a huge reception area with more couches and armchairs, before reaching another glass door. This time, I swiped my card, and then placed my index on the reader for fingerprint recognition.

Laura commented: 'This seems more like a bank vault than a care facility'. She was right, of course and I felt compelled to explain: 'Now that you have signed all these NDA's and legal stuff and you have been appraised of the sensitivity of this job, I gather you can understand why all these precautions. And you have no idea how paranoid our Head of Security is; the guy even suspects himself of misbehavior'.

'If you mean this Jan Thompson character, I have met him, and I agree with you, not a funny person. And by the way, this was just to lighten the mood. I have no problems with security'.

We had arrived in front of the thick mahogany door of my office. There was nobody else around, and I had no need for a full-time secretary here. I opened the door to let her in, in front of me: 'Please sit down and make yourself comfortable. I'll make us a cup of coffee'

She sat in one of the comfortable black leather chairs in front of the huge glass desk, while I went to the side table with my beloved Saeco Royal Professional coffee machine. I take my coffee very seriously, and pride myself of being a connoisseur. She has a look around the office: the sparsely decorated walls, two paintings only and nothing extravagant, a lot of space, the clean desk and the fantastic countryside view from the two huge balcony windows, so typical of the early 1900ies. I saw that she noticed the fresh flowers on the side dresser; Myla, of course, had phoned ahead and had made sure I had my little perk.

The pleasant aroma of brewing coffee started to fill the room. I had once read and that coffee aroma had a conducive effect on the thought process, and that inventor Nikola Tesla used to make coffee just to smell it, not to drink it.

I filled in the silence with small talk, like a smitten teen-ager: 'Did you know that in East Africa, coffee was used in religious ceremonies and that, as a result, the Ethiopian Church banned its secular consumption?'

She nodded negatively, smiled and waited for me to get down to business.

'Doctor Wheelan, please tell me what you have understood this position is about, and what are your thoughts?', was my way to mask my annoyance at realizing I had left her file in the car.

'First of all, I understand that Dr. Zimmerman who interviewed me several times and whom I was supposed to report to, has suddenly passed away. I feel terrible about that, and want to extend my condolences to you. From my meetings with him, I understand you two were close friends. These are terrible circumstances, and I am truly sorry'.

It was the right thing to say, but she sounded really sincere. My eyes glistened and I nodded, not trusting myself to speak.

'I was looking forward to work with him. He was quite renowned in his specialty. As you know, my only practical experience is limited to my thesis work. I am just out of School, a fresh Ph.D. and I really was surprised to be considered for the job'.

I had read Jack's notes and I knew why. And I was starting to agree with old Jack. She was sharp and straight.

She continued: 'I see my job as giving the best available twenty four/seven care to the few autistic people in this facility, four I think, with a fifth one on the way. My first goal would be making them better by improving their social skills as much as possible. The second goal would have them do meaningful work on the analysis of trends in the money market, and translate their results or input into actionable trading strategy, with the help of your on-site mathematicians. On the side of all this, we should do some research work on improving the selection process for savants, and on understanding their thought patterns in order to refine the trading platforms. I must make very clear that patient welfare would always be my first priority'.

'I would not like it to be otherwise, doctor. What do you think about the logic behind this idea, and the ethical aspects?'

'I have discussed all that with Dr. Zimmerman, Mr. Van Dijk, and I would not be here if I had reservations: I think it is a very ingenious idea, and the results show that it works beautifully. So it is probably a stroke of genius, and I wish I had thought of it myself'

I was flattered to hear that, but was it nose-browning? I wondered; she looked sincere, but my objectivity with her was long gone.

She continued: 'Dr. Zimmerman underlined how difficult it had been to achieve those results and that there is still a lot of work in progress. I think this is the most interesting project I have heard of in a long time'. She stopped for a few seconds. 'On the ethical side, I also did have long talks with Dr. Zimmerman. I fully agree with him that giving autistic people legal and worthwhile employment based on their specific qualities is a no-brainer in terms of normalcy. Of course, their working environment should be caring and they, and their families, should be proportionally rewarded. To sum it up: no problems there'.

I looked at her silently while she took a sip of coffee.

She continued: 'But I have talked this over and over with Dr. Zimmerman and I have been checked, tested, and even interrogated by your Security guy, and your partner. So you already know all this.'

I liked her straightforward approach. She reminded me so much of young Jack Zimmerman, it hurt.

'Dr. Wheelan, you are right, but I just wanted to get a first-hand impression of you. As you also know, we are in a bit of a jam because of Jack... of Dr. Zimmerman's untimely demise. You have been in this interview process for over 4 months, and you came up as his favorite. And I can understand why. But we are now not looking for an aide any more, but for someone to take over the program'

I looked at her, and drank some coffee while thinking. I then went completely off-road, against all the interviewer's rules: 'Did you know that when I hired Jack over six years ago, he was the worse candidate on paper, but I went with my gut? And I never regretted it.... You lack experience, but I see a lot of what I saw then in him in you: the drive, the full support to the idea, the out-of-the-box thinking'

She was impassible, no tell-tales on her face. Inscrutable Asians ....

'I am offering you the job at a 30% higher salary than originally discussed, as you are now replacing Jack. If things work out, and there is no reason why not, you'll get another 30% raise in six months, and you'll get into the annual bonus pool. All the rest is as discussed. But there are two conditions'.

She did not flinch or answered, still inscrutable, but waited for me to continue. She would make a fierce poker player.

'One: You start immediately. Two: You call me Olivier and I call you Laura. Mr. Van Dijk was my father'.

I was disappointed it did not make her smile, self-conscious of my attempts to make her like me. She rose up slowly from her chair and extended her hand: 'Deal, Olivier'. And finally smiled, showing small dimples and perfect white teeth. But there was something disturbing in her eyes, or was I overanalyzing?

I smiled back, hoping I had done the right thing for the Fund, and that her silky black hair and her good looks did not have too much to do with it.

She sat back, still smiling. 'Where do we go from here, boss?'

'I understand Jack has shown you around the facilities. So I won't have to. I'll take you to your office. Jack's still needs to be cleared, and I would not be comfortable with anyone sitting there. You'll see I am the most delegating boss in the world: You organize yourself and bring results and I give you all the support you need. Talk to me when you want. I am usually in Manhattan, but you'll have my cell number. Jack probably told you about the serviced flats on the second floor. I'll have the biggest one prepared for your exclusive use. You can commute if you want, but any time you need, this is your place. You can also use it permanently if you want'

'Thank you. I'll check it up. I'll organize and start full time next Monday, if it's OK with you'.

'Monday is fine. You are in'

At these words, something glittered in her eyes. But I was too smitten to notice.

***

St George Hotel, Manhattan, New York City

Doug Svenson was living the good life. Too good. Money, good food, man gadgets, mistresses, boat, cars… How long the Bible-famed seven fat years could go on before enter the seven lean years?

He was lying on the bed, naked, spent and relaxed, but philosophizing. She bent over to kiss him on the lips: "Got to go back to work. Lunch time is over".

Doug tried to grab her, but she twisted out of his embrace and walked to the door. He could not help admire her fantastic body as she walked away on her high heels. She blew him a kiss before closing the hotel door behind her.

Doug sighed. Sarah was a fantastic-looking girl, and although they had been having these nooners for nearly a year, she had not started talking about him leaving his wife. Yet. He knew the time would come and he would have to dump her. But, fingers crossed…

He was shaken out of his reverie by a discrete knock on the door.

"What is it?" he shouted while standing up from the high hotel bed.

"Complimentary room service, Sir"

That was strange. Doug had been using the boutique St George Hotel for over six months now and had never been offered anything complimentary. He had never ordered room service either. But if there was one word he could not resist to, it was the magic "complimentary" one. The hotel owed him that much, as a faithful bi-weekly patron. He did not know that his uncontrollable greed, common to all financiers, had been taken into account.

"Just a minute, please". He slid into the hotel's plush bathrobe.

He opened the door to a uniformed waiter who pushed a cart through: "Compliments of the St George, Sir".

On the immaculately white tablecloth, stood a Champaign bucket, two glasses, a bowl of strawberries and, oddly, a playing card. A Jack of hearts. But Doug was too busy trying to read the bottle label to wonder. It was "Moet et Chandon", the real stuff.

The white-gloved waiter was standing near the cart, waiting. He looked like a gaping idiot, with big horn-framed glasses and a full mane of hair that looked more like a toupee than real hair. Of course, the tip. Nothing is really free nowadays, is it? Leeches! Doug turned around to reach for his wallet on the bed table.

He suddenly felt something whirring in front of his face, but he had no time to think. His throat was suddenly constricted. He could not breathe; but, worse, the flow of blood to his brain had stopped. His primal brain took over and ordered adrenalin sent through his veins. He started to fight back, thrashing and trying to remove what was strangling him. But the piano wire squeezing the life out of him was well into his flesh, definitely out of reach. He just succeeded in scratching deep into his own neck to no avail. Strangulation was a fast way to debilitate a victim, sapping his strength and resolve while killing him. The waiter behind him was acting calmly, twisting the wire even more. Doug knew he was dying, but why? Sarah was not married, so no husband. His wife maybe? Who else? Why?

Doug died wondering. He went limp and soiled himself as life left his body. The waiter kept the choke tight for another minute as the lifeless shell that had been Douglas Svenson crumpled to the floor. The waiter pulled the body on to the bed and rearranged the soiled bathrobe that had opened up during the quick struggle. Doug looked as if sleeping now, at peace. The man disguised as a waiter opened the corpse's mouth and started to stuff it with one-hundred dollars notes from his pocket. He then fetched the playing card from the cart and proceeded to stuff it too into the still warm victim's mouth. After a pensive look at his handiwork, the killer proceeded to the door. He left without looking back. One more blood-sucking thieving banker-parasite had met his maker prematurely.

Chapter 7

Ne3 Nf6

Central Park, Manhattan, New York City

New York City is a grey place when it is drizzling in the fall. It is as if its fiery dynamism starts to slow down towards the winter. Of course the same people stroll around, the same hot dog stands crowd the pavement, but people are less rowdy. Just an impression thought Laura as she climbed the steps out of the Central Park West Metro station. She lifted up her collar against the cold and the light rain. She was wearing a grey track suit, a short fluorescent sleeveless coat and sneakers. Her lustrous black hair was held back in a pony-tail, emphasizing her high cheekbones. She hurried towards Central Park, gradually starting a light jog. As she entered the park pathways, she unobtrusively pressed the call button of the cell phone in her pocket. After 2 rings, a male voice sounded in her earphone: 'Yes?'.

'In the park'. And she ended the call.

Now she could increase her rhythm into a full run towards Park Drive. Laura had always kept in shape, and she easily lengthened her strides, falling in a calming regular rhythm. Running always helps clearing your mind; even entering a quasi-meditative state. No wonder so many people jogged in this World Capital-of-Stress-city. The Park was such a relaxing setting for jogging. It looked so close to Nature, it was hard to believe that it was in the middle of a sprawling World Megapolis and was, in fact, fully landscaped; nothing natural. There were quite a lot of runners around, in spite of the light rain and the office hours. Do all these people have jobs? After twenty minutes, she broke into a sprint, counting to thirty, and then gradually slowed down. She stopped, panting and checked behind her: There were a few joggers, but nobody sticking out as familiar. She suddenly started running in the opposite direction, the one she had been coming from, fast. None of the other joggers looked interested or changed direction. She kept running up to a small path between trees on her left. She took it and stopped abruptly after three steps. And she waited. There was nobody around. She counted to fifty, and when she reached forty two, a male jogger in a rain track suit stormed into the path. He did not give her a second glance and kept running at a punishing pace. He did not seem familiar to her, and she did not remember seeing this outfit behind her today. She got back onto the main track, reversing directions once more. When she got close to the North edge of the park, her phone rang in her ear. She pressed the button in her pocket: 'Clear', she heard. She cut off with no word and gave a sprint towards the Taxi stand on the outskirt of the park. She opened the door of the first taxi in line and crumbled inside. 'Penn Station, please. I am in a hurry'.

As the taxi drove out, easing into New York City's brutal traffic, she checked the rear window. Behind her, she saw an African American man, in a trench coat, taking his time getting in the second cab in-line, arguing with hand movements, looking around, and making sure nobody else could catch a fast cab from there.

When Laura's cab disappeared, trench-coat-man finally sat in, and asked the driver to be driven to Federal Plaza. After a minute, he took out his cell and pressed the call button: 'Looks like you are clear'.

In her cab, Laura cut off, and told the driver: 'Sorry, change of plans: Please take me to Federal Plaza'. She sat back in the back seat of the car, inhaling the smell of strong ethnic culinary spices coming from the driver's cabin, Indian sub-continent obviously. After a few minutes of closed-eyes relaxation, she contortioned to take off her short reversible sleeveless coat and put it back on with the white color out. There was a white cap in the pocket that she placed on her head, covering all her hair.

This was no ordinary psychiatrist behavior.

***

The generic ringtone of a cellular phone sounded.

'Yes?'

'I have lost her'

'Fuck! How come? You are supposed to be a professional'

'She was running in the Park and changing directions all the time. No way could I have kept tailing her on my own without being noticed.'

'Was she deliberately trying to shake you off? Did she notice you?'

'I am sure she did not make me. But she would have if I'd kept the tail. I cannot say if she was just running around or if she was trying to lose me. I do not think she was, but I cannot be sure'

'OK. Wait for her around her apartment. I'll send you back-up for the coming days. Make sure you stay on her next time. We need to be sure she is clean'

'We'll need at least two more people'

'OK'

Click

***

Ringing

'Speak'

'We need to be extremely vigilant with the new lady doctor. She has shaken a tail, and it could have been on purpose. She could be trouble'

'Keep on her 24/7. We need to be absolutely sure. In any doubt, we get rid of her. Spare no expenses'

'OK. Check it up from your side too'

Click

***

Laura was unaware of being the subject of such ominous chatter.

She left the taxi and hurried to the entrance of the Jacob K. Javits Building at Federal Plaza. She overtook the usual line of immigrants waiting to go through the security checkpoint and enter the building for USCIS services. Showing her special card to the screening people, she was given priority and went through the portal and a fast check. She jogged to the elevators, and took one half-filled car. She left the lift at the eighth floor, just it just as the doors were closing. She then took the stairs down to the seventh floor where she punched a code number in the security pad to gain access.

She stopped in front of the door marked: "Organized crime task force". She entered without knocking. The room was surprisingly big for a government office, but it still managed to look cluttered. It smelled of stale coffee. There were three desks, all invisible under mountains of papers. The walls were covered by pin-boards with pictures linked by lines and post-it notes. There were two men inside, one behind what looked like the main center desk, one sitting in front of it.

'Hi Laura' said the man behind the desk, Special agent in charge John Reilly.

 John was completely bald with a shiny scalp, but he had the square jaw one would expect of an incorruptible FBI agent in an old movie about "G-men". He was also dressed as a film enthusiast would expect from the FBI: dark suit and dark tie, even in the office.

'Hi J.R.!' Laura answered. The nickname stuck to John Reilly since the seventies "Dallas" TV show. The other man in the room, the trench-coat man from the Park, nodded silently. Dave was an-always-neatly-dressed tall African American. Only his eternal trench coat did lack style.

'Dave is pretty sure you were not followed. What do you say?'

She let herself fall into the second chair: 'I am not sure I was tailed, but I could have been. There was this guy who followed me into a side path. I cannot say for sure'

'If he did, he let go after your volte-face. There was nobody behind you both times you passed my bench, and when you climbed in the taxi. You were clean'

J.R. cut in: 'In any case, no complacency, do not let your guard down. Do everything by the book. Now where do we stand?'

'I am in, I have the job. As we expected, instead of the aide job, I'll be replacing Dr. Zimmerman, which will perhaps give me the seniority necessary to poke my nose around faster than we thought. I should not be happy this guy died; he looked OK. But this is a golden opportunity'

'How was this Van Dijk guy?'

'Smooth, easy going. Incredible how crooks can look deceivingly trustworthy'

'If they did not, they would not be very successful crooks, would they? When do you start?'. J.R. was always talking in short sentences and to the point. And he was always accompanying his short outbursts with nervous hand movements. He had no life but for the Bureau, and it was taking its toll.

'On Monday, but I am already hopping in and out. The bad thing for us is that their operation is compartmentalized: The trading and the client meetings are all happening in Manhattan. And I am based Upstate with the autistic patients, running math models. It will probably take time for me to be trusted enough to sniff around the main office. Anyway, we knew we'd have to take it slowly. Head of Security is a paranoid Nazi'

'Yep. Jan Thompson is quite a character. We have a file on him, and he was probably involved in pretty ugly stuff in Apartheid times. Be very careful around him. Now, did you get the name of the new autistic kid they are trying to bring in?'

'Yes, Patient Number Five. The father of this boy is Joshua Applebee, from Norwalk, Fairfield County in Connecticut. I have the address here'. She passed on a crumpled piece of paper extracted from her sneaker. J.R. took it with a moue of light disgust.

'Ok. We'll take it from here. Now, a short reminder of the protocols and here are ten SIM cards'. He passes on a small plastic bag. 'We have been over this several times, but once more cannot hurt: If you need to contact us or we need to contact you, you send to or receive an email from: Your sister in Albuquerque. If it is urgent, it will be from or to your brother in Chicago. You have the addresses memorized. In both cases, after the mail, in or out, you use a new SIM card, in numerical order, into your phone and call Dave's cell for instructions. Destroy the card as soon as you have finished. In case of emergency, you call your gynecologist for an appointment; you have the number on speed dial. If you need immediate support or extraction, you call Dave directly, and excuse yourself for the wrong number. There will be no meeting outside those set-ups: You are now on your own. Hide SIM cards on yourself or in your handbag, and remember that these people have bugged your place and will bug your office. They'll be watching you very carefully, especially in the first weeks or months'.

'I got it, J.R. They have been sniffing around for months now'

'Be very careful, Laura. The people behind this fund are dangerous people. And remember we are looking for a proof of their connection to organized crime. We know the Latvian Mafia bankrolled this fund, and not for charity purposes. We need to know what is happening there, so we can bring these scumbags down'

'OK, boss. We'll be in touch. Keep my back safe'. Laura stood up with the plastic bag, hi-fived Dave and left.

Both men watched the door close. After a minute, Dave asked: "Why did you not tell her about Jack Zimmerman? The guy dies mysteriously after he contacts SEC. She shouldn't know that? She should not know about the SEC?'

'Dave, I had no choice here. This is need-to-know. She knows her job and knows it is dangerous. She must be able to behave normally. And we cannot be sure he was murdered, it could be a heart attack; the guy was fat, wasn't he? And anyway these SEC people are useless'.

Dave knew his boss was angry: He had been reprimanded by higher-ups at having pushed the SEC to do an emergency audit that gave no results. This inter-agency politics were never good for your career. Reilly suspected, but could not prove, that there had been a leak at the Securities and Exchange Commission.

'Yeah. Hell of a coincidence. I still think she should know; she could be in danger'

'Duly noted, Dave. But it is my call, not yours'

Dave did not relent. John Reilly was too intense, and prone to take unnecessary risks. 'She could be next in line, J.R. Remember it. She is replacing a guy who could have been murdered. You do not want her death on your conscience do you?'

John looked down, but did not answer. He was still seething about the reprimand from the higher ups. And he had a lot on his plate; even a serial killer on the loose. He really cared about his agents, but they had a job to do, and it was not the boy-scouts, was it? He admitted to himself that he also cared a lot about success, even at a cost.

***

Folger Park, Capitol Hill, Washington D.C.

John Kwan was a 35-years old American-born ethnic Chinese, from San Francisco. He was a poster boy for integration, having grown up in one of the most liberal cities in America. He had been a brilliant student, played football, eaten apple pie and done everything his friends from all backgrounds had done in this melting pot. He had not been discriminated against in any way. Neither had he been subject to racist slights. It was therefore difficult to explain why he had immersed himself in his ethnic culture while in college, and had he started feeling Chinese first and American second. It is in a study group for perfecting his written Chinese that he had become prey to Communist Chinese mole recruiters. Many good things can be said about Chinese culture; one of the most differentiating from the West's instant-gratification syndrome would be the ubiquitous importance of patience. John had been slowly manipulated, in a process supervised by specialist psychiatrists in China, to become more and more alienated from his American background. With Confucian patience, it had taken over six years before he had been officially recruited by the Ministry of State Security, the Chinese spy agency, as an official mole. He had been thoroughly trained in China and then sent back for a period of dormancy. He had set up, in Washington D.C., a travel agency specializing in the Orient, and he had been ordered to concentrate on making it a successful business. Only after five innocuous years, had he been activated for small but gradually more important missions. The Chinese knew a thing or two about safe procedures and long term goals.

John was now sitting on a famous "fountain bench" in Folger Park, working on his iPad. There were another two strollers sitting on the bench, but on the other side of the fountain. A Caucasian man of about fifty approached the bench and asked if he could sit beside him. John nodded his agreement, and kept fiddling with his iPad. The man sitting near him opened his back pack and proceeded to take out a lunch box, with strangely trembling hands. He left his back pack on the bench. It very much looked like John's. The man was still eating when John picked up the bag in a natural gesture, stuffed his iPad inside and stood up, leaving behind his own, empty, bag. He proceeded out of the park, strolling slowly to check for a possible tail, as he had been taught. In the bag, -not his-, was a USB key, hopefully holding secret data from a private company under contract with the Pentagon for stealth technology. Should the data be what his masters in Beijing were looking for, the Swiss bank account of the lunching man would be credited with 500,000 dollars. John despised those greedy people who would betray their country for money. No real Chinese man would do anything like that, ever. Or so he surmised.

He saw a pair of uniformed policeman walking towards him, and his heart jumped. What should he do? Run? One of the law men looked at him. It was curious.

He kept his cool and kept walking until they crossed paths, nodding a polite hello. John had not noticed he had been holding his breath. He exhaled and quickened his pace. He had to get away fast.

From the shadows, an oriental-looking man had been watching him intently.

Chapter 8

Bc4 c6

Norwalk suburbs, Connecticut

Joshua Applebee was not a man to be trifled with. Be straight with him, or be ready to suffer the consequences.

He was standing on the path in front of the typical American white picket fence house, waiting. This was an upper middle class suburban house with a porch entrance and big French windows. The front garden was well kept and appealing. The "For Sale" sign near the mailbox bore the name of his realtor company, Applebee's. Joshua looked at his 'Grand Complications Platinum Patek Phillipe' watch; men like their toys, among them expensive watches. Of course he was always early, waiting for his clients to show up. Joshua cut an athletic figure at 45, testament to his previous career as a special-forces soldier and his commitment to healthy living. Another souvenir of those Navy Seals times was a rather long scar beside his right eye going down to mid-cheek. Joshua was keeping active and had a tanned face from his day-time jogging. Despite thinning hair, he had rugged good looks and a trustworthy appearance. This had been a crucial factor in his professional success, and Applebee's had become the leading realtor in the area.

Norwalk had long been a problematic lower-income city in one of the richest counties in the United States, but hard mayoral work on the quality of schools and urban renewal, had succeeded and caused a renaissance of the town and a gradual improvement. Nowadays, the suburbs of the city were sprawling and attracting upwardly mobile middle class families. Joshua had been a prime beneficiary of this movement by positioning himself early and right in the soft spot.

A black sedan stopped in front of the house, five minutes late, and an African American couple climbed out. They were well-dressed and obviously educated, just the type of clients suitable for this kind of neighborhood. Joshua approached, hand extended: 'Mr. and Mrs. Smith?'

'And you are Mr. Applebee, I presume. Nice to meet you'. The husband shook his hand.

'Let us go inside and have a look', Joshua proposed, while shaking hand with the wife. 'Check up the entrance and the garden first, I think you will like it'.

'Thanks Mr. Applebee. We have got it. We really are more interested in the interior of the property, if you don't mind. Let us go in'.

'No problem, the client is king. Follow me please'. Joshua was slightly nonplussed and opened the big heavy front door. After moving aside to let them in, he closed the door behind the couple and prepared to start his pitch, but Mr. Smith interrupted him: 'Mr. Applebee, please do not be alarmed, but we are federal agents and are not interested in the property'.

Mr. Smith slid his hand in his jacket, and found himself pinned against the wall, his hand immobilized and with Joshua's elbow across his throat.

Mrs. Smith, obviously startled, spoke slowly and lifted both palms up to emphasize the lack of aggressiveness in her stance.

'We really are FBI agents. You are not in any kind of trouble, Mr. Applebee. Please relax. Let him go. We need your help and we had no choice but to approach you this way. We apologize'

'I do not understand. No sudden moves, please'. Joshua did not let go of Mr. Smith and kept his eyes on Mrs. Smith. 'Explain'.

'We just need to talk to you discreetly. Please let him go'.

Joshua let Mr. Smith free and took a step back into a non-aggressive but ready position.

Mr. Smith coughed and shook his arm. He was pale. That had been unexpected.

'Please have a look at our credentials, Mr. Applebee, I'll place them on the table. And again, do not worry please, you are in no trouble whatsoever'. Mr. Smith took a FBI shield from his jacket pocket and placed it on the hallway table, and then took a step back. He then extended his hand to his wife who handed him a similar badge from her purse. 'As you can see, the names are not Smith. Please check us up by calling the New York City FBI office directly. My name is Dave Freeman, working for special agent in charge John Reilly'

Joshua took the shields and had a look. They looked genuine enough, heavy and official-looking, but these things are probably easy to fake. Joshua remembered that a New-York congressman had been making a lot of noise a few years ago about the free sale of fake police badges, because some had been used in abduction attempts. Congressman Weiner, or something.

Joshua waved them in, unapologetically: 'Let us sit in the lounge. I'll call'

'But please do not use your own phone, Mr. Applebee. I'll explain later. Please use mine'. Dave gave him his Blackberry.

They sat down on the leather couches of the spacious lounge, around the coffee table, tastefully adorned by a few books and magazines. Joshua was a pro, and his listings were always ready-for-sale up to the last detail. A frowning Joshua used the Blackberry to Google

FBI NYC phone number. The two agents sat quietly across, really careful now not to upset him.

'My name is Joshua Applebee, and I would like to talk to agent-in-charge John Reilly please'

'Just a moment please'. Music, of course, and then another female voice: 'Mr. Reilly's Office, how can I help you?'

'Good morning. My name is Joshua Applebee and I would like to talk to Mr. Reilly please'

'Mr. Reilly was expecting your call, Mr. Applebee. I am transferring you'. No music this time, and after a few seconds: 'Mr. Applebee, good morning. I am special agent in charge John Reilly. I am sorry we had to contact you this way, but my agents with you will be able to explain'

'So these people are legit? African American couple in their mid-thirties'

'Yes, Mr. Applebee. These are real FBI agents and they will tell you we need your help. Please keep this confidential. And again our apologies for the way we had to contact you but we had no choice, as you will understand'

'OK. I'll listen, but I am a busy man. Have a good day, Mr. Reilly'

'You too. Thank you for your understanding'

Joshua signed off and looked up. 'OK. Shoot! ', with a faint smile, 'I mean, do not shoot but talk away. I am listening, but do not forget I have a business to run. What is this about?'

Dave took out a bunch of papers from his attaché case: 'This has something to do with the Rain Fund and a running investigation'

Joshua looked surprised at hearing the name, but kept silent.

'We need you to sign a federal NDA before we can explain. Bureaucracy and procedures, you understand. Sorry'

'So you come to me under false pretenses, you take up my time, and on top of it, you want me to sign stuff before you tell me what it is about' . Joshua still had a thin smile on his lips.

'Mr. Applebee, we are sorry, but again, these are procedures we are obliged to go through. Divulging information about a running investigation is a criminal offense and the lawyers insist we get the paperwork done. If you refuse to, we cannot force you to in any way. We would not, in any case. Not after that any way'. Mr Smith rubbed his neck, still red from Joshua's choke. 'We need your help, but without these NDA's, we would have to thank you and leave without proceeding'.

Joshua's interest was piqued now. How did these people know about the Rain Fund connection?

'OK. I want to hear the story. Pass on the papers and let us get on with it. I still want to sell houses today'

Joshua glanced over the papers and scribbled a signature on all them, one by one. He laid down the pen and looked up.

'OK. I am listening'

'Mr. Applebee, thank you for that. We know you have signed a whole bunch of NDA's with the Rain Fund and are not supposed to talk about that. Therefore, we shall tell you what we know and you do not have to comment. We know that you have signed a contract with the Prometheus arm of the Rain Fund which will basically employ your autistic son as a mathematics and statistics research analyst. Your son will receive the best care available today for his condition, 24 hours a day, and on top of that will be handsomely paid for whatever he will be doing there'

'As you said, I cannot confirm anything, but this is not illegal by any standards'

'No, it is not. But the Rain fund is run by organized crime and is under investigation. That is the part that is to be kept secret. We have established that the money used to buy half of the fund 3 years ago came from an East-European criminal organization active in the

US; Really bad people into sex slave trade, drugs, extortion and violent crimes. The fund is laundering money for them, but we do not know how. It has reportedly the highest return of all hedge funds in the business, and, given the mob angle, it is fishy and extremely unlikely to be legal'.

Joshua cut in: 'But this is where people like Tom, my son, come in. The psychiatrist who reeled us in explained to us how good his patients were to spot trends, and they use that for their trading. He showed us data and we saw the other autistic workers there on the job. There is some logic there, isn't it?'

'There is some logic and we believe they carefully polish this image to justify these exceptional results. But the experts we consulted all agree that the successful use of autistic patients for such work is highly improbable. So there must be some other explanation'

'Excuse me Dave. It is Dave isn't it?'. Dave, "Mr. Smith", nodded.

'As you can easily understand, I am not unfamiliar with the subject. Forget my son for a minute.I could refer you, for example to well known Daniel Tammet, a high functioning autistic savant. The guy can perform mind-boggling mathematical calculations at breakneck speeds and he also can describe how he does it. He also speaks seven languages'. Joshua stopped and looked at them intently, his eyes softening: 'And my Tom is also high functioning, he just lacks the ability to empathize and socialize'. After a few seconds, Joshua regained his composure: 'And I have seen their facilities, and I have seen people like Tom sitting in front of computers, and I have seen the staff analyzing their input. There were mathematicians and statisticians around, real geeks, interpreting and checking the data. I have seen this operation and these people are all working, really working on that. So I am not convinced. Anyway what do you want from me?'

'And here we are getting to the point. We have been trying to infiltrate the fund, but it has proved very, very difficult. The security checks and the continuous surveillance they apply on their employees are incredible, again not at all in line with typical business procedures. We need somebody inside, to help us understand how their operation runs, how is the money laundered and where are these returns coming from. We have had the SEC check them with no results. You can help us by getting us some information from the inside: You are not a future employee and you come as a package with your son. Their selection process does not apply, at least not fully'.

'Wow! You want me to spy on them?'

The woman introduced as Mrs. Smith answered. She had a surprisingly soft voice for a law enforcement officer: 'Mr. Applebee, please listen to me. I shall be blunt. We know a lot about you. We know you are a patriot, we know of your two tours in Iraq with the Special Forces and your commendations. We know you would have nothing to do with scum like the mafia bosses involved here, with the kind of crimes they are committing and with the laundering of their dirty money. We also know your wife bailed out when she understood how difficult it would be to raise Tom. We know you love your son and would do anything for his well-being. We know you are doing very well in your business, but that the special needs of Tom are a big drain on your resources. We know, this contract is a great opportunity for Tom to get the best possible care while even being paid for it. We know this would allow Tom to lead a life as normal as possible with his condition. But, this thing will not last, because we are taking these slavers and drug lords down, no matter what. And you do not want to be part of such a sleazy operation'.

'It looks like you know a lot about me. This is quite disturbing'

"Mrs. Smith" countered fast: 'We know much less about you than your friends at Rain. Why do you think we approached you here? You are followed, observed and listened to. They have checked every inch of your past, and I bet that your interviews with them were numerous and very thorough. Maybe more like interrogations'

'What do you mean? Followed? Listened to? Do you say they have my phones tapped?

'This is a fact we have checked and ascertained, Mr. Applebee'.

Joshua darkened but stayed silent.

Dave, a.k.a. Mr. Smith, took back the pulpit: 'Mr. Applebee, we want to ask you to join the program and simply leave your eyes open, try to understand how things work, befriend people there. We know that if you take on this task, you will do it because you are a decent American, not for anything else. But we still would consider you an undercover agent, deputize you and pay you. Of course, these are not the amounts of money that would allow maintaining the kind of care your son would get there, but it is the best the government can do. When we bring this operation down though, there is the possibility of a reward fee on illegal money confiscated to be shared between the citizens having helped. It is based and on top of the whistleblower IRS scheme. You probably are aware of this scheme, in which every citizen can fill a form and give the IRS information about tax evaders. This thing has been going on for 140 years already, and the whistleblowers can get up to 15% of the recovered unpaid taxes. But since 2006, the IRS really started cracking down on big time cheaters and introduced a new program, in which informants are paid a *minimum* of 15% and a maximum of 30% of the amount owed in taxes. But there's a catch: In order to collect a reward, the taxes, penalties and interest in dispute must add up to at least $2 million, which in this case is far below the expected bust'.

'OK, I get the money part. But would this job be dangerous?'

'This is the white collar part of the operation and we would always be a step behind you. So I would say you should be safe, although anything is possible, there are no guarantees'.

'I meant for Tom, not for me'

Dave, an experienced recruiter, wondered how he had missed that. This guy was a fighter and only cared about his son. The operation looked good though, already half in the bag.

'I see no reason why Tom should be in danger. He is no threat to anyone, he cannot be a witness. Really, no. In any case, for as long as it runs, the experience should be good for Tom, he'd get the best possible care and maybe get better. Who knows?'. Dave corrected himself immediately: ' I do not mean he is not OK, but you understand my meaning. It is in no way condescending or derogatory'.

Joshua nodded pensively, seemingly unaware of how scared they were of him.

Mrs. Smith cut in again: 'We realize you need to think about it. We understand there is no way you can give us an answer here and now. And in any case, we need to get out of here. More time here would look suspicious'. She stood up.' We shall contact your office in two days for an appointment to see another property, and you can tell us what you think. Do not, I repeat, do not under any circumstance talk on the phone about any of this. Or tell anybody for that matter. *That* would be dangerous. And now, let us sign your visit report: Everything should be as with regular clients'.

The ball was now rolling, fiddling with the law of the unintended consequences.

***

Manhattan, New York City

Adam Weatherspoon was sitting for lunch at his favorite Mac Donald's, across the street from his place of work. He just wanted quiet and some comfort food.

 He liked to come here, just for the opportunity to unwind and get out of the office, unlike his boss and most of his colleagues who ordered take-out. Adam loved fast food and did not care about the health fad: He always ordered the biggest greasiest burger out there, and with a supersized milkshake. He went to the gym three times a week to get his small paunch under control; that was good enough.

The place was packed, as it usually was at this hour, but he had a table for two just for himself, on account of his bag on the chair in front of him. Suddenly, there was a woman standing in front of him with a tray in her hands: 'Do you mind if I sit here, please? I see there is a bag on the chair'.

Adam hated the idea, but how could he refuse? It was annoying; most people got the message that you wanted to be left alone, and looked for easier seating.

'Please, do sit down', as he was removing his bag and placing it in his lap. He looked at the woman and thought: 'That is my luck. Not only crowded at lunch, and it must be by an ugly woman'.

The woman sitting in front of him looked about forty. She had grey unruly hair and librarian glasses which made her look mousy. She had a hint of a mustache, and was dressed like an old maid, long dress, flat shoes and a cardigan. On her tray, there was a salad and a paper cup of tea. Adam was thinking: 'Why go to Mac Donald's for a meal like that?'

The woman, now sitting, started talking immediately: 'Mr. Weatherspoon, my name is Nathalie Zini and I am a journalist for Inside Business Weekly. I would like to ask you a few questions about your place of employment'.

Adam choked on his food; he just had had a big bite of bacon, beef and bread. As he was coughing crumbs up, she was proceeding: 'What you tell me is in total confidence. I never reveal my sources, even in court. I am also in position to offer you some money for information about the Rain Fund'.

At the end of a cough fit, Adam, answered: 'Leave me alone. I have nothing to tell you'. And he restarted coughing.

At least he was answering something; this one was weaker than the previous ones she had approached. He probably had been well-raised and conditioned to answer when addressed politely. 'Please

Mr. Weatherspoon. Do not worry; you do not have to answer any question that breaches your contract or anything. My questions are simple and of the public domain'. They must be hooked first, and then reeled in slowly.

'I cannot answer anything about the Fund. Please leave me alone'.

'Can you at least confirm that you are an IT technician there? This is nothing confidential, is it?'

'I am a computer technician, but there is nothing I can tell you about the Fund. It is strictly forbidden'

Great. He was starting to talk. 'Why so much secrecy? There is nothing illegal going on, so there must be things you can tell me that are not proprietary. I can reward your services in perfect discretion. What exactly are you doing at the Fund, Mr. Weatherspoon? '

Adam was scared, looking around him. He was under tremendous pressure, not knowing what to do. He suddenly remembered what he had been told to do at his induction, should anything like that happen: "R.B.R. - Refer to Public Relations, Break contact, Report". It had been drilled into them by the Security guy.

'Are you feeding data into computers?'. She was relentless.

Adam stood up, grabbed his bag and his half-finished burger and ran outside. His jump had tilted the small table and let slide to the floor both his milkshake and the woman's tray. He did not care. She did not run after him. She was looking at his back, wondering what kind of secrets made people that afraid.

She would not let go, she would learn what was going on there. And let the world know!

***

Citex Building, Manhattan, New York City

Murders happen unexpectedly, it is a given. Or they do not.

The security guard, in full uniform, was strolling in the hallways of
the eleventh floor of the office building. It was nearly eight p.m. and
most offices were deserted. He was strolling nonchalantly, fiddling
with the baton hanging from his instrument belt. He stopped in front
of the glass doors marked "Rice and Jones Securities, Inc", and
looked inside. There was light seeping from the Venetian stores of
the last office on the right. As expected. Mrs. Jones was a
workaholic, always last to leave the office. Of course, when you
make millions ripping people off, it is worth your while. The guard
started humming quietly under his moustache the Ray Charles tune
"Mrs. Jones" that had just popped in his mind, by association. He
used the stolen master key to open the glass doors and passed in
front of the deserted reception desk. When he approached the lighted
office, he could hear a muffled voice, obviously in a heated phone
conversation. He would still have to check whether Mrs. Jones was
alone, although a near certainty, but one cannot be cautious enough.
The guard retreated into the shadows of the open space and took out
a deck of playing cards from his pocket. He started to shuffle the
cards, absentmindedly, his eyes becoming glassy and focus-less. He
was getting into "the zone". He took a deep breath, exhaling slowly,
relaxing, and turned over the card on the top of the deck: Ten of
spades. Shit! A black card! He felt a stab of disappointment
engulfing him. But the rules were the rules. It was the first time that
it had happened, but a black card meant that Mrs. Jones was meant
to live, in spite of her swindling ways. He kept looking at the card,
hoping it would turn red by some conjuring trick. But he knew that
was it. A few months of research, a few weeks of shadowing her,
everything down the drain. Nothing doing!

The guard impersonator retreated slowly towards the entrance, deep
in thought. He was already planning his next mission. That is why,
maybe, he did not hear the door of the office open behind him.

"Hey! You! What are you doing here? You are not supposed to enter
the offices"

That had been a mistake! Always be vigilant. The crusade depends on it. What was he going to do now? Run, bluff, kill anyway? He decided to play it by ear. He half-turned over, in place, near the door: "Sorry ma'am. I thought I saw something move in the dark, but it was nothing. I just had to make sure". He could easily fake a slight Spanish accent, and his moustache would be the useless focus of any description.

She did not reply immediately, glaring at him with all the self-assured might of the successful power-woman in presence of an underling.

That's it! A consummate bitch. If she makes a fuss or takes another step, she is dead.

"Next time have the office ring up first. Now get out!"

"Sorry ma'am. Won't happen again". He closed the glass door with slightly shaking hands. That had been close. It would have been easier, and more rewarding, to kill her anyway, red or black card. But rules were rules…

Chapter 9

d5 Be7

Norwalk suburbs, Connecticut

Two days later, Joshua was again standing in front of a house for sale, waiting. 'Same kind of house, by the way, but this is no real sale again', was he thinking. The last two days had been difficult; he had lost some sleep on soul-searching. Pros and cons. During the day he was irritable and un-focused. He was constantly checking around whether anybody was following him, or even just looking strangely at him. He had snapped at his assistant, for the first time in years and she had been truly shocked; it was so unlike him. Yesterday night, he had been short with Tom's caretaker when coming back home from work. He quickly apologized, but realized that he had to come to a decision and leave the uncertainty behind. One way or another would be better than over-thinking this dilemma.

It was drizzling, very lightly, but he was standing in the rain, deep in thought. His eyes were scouring the beautiful trees lining the street and starting to lose their foliage, but not really seeing them. His face was wet, but he did not seem to realize it. His right hand was nervously playing with the keys in his blazer pocket: He had not made a decision yet. This was going to be one of those on-the-spot things.

He was early and had to make this decision before the FBI agents arrived. They had called, as agreed, and he had proposed the sighting of this house. His eyes were again wandering down the typical suburban street, when he noticed the black Camry parked a few houses down with the driver still inside. There was something familiar with the car, like he had noticed it before. Irritated, he started to march briskly in its direction to have a look at the driver. But just at that moment, the "Smiths" stopped their car beside him, looking at him strangely. He regained control and stopped to greet them.

The agents climbed down and shook his hand in turn, slightly over-playing their house-hunting roles. They were again fully credible and dressed as the typical professional couple living in this neighborhood. This time, "Mrs. Smith" had a shorter dress showing off beautifully-shaped legs, Joshua could not help notice. He turned his back to the Camry and told them quietly: 'I think the black Camry behind me has been following me. I really want to check it up'

Mrs. Smith took his arm gently and prodded him towards the House for sale.

'Do not confront them under any circumstances, Mr. Applebee. Trust me, it would only bring trouble and serve no purpose. Let us go in and talk'

Joshua let himself be lead and opened the door to let them in. They all went directly to the living room and sat down, barely having a look at the house, although it was more upscale and better designed than the previous one they had met in two days ago. There was a faint odor of lavender in the air, probably from one of those plug-in continuous air fresheners.

Dave cut to the chase: 'What have you decided, Mr. Applebee?'

'The truth is that two minutes ago, I was still clueless. It is a very difficult decision, and I especially need to choose what is best for Tom... But seeing this car shadowing me, just made me flip. This invasion of privacy, and what you have told me about the people behind the fund, it all stands against everything I believe in'

The agents stayed silent, watching Joshua intently. Dave changed position on the black leather couch, but said nothing; he was an experienced recruiter and knew when to shut up. Joshua continued: 'You probably don't know this, but my parents, now both deceased, have been seriously hurt by the Bernie Madoff affair. They were wealthy but as good as ruined when the Ponzi scheme collapsed. If there is something fishy behind this fund, I owe it to them to ferret it out'.

Dave nodded. He had known about Joshua's parents, but had kept this argument in reserve if further convincing was needed. He knew everything about Joshua, even his being in the long list of potential suspects for the serial killing of East Coast bankers. Joshua's name was at the intersection of having the required killing experience from his army days, having a motive to attack financial crooks and having sold the house to a Connecticut victim.

It could not have been better than Joshua agreeing to cooperate without having to show that they knew about the financial swindling of his parents. Dave felt a little guilty pushing and manipulating Joshua into taking the job, but it is not as though there was an alternative. Anyway, he had a job to do and a career to further; he was honest, but not less ambitious than the next guy.

'So you are taking the job?'

'Yes. I'll do it, I'll do it'. Joshua looked relieved, now that he has made a decision. *'Alea Jacta est',* he thought; this was a life-changing decision. 'I am definitely not doing it for the money, but

I'll want the agent's pay you talked about and the reward money if it comes to that. I have googled the IRS whistle-blower scheme for big cheaters: It was astounding. In 2008 only, the IRS has received tips from about 500 informants identifying over 1000 big-fish cheaters. If any money is made this way, that will be all for Tom's future. I'll also want insurance covering Tom's all future care, if anything happens to me'.

'You have got all that, Mr. Applebee. We have the papers here for you to sign. Nothing stays with you, but all will be handled by the legal department at Federal Plaza in Manhattan. The money will be paid monthly in a trust managed by the head of the department, Mr. Zacharia Levi. Just remember his name'.

Joshua signed the papers extended to him without reading. 'What exactly do you want me to do?'

'First of all, you go in slowly and get acquainted with the people. Remember that information can be gathered from the most menial workers up to the top. Keep your ears and eyes open. Befriend the staff and become part of the landscape with frequent visits. You are looking for clues on how the money gets in and how it is managed, which people do what, and what is especially secret and protected. Try to befriend the heads of the fund if possible, Alex Prilutski and Olivier Van Dijk. Once you are well inside, you could ask them to handle your money in spite of the fact it is small potatoes for them. That would justify your asking financial questions'

Joshua was now leaning forward, concentrating on what was said.

'We shall give you a very special USB key that looks innocuous but can copy all files in a computer in a few minutes and without leaving any traces. Try to stick it in any computer you come across when you are sure you are not observed and can get away with it. But remember, there are security cameras everywhere, and not necessarily visible. We'll contact you every few months for a short debrief, the same way we met today: Mr. and Mrs. Smith will want to see another house. Now, if you need to contact us, you have your office call us about a viewing of something suitable. If you need to see us urgently, do the same but call directly yourself. Our number always goes to voice mail, but is always listened to in real time. If anyone is in danger, or you need to be extracted, you call the same number but mention that the house you have to propose is outside the city limits. Did you get all that? Any questions?'

'I think I have it. Do I have any help on the inside?'

Joshua noticed a tiny frown on Mrs. Smith's part.

Dave answered: 'Mr. Applebee, even if we had anybody on the inside, we would not tell you, for everyone's security and best interests. But we don't. You are our only resource to bring those bad guys down'. Dave hesitated, and continued after a brief pause:' Remember at all times that you are always under some kind of scrutiny. People are watching or listening, or both. It will probably ease with time, but do not confide in anyone, no matter what'.

Dave passed him a small USB key, with a key holder. 'This is the hi-tech key. Put your keys on it so you always have it with you and people get used to see it around'

'Thanks' said Joshua. It really looked innocuous. While fitting it to his current key ring, he was already wondering whether he was not doing something stupid. His hand went to the scar below his eye, in a nervous tic he had when stressed.

'Do not thank us, Mr. Applebee. We should thank you. You are the kind of man that has made this country great. We know Tom is joining in a few days, so you are now on your own. We shall be leaving now, and contact you in a few weeks. Take care of yourself. Be very careful, take it easy and ease in slowly. And God Bless You; this is not going to be easy'

Joshua answered with a wry smile: 'Do you know what the SEALS motto is?'

Both agents nodded no.

'It is not the only motto, but the most popular with the troops: Yesterday was the only easy day'.

Both agents shook his hand gravely and left. Joshua stayed on the couch, playing with his scar. What was wrong with him? Again doing the right thing? He had learned long ago that most people cared about themselves first and not about things bigger than themselves. Had he not done more than his part for his country already? People do not really change, do they? Still, this time was different; there was Tom to take into account.

Joshua left the house and locked the door. He went to his car slowly, scanning the street. No sign of the black Camry. Joshua climbed into his Lexus SUV and drove away, deep in thought.

After ten minutes of leisurely driving back in the direction of the office, he suddenly caught sight of a black Camry, two cars behind him. His blood reached boiling point in a jolt. Sometimes, he did not let himself think before doing; he was more of a man of action than an undercover agent. There was a side road coming up on his right, and he took it suddenly, before slowing down sharply after the corner. And here it came: the black Camry had taken the same turn and increased speed, most probably to keep him in sight. Rage-blinded, Joshua slammed the brakes, bringing the car to a sudden stop, and the Camry behind was forced to apply an emergency braking maneuver, with a deafening screeching of tires. From the corner of his eye, Joshua could see a woman pushing a baby pram on the pavement startle mightily. The Camry crashed a few inches into Joshua's bumper. Joshua was braced for impact and avoided whiplash, but the shock of the collision was still more than he expected. He started scrambling out of the car, but forgot to first unbuckle his belt. The Camry used these few extra seconds to reverse fast and then overtake the Lexus, just as Joshua managed climbing out. It sped away, with Joshua watching, standing in the middle of the street, trying to make sense of the plate number. There was a pervasive odor of burnt rubber, and the woman with the pram was looking at him in a state of shock.

This was definitely somebody following him! No horning, honking, swearing, fist brandishing: This was not normal road behavior. The FBI was right. Joshua got only a glimpse of the driver: black hair,

Mediterranean type, no beard. Not much. He would not recognize him if he met him on the street.

He climbed back into his slightly damaged car to write down the plate number as he remembered it. He did not know what he was going to do with it, but better having done something than being a passive victim. He had an old friend from his army days who had a Private Investigation company, maybe he would ask him to check it up. He felt stupid for what he had done, but good at having confronted the punk. He was, after all, a warrior at heart- *Miles Militis*.

They had better not come near him again.

***

Guangzhou, China

Colonel Jeung was on his knees in a dark damp cell with no windows. His hands were tied behind his back. He was cold, but still sweating. His knees hurt from the concrete floor and his wrists were tingling from the lack of blood circulation. There was a figure in a white lab coat in front of him. The figure approached and bent toward him: It was Ting, the Chief Engineer of the Peng project at Sin Kiang. Ting had big and thick glasses, making his eyes look small and mean. He was smiling malevolently. Another figure approached from the shadows, holding a handgun: It was General Wong. General Wong was smiling too. He passed the gun to Ting, telling him: 'Do it. Three can keep a secret, only if two of them are dead. Do it'. And suddenly, Ting's head exploded, throwing pieces of flesh around. Curiously, his thick glasses fell intact to the ground even before his gun and his dead body. Jeung was covered with gore, feeling sick with revulsion and scared to death. He felt his heart racing and his throat constricted. Wong had taken Ting's place, with a smoking gun in his hand. He placed the hot barrel of the gun onto Jeung's forehead and started to squeeze the trigger slowly.

Jeung screamed and sat up in his bed. His wife, startled out of her sleep, gripped his arm: 'Quiet, quiet. Everything is fine. It is just a nightmare. Everything is fine'.

Jeung's heart was beating fast. He was covered in sweat. It was incredible how those nightmares were feeling real. This had been going on since he was back from the Gobi desert, making his life and his family's unbearable. Tonight, his screams had not awakened their young daughter, but it was more the exception than the rule.

Jeung had not pulled the trigger himself in the execution of the civilian employees of project *Peng*, but, unlike the Nazis of World war Two, Jeung did not believe that "just following orders" made things right. His conscience was torturing him for his supervisory role and for not fighting more to have this absurd decision cancelled.

He stood up and went to gulp down a glass of cheap whisky. He was becoming addicted to alcohol. Wiping his mouth, he took the decision to seek a private and discreet psychiatrist to treat him, even though it was against all regulations.

Chapter 10

a4 Nbd7

Prometheus Foundation, Washington County, New York State

I was a much lesser man than Jack had been. I had admired him and even had been a bit jealous of his integrity. I was more calculating and egoistic than him, and I decided to try to emulate him from now on.

I was sitting in what used to be his office. Everything looked and smelled like Jack here. I do not think I'll ever think of it as anything else other than Jack's office. It was, in fact, more of an oversized cubicle. It was all windows and at the newly built mezzanine floor above the huge working space for the patients. The "big room" that had been the main lounge of the original mansion and that could have housed three times my apartment. It had high ceilings, stone walls and supporting columns, and before our redecoration, it had looked like a Templar's Hall of Crusades' times. I liked the Foundation, because everything here looked like laden with history and grandeur. It was, in some way, lifting. I was sitting in Jack's chair, and from there I could see the entire work-room. From the intercom on the table, I could have listened to what was said in any part of the room if I had known how to use it. Behind me were the side tables, desks and filing cabinets, all very neat and organized. On the side opposite to me, I could see, through the windows and down on the ground floor, six distinct working areas with large computer screens on wide tables. It looked very much like a posh office with outsized furniture, but in bright colors. Three patients were actually working on their computers, with a caretaker assigned to each, keeping an eye on them. Behind each of the workstations there were couches and armchairs and thick carpets. It was cluttered with games and books. It did not look like an ordinary office. Each of the patients had his own space for relaxing or recharging his batteries. In fact, one of them, Number 2, was lying down on his couch, his caretaker sitting on the nearby armchair and talking to him. Number 2 was not even looking at him. For Number 2, eye contact was nearly unheard of, and so was physical contact. When passing through, I had gathered that the caretaker was working on discouraging the repetitive behavior of Number 2, who had started lately to walk endlessly around a piece of furniture. Of course, what I could see from here were only the patient's working spaces; they had living quarters in the back of the mansion, on the same floor.

I let my eyes wander around the room. This was very much Jack's creation and the heart and soul of the Fund I had dreamed of. The colors were bright and happy, but every individual space was slightly different. Jack had pioneered an individual approach to patient care and work inducement. Jack was a good man, a pioneer in his field, and probably a genius in his own right. He did not deserve to die. Why is life so unfair?

'Olivier?'

I snapped out of my reverie. Laura was standing in the doorway, leaning on the side, and she looked like she had been there for some time. It slightly embarrassed me and I wiped my wet eyes discreetly. She had the effect of making me feel self-conscious; I was not used to that, and it was annoying me. Laura had probably noticed but did not show it; she just sported a friendly smile. She wore, like always, a white doctor lab coat. She had told me after our first meeting that she saw this as a uniform, placing herself in the right caring frame of mind. I liked her professional and serious attitude. Especially, as the coat could not hide how gorgeous she was. I was surprised at my emerging feelings for her. It was not like me, at all…But I had sadly not felt reciprocity from her part; she was always nice, but coolly professional.

'I hope I am not disturbing you'

We had had a few short meetings since she had started here, but mostly about her fitting in and getting started. I already had had the distinct impression that she was very good with the patients, and it was confirmed to me by the Head of the Nursing team.

'No, no, Laura. Sorry, I was deep in thought. I did not see you there. Is everything OK?'

'Yes, thank you. I was just passing in front of Jack's office, and I saw you inside. Just saying hi'

Her office was very similar to Jack's, slightly smaller, but further on the open hallway of the mezzanine.

'I was just collecting Jack's personal things and putting things in order. I had not gotten around doing it yet. It has been difficult'. I pointed at the 2 carton boxes on the coffee table. 'Can you believe that those are Jack's personal things? Two boxes filled with a few diplomas, family pictures, mementos and trinkets: That's what is left of my best friend's six years here'

Laura just nodded. She understood that there are no words.

'I'll bring those to his wife later today, and then I'll start working on his files and work projects. We'll sit together and comb through everything when I have put some order in it'

Laura took a step into the office, and I got a whiff of her perfume. It smelled like Nina Ricci's *Rive Gauche.* Everything about her fascinated me. She answered: 'OK. In fact, I have taken a head start on his data interpretation work. I have done some reading of his notes, and it is quite fascinating. Unorthodox, but fascinating. I also called his wife this morning, maybe I should have gone through you, but there are some references in his notes to files I have not been able to find. I wondered if he used to take some files home. It was somewhat awkward, but she was very nice, it is the first time I spoke to her'.

'Caroline is a great woman, she is devastated, but strong. What did she say? I do not remember Jack ever taking work home. He used to work late when necessary, but had this rule about work and family not being a healthy mix'.

'She said she'd have a look in his study, but not today. They are having a remembrance ceremony this afternoon. I was a little embarrassed to have called'

'Yes. Today is Jack's *shloshim*. It is a Jewish tradition: the uncovering of the tombstone thirty days after the funeral. It is also the end of the formal grieving period for the relatives. I'll be going'

'Never heard of that. It sounds very respectful. Anyway, it is a little bit awkward, so I'll wait a few more days before I call her back. Perhaps I'll visit to pay my respects'

'Good idea. Maybe I'll come with you to make it easier', I added quickly: 'If you want me to, of course'.

'I'd like that. Thank you'.

'OK, then. Now, how are things going here in terms of care?'

'I think I have things under control. Jack's protocols are very detailed and thorough. And he has built a great professional staff. They have not all fully accepted me yet, you know: the young-and-just-out-of-school syndrome; but I concede I am getting into pretty big shoes. I'll get there. I am pretty new, but I already have the feeling that the success of the trend-discovering work is rooted in the intensive and thorough care given to the patients. Before you can have them look at patterns and ask them to complete the graphs, you have to get them motivated and interested'

'It has taken a few years to get there, Laura. When I first thought of these savants helping us, I thought it would be easy. You know, just show them the math and collect the money. Did you know…'

I was suddenly interrupted by a startling scream coming from below. It sounded again like: 'Beast, beast!'

Laura was immediately running out. She was already climbing down the stairs as I got to the door. Number 3, a young African-American adult named Tim, was shrieking with his eyes glued onto the screen. Tim was very special in that he was not born autistic, but had gotten his very special abilities after a head injury in a car accident when he was nine years-old. There was, to the best of my knowledge, only one other case of injury-induced savant syndrome: the famous Orlando Serrell, able to do incredible calendar calculations and remembering the weather of everyday he ever lived through. After recovering, Tim had some loss in social skills and movement control; he was confined to a wheelchair. But he had gained, just like Orlando, fantastic mental mathematical skills.

'Beast, beast!'. He had been working quietly until then, but was now in a kind of trance. I got down the stairs. I saw Tim's caretaker holding him lightly and pulling him gently away. Tim was different from the other patients in that he was much more tolerant of physical contact. Laura came from the other side and started to talk quietly to calm him down. Number 2 stood up and looked on curiously, but did not look alarmed. Number 1 and Number 4 were working on, as if nothing had happened. I stayed a few feet behind, not to disturb their intervention. Tim was not shouting anymore but looked entranced. I saw that the computer screen did not show the usual graphs or text: it was covered with moving lines of characters. It looked like base code. I pressed the screen off-button, and watched as Laura and the caretaker brought Tim out of his chair and on to the couch.

Another episode, and with Number 3! This is definitely not good. We have to get to the bottom of this. I signaled his caretaker, a promising new orderly, to come to me while Laura talks quietly to Tim, on his couch. He was a tall athletic African American named Rishad Jackson, already renowned for a wide ubiquitous smile.

'Did you see what he was working on when this started?'

'Nothing special, Mr. Van Dijk. He was just typing normally. I did not see anything special'

'Did you see how long he had been looking at strings of code instead of graphs and numbers?'

'Not really. It looks all the same to me. Sorry Sir'

'No problem. We'll have to check it up and monitor it. Do not worry. Good work, Rishad. You reacted fast and well

'Thank you, sir'

I sat there thinking. While Laura was calming Tim, I had my brain juices flowing. Was there any link with the base code? Any specific part of it? I'll have to talk to Laura about it: We'll have to try to ask Tim later, and get something out of him. We'll have to correlate with previous events. We'll have to check the computer's records and monitor them for future events. This was a serious problem for an operation like ours. I made a mental note to work out a specific detailed program to check all that. It felt good to be back immersed in work. Maybe I had let myself flow too much into idleness and hobbies. Nearly as an afterthought, I also reckoned that we owed to Tim to solve the problem for his own well-being. Not only for the sake of money. An afterthought maybe, but it was the first time and did more than pay lip service to the ethical side of the problem. Maybe I was slowly becoming a better person. For Jack, for Laura, for myself? Who cared? The truth is that it felt good.

I checked my Rolex; I had to leave now to be in time for Jack's *shloshim*. I signaled Laura quietly and stood up. She looked definitely on top of the situation. I mouthed silently: 'Will call you'. She nodded and turned back her attention to the now calmer Tim, our Patient Number 3.

Chapter 11

a5 Ne5

Peaceful Pines Cemetery, Southport, Connecticut

I was standing near Caroline Zimmerman, with a yarmulke on my head, over Jack's final resting place. The Peaceful Pines Cemetery was just that, a peaceful pastoral field with scattered pines. Everything green as far as the eye could see, and it smelled,- what can I say?-, piney fresh. Even in death, wealthier is greener.

The rabbi was singing "*El Male Rachamim*", the traditional Hebrew prayer for the dead. Attendance was much lighter than for the burial one month ago, only family and close friends. My God, already one month had gone by without Jack! One month that Jack is buried in a mound of dirt, exposed to rain and worms. I, myself, would rather be cremated, when I think about it. There were about thirty people for this ceremony, when the actual interment sported about three hundred. I was pondering how fast people move on. Life is for the living, and once you are gone, they go on and slowly forget you. And people have so much to do in their own lives. I was upset though that Alex had not showed up. The callous bastard was really getting on my nerves.

The rabbi finished his prayer on a long low-pitched note, and it looked like the ceremony was closing with Jack's two boys reading together a last prayer in voices broken by sobs. I recognized from the burial the *Kaddish*, a ubiquitous sanctification prayer of Jewish liturgy.

The rabbi, a bearded young man with thick glasses, invited the participants to the guest house for a celebration of Jack's life, basically an excuse for food and drinks. Organized religion is a social thing, in my view, just like Facebook. People started moving away from the tomb, with its new shiny black marble headstone, but I did stay a few minutes to pay my more personal respects. Caroline was still beside me, and I hugged her warmly. 'This is so unfair', I managed to mutter in a strangled voice.

After a minute or two, I regained my poise and told her, releasing the hug: 'You know I am not into food at those occasions. I'll hop by your place to drop Jack's personal effects, they are in the car. You will be all right?'

'I'll be fine, Olivier. Thanks. Thank you for coming, go ahead'

'I'll be in touch; call you in a day or two. Take care of yourself and the boys, Caroline'. I waved at Jack's sons.

She moved away and I started jogging to my car; the faster away from those places, the better. Superstitious Jews would even wash their hands and wipe their shoes clean on leaving a cemetery. So Death would not stick to them, as if it was contagious. I just took off the yarmulke and placed it in my pocket; in my opinion, that would be enough.

While driving to Jack's house towards Southport, my thoughts came back to Number 3's outburst earlier today and what it meant for the operation. It had happened before, so what had Jack been doing about it? He did want an urgent meeting before he died. Was it to talk about that? Was he on to something? This was a problem that I had to solve fast, and now, tragically, without him.

I was on autopilot, deep in thought and nearly overshot Jack's house. It was a big palatial mansion with an open driveway, and no gate. With the company's life insurance money and the survivors' clause in Jack's contract, Caroline would have no problems keeping the house and her current lifestyle. And pay for the boys' education. In any case, I would not let them down. I stopped in front of the main entrance, and climbed down. Times when you hid a spare key under a flower pot are long gone, especially in these upscale neighborhoods, but I always had had a spare key to Jack's house, and vice-versa. Just in case. I opened the door and went straight for the alarm pad. Both our codes are the Pi number, 314159, an old inside joke. But I realized suddenly that the alarm was not on. This was strange: You do not go to a public family affair and leave your house unprotected. Something was wrong. Maybe the cleaning staff or something alike? I called out: 'Anybody home?'

I thought I heard a faint noise upstairs, but no reply was forthcoming. I climbed the wide oak staircase, two steps at a time, calling again: 'Is there anybody here? This is Olivier'. Upon further reflection in hindsight, this was not a wise thing to do.

From the top of the stairs, I could see Jack's den as its door was half opened, and it looked uncharacteristically cluttered with books and papers on the floor. I started running towards the den, adrenaline pumping into my veins, without really analyzing the situation. I immediately thought of burglars and it got my blood boiling. I tend to be short-fused in the face of iniquity. And at nearly forty, I was still behaving like a teen-ager: extreme sports, loose women and, specifically now, machismo. As I passed in front of the master bedroom door, I felt rather than saw a shadow lunging at me. I instinctively ducked aside, just enough to avoid most of the impact of a retractable stick intended for my head. It still hit me hard on the shoulder, causing me to fall onto the carpeted floor of the hallway. Thanks to years of *Parkour* training, I instinctively rolled forward and stood up in one move, turning to face my hooded assailant who was already coming onto me with his stick brandished. Definitely a burglar, dressed in black with a black ski mask. You do not get closer to a burglar uniform than that. I believe myself to be a pretty nice guy, but once the adrenaline takes over, I forget social graces, and let the primal brain do its thing. Instead of retreating from the stick as he expected, I shot low for this guy's legs and lifted him up to slam him hard back to the floor. A classic Mixed Martial Arts *shoot* move. He let go of his stick and was so stunned by the takedown that he could not avoid my falling down on his face with an elbow strike powered by my entire body's weight. I felt his nose cartilage break, and lifted my body and elbow for another strike. First rule of fighting: When something works, do not try anything else! Keep at it! It felt good to fight on the side of justice and win. Like a regular super-hero.

But I suddenly felt a searing pain in my exposed side: a full-powered kick in the ribs that dismounted me. 'Shit, he was not alone, stupid', I could have heard myself thinking. What did I say before about short fuse, teen-ager and not thinking? I rolled on my side and felt another kick graze my head. This was no fun. I rolled up, but this time I did not make it in time to see a punch coming to the side of my head. But I felt it and it hurt. I ducked and pressed forward with my hands covering the head for protection. This guy was tall and strong, and he also had a balaclava on the head. He kept punching, but I suddenly stopped in place, breaking his rhythm, and delivered a low roundhouse kick to his forward knee, with all the strength I had. The intruder's last punch connected, but he crumbled in place; I had gotten him hard and bad. The knee is the weakest joint in the body, and you need it just to stay standing up. So remember: Kick someone's knee in the wrong direction, and he his yours. As he bent over, I kneed his offered face, and then... everything went black. His accomplice, whom I had forgotten about, had picked up his stick and finished what he had begun. No matter what you see in movies, fighting two adversaries is always a losing proposition! If I live, I would be wise to remember that.

***

I opened my eyes, slowly. 'What the ...?' I was still disoriented. A throbbing pain in the head made me wince. Where was I? What had happened? I had no idea, everything was blurry. It then slowly came back to me: Jack's house, the burglars… I was looking at the moldings on the white ceiling. How long had I been out? Are they still here? I tried to stand up, but the searing headache made me lie down again. The place sounded quiet, so I gathered that the intruders were gone. I tried to wriggle my cell phone from my pocket, but every movement got my head throbbing more. I rolled on my side and managed to take out the phone, when I heard the main door open.

"Olivier? Are you there?' This was Caroline's voice.

I tried to shout back, but just managed to croak. She must have heard something, because she went for the stairs. 'O My God! Olivier!' she exclaimed as she reached the top, and ran towards me. 'What happened?' She kneeled besides me and then saw the state in which Jack's den was. 'What has happened?'. She stood up and retreated a little, with a scared look on her face. Poor Caroline, as if she had not had enough today?

I managed to talk: 'Burglars. Looks like they are gone. Call 911'. I let myself lie down again. While she placed the call, asking for both police and an ambulance, I stood up slightly on my elbow, still checking around. 'Where are the boys?'

'They went with their Uncle Danny; they are staying with their cousins for a few days. What happened, Olivier?'

She helped me slowly onto my feet and led me towards Jack's den. The place was ransacked: The floor was scattered with papers, empty drawers, files and books. The shelves were empty; the pictures were all off the wall as if the burglars had looked for a hidden safe. I sat in the corner armchair: 'What time is it, Caroline?'

She checked her watch: '6.45'

'I guess I have been out for about 15 minutes. These guys were professionals, what were they looking for? Is there anything around of value?'

Caroline stood up, prodded by my question, and went towards the master bedroom, mumbling something about jewelry. I followed slowly; my head was hurting like hell. The master bedroom looked fine, but Caroline went for the walk-in closet. The closet was also in shambles, and the safe was in clear view inside one of the cupboards. It looked unopened. I suppose I did interrupt their work after all. At least I did not get my head bashed for nothing.

Caroline broke into sobs and went to sit on the bed. This was too much for her. First Jack, now this. The burglars probably knew about the ceremony. Who the hell is despicable enough to burglarize the house of a grieving family? Animals!

I took Caroline in my arms and she sobbed on my shoulder. I wanted to caress her head, but I saw my hand covered in blood, probably from my own head.

We heard a shout from below: 'Emergency services. Coming in'

After a few minutes, the place was swarming with people. I saw uniformed police officers talking to Caroline, while a paramedic was checking my head wound. 'You'll need stitches, sir. And definitely an EEG. We'll take you to Bridgeport General; no way you should drive after a head wound like that'. I did not really want to leave Caroline alone, but I relented. 'Just let me make a call, please'.

I sped-dial Jan Thompson's number and got a busy signal. 'Shit'

I tried Alex; he answered on the second ring: 'Alex! Olivier, here. There has been an incident at Jack's house. Please tell Jan to send two security guards to keep Caroline safe. I have to go to the hospital for a few stitches. Then we'll see what to do'

'What? Are you all right? What happened?'. Alex sounded genuinely concerned; it was definitely a first.

'Don't worry, I'll be fine, Alex. Burglars or something, and I have just got a scratch. Just get people here to make her feel safe. We'll talk later'.

'OK, Olivier, I am on it. Just be careful'. And he hung up. I must say I was slightly surprised to hear so much worry in his voice. It had been a long time since he had me feel like a real friend, and it made me feel good about him for once.

***

Wan Chai, Hong Kong, Special Administrative Region, China

John Kwan paid his check and left the *Tiffin* restaurant on the mezzanine of the Grand Hyatt Hotel in Hong Kong. He stayed on the same floor, and went directly for the designated passageway going directly from the luxury hotel to the huge adjacent Convention Center. It was only a few minutes' walk, but the place was packed, and John had to negotiate his path in between the many attendees of the Travel Fair, going to or from lunch.

As he entered the Convention Hall, after showing his ticket and going through the inevitable magnetometer portal, he was struck, again, by how organized the Center was in spite of the uncountable number of people scuttling around.

John went from booth to booth, checking for interesting deals to offer his clients. His agency in Washington D.C. was mainly working for companies and business travelers, but there was always a better or a cheaper way to do things.

After two hours of stopping at the most promising booths, his bag was full of prospectuses and business cards. He had made a point, like always, to speak only English, and denying any knowledge of Chinese, be it Mandarin or Cantonese. He was finally standing in front of booth 1231A, of the International Chinese Tourism Corporation. He introduced himself and his interest in cheaper Travel between the US and China, and was taken into an ornate glass cubicle in the middle of the relatively big booth.

This cubicle was in fact a soundproof area with electronic jamming; making sure that no eavesdropping could take place. The ornamentation also made sure that no lip-reading could occur. Once inside, John switched to Mandarin Chinese, when addressing the suit-and-tie-clad Chinese man in front of him.

This was his yearly meeting with his handler, known to him as Jeung, and much had to be discussed. John was thoroughly debriefed, and also took the opportunity to discretely hand over the USB with the Stealth technology data. After twenty intense minutes, he was congratulated for his good work. He did not know that Colonel Jeung had had him shadowed and covered to evaluate his proficiency, and that he had passed with flying colors.

Jeung concluded with new instructions: 'On top of handling the two assets of the last two years, you are now ordered to try to make contact and find a source in the American Cyber-Security Unit of Homeland Security. In the data I have given you, is all we know about the personnel of the Unit. You are to check and increase the data, and identify the best candidate for recruitment. At first glance, it will have to be, again, money-driven recruitment. It is imperative that we have someone informing us about what the Americans do about cyber-security, and more importantly, what they do know about ours'.

John, proud of his increased responsibilities, took his leave after shaking hands with Jeung, and made sure he was taking many legitimate prospectuses from the International Chinese Tourism Corporation.

He covered a few more booths, before calling it a day and returning to the Grand Hyatt. He would be flying back home tomorrow, back to his wife and daughter, to his travel agency, and …to his spying duties against the country of his birth.

Chapter 12

Be2 0-0

Bridgeport Hospital, Fairfield County, Connecticut

I was lying in my hospital bed, feeling fidgety and impatient. I hated hospitals and I hated idleness, and their combination is synergistic. The doctor,- and I hate doctors too by the way-, wanted me there overnight for observation, and in a low light environment to give my brain a rest. First, he tried to show off by calling my illness by a Yale-learned acronym: Grade 1 MTBI, which stands for mild traumatic brain injury, or basically, "you have just been hit on the head". So: no TV, no reading, no phones, just resting. That is probably how the antechamber to Hell looked like. They had stitched me up, 4 stitches which I could later show off proudly, and then they gave me an Encephalogram that had showed a clear concussion. They had done a few cognitive and neuropsychological tests. For all that, they had first razed my hair and turned me into an egg-head. Though, with the stitches, I looked more like a skinhead punk.

My head was still throbbing and my ribs hurt like hell, in spite of all the painkillers, but I did not feel like sleeping. Every move resulted in lancing pains in the side. In fact, I was now replaying the fight in my head, this time winning it! If only I had seen the other guy and evaded the kick… Wishful thinking, of course. I'd have to talk about that with my Ju-Jitsu coach. Be ready for next time. Just a minute: Which next time? What am I, a brawler? First time in my adult life that I had been in a real fight! But still, having practiced martial arts all my life, I was somewhat disappointed in the results of my first real fight ever.

The door of the darkened room opened and Alex came in silently, his index finger on his lips. 'Shhh'. He closed the door quietly and told me in a low voice: 'They do not allow visitors for your kind of injury. I had to create a diversion to sneak past the Head Bitch Nurse'. Typical Alex lingo, but I was happy to see him.

'Yeah. I know. They took my phone too. They wanted to cover my eyes for total rest too. Didn't let them. Good to see you, Alex. I am bored out of my brains'

'So what's up, Olivier? What happened?'. He sat on the side of my bed.

'I really don't know. I left Jack's ceremony early to drop his personal things at the house, and there were two guys there burglarizing the place. I got one, but I did not see the second one sneaking on me. They beat me up pretty bad, but I got a few good ones through. I know I look bad, but as we used to say, you should see the other guys!'. I was smiling, but it turned into a wince, as my head rewarded me with a serious pain signal.

'This is no joke, Olivier. You could have been killed playing hero. What did they look like?'

'Ninjas! Haven't seen their faces. These people were professionals, not junkies looking for laptops. They had balaclavas and gloves. They were dressed in black, motorcycle leather stuff. They were tough too. When I think of it, they were silent all the time we fought. Not a word. Real pros'

'What the hell were people like that looking for?'

'I gather they knew about the *shloshim*, and chose to go for Caroline's jewelry. By the way, why did you not come to the ceremony? You are the Jewish partner, not me. You could have made the effort!'

Alex did not answer. Typically, he did not look embarrassed or ashamed either.

I continued: 'Something has been bothering me: They ransacked Jack's den thoroughly, and the master bedroom closet a little bit. That's all. Professionals like that work on info, not random. And if they knew about the *shloshim*, they were cutting it pretty close.

'Who knows? We'll probably never know what they had in mind. You are a lucky bastard though'.

'I guess. Did you have Jan send people over?'

'Yeah. He'll have one guy in front and one guy at the back 24 hours a day, for a few days, and Caroline has them on speed-dial. She was pretty shaken up. Jan will upgrade her security system on our dime'

'This is the least we can do, Jack is like family. *Our* family, we owe him so much… It is really tough for her. First Jack, then this.'

'Yeah, you are right'. He then switches subjects, abruptly: 'What do you say about the lady replacing Jack?'. It sounded a bit out of place.

'Still early, Alex, but she looks OK. She reminds me a lot of young Jack. She has an open mind and works hard. And she cares. I will have a first in-depth meeting with her when I get out of here. .. Maybe I'll wait for my hair to grow back a little', I crack a smile.

'Ah Ah! You care what she thinks! She is a looker all right Olivier, but don't get us a sexual harassment lawsuit please'. Alex was smiling now. It had been a long time we had not bantered this way. I should get my head cracked more often.

But I got serious again: 'Just before I left, there was another episode with Number 3. I was there and it did not look good. No violence, but a very strong episode. I'll sit with Laura to get a program going to solve this thing one way or another. Fast'

'OK, Olivier. This is your thing. You get back on your feet and solve it your way. Get back to work. I understand there is a new patient coming in anyway, a promising one'

'Yes there is, but remember that it also happened to others patients one way or another, it looks like a general symptom. If you are hinting again at firing Number 3, forget about it. We have to get to the bottom of this. Anyway, what is up on your side of the business?'

'You know; same old, same old. Got a few new clients, big money. I let them simmer a bit, but people are really lining up. We are …

The door opened suddenly, and the shift nurse, an overweight and stern Latino woman with a hint of moustache, came in frowning. She succeeded in both whispering and making it sound like shouting, no mean feat: 'What is going on here? No visitors. Please leave, immediately'. She was a scary woman all right!

'Sorry, I did not know' Alex winked at me. 'Anyway, I was just leaving'

As he stood up from the bed, I mouthed silently to him: 'Cell phone'. He threw his on my lap discreetly while turning to say goodbye, and left silently under the disapproving eye of the nurse. I hid the phone below the covers. Once alone, I would call Caroline first; then I would do my international chess moves; and then I would look for people to bother.

***

1982, Kanosta Prison, Liepaja, Latvia

Young Aivars Bartolis was standing in line in the prison courtyard with the other thirty or forty new inmates freezing in the January cold. He was seething with anger, forgetful of the temperature. The Russian prison administrator was shouting rules and threats, but he was not listening. His eyes were roaming the green piney countryside outside the barbed wire fence, and he could smell the sea in the distance: Things so close, but yet out-of-reach for a few years now.

Aivars had always been headstrong and proud, but honest. His hard-working parents, his father manual laborer in a tire factory and his mother seamstress in a garment shop, had raised him to be respectful of his fellow citizens. But not of the Soviet occupation of his country. Aivars had grown up listening to stories about forced conscription into Soviet and German armies, about resistance to the Soviet occupation after the war and the resulting deportations, massacres and arrests. The grandfather he had been named after had died in Siberia in 1952, after being arrested in the infamous Soviet Priboi *operation that had deported nearly 200,000 Latvians in a few years. Aivars had always been a proud Latvian, hard working in coal-hauling since age 14 to help his family survive. But now, at age 17, he had been caught painting anti-Soviet slogans on public buildings with a few friends. A same-day kangaroo court had sentenced him to 3-years in prison, and here he was, with compliments of the occupying power. He just hoped his parents had been advised and would not worry too much. Aivars knew his life would be different now, and that he would have to be strong and heartless. He hoped this would not change him, he just wanted to keep quiet and survive. At that very moment, a guard who saw him day-dreaming hit him in the solar plexus with his truncheon.*

It was ominous.

Chapter 13

0-0 Bd7

Jack Zimmerman's house, Southport, Connecticut

I was back at the scene of the crime! As I climbed out the taxi in front of Jack and Caroline's house, I felt the anger swelling in me. If I could just get my hands on these two scumbags …

I had been released this morning, after a lot of whining and complaining. They brought me out of the hospital on a wheelchair, as per regulations and procedures. I hate hospital administrators even more than doctors now.

There was a car on the curb, our security most probably, and another car, near mine, in front of the house, the police I supposed. When I called Caroline discreetly from the hospital on Alex's phone, she told me the Police wanted my testimony, so I asked her to set up a meeting at her place. I wanted to look her up at the same occasion. I saw the guard on the curb looking up at me and mumbling something on a cell phone, and I jokingly waved at him.

Caroline was at the door, and I hugged her. I grimaced as my ribs still hurt. She looked at my bald head and smiled mischievously: 'Sorry! I did not mean to smile but it does not suit you too much'. It was the first time I saw her in colorful clothing since Jack died; she had stuck to widow black until today. It was also the first smile I had seen on her, in a long time. Her face was still lined with sorrow though: Jack and she had been the closest thing to the perfect couple that I had ever seen.

'Yeah, thanks for mocking me. How are you holding up?'

'I'll be fine. Losing Jack has destroyed my world. So, a little burglary pales in comparison. Thanks for the security, but I don't think they'll be back'

'Just keep them for another few days. You'll feel better. And so will I. Then we'll discuss it again'

I saw a woman in uniform standing in the hallway; but regardless of the uniform, there was no doubt she was a cop. I cannot say why but she looked like the arch-type TV policewoman, a little masculine and trying hard to look tough. She extended her hand: 'Detective Steever, nice to meet you Mr. Van Dijk'. As expected, she had a strong grip and a "serving hero" attitude.

'Hi detective. Nice to meet you too. Let us get this over with, if you like. I really hurt'

She nodded and I continued, getting on with it at once:

'I was at the cemetery with Caroline and left early to drop two boxes at the house'. I pointed at the boxes on the floor in the entrance.' I arrived here around 5:30 p.m. I came in…'

'How did you open the door?'

'The door was locked, but I always have had a key. And Jack had a key to my place too. You know, best friends... The door was locked, but once I was in with the two boxes, I went for the alarm, I know the code too, but the alarm was not on. I heard noise upstairs, and so I called out, and then climbed the stairs'

I was climbing the stairs with both women behind me.

'From the top here, I saw the den was ransacked, and I started running towards it. One of the guys attacked me from the bedroom as I passed in front of him, with a stick. He hurt my shoulder but I managed to fight back and at least broke his nose'

I looked around and pointed at the approximate place I had tackled my assailant.

'But there was another one, he kicked me and then I got whacked on the head. I was probably out for ten or fifteen minutes'. I pointed at a big bloodstain on the carpet. 'That's probably mine. I came to when Caroline arrived. The guys were dressed in black motorcycle gear and they had ski masks on their faces, and gloves. They were tough, silent and professional. They did not say a word. I think they were Caucasian, from what I can remember around the eye holes of their masks. But I would not swear by it. What else could I tell you?'

The detective was jotting a few notes on a pad. She lifted her head: 'What were they after, in your opinion?'

'I suppose jewelry, cash,… How should I know?'

'There is something strange with this burglary, Mr. Van Dijk. Two professionals, as you describe them, get into the house from the back door. There are signs of sophisticated lock-picking, not crowbar or breaking stuff. They also had to know the alarm code and punch it in. No other explanation, Mrs. Zimmerman is sure she switched the alarm on. They then go directly upstairs and concentrate on this home office. Downstairs, there were iPods and an iPad, cash, and obviously expensive silverware. But no, they ransack the office, obviously looking for something. On the other hand, they go easy on the bedroom. I'll tell you something. I have been doing this job for a long time: The closet job looks like a cover-up for what they were doing in the office'

She looked at my surprised face. Do not underestimate short-haired female detectives, ever. Some of them are sharp, was the immediate thought going through my head.

She kept going: 'Usually, burglars trash the whole place fast, and get everything that is valuable. Nothing looks like it is missing. There were no marks on the closet safe where the jewelry is. My gut feeling is that they were looking for something specific, in the office'.

'Maybe they were interrupted; they did not have the time to do more than the rooms upstairs when I arrived'

'Maybe, but remember that they looked and acted like professionals. Or so you say…'. She looked at me pointedly. 'So they should have known, be prepared. Something does not fit. What is your relation to the Zimmerman family, Mr. Van Dijk?'

'Jack was my best friend, and he was also working for one of my companies'.

'Did you have any special relationship with Mrs. Zimmerman?'. She kept it coolly professional, but it was still hard to swallow. Caroline did not see the innuendo at once, but I did.

I barely kept myself under control: 'If you are asking if Caroline and I had an affair, the answer is no and this is extremely rude of you under the circumstances! And this would have nothing to do with a burglary anyway'. Caroline was reddening, from anger or embarrassment, or both.

'I am sorry, I had to ask. This is procedure. I truly apologize if I have offended you two'. I stayed silent and she continued, not looking sorry at all: 'Could this burglary have anything to do with business? The computer was on and it looks they were looking into files and papers'

This got me thinking for a while. This woman was a bitch, imbued in the authority her job gave her, but she was not stupid. 'I really cannot see what would justify anything like this. Jack was a psychiatrist caring for people. Patient files would have no value whatsoever. I'll think about it and let you know, but I really cannot see what'.

Cops, for a start, never believe you *prima facie*. She looked at me dubiously, but then continued: 'OK. Now please leave me your details, in case I need to contact you'. I handed her one of my cards. She took it, looked at it thoroughly and then pocketed it. 'You said Jack Zimmerman was working for you. What does a psychiatrist have to do with a hedge fund?'. She looked like a cat that has just caught sight of a mouse.

Like it is the first time I have had to answer that! I gave her my standard reply: 'Very simple: Investing is based on the psychology of markets and investors'.

She got it, or at least behaved as if she believed me: 'Here is my card, if you think of something. Take good care of your injuries, Mr. Van Dijk. Goodbye Mrs. Zimmerman'.

I called after her as she climbed down the stairs and headed towards the door. She turned back.

'I thought of something yesterday. When I arrived here they were no cars parked nearby or in the driveway. How did they arrive here?'

'Oh! That's quite simple, Mr. Van Dijk. We found tracks of all terrain motorbikes in the back. The problem is that no neighbor we interviewed saw or heard anything when they came or when they left. And you know people tend to be nosy in those neighborhoods'.

She waved a goodbye with her hand and left.

After the door closed, I looked at Caroline: 'What the hell did these people want? You are sure nothing is missing?'

'Yes, I checked twice'

'Jack did not usually take work home, did he?

'No. You remember he was quite particular about that. It is true he did spend some more time on his computer at home before the conference but I think he was preparing his speech. He even bought one of those USB keys for the speech. I remember it because he never had one before, just to avoid the temptation of taking his work home. I also remember he asked our eldest to explain how to use it'

'Jack was a great family man'. I sighed. 'I miss him so much. He was my only real friend'

Caroline did not answer; her eyes just glistened. I continued: 'I'll put some order in the den before I go. Anything else I can do for you, Caroline?'

'Thanks, Olivier. Nothing. I'll just go and rest now. Be in touch'

'Hold on, Caroline. I'll see you in a few days. I'll let myself out'

I brought up the two boxes with Jack's personal effects upstairs. They had remained near the entrance where I had left them the day before. I straightened up Jack's office, having a look at all the papers and files. I hung back the diplomas and pictures, I swiped the debris. There was absolutely nothing about work in Jack's office, as specified by his contract and reinforced by his habits. I checked his laptop brought back from Scandinavia, his password was of course "Caroline"; and there was nothing about work. On the desktop I found a first basic version of his speech, nothing new there.

After 45 minutes, I logged off and left silently, locking the door behind me. The master bedroom door was closed and I assumed Caroline was sleeping or just resting. I thought I heard quiet crying. I made sure to be as silent as possible.

I locked the front door and signaled the security guard in his car, then climbed into my own car, and started driving in the general direction of Greenwich. My head and ribs were hurting real bad, and I felt exhausted. I should maybe listen to the doctors for once; I probably should rest more and take it easy.

I wrestled with the idea of going to work; I was anxious to get started on the episodes our patients were having. But reason prevailed and decided to call it a day and drive back home to Manhattan. I stopped on the side of the road to prepare for a U turn, when I suddenly noticed a silver Audi slowing down behind me.

I swore like a sailor. The Audi definitely looked like the same which tailed me to Greenwich last time. What the heck was happening?

I did not feel I could confront and fight someone again today. So I pressed speed dial 5, and Jan answered after three rings: 'Oliver?'

'Jan, the silver Audi is again behind me. I am two miles north of Jack's house, planning on a U turn and back to Manhattan'

He did not have to think or anything of the kind. He just answered, as if this was the most natural situation in the world: 'OK. Here is what you do: Do the U turn and drive just below speed limit towards Manhattan. Stay on the main road, do nothing and I'll take care of everything'

'OK. Keep me posted, Jan'. He cut off.

I had been driving south for about twenty minutes, spotting the Audi in my rear mirror from time to time, but not in the last five minutes.

The car phone suddenly rang: 'Oliver. It is Jan'

'Yes, Jan'

'You can drive on normally now. We have delayed your tail. You will not be bothered, and we'll check what it is about. I'll let you know when we know more'

'Thanks. Let me know ASAP please'

'My job. Bye'

I was over the bridge into Manhattan when the phone rang again. The screen showed "Jan". I really did not like the guy, but this time, I was eager to answer.

'You have been followed by a journalist, a woman named Zini. We have boxed her in between two cars and slowed her down. Slowed her down a lot. She dented one of our cars in a fit of rage, and we made her stop to exchange details by law. She is pissed, but she knows now we are on to her. I think she'll leave you alone. Anyway, we'll keep an eye on her. Always check your back when you drive Upstate'.

'OK. Thanks, Jan'. And I cut off. This guy was effective. How did he get here so fast? And what did this journalist want from me? This is the" Inside Business Weekly" lady. Persistent broad; that was not good news. Was she on to our secrets? I hoped she would leave us alone, now.

But, truth be said, I seriously doubted that. Trouble was most certainly on the way.

Chapter 14

Kh1 Kh8

The Prometheus Foundation, Washington County, New York State

The door was open, so I knocked while entering Laura's office, without waiting. I stopped in mid-stride: 'Sorry. I did not see you had a visitor'.

There was a man sitting in front of the desk. Laura's office did look different from Jack's: everything also organized and in its place in neat piles, but an undefinable woman's touch. Maybe the impressionist print on the wall.

'Good morning, Olivier. I like the new look. This is Joshua Applebee, Tom's father'. She was jokingly referring to my newfound baldness.

'Oh yes. I did not realize today was Tom's arrival. Good morning, Mr. Applebee, nice to meet you finally. I am Olivier Van Dijk. We'll do our best to give Tom the best of care here. Welcome on board'.

As I extended my hand, I saw Laura frown, from the corner of my eye. She had probably just seen the stitches on my head. Mr.

Applebee's handshake was strong, and I noticed immediately his rugged good looks, with an unexpected pang of jealousy. What is wrong with me? I barely knew Laura, she was working for me, and my usual girlfriends were models nearly half her age.

Laura enquired: 'Sorry! I did not realize the haircut was injury-related. What happened to you? An accident? Is it one of your sport excesses?'

'I am fine, Thanks. It looks worse than it really is'. I felt good at the attention. Get a grip, Olivier! 'As a matter of fact, it is quite a story: I surprised burglars at Jack's house when I went to drop his personal effects, and they attacked me'. I could not help adding: 'Though you should see the other guys!'.

'What? Did they get arrested?'

'No, no. One of them hit me with a stick on the head from behind. No sense of fair play, these burglars nowadays!', I said with my best macho smile. 'They fled'

Mr. Applebee cut in: 'It looks nasty. You are lucky, I think'

'I have had luckier days, but I guess you are right, it could have been worse. I have also busted ribs, not broken though'

Laura looked concerned, more than she should normally be; I liked that: 'Were you alone? What did they steal?'

'Yeah, I was alone. Good it happened to me and not to Jack's wife coming home, and from the cemetery on top of everything! Poor woman. Anyway, according to Caroline, nothing is missing. They thrashed Jack's home office and Caroline's walking closet, but I surprised them before they found anything. They were looking for valuable stuff; these people were not starved junkies. They left behind iPads and stuff like that, but they checked for safes behind all the wall pictures. Anyway, all's well that ends well. I have organized upgraded security at the house. I just wish I could lay my hands on these scumbags!'

Laura looked pensive. Her guest had a very discreet smile, probably at my bravado. I continued:' Anyway, Laura. Sorry to have interrupted your meeting. I just wanted to sit with you about our program of action regarding …' .I wanted to say "the incident", but I stopped myself, because of Applebee.

'Regarding what we discussed, of course, Olivier'. She is a bright lady, no doubt.

'You know what? I'll have Myla set up a formal meeting with you'. The truth is I hate scheduled meetings; that's why it is so good to be the boss, being free to decide the when. I turned to Mr. Applebee:

'Where is Tom, Mr. Applebee?'

'Please call me Joshua. Your nursing people took him to his room, we just left him there. Place looks great. I'll be helping get him comfortable with the place and the people'

'I am glad you feel that way. We'll do our best for him. He is in good hands with Dr. Wheelan here'

'Laura', she cuts in.

'Laura. OK. And please call me Olivier, Joshua. I am glad you'll be helping with the induction. I understand Tom is highly functional, but this is the critical period to get him comfortable with his surroundings'

'I definitely want to be around and be a positive influence for him. As I discussed with Dr. Zimmerman, and now with Laura, I will not just leave him here as a burden I want to get rid of. Tom is a big part of my life, and I'll stay very involved'.

I found myself liking the guy, in spite of him being too familiar with Laura. He had this aura of outdoor-guy sincerity.

'This is totally to your credit, Joshua. This is fantastic, and I must say that we have very high professional hopes for Tom'.

'Great. I must say that I am very glad he'll be working a real job. I want him to feel as a full and constructive part of society, it will do wonders for him and for his future'.

Laura cut in: 'Tom is the most social of all our patients to date. I think that thanks to Joshua, he has developed uncommon social skills for a savant. He is able to verbalize a lot of his thought patterns. This should be very good for him'.

'OK. I'll leave you to it. Laura, Myla from Manhattan will set up the meeting. Joshua, please feel free to contact me if there is anything I can help with'. I extend my hand. 'Welcome on board, it was nice to meet you'.

'Likewise'

'Bye'. I left for my office.

Laura sat pensively. She looked up at Joshua: 'Shall we have a look at the workstation downstairs?'. She points through the large windows to the fifth workstation in the big common room. 'Just give me a minute please; I need to send an email'.

'No problem, go ahead. I'll go down and have a look. I'll wait for you downstairs'.

As Joshua left the room, Laura frowned and turned her attention to her computer. She started an email to her "brother" in Chicago.

***

I went back to my office in the other aisle of the floor. I liked my office at the Foundation, because it was eerily quiet. I had no assistant here and it was more difficult for people to disturb me. Myla had made sure there were fresh flowers, which subtle aroma of rose greeting me in.

I prepared myself a cup of strong espresso coffee, and sat on the office leather couch to do some reading. I had all of Jack's unread reports in a pile and I wanted to go through them. I had been very sloppy lately, and enjoyed my golden playboy life. I had let myself believe that I could let Alex run things and relax. But it looked like I could not just enjoy the fruits of my entrepreneurship.

My thoughts kept coming back to Laura. What made her tick? 'What's up with you, Olivier? Are you falling for her? Or is it an infatuation? Or maybe is it time to grow up and get serious? How many more bimbos do you need to screw? Maybe you are finally maturing? Laura is an intelligent and articulate woman, sure of herself. And beautiful...OK, Olivier. Stop it! Back to work'.

I began reading, starting with the oldest unread monthly report by Jack; it was four months old. Thanks to regular training in the renowned Ultimate Study Method, I could still speed-read and concentrate like in College; and as I put my mind to it, I had finished after about fifty minutes.

Something was gnawing at me. I had read Jack's reports since we started together six years ago, and there was a clear evolution in those last ones. There was a hint of self-criticism growing, as if Jack started to doubt the success we were having with our system. He seemed to slowly become unsure of the way we analyzed the patients' input. It did not add up.

I took out my cell and called my assistant: 'Hi Myla'

'Hi Olivier. How do you feel?'

'OK, thanks. Better. Still a headache, but I'll be fine. Myla, please set up a meeting with Laura, sometime tomorrow, here at the Foundation'

'OK. Will do'

'And please get me Alex on the phone'

After a few clicks, Alex answers: 'Hi Olivier. Anybody kicked you in the head today?'

'Funny. You have a minute?'

'Just make it quick, I am with a candidate-client'. Alex is always the consummate salesman: Not a client, a candidate!

'I just wanted to ask you if you had talked to Jack in the few weeks before he died.'

'What do you mean, talked? About what? Of course I talked to him'

'Did he talk to you about any doubts he may have had with our methodology? Or did he look depressed, or less self-confident?'

'No, of course not. Not at all. Why do you ask?'

'Just a feeling. You know these last months I have been away a lot, and I was just reading up on his last reports. I have this feeling something was bothering him'

'Come on, Olivier. Leave it be. I know you miss him, but this is nonsense. He was fine, nothing special. Life must go on, especially yours. I have to continue this meeting. We'll talk later"

'OK, Bye'

'Bye. And do not start to talk around about this nonsense, please. People need to feel confidence'

He cut off. Alex is always blunt and marketing-oriented: Do not rock the boat, and keep up appearances. But his reaction bothered me; there was something ringing false. Why insist to keep this quiet?

I decided to stretch my leg around the facility. I would have gone jogging, but the doctors had forbidden me from doing so for another two weeks. Did I mention I do not like doctors? I left my office, still wondering about Jack.

My steps took me back to the other aisle. From the gangway, I could see the Big Room. Number 1 and Number 3 were at their work stations. Number 2 was playing video games and Number 4 was resting. And our new Number 5, Tom Applebee, was sitting at his computer with Laura and Joshua on both sides, and our Head caretaker behind him.

I climbed down the stairs and approached them silently. They were silent while Tom was clicking on and watching the double big screen. This was probably the familiarization phase of the work induction. The new patients were shown historical graphs and tables of numbers. The others were watching intently and did not hear me approach.

I heard Joshua asking his son: 'So, Tom. You like it? Is it interesting?'. No reply. But Joshua kept asking, in a soft and loving voice: 'Is it interesting, Tom?'. You could really feel the love and devotion this guy had for his son. I remembered from the files that his wife had left him because she could not cope with raising a special-needs child. The straw that had broken the camel's back had been Tom's compulsive habit to watch the drum of her front–load washing machine turning during the whole of the laundry cycle. But Joshua had love enough for the both of them and had done a great job.

I was surprised to hear Tom answer: 'Yes, dad'. Usually it is very difficult to interact with autistic savants like Tom. And he added: 'It is easy. Simple graphs'. Joshua had done a great job indeed. I cleared my throat and Laura turned to me: 'Olivier! I did not hear you. We are showing Tom the workstation. He was enthusiastic and literally started working at once. It looks like he is going to be a very special patient'. She moved aside: 'Please meet him'. Tom a lanky fellow dressed rather elegantly with slacks and a buttoned shirt. He cared about his appearance, and really looked like a normal 19 years-old.

She leaned near Tom's ear: 'Tom. This is Olivier, he is in charge here. Say hi'. Tom did not answer, but I did not expect him to. 'Hi Tom. Welcome. I am Olivier'. He did not stop clicking with eyes glued on the screen. But, to my surprise, he lifted a hand in a Hi gesture without looking. 'Hi, Olivier'. A great job indeed!

I was then stunned to realize that Tom was way past the induction phase: He was working and completing patterns, filling in the expected future values.

We had designed programs showing up-to-the-second trends, and luring the patient to playfully complete the trend into the future. Simple concept, but that had proved difficult to put into mathematical practice. But I could see that Tom had already got the knack of it.

Tom did not look at me and kept clicking, but he had actually greeted me. Mathematical geniuses of this caliber were usually very closed-up socially and deeply autistic. I was flabbergasted. Jack, and now Laura, had been right: This was a very special kid.

Laura saw my surprise and winked.

'How long has he been at that?' I asked quietly.

'Just a few minutes! Can you believe it?' Laura answered in a whisper. Joshua was looking up at us, beaming as the proud father he was. His wide smile had the effect of pulling up his scar, making his joy even more noticeable.

'How did he do with his room and the staff?'

'He is really an easy young man. It was really simple. His dad will stay around for a few days, and Tom will start working at once'.

I felt again a pang of jealousy. So this tanned and likeable guy will be staying around Laura all this time. I suddenly felt annoyed. And the guy even had dimples, for God's sake.

'What about you, Laura? It is pretty late. Are you staying in?'

'As a matter of fact, I am tonight. I have to go into town tomorrow. And I meant to tell you that I'll take you up on your offer and will probably move in and stay permanently here during the week'

'No problem. Glad you will. You have organized a room for Mr. Applebee?'

'Yes I did, I have asked Anna. In fact, he was just going to fetch his gear from his car when we stopped over to check on Tom'

Joshua was taking his keys out of his pocket and I noticed his key holder was a USB key. This caused a connection in my brain, which immediately eluded me. That was important. I made a mental note.

Joshua climbed the stairs and left through the gangway door. I kept talking to Laura.

'Did Myla set up an appointment with you?'

'Tomorrow 4 p.m. As I told you, I am going into town tomorrow morning'

We parted. My heart was heavy from the business-like tone she used with me. Some things are not meant to be.

***

Tom was typing at the computer. He felt satisfied, even happy, if that really meant something. The strings of numbers shown on the computer screen meant something to him; the progression was logical and leading to an obvious conclusion. Everything in the world was linked by numbers, it was so easy. How come the people around him did not see that? They are all like drones, too busy to care about relationship stuff and social conventions. Even Dad, who was a great guy and was always supporting him, could not see the patterns and spent too much time trying to get him interested in other people. Tom was baffled by what he understood clearly other people wanted from him: acknowledgement, salutations, feigned interest in them and their stories. But he would try his best to please Dad, to a point. He understood how deep was Dad's love and support; but why dwell in these things at all.

This new place was cool. The numbers sequences they had showed him at first were pathetically childish, but now the computer was churning real data and it was interesting; not much of a challenge, but interesting. In fact, the last time Tom had been that interested, was when he had taken part in international hacking operations with a few like-minded people met on the internet.

Tom was going to like it here: He had a big room to himself, an orderly following him around and getting him whatever he needed and the fastest computer he had ever had to play with. He understood that what he was doing had economic value and he understood he and his Dad were getting some of it, but he really did not care; so long as he could play with those numbers patterns... He could correlate strings of numbers those people did not even dream were linked in some way, like everything in the Universe. But they were too dumb, they would never understand that. Even Dad.

***

South East Side, Manhattan, New York City

Nathalie Zini was in her tiny apartment, working furiously on her laptop.

She was a driven woman. She was intelligent but bitter. She knew she had always been, not really ugly, but homely. She had been shunned at school and in college because of her appearance, her lack of grace and complete lack of aesthetic taste. She was only thirty three, but looked well over forty, and she was alone. She fitted the archetype of the old maid, from the mole and moustache, all the way to the dress code. The only things lacking were the cats. She did not like cats. She did not like dogs, nor people for that matter.

Nathalie Zini was on a mission: To prove that people were rotten and that most endeavors were based on greed and a lack of morals. She was convinced that all rich people were thieves, and that all poor people were lazy, and a few more generalizing axioms along the same lines. She had chosen the perfect profession for this mind-set: The holier-than-thou journalist.

And this self-hate drive had made her a good investigative journalist. Once her sights were on a prey, she never let go. She had not won any prizes yet, but she was definitely on her way. She had now decided to find out what was behind the Rain Fund, and she would not relent. Her inability to get any of the employees of the Fund to talk to her was a setback. So were her failed attempts at following Van Dijk on his trips Upstate. The gall of these people! Boxing her car and slowing her down. Thugs! She was fuming just from the memory... There was no doubt in her mind that something fishy was going on at the Rain Fund. And she was going to get to the bottom of it!

She was reviewing all her data about the Fund when the doorbell rang. This was a relatively safe area, but the building entrance was locked and it is the downstairs bell that should have rang. She went to the door and looked through the peephole, asking: 'Who is there?'

There was a woman with a cap and a uniform at the door, holding a package: 'Fedex for a Ms. Zini'.

The uniform and the fact that it was a woman extinguished any remaining suspicion that anything was wrong. She probably had entered the building while someone else was coming in or out. She opened the chain, then the door: 'Who is it from?'

But she was startled to see that the uniformed woman was also holding something else.

Zini was tased before she could open her mouth. She fell to the ground, shaking uncontrollably. The Fedex woman threw the parcel inside, came in, pulled Nathalie into the tiny hallway, and closed the door. She then proceeded to extract a silenced pistol from her vest, chamber a bullet and shoot Nathalie twice in the head. Just like that. The killer took a look around, her nose frowning at the smell and at the squalid appearance of the flat: the hairless rugs, the scratched IKEA furniture and the see-through curtains. And now the growing pool of blood around the corpse.

The killer retrieved the Taser hooks and placed all her weapons back into their holsters. She opened the package she had brought, and emptied it: A few files that were to be opened and scattered around, and a carefully wrapped empty coffee cup to be left lying on the lounge table.

After a look around, the killer, still in Fedex garb and with her cap shadowing her pretty face, opened the door and checked the hallway. Empty. She left, simply closing the door behind her, and thinking that this one had been an easy and fruitful assignment. But as she was pressing the call button of the elevator, a door opened in the hallway, two doors from Zini's, and a young man in a suit came out, hurrying towards the elevator.

'Shit' thought the woman, hoping she would not have to kill him too. She turned her head away, pulling the cap a little more on her head. The elevator doors opened just as the man got close, and she entered first. She immediately lowered her head, fiddling with her fake electronic terminal. The young man was oblivious to her presence, busy messaging on his smartphone. He did not look at her, and left the elevator first at ground level, ungentlemanly. He did not know it, but it had saved his life.

The killer swore under her breath as she left the building. The man had not given her a second look, which was good. But he would certainly remember a female Fedex employee when the police would be all over the case. That would weaken the effect that the documents she had left there were trying to make. She still had done her job though, and payment was forthcoming.

Her nest egg was growing, and it looked that there was more and more business coming from this client.

Chapter 15

Nc4 Nfg4

Rain Fund Offices, Manhattan, New York City

Laura was angry and tense.

She put on the ear piece, and switched on the cell phone. It was the new SIM card, the second on the list. She made sure her hair was down and covering her ears, and then left the building housing the Rain Fund offices by the main entrance. She had left her car in the parking reserved for the funds employees, and then gone up to the offices to check up on Olivier. He was not in and there was no way for her to sniff around. She flagged a cab, which deigned to stop, and ordered the driver: 'Macy's please'.

Once she arrived at the famous department store on 34th, she started browsing, suddenly changing directions, stopping abruptly and checking behind her for familiar faces. She was thinking about when was the last time she went leisurely shopping? She decided to enjoy it, and bought herself a blouse and a pair of Jimmy Choo's. With her purchases paid for, she went to the lifts and entered the packed car with a bunch of people. As the doors were closing, she suddenly stepped out, making sure she was the only one dropping off. She then hurried away towards one of the exits, and tried to make herself smaller in the lunchtime crowds. She took out a cap from her bag, put it over her head and kept walking. She entered the first Starbucks and went directly for the ladies' room. She had to wait in line for a few minutes before entering a stall, and pondered the philosophical question of the relative length of men and women queues to public toilets. She also had the time to be melancholic about the good old times when Starbucks' toilets were shiny clean. Once in her stall, she then turned over her twin-sided jacket, the most basic but simplest trick in the book, and put a scarf around her neck and the bottom part of her face. She then pressed the call button of her phone, and just told the person answering: 'Coming out now'.

She left the Starbucks without ordering drinks and went directly to the first in line at the taxi stand and climbed in: 'Houston Street, please', pronouncing the "Houston" in the typical New York way. The driver did not answer and just eased out into the traffic.

She looked through the back window and saw Dave, in his eternal trench coat, arguing with another man at the door of the second Taxi, with big hand gestures. It looked even like some pushing and shoving went on. She was still in sight when the third taxi eased out into the traffic, before the argument for the second was settled. She kept her eyes on the third taxi, but after a few blocks, it turned right and disappeared from sight.

She called Dave again: 'Everything OK?'

'You were definitely followed, at least 2 guys. I had to physically stop one of them from getting in the taxi behind you. Looks like you are in the clear now, but be careful. Take the parking entrance anyway'

She stopped the cab well before Houston, near a taxi stand, where she took another cab, this time for Federal Plaza. Laura was pensive: They were still tailing her, and very tight. A two people-team following her was thorough and expensive, and meant this was a hell of an operation. She would have to be even more careful.

She had the taxi stop just at the entrance of the underground parking, gave two twenties to the surprised driver, and ran inside the parking. She showed her credentials to the attendant to gain access and took the lift up to the lobby.

Five minutes later, she was in John Reilly's office. Same smell, same clutter, even same suit on J.R.

'OK, Laura! So what was so urgent?'

Laura was sitting in the chair in front of the desk. Dave had not arrived yet.

'Olivier was attacked in Jack Zimmerman's house, and caused serious bodily harm. The place was thrashed. I suppose you knew and did not tell me!', she said angrily.

'We know that, Laura. You know that everything with tags that pops, we get copied. Of course the names Zimmerman and Van Dijk are tagged'

'But did you know that the burglars went there a few hours after I talked to Jack's widow about files in Jack's home office? And about going there to have a look? And Olivier says that the den was thrashed, but not much else'

John lifted an eyebrow at the familiarity of "Olivier", but did not dwell on it. He looked genuinely surprised. 'No, that we did not know. So you think there is a connection?'

Dave came in with his jacket on his arm and sat down silently in the second chair.

'Of course I think there is a connection! This was not a real burglary, they did not take anything and they were super-professional according to Van Dijk'. She had caught the look and corrected herself.' And I start wondering about Zimmerman's death. What do you think, is it not too much of a coincidence?'

John and Dave exchanged a look. It was clear they were hesitating.

'What?' It suddenly dawned on Laura: 'What is it else you did not tell me? What is going on?'. She was looking alternately at both of them.

Dave looked embarrassed and looked at his feet.

Finally, John blurted: 'OK, Laura. Sorry, we did not know for sure and wanted to keep things compartmentalized. The thing is that Jack had contacted the SEC a few days before his death. We do not know if he was murdered, but...'

She interrupted him: 'Fuck! You sent me undercover without warning me the guy could have been murdered! You son of a bitch! When were you planning to tell me?'.

John had his hands up. 'We still do not know what happened. There was no evidence whatsoever of foul play, it could be a coincidence'

'Come on, J.R. The guy works for organized crime and contacts the SEC, and he turns up dead after a few days. That is not a coincidence; that is a normal chain of events in the world I live in. And you do not think I should have known about it?'

'Please, Laura. Calm down. We did not know when you went in. And we still don't know if he was killed or if it was a heart attack, the guy was fat for God's sake!'

'But I hope that, now, you agree that it looks suspicious. Especially with those burglars looking into Jack's papers a few hours after I talk to his widow about missing files'

J.R. held his hands up: 'Yes, yes, I agree. This smells bad'

Laura pressed on: 'And am I allowed now to know what Jack told the SEC?'

'That's the thing, nothing. Dr. Zimmerman contacted the SEC but set a secretive meeting for after his conference abroad. I talked to the SEC agent who handled him on the phone: Jack suspected there was a huge cover-up of illegal activities, but he did not know the how or what. He said he was compiling a file showing the discrepancies, and wanted to come in and present it. That's the length and width of it. Now understand that to the SEC, it was just another routine call-in. They did not know of our interest, and it came up flagged to us only a few days later and in a routine report. And we were lucky because it was only thanks to this new inter-agency software'.

Laura was pensive: 'I wonder if those missing files are the same I have been looking for at Prometheus… Those had to do with results-correlation studies'.

'That could be it, but what are they about? You need to find them, Laura; this could be a breakthrough for this investigation. If that is what he wanted to hand over to the SEC, and why he died…'

'I get that, but where are they? Maybe the burglars found them'.

'Maybe not. They were interrupted by Van Dijk'

'I'll visit Jack's widow as promised and try to go through his papers. This is totally legitimate data for my work there. If it does not work, I could try to get Olivier's help'.

'Olivier? You are crazy', Dave interjected with a strange look, 'he will help you to frame himself?'

'How do you figure, Dave? His own people tried to break his skull? There is something else here we do not understand. Since I am in, I have been trying to get a "bad guy" vibe from him, and I cannot. It is as if he has no idea what's going on in his own fund'

'Come on, Laura. Do not tell me you are falling for this Van Drek, Dave shot back. 'You have to keep your objectivity'

Laura looked up uncomprehendingly. J.R. shot a sharp glance at Dave to hint him to quiet down. He explained: 'Drek is New York slang for garbage. Maybe less common in LA. Comes from Yiddish. But Dave just got carried away'.

Laura's cheek reddened slightly and answered both of them: 'I am not falling for him, I am expressing an opinion based on observation, and that's my job. I am in and you are not. He could be in the dark, we do not know for sure. And if he is, he could help us, who knows?'

J.R. stopped the argument: 'Enough, you two. Laura, I think your first priority is now to find those files. But be even more careful, these people are very dangerous: we know they follow you, we know they listen to your conversations, we know they have no problems burglarizing and battering, and probably murdering in cold blood. We cannot be too close, but make sure you have your phone and emergency SIM always with you. Anything special you do, like going to Jack's house, try to let your brother in Chicago know in advance under innocuous codes'

'OK. I'll have a look at the SEC report, and then go back upstate. I have a meeting with Olivier later this afternoon'.

Dave was on the verge of saying something, a scathing comment probably, but saw her challenging eyes and thought the better of it. They sat in silence while Laura read the short SEC memo. When she finished, -nothing notable in the memo-, she lifted her eyes and Dave asked: 'Anything else to mention, Laura?'

'The new patient is in, whose father I told you about. He looks promising. Besides that, I am just fitting in. I like the job, as a matter of fact. I have a meeting with the Prilutski guy next week .About the project, but I will try to talk to him about investing in the fund and see what happens'.

'OK, Laura. Good job. Sorry about the SEC story, we have your back. Go back and be careful. Maybe this is the start of cracking this case wide open'.

Laura stood up and left without a word, she was clearly still angry. As the door closed, Dave said quietly: 'You did not tell her about Joshua? She will be ballistic when she finds out'

'Shut up, Dave. This is totally different. They need to interact naturally and should not know about one another. If things go awry, we can let them know and have one help the other. This is standard procedure, you know that'

'Yes. But you have lied to her again, and she will not like it!'

'By omission only, Dave. By omission only. If she cannot take it, she is in the wrong business. And you stop busting her balls about this Van Dijk character'.

***

Cell phone ringing: 'Allo'

'The lady doctor is definitely shaking tails on purpose. I think we have a problem. It looks like she had help from the same guy we saw in the Park last time. Something is wrong with her'

'Shit! Are you sure?'

'About the guy, no. We tried to follow him after we lost her, but lost him too. But the lady is up to something, this is not natural behavior'

'We have to be sure before we do anything. There has been too much boat-rocking lately, we need some quiet. Double the manpower, again, and cling to her like glue. This is high priority. But keep your distance'

'OK'

Click

Chapter 16

Qe1 Rf7

The Prometheus Foundation, Washington County, New York State

I was in my Foundation office and I had no idea how my life would be turned up today. I had just completed my daily international chess moves. Only four, because I had just been checkmated by a player from somewhere in Eastern Europe. Annoying because I had not seen it coming, but it was just a game.

I was watching the relaxing landscape with a great cup of Robusta coffee and thinking about our "Beast" problem. I had hit an idea earlier: our new Number 5 looked brilliant and more communicative than our regular patients. Could we not expose him to the base code that triggered Number 3's attack and ask him what he saw? Of course, it was still early. We had to acclimatize him first and get him in the zone. But I would have to talk to Laura about that.

Laura. My thoughts slid naturally to her. Why was I becoming obsessed with her? She was of course a beautiful woman, but so was the swim-suit model still asleep in my bed in Manhattan. Laura was the consummate professional and had not shown the slightest hint of romantic interest in me. But there was something about her that fascinated me.

This train of thoughts was interrupted by my cell phone ringtone. The screen showed Alex calling.

'Hi Olivier, how is the head?'

'Better, thanks. And the hair is starting to grow back, slowly. In fact, my ribs hurt much more than the head. I have not been training since it happened, and I feel bloated'

'You can train less and work more in the meantime'. Alex was always been teasing me about my work ethics, though I suspected he was quite happy with my letting him do as he pleased.

'So you called to prod an invalid to work?'

'No, not really. I called about Dr. Wheelan.

'What about her?'

'Jan seems to think she could be, how could I say,… not totally on board'

'What does that mean, not totally on board? What does he base himself on? What happened?'. Laura was becoming a touchy subject for me.

'Nothing happened; it is just a gut feeling he has. But you know, he is a professional and we should trust his judgment. He just says she could be a potential leak, and we should just be careful and go slowly'

'But, he vetted her, he checked everything. She passed days of tests. And what could she leak? That we work with autistic employees? You have probably already done that, and, with her contract, she'd be sued for everything her grandchildren may at some point earn!'

'Just passing it on, Olivier. Relax. It does not hurt to be careful'

'What do I have to do to be *careful*? What is really going on, Alex. What is the matter?'

'Just playing it safe, Olivier. We have business secrets to protect. Remember this journalist who was following you and stuff…I am just asking you to keep your eyes open'

'OK. I have a meeting with her later, and I'll remind her of the secrecy issues. And you tell Jan to relax. Next time we meet, I'll want to discuss Jan with you and a few things that have been bothering me'

I rang off and finished my coffee. Something was definitely in the air. It was like a chain of events, like fate had just turned on me and bad things were occurring around me: Jack dead, being followed, being attacked, Alex's strange behavior, my obsession about Laura, the fund story starting to really leak out. My world was starting to change.

My thoughts were interrupted by the buzz of the suite's door. I checked the video monitor and,- speak of the devil -, Laura was standing at the door, with a bunch of files under her arm, wearing, of course, her white doctor coat. I checked my watch: Our meeting was up. I buzzed her in and went to open the office door.

'Hi Laura! I think we had better do that in your office: All the data will be more available'

'I brought most of it, but I think you are right. But if you want good coffee, bring your own. Mine is shitty overheated filter ' She smiled. Could she be a spy? I cannot believe it, not with a smile like that.

While we were walking to her office, she told me about the progress with Number 5. It reminded me I had to broach the subject of the base code with her. But I would wait a bit.

We sat, both of us on her side of the desk, and started to go over the health care reports of all the patients, excluding new Number 5. We then checked the performance reports of their work hours and chart completion percentiles. There was nothing out of the ordinary there. It really looked like Laura was as good as Jack in getting the patients interested in their task. She was insightful, professional and delightful. I was really attracted to this woman, and there was no way I could keep trying to convince myself otherwise. And the hint of cleavage she was showing was no spoiler although I think she noticed me watching. Come on, Olivier, what is the matter with you? Stop behaving like a schoolboy with a crush!

This made my next sentence all the more difficult. 'Before we go on to the "Beast incident" part of this meeting, I have been asked to remind you of the utmost secrecy that is part of your contract, Laura'

She visibly startled and it really made me feel bad: 'No offence, Laura. Just procedure. There has been a journalist sniffing around and strange things going on, like the burglary for instance. Remember that the whole idea behind the fund is to keep our methodology secret'

'You do not trust me?' She truly looked offended, and pulled away slightly.

My heart sank. 'No, no. Come on, Laura. You are doing a fantastic job, and I really appreciate you. I even…' I let my voice trail. 'Anyway. I have just been asked by Security to do a routine reminder. Please do not take this personally'. This nearly sounded like pleading.

'OK, Olivier. But promise me you'll never remind me again'

'Done. Sorry, had to. Won't again. Let us proceed'

'OK. But before we talk about what happened with Number 3, I wanted to talk about results correlation'

'Ok. Shoot'

'The missing files from Jack are all related to his validation project. There are references in other reports to this work and I cannot find it. He was basically correlating and analyzing the trends asserted by the patients with the actual trading results. He was trying to check for actual performance differences between the different patients and their specific mind frames'

'I see. Yes, I talked many times about that with Jack. He just did not have enough time to seriously work on that. You have to remember this is not a research organization, but a business-first money maker'

'This is clear. This is not being done at the detriment of care or everyday work. The thing is that Jack's files are nowhere to be found, and on the other hand, Alex seemed reticent to let me have the Manhattan data on the actual trades'

Everything then clicked in my head. It was nearly audible. That is why Alex had called me. Turf. Laura stepping on Alex's turf. I smiled lightly.

'Did I say anything funny?

'No, no!', I lifted my hands in defense. 'I now understand why the security reminder. You have asked for data from the heart of our operation. You have rattled the cages. Our head of security is paranoid and Alex is jealous of his turf. There are some politics here you are probably not aware of: On an everyday basis, I handle this side of the operation; and he handles Manhattan'

I continued: 'We'll get the data together. I'll go with you. This is interesting work'

'Great, Olivier, thanks'

'What I wonder, though, is where those missing files are?'

'There are three files missing from Jack's cabinet and computer: C183 to C185. Could that have anything to do with the burglary?'

I reflexively touched my stitches while answering: 'Jack did not usually take any work home. It does not fit'

'But maybe the burglars did not know that'

'Maybe not. But I did clear the mess in Jack's den, and did not see any files. Neither did I find anything work-related on his computer. You could give it a try, though, I can ask Caroline'

Something is bothering me while I talk: I have something in the back of my mind that wants to pop up. But I still cannot put my finger on it.

'OK. Now to the "Beast" incident. Have you reviewed Jack's files about the previous incidents?'

'Yes, of course. Not very much, though base code is mentioned in one previous incident'

'And Jack had no theories? I ask you that, because he wanted an urgent meeting with me before he left for this fateful conference. I thought this was about this problem'

'Nothing in the files. But I have come up with a research plan, to try to monitor better the patients and try to discover the trigger of these attacks. I should talk to the computer guy, though, and he has been ducking my calls too'.

'OK, Laura. I'll also set up the meeting with him, and I'll sit in on it. But before you show me your plans, I wanted to run something by you, just brainstorming'

She looked curious: 'OK'

'You have told me, and I have seen it myself, that Tom is an exceptional patient in terms of his trending skills, but also in his ability to communicate. So I thought we could show him bits of base code and check his reactions. We could do that in a very controlled environment, and we could also probably get a better insight from him if anything happens. What do you say?'

Laura did not jump up as I feared she would; she sat in silence, thinking. 'This is not a bad idea, Olivier. But this should be very closely controlled, and I should ask for his father's permission. And we should wait for him to be fully familiar with his environment'

'Sounds like a plan'. I stuck my hand out. She shook it, and I felt a jolt. I did not let go at once and locked eyes with her. I let her hand go, and I am pretty sure she was slightly blushing. I was dying to invite her to dinner, but instead I said: 'We are going to do great work together, Laura'

I stood up to leave.

'Thank you, Oliver, I appreciate the compliment. You are OK yourself'

That emboldened me. I turned back at the door: 'We should have dinner sometime. I would like to know you better. See you Laura'

I did not wait for her answer and fled into the gangway, like a shy schoolboy. But I still felt good at my Parthian arrow: Fire and flee. As I walked back to my office, I saw Joshua downstairs with his son at the workstation. Joshua was kneeling near his son's chair.

I climbed down to say hi, and approached them. The care-taker was sitting in the armchair behind them, dozing.

'Hi, Joshua. Hi Tom'

Joshua stood up and turned towards me. I did not know why, but I had the impression that he had a guilty look. 'Hi Olivier. What's up?'. Tom did not answer, but kept clicking at his computer.

'Just working late. How is everything?'

'Fine. I think this place will do wonders for Tom. It really looks like he likes it here'

'I think Tom looks like a fantastic young man, and there is no doubt you are a great dad'

'Thanks'. He threw the keys he was holding to his left hand, and extended his right hand.

I shook it. But I again noticed his USB key. And it finally clicked in my brain, perhaps because I was not trying: Caroline mentioned Jack buying a USB key for the first time and doing some work at home, allegedly about his speech. That's it: The USB key. Maybe the files are in there. Joshua was looking at me strangely, probably on account of my spaced-out look.

'Welcome, Joshua. Sorry, I was just thinking of something. See you around'

And I ran away, making a mental note to call Caroline. I was on my way back to my office, excited, when my cell vibrated. The screen again read Alex.

As I pressed "on", Alex started whispering at once: 'Olivier! The police are here, looking for you. They are talking about a murder'

'What? Which murder? What are you talking about'. I did not fully process his words.

'The Zini broad, the journalist. Apparently she has been murdered, and you are a person of interest. I called our lawyers. Rosenthal is on his way here to talk to the cops. I have not talked to you and I do not know where you are. So, switch this phone off and get organized. This is serious'

And he rang off.

My world was definitely crumbling.

■■

I was standing in my office, thunderstruck. This is not the kind of news you expect at any time. I went to the window, my brain churning. Things were getting weirder and weirder: Jack, Caroline, now Zini… There must be a connection between all those these incidents, and the only connection coming to mind was the Fund.

The last time I heard of the journalist, was when Jan told me they had stopped her following me. I called Jan from my cell phone, but he did not pick up. Jan snubbing me was happening more and more, and it was intolerable. But maybe the police was around? I had no idea what happened to the woman, where or when; but I assumed that the police wanted to question me because of the article she wrote. Or was it more?

But what if it did have something to do with Jack, with the missing files, with the burglary? We had secrets to keep, just like every other business. But nothing worth breaking and entering for, or worse, murder for! Had I lost control of my own company?

I suddenly felt my heart constrict: And what if Jack's death was no accident? I needed to find those missing files, and my last hope is that they may just be on Jack's key chain.

I took out my cell phone to call Caroline, when I suddenly saw blue and red lights coming from the right side of my field of vision: It looked like a police car was coming down the driveway. They are probably coming to pick me up for questioning. I would have to meet up with my lawyer, Eli Rosenthal, before I even start answering their questions. This could take ages.

I was psyched up and really wanted to check for those files before I lost precious time cooperating with the police. I rationalized that I had no information whatsoever about the murder, and I had not yet been formally notified of the police's interest in me. So, I switched off my phone, took out the battery and checked the security cameras feed on my desk's computer screen. After a few minutes, I saw two policemen entering the reception area. I quickly strolled to the balcony window, opened it and climbed onto the generous ledge. I managed to close back the window. Of course, I could not lock it from the outside, but it looked good enough. Luckily, my office windows were on the side of the building, and nobody could see me from the driveway or the gate.

Jumping from the first floor should be no problems for an experienced *traceur*, as parkour practitioner are called. I jumped towards the grass, dissipating the energy by the bending of the knees and a forward shoulder roll that took me away from the lit-up building. I still felt a stab of pain in my head and ribs, which forced me to stop and regain my breath. This was no way to care for my injuries. I touched my head wound with my fingers. My fingers came back wet; I was bleeding a little between the stitches. I stood up and went for my car, near the main entrance, making sure I walked normally. There was an empty local police cruiser in front of the stairs.

No need to hurry suspiciously, but I still had to get away fast. I climbed into the car, started the engine, and drove to the gate. A guard I did not know came to the passenger window:

'Good evening, Mr. Van Dijk. Have you seen the policemen looking for you?'

'Yes, thanks. But I am in a hurry now, please open the gate'

The gate was already opening, and I roared out, driving towards Southport. Our receptionist being a stickler for procedures, it was likely that the policeman had not even reached my office suite yet. I drove fast; I was high on adrenaline now, and it dulled the pain in my ribs. It was already dark, and I slowed down gradually to the speed limit: No need to get arrested for speeding now.

When I finally got to Jack's street, about half an hour later, I drove really slowly. There was a dark sedan opposite the house with a shape in the driver's seat. It was probably Jan's man. So the security I requested was still on, and there should also be another man watching the back. These people were technically working for me, but Jan was the last guy I knew who had had an interaction with the Zini woman. And something at Rain Fund was definitely off. I drove by the guard and took the first side road. I parked, shut off the engine, and climbed down.

I started walking, leisurely, like a resident out on his evening walk and went around the block to stop two houses away from Jack's backyard. How was I going to get inside without being seen? The moon was not full, but the night was not moonless either, and public lighting all around was pretty pervasive. I had to get in without being seen by Jan's goons.

I hoped fervently that I would find answers inside.

Chapter 17

h3 Nf6

The Prometheus Foundation, Washington County, New York State

Laura's brain was working in overdrive. She was trying to sort out all the thoughts and feelings that were assailing her: her budding sentiments for Olivier tempered by his maybe being a crook, her newfound love for the work she was doing with the autistic patients, the progress and dangers of the case, the office politics at the FBI,…

She was still sitting in her office. It was late, but she was staying the night in the service flat. She had been organizing the trending results from the patients, to have them ready for testing versus the actual executions. There was something important there, she felt it.

She stretched her upper body, to relieve neck strain, and glanced at the big room downstairs. She could see that Number 1 and Number 5 were at their desks, while Number 3 was sitting on his couch. Number 2 and Number 4 were probably in their rooms, resting or eating or grooming. There were three caretakers around, and Joshua was behind his son, Number 5, on the workstation.

Joshua had become quite a fixture at the Foundation: he was often around, especially in the evenings. He was taking an active part in Tom's care. She liked Joshua: He was caring but also virile and powerful-looking. He was always straight with his answers; you did not feel any of the hypocritical veneer so many professional people were adept at. He was one of those likeable 'What-you-see-is-what-you-get'- kind of man. And there was no hanging doubt about his being a crook.

She felt that she could ask him straight about the little experiment Olivier had suggested! She left her office and climbed down the stairs into the big room. She approached Tom's station silently, and heard Joshua talking to him in a soothing voice. She could not make out exactly what he was saying though.

'Hi Joshua. Hi Tom!' she said to let them know she was there, a little bit embarrassed at her eavesdropping attempt.

Joshua turned towards her, while Tom ignored her, characteristically.

'There is something I would like to talk to you about', said Laura. 'Can we sit down for a moment?'.

Joshua looked intrigued: 'No problem. Everything OK?'

'Yes, yes', as they sat down in Number 5's foyer behind the work station. 'I just want to have your opinion on something, and please, take it for what it is: Just a preliminary check for an idea born in during a brainstorming session'

'Go ahead, Laura. I am listening' He was keeping an eye on Tom while talking.

'You remember I told you about something upsetting some of the patients from time to time, always while they are working on the program. They suddenly get frightened by something they see on their screens, and become hysterical'

'Yes. I remember it is something you mentioned, and there was an incident like that a few days ago.'

'Yes. This is something that has happened to three subjects a total of seven times, and we do not understand it. The patients mumble incoherently about something black, frightening or a "beast". It is a matter we must understand for their sake'

Joshua was listening intently: 'What do you want my opinion about?'

'Tom is by far the most gifted and the most communicative of the patients here. He is a great kid, and your support and encouragement has a lot to do with that. Now, we know for sure that in two cases, including the last one, this has happened when the patients were looking at the base code of the software. How and why they got there, we do not know. But you know they fiddle around and they are all geniuses. We were thinking that we could, with your permission and help, show bits of the base code to Tom, or try to lead him there by himself, to see if he would react to anything and perhaps be able to communicate with us about the experience'

Joshua sat silently, deep in thought. He finally sighed and spoke slowly, as if thinking out loud: 'At first glance, I do not see why not, if it is done under my close supervision. This is important for him and for the other patients. It is better to do it in a controlled environment, than to have it happen suddenly out of the blue. Why not? We need to iron out the details, but I think it is, in fact, a good idea. Let me think about it tonight, and we'll talk about it again tomorrow'.

Laura was suddenly relieved, it had been quite a forward request; Tom was still new and it could prove itself traumatic.

'Thanks Joshua. Let us discuss that tomorrow. You and Tom are very special people'

She stood up

'You are a fine lady yourself, Laura. See you tomorrow'. The hint of a smile made it clear he was flirting in a good-natured manner. He was a handsome man, she thought, noticing again the small dimples as he was smiling. You got used to the scar and did not see it after some time. He stood up to go back to Tom, and Laura went back to her office.

She climbed back the stairs, smiling to herself and flattered by the attention.

When she sat back behind her desk, she immediately saw the flashing window of a new email. She clicked on it; it was from her "brother". The content was inane but included the code words for an urgent call back.

Her heart started beating fast. When undercover, this kind of contact usually meant very serious trouble. She went to her serviced flat and dressed quickly in her jogging outfit. She exited the building by the main entrance, and started running lightly around the mansion, taking the path going towards the enclosed grounds. She stopped a second in a darker area, kneeled as if tying her laces and deftly changed SIM cards in her phone, to and from her sock. She stood up and started running again, faster this time, while switching on the phone.

'Laura' she said close to the mike.

'There has been a development you must know about. A journalist covering the rain fund has been murdered at her home, and Olivier is a person of interest'

'What? When was that?' And she added defensively: 'He was with me this afternoon'

'No details yet. But you should be very careful. Antagonistic connections to the fund are eliminated'

'I have a feeling that things are moving fast now. I think we should give a push to get things tumbling around and see what comes out. I'll go to Jack's widow to look for the missing files, as soon as possible. I feel there is something there. Let us stir the pot and see what happens

'You are the one undercover. I trust your instincts, but be very careful, Laura. And do not trust this Olivier character'

'OK. Will keep in touch with next SIM'

And she cut off. In for a penny, in for a pound; she decided to do a bit more jogging to clear up her mind. The grounds were fantastic for training, green and lush; a far cry from city-running. After doing ten lapses around the building, she did a series of ten sprints and then jogged back to the Mansion. As she climbed the stairs, she heard a commotion from the big room area. She ran up, punched in the code to open the door, and entered the gangway. She could see downstairs that Joshua was standing in Area 3 with two beefy uniformed security guards around him. They were shouting menacingly at one another. One of the guards was waving a baton.

***

Laura, in her jogging suit, stood frozen on the mezzanine hallway, looking down at the altercation in the big room.

'Stop! What are you doing?'. She started running down the stairs. 'You are upsetting the patients! Stop!'

She was running towards the three men, now looking at her, all with undivided attention.

'What is the matter here?'

One of the guards, a hulk of a man she had never seen before, answered: 'This guy here was fiddling with the computers, spying around. We have to restrain him and check him. Please do not meddle in this'

'I am Dr. Wheelan in charge of this center, and you are upsetting my patients and attacking their parents. I demand you stop immediately!'

This did not seem to make any impression on the guards. 'And we report to the Head of Security only, and this has the highest priority. Please move away and let us do our job'

Laura looked at Joshua, placing herself between him and the guards: 'What is the matter, Joshua? What happened? Did you do anything to upset them?'

'Of course not. I was just strolling around, looking at the equipment. I have just put Tom to bed and I was making my way home'

The other guard now interjected, moving sideways to go around Laura: 'If you have nothing to hide, let us check what you have on your person. We have seen you on the security cameras, fiddling with the computers'.

Joshua answered in a low, but menacing voice: 'You will do no such thing. Keep away from me!'

Laura tried to intervene: 'Your shouting and aggressive behavior is causing great psychological damage to the patients present. Stop at once! Let us go to my office to settle this like civilized people'

But the guard who had asked to frisk Joshua kept moving forward, and suddenly, with a speed belied by his bulk, jumped forward with his stick held up. He bumped slightly into Laura, throwing her to the floor.

Joshua was ready though, and years of army training kicked in, as if yesterday had been his last close-combat training session. He side-stepped forward, rolling into the downward strike and letting the entire attacker's energy dissipate forward. He caught the guy's hand, inversed his pivot and threw him to the ground while cranking his wrist joint. An expert would have recognized a classical *kote gaeshi* throw of Aikido. It had taken a fraction of a second only, and Laura was still in shock, on the ground. Before she could recover, she saw the second guard going for his belt holster. He was going for a gun! This was totally out of proportion.

But Joshua was now in fighting mode, pumped up with adrenaline. It is funny how your body does not forget those years of grueling training. He saw the other guard going for his gun while he was still finishing the first guard by stomping him on the face. He jumped forward and kneed the second guard in the groin while getting control of his gun arm. He followed up with a second knee strike to the face, elbowed down the back of his neck and pushed him down the floor. He took the gun from the holster and jumped back to the other guard moaning on the floor. Joshua fell with all of his body weight into an elbow strike to the head, and immediately went for this guard's gun holster.

Joshua was already up, with two guns in his hands. 'Laura. Do not be alarmed. I am working with the police and those are bad guys, very bad guys. I have to take Tom and get the hell out of Dodge. Please do not get involved'. He was putting both guns in his pants belt.

Laura was slowly recovering from the shock. This had happened so quickly. And wow! Can this guy fight or what? And what did he say about the police?

Laura stood up and had a look around the room: the two guards on the floor, one moaning, holding his injured wrist, and the other out cold. The patients were looking on curiously, but did not look especially alarmed, unlike their caretakers. Laura's brain was working furiously. She had wanted to stir the pot! She had her wish. She had intended to go to Jack's house for the files, but now all hell was breaking loose here. And with a journalist close to the story murdered, this situation was accelerating out of control. Laura took an instant gut-based decision: 'I am coming with you. You have to move fast, I suppose we are being watched on the security cams'

Joshua was bending over the downed guards, using their own handcuffs to restrain them: 'You do not have to do that; you do not have to be involved'

'I am involved. You'll need my help to get out and we'll talk later. There is more to this than you know. Let's go quickly'.

They ran towards the living quarters, and Laura shouted to the caretakers: 'Get all patients to their quarters and make sure they all stay there away. NOW!'

As they hurried towards the patients' living quarters, Laura told him: 'Get Tom and bring him to my car, a grey Honda, in front. I'll be waiting with the engine running'.

Laura took the side entrance to the Parking lot, jumped into the car and started the engine. After two minutes, Joshua appears half-carrying Tom in his pajamas. He opened the rear door of Laura's Honda Civic and pushed Tom gently inside.

'Tom, just lie down and relax, Dad will be back' and to Laura: 'Drive to the gate, play stupid. I'll get the gate opened'.

He slammed the door and ran into the darkness.

Laura drove toward the gate at normal speed. As she approached, the guard came out of the booth and she saw that his demeanor was normal. Maybe they are not yet aware of the events that just took place in the big room.

'Evening Jim'

'Evening Doctor'

As he signaled the other guard in the booth to lift the barrier, the communication device on his lapel came to life: Gate! Gate! Come in'

Jim stopped in his tracks to listen in.

'Come on, Jim. Open up. I am in a hurry' Laura pleaded, trying to look natural.

They both missed Joshua in the booth, holding the second guard in a sleeper hold, a strangulation move cutting blood to the brain and causing loss of consciousness in less than a minute.

Jim looked at Laura: 'Just a sec, doctor. I have to check this'. As he turned around towards the booth, Joshua slammed into him like a ton of bricks. Another sleeper hold and Joshua carried him into the booth, from where he also lifted the barrier. Laura opened the front door to let him dive in and rushed out with all the speed her car could muster.

As the property became smaller in her rear view mirror, Laura started talking: 'Did you do something there, Joshua? And what did you say about the police?'

Joshua was leaning on the seat to check on Tom in the back. 'I did snoop around, and I do really work with the police. I am sorry. The people you work for are very bad guys, Laura. And the guns they pulled on me really show you that. But you did not have to get involved'

'Who do you work for, Joshua. Which police department?'

'Why does it matter? And where are you driving to? I need to get Tom to a safe place'

'I am taking us first of all away, and fast. Then we'll have to drop you somewhere safe, I know where. So bear with me, please: which police unit do you work for?' Laura was seething: 'Tell me the name of your handler, NOW!'

Joshua startled. He had never heard Laura shout. 'Dave Freeman of the FBI. Why? Do you know him? '. He saw her face and it suddenly dawned on him: 'You know him. You also work with the police'. This was more of a statement than of a question.

'The fucking son of a bitch!' Laura hit the wheel with her palm. 'I do not work with the police, I am an FBI agent working with Dave and reporting to son-of -a –bitch-in-charge John Reilly. He did not tell me about you, and it is not the first time he kept vital information from me. And now the whole op is blown up'.

Joshua looked at her with renewed interest: 'If it helps, he did not tell me about you either. And I asked'

'What did they catch you doing there, Joshua?'

'I was copying computer's data to my USB'

'Stupid! This data is available to me on a routine basis. You are just in and already burnt. And now everything went down the drain

'Why did you not stay behind then?'

'Things have been moving lately; there has even been a murder, probably related. I think it has something to do with missing files. Time to let the shit hit the fan and look where it lands'

Joshua smiled: 'You are a handful, Laura. I am surprised to hear you talk dirty, but I like it. What do you suggest we do now?'

'You need to go somewhere safe with Tom. I'll go to my predecessor's house and look for those missing files. I also have to report to my son of a bitch boss'

'We can leave Tom at his old caretaker's house. She'll be happy to take him in. Then I'll come with you. You need protection'

'I have seen you fight and I'll be glad to have you by my side. But you are sure Tom will be OK?'

'One hundred per cent. I would not leave him if I was not sure'

'OK, then. Do you still have the guns?'

'No. I threw them in the bushes in the compound. Pity'

'OK. Where to?'

'Drive towards Norwalk, I'll guide you then'

Laura took out her phone and pressed "send".

'Allo, Dave. Are you in the office?'

'Yes. A direct call? Everything OK?'

'Put J.R. on'

'Why? What's up?'

'PUT J.R. ON! NOW' Laura shouted.

John took the phone: 'Yes, Laura'

'You son of a bitch! I have here with me someone who wants to talk to you'

Then she passed the phone on to Joshua.

Chapter 18

Nxe5 dxe5

Jack Zimmerman's house, Southport, Connecticut

I was standing on the corner, two houses away from Jack's. Nobody around: time to go. I jogged lightly towards the first wall separating the first two gardens, just like the start of a *parkour* practice. I was over the wall lightly and silently in a second, landing in Jack's neighbor's garden. There was a lawn and landscaped bushes, ideal for quiet and concealment. I climbed lightly on the brick shed close to Jack's wall and had a quick peek over: Nobody there. I was expecting a second guard in the back; this was unsettling. I jumped down and grabbed a river stone from the bed flower. I climbed back slowly on the roof of the shed and waited silently, making sure to stay immobile. After a few minutes, I finally saw him: The second guard was walking on the far side of the house; he must have been strolling from back to front. No need for a diversion then, I left the stone on the roof. With my eyes rested and now used to the darkness, I kept watching him closely. As soon as he passed the corner of the house on his way back to the front, I crouched and jumped into Jack's garden. Then immediately back up onto the backyard tree, climbing silently. From the first fork in the branches, I jumped towards the balcony, catching the banister and pulling myself up easily. I crouched behind the colorful flower pots and stopped moving, getting back in control of my breath, and looking out. After a few minutes, the guard was walking past again. This time, he turned into the backyard and strolled around. My luck! After a few moments, it became clear why he had changed his routine: He lit a cigarette! This was second-hand smoking at its worst: Nothing I could do! I kept quiet until he completed a few inhalations, threw the half-finished cigarette down and stomped it out. The cigarette smoke was still lingering around. He'd better not have Caroline smell that!

As soon as he turned the corner, I dialed Caroline's cell. She answered after four rings: 'Allo?'

I whispered: 'Caroline, it's me. Please be quiet and do not answer. This is important. I need to talk to you and I am now on the balcony of your master bedroom. Please come open the window fast and without noise. Please be quick'. And I closed the phone before she could keep talking.

She could not have been far, because after a few seconds the large French window opened. She had the good sense of not lighting up. I slid in quietly and closed back the window gently, being careful not to alert the guards to my presence. Caroline was staring at me with an anxious glare, trembling. She was still dressed, in a comfortable home tracksuit. I closed the curtains, and then sat on the bed. She sat on the bed too, gazing at me with a confused look on her face.

'Caroline, I do not want to cause you pain or fear, but you deserve to know that I think that Jack's death is suspicious and could have something to do with some missing data'

Her hands went to her mouth with a look of anguish. I felt bad with reopening the wounds but I had no choice. I took her hand.

'I am trying to get to the bottom of this, but it is becoming dangerous. I need to ask you where Jack's key set is. You told me about a USB key memory stick he bought, is it on it? The data could be there'

'As a matter of fact it is, and I have the key set here in the closet safe. You really mean to say it was not an accident? That someone killed him?' There are tears in her eyes.

'I truly do not know. I know it was declared a confirmed heart attack, but too many strange things have happened since'.

She was turning the dials on the safe, looking distraught. She had to redo the sequence, her hands trembling fiercely.

'I am so sorry, Caroline'

She threw me the keys, and then looked at me with a sad look. 'Please leave now, I need to be alone'

I nodded. The key holder was a USB memory stick, bingo. I had to check it up somewhere; I had to find a computer immediately and see what it contained.

'Can I use the …'. We both heard a noise downstairs, and I stopped talking. I went to the door silently, with my index finger covering my lips. I looked down carefully and saw two masked men with guns treading carefully downstairs. I had been so stupid; this place or our phones were obviously bugged. The intruders did not see me but would be here in a minute or two. I stepped to Caroline and whispered in her ear: 'Lock the door quietly behind me, then lock yourself in the bathroom and call 911 from your cell. Now!'

I sprinted out without looking back and heard her closing the door behind me. The goons were on the stairs, but I totally surprised them: I ran to the den's door before they could shoot or react, locking the door behind me. I heard them running after me, grunting. I went to the window, opened it and jumped out, catching myself for a second on the bottom of the master bedroom balcony. That dissipated the energy and allowed me for a long jump down to the yard, and a roll forward. In a second I was on the garden wall, somewhat elated by the jumps and the flowing adrenalin; but the intruders were already at the window. I heard a pop and felt something grazing my arm. Wow, that was close! I assumed that it was a silenced weapon, although I had never heard one before outside of a movie theater. These people were playing for keeps. I hoped I had lured them away from Caroline, and that she would be all right. If she had called 911, the police must be on their way. And the opposition already knew their time was limited, from their listening in.

I was already behind the wall and I thought I heard a few more thuds hitting it. It could be my imagination, but nothing like chasing bullets to give you a power boost. I ran close to the neighbor's house façade to avoid being in the line of fire, but that lit up the motion-detector projectors. In a second, I was over the second wall, running like a madman. I was glad I took up *Parkour* a few years ago. Who would have known how helpful it would be? It had definitely saved my life today.

I had to decide where to run to and I was trying to think while running. In order to get to my car, I had to pass in front of Caroline's house. My assailants were probably behind me and I could try this direct route. A detour would help them cut me off, but on the other hand there could be more bad guys in front the house.

In a split second, I decided to go for the shortest way: the curb opposite the house. I turned left and started running like crazy. The street was deserted as I began hearing police sirens in the distance; this had the effect of making me slightly more hopeful I would make it.

Einstein once said: "Man plans and God laughs". He knew what he was talking about: As I was closing on the house, I suddenly saw a shade running out of the driveway and onto the road, looking straight at me. Shit! This was one of them and he was lifting a gun towards me.

At that precise moment, something incredible happened: A car parked a few yards from there, with no lights on, suddenly roared to life and simply ran my would-be killer over!

I heard the thud, but I was too pumped up to stop or ask questions. I swerved and ran even faster, heading for my car. I had ever been that scared in my life! I heard shouts behind me but did not slow. I even zigzagged, like in the movies.

But before I arrived at the intersection, I saw the blue and red lights of a police car coming towards me, siren on. Instead of running for my car, I ran towards the police cruiser in the middle of the street, hands extended up and shouting.

The police car stopped in the middle of the street a few yards from me with full lights on and the passenger door opened. The police officer shouted: 'Lie on the ground, hands in plain view. NOW'

I lay down fast on my belly hands extended forward, and shrieked to the approaching cop: 'Please go to the Zimmerman residence down from here. There is a woman there in danger; she is the one who called 911. Please go fast'.

The policeman approached me carefully, handcuffed me and muttered something in his microphone. There was another police car arriving on the scene and he waved it through towards the house.

'Please, please make sure she is fine. She is in the upstairs bathroom'

'Taken care of, sir'. He helped me stand up from the cold pavement and took me towards the back of his cruiser. He looked at my disheveled state before asking: 'What is your name, sir, and what is happening here?'

'My name is Olivier Van Dijk. This is my friend's house, Mrs. Zimmerman, and we were attacked by armed intruders'

'We'll check it up, sir. Mind your head'. As he eased me in, handcuffed, into the back of the cruiser, I saw that the car which ran my assailant over was a grey Honda. In front of it, were two persons with their hands in the air, talking to two more police officers. I recognized them immediately in the strong headlights: Laura and Joshua! Together. They had run my assailant over! I was shocked. What were they doing here?

***

Fairfield Police Department, Reef Road, Fairfield, Connecticut

I was sitting in a brightly lit interrogation room at Fairfield PD. It did not look much like interrogation rooms on TV: no one-way glass, no padded walls, and no bolted-to-the floor table and chairs. It was just a simple room with a desk and three plastic chairs. The policemen had taken the handcuffs off me already on our way over here. Finally, a middle–aged, obviously bored detective had come for a deposition about what had happened at Jack's house. He was dressed in jeans and a flannel shirt and brought me black coffee in a paper cup. At least he called that coffee, may God forgive him. He confirmed that Caroline was OK, but did not offer any more details, mumbling something about investigation procedures. I asked about Laura, and Joshua, and the car crash, but I got no answer. I also asked about my old friend detective Steever; she was not on duty, but was looking forward to grill me tomorrow morning.

The detective told me I was also a person of interest in a NY murder case, and that they had called NYPD. After a short argument, he brought me a phone to call my lawyer. I wanted very much to tell the story of the incident at Caroline's house, and I had nothing to hide, but I have learned early in life that, when dealing with bureaucracy and the law, you needed counsel, no matter whether you were innocent or guilty. Many innocent people who had never heard of that Golden Rule were sitting in jail: The justice system is about process, not about justice. It is a fallible human creation with inherent flaws: You always needed to ensure that you did not get even the tip of your finger in its jaws, just because you wanted to do the right thing, or just because you wanted to look nice and helpful.

So, I sat there waiting for my 500 dollars-an-hour lawyer to come all the way from Manhattan. It was already midnight, and I was exhausted. They were good enough to bring me another very bad coffee and a stale bagel, and then, to leave me alone.

About forty five minutes passed, and I was dozing off in my plastic chair, when the door burst open. It startled me awake, and Laura was standing in front of me, in the track suit she had been wearing in front of Jack's house, when having, allegedly my lawyer would say, run over the guy who was about to shoot me.

I was more than a little surprised. 'Laura! You are all right!'

She was not into small talk. 'Olivier! Listen to me. And listen carefully. There is no time, so no interruptions. I am a psychiatrist, but I am also an FBI agent'. My jaw dropped open, and her words took time to register. She continued: 'Your Fund is under investigation because of its links to organized crime. My boss is sure you are in on it. My gut feeling and what I have seen in the company to date, tells me that you are not. You are a stooge, taken on for a ride'. I started to say something in protest but she held up her hand. I had to process this, and just shut up. She continued: 'You are in a shitload of trouble: you are the suspect in a murder case, and even if you had no idea about what is happening in your Fund, you bear the legal responsibility for all kinds of misdeeds. Now, this operation is imploding, people are dying and things are happening fast. You could help me to nail this case, and I'd do what I can to help you. I know you did not murder Zini, because you were with me around the time of death and could not have been back in Manhattan in time to do it. But the cops will take time convincing, and anyway you could have had it done by somebody else! My boss wants to go by the book, send an army of agents and accountants and scrutinize all the files and computers. He wants to arrest and prosecute everybody, including you and let the lawyers sort it up. I am convinced that if we do not act fast, the bad guys will disappear with the money and the evidence. What I want from you is this: It is your company. We could go now and get all the evidence needed before morning. I would put that to your credit and make sure it helps you in your future legal woes'

This entire monologue was in one go; then she suddenly stopped, as if out of breath. She looked at me sternly.

I had finally got it: my whole world was crashing down, and I had to do something, and stop taking the events as they happened, simply as an observer: 'I do not believe there is anything wrong with my company'. But it lacked conviction, and I knew in the back of my mind that there were things I should have pieced together before. I had led a playboy's lifestyle and taken second fiddle to Alex, and now, tonight, in this soulless room, was the reckoning. I had to save my company and set things right. And I cared what Laura thought of me, even now.

My brain was churning: Should I wait for my lawyer and let him take care of everything. He was one of the best around and probably would cost me an arm and a leg, but he could get me out with a slap on the wrist; in fact, I had done nothing wrong and I had no knowledge of any wrongdoing. On the other hand, I was slowly getting mad: Somebody had messed with my life's work, and taken me for a fool. I needed to know for sure. And do something about it. I considered myself a regular guy, that had been lucky, but now I had been banged on the head, shot at, lied to and framed for murder. It was time to become proactive.

'I am with you, and I'll do anything to get to the bottom of this. What can you do to get me out of here?'

'I can have you transferred to my custody, no problem. Remember that I am a fully-credentialed FBI agent. My boss will almost certainly want to fire me, then kill me, not necessarily in that order. But not if we succeed. And anyway, he pissed me off tonight'.

This was a Laura I had never seen. An angry tiger.

Suddenly, I got over my surprise and became the man of action I needed to be: 'Get me a computer then, fast'. I took out my keys, with Jack's USB stick. Her beautiful Asiatic eyes rounded up in surprise: 'You found the missing files?'

'Yes. At Jack's. They were simply on his key ring, hiding in plain sight. And by the way thank you for saving my life down there. We'll have to talk about that later'.

After a few minutes we were on a computer at a random desk in the common room of the police station, under the surprised eye of the flannel-and-jeans detective. Laura was moving the mouse, but we were both reading Jack's reports. After twenty minutes, we had gone fast through everything. I was in shock! Laura looked at me and summed it up in words that cut through my heart: 'The patients' trending is ineffective. Your whole operation is based on a lie'

I was crumbling; my whole life's dream was a hoax. I was so proud of this idea of mine, so sure it worked. It had made me succeed, become rich. But the data was irrefutable: Jack had checked the actual effect of trading on the direct basis of the trends extrapolated by the patients. Results were equivalent to random.

'How is your fund making money then? This is proof there is something illegal going on. These files show that there is no correlation between the trades recommended by Prometheus, and the ones recorded in Manhattan'

She thought for a minute and continued: 'We need to check the files in Manhattan. The records will not fit, and this will be the legal proof of the hoax. And Jack has probably been murdered because of these files'.

I am starting to get very angry, emerging from the state of shock I was in. But something still did not fit: 'But they have been checked by the SEC. We shall not find anything'.

After a minute, I seethed: 'Alex. Alex must be behind all this. I always suspected his seed money was from dubious sources. There is no way he would not know. Let us go confront him. Now!'

Laura readily agreed it was the best way to proceed: Rattle the cages before daybreak, before the opposition could organize.

'Call your lawyer: I'll arrange your release from here. But everything should look as if you are being remanded here for Zini's murder. Tell him to play along, and tomorrow he'll sit with my boss to clear all this mess up and get you a deal'

Fifteen minutes later, we were driving towards Manhattan in her small Honda.

I asked her: 'How is a truly gifted psychiatrist in fact an FBI agent?'

'Very simple. I had always dreamed of being a profiler, like on TV. They drafted me especially for this case from the relevant courses I was taking on the criminal mind. I have an autistic brother, and I was familiar with the condition. I even like the work with autistics. And for what it is worth, I still think you had a great idea, and that it should work, with a little tweaking'

'Thank you Laura'. I was grateful for the much needed encouragement.

After a few minutes, I asked her: 'What was Joshua doing with you at Jack's house?'

If she did notice the hint of jealousy in my question, she did not show it.

'You are not going to believe this, but Joshua is also working for the FBI, although I did not know about it until tonight. He started the whole mess today by trying to copy files from the patient's computers, and was caught by your security people'

'Joshua too? My God. Is there anything real about my own company? What happened then?'

'He took care of the security guys like they were nothing. You will not believe how he fights, he is ex-army. In fact, I wish he was with us right now'

I felt another pang of jealousy. But she did not notice and finished: 'Anyway he took Tom out and we drove to Jack's place. We were just parking the car before going in to ask Caroline for Jack's papers, when we saw you running, and a guy jumping on the road with a gun pointed at you'.

I stayed silent the rest of the way to Alex's place, trying to make sense of the whole mess I was now in.

Whoever had screwed my life's work would pay for it, I swore to myself.

Chapter 19

Bc4 Rff8

54th Street, Manhattan, New York City

Laura's car was parked, illegally, in a side street, one block away from Alex's building. We exited the car and I asked her: 'How do we proceed? We just go up to him and ask him to confess?'

'We'll have to play it by ear. Let us confront him and see what happens. I'll use my cell to tape him; we will not tell him I am FBI at first. Either way, I can still arrest him if I need to, and tomorrow, his office will be crawling with agents'

We walked briskly to the building's entrance, one of those prestigious places with concierge and dais stretching out on the pavement. The glass doors were closed, as it should be at this ungodly hour, but I knew the uniformed doorman on duty. I signaled to him through the glass and he came to open the doors.

'Night , Mr. Van Dijk. How are you?'

'Thank you. I am here to see Mr. Prilutski'.

I did not remember the receptionist's name; I do not think I ever did know. He nodded hello to Laura. 'I'll have to call up; you know the procedures at this hour'

'No need. I'll call him myself. He is not expecting me but this is urgent. You know, business'. I took out my cell to show my intention to call. The receptionist nodded gravely, as though he was an important businessman himself.

I dialed Alex's number, and after seven rings he answered in a sleepy voice: 'What?'

'Alex, it's Olivier. It is an emergency; I am down in the foyer. Please tell the doorman to let me up'. I did not want him to hear that Laura was with me before we were up.

He was silent for a few seconds, trying to process it. 'OK. Put him on'.

After a few minutes we were at the door of his luxurious apartment. I did not need to signal Laura to stay out of sight of the peephole. I rang and the door opened nearly simultaneously. Alex was in a robe, doubtless some designer made from some kind of natural and expensive fiber, over his silk pajamas. His eyes were puffy with sleep and his voice throaty. He obviously had been asleep; which did not compute with him being involved. The people behind this had been very active tonight, they knew about Joshua's fight, about Jack's house, about Zini and the police and about me escaping their clutches. Could it be that Alex was a stooge too and had no idea what was happening? My heart jumped with hope; I really did not want to have been betrayed by an old friend.

Alex yawned: 'Come in. What happened that is so important?'

He then noticed Laura standing behind me, still in her tracksuit. He was surprised but did not comment. Not even a snide or crass comment; it was so unlike him, that I was sure he had guessed trouble was on its way. I asked: 'You are alone?'. Alex often brings bimbos home, sometimes more than one at a time, for all kinds of parties where alcohol, drugs and sex mix in various proportions. He was quite dissolute, since our college days, and had not outgrown it.

He nodded and let us in, leading us to the huge living room. The drapes were closed, depriving us of a fantastic view of the New York skyline, but, on the other hand, giving us some privacy. Alex's apartment was grandiose, but soul-less, the fruit of a greedy interior designer in love with glass, stainless steel and modern art. We were all sitting around the glass-and-marble coffee table, in nervous silence; and I did not know how to start the questions.

I finally blurted: 'The trading of the Rain Fund is not based on the patients' input, because it does not work. Tell us what is really going on, Alex'. I spoke in a calm but very determined voice, and the quiet and apparently calm tone was in fact a further emphasis of my seriousness.

By now, Alex had had ample time to wake up and rebuild his composure. He sounded nearly emotionless, which in itself was a give-away: 'I do not understand what you are saying, Olivier. You came to me in the middle of the night, for this nonsense? What is wrong with you? And should you not be with the police or something?'. It definitely sounded false. At the very least, he knew.

This outburst of patent lies really broke down the dams of my patience and the last remains of my friendship feelings for him. His tone and demeanor caused the pieces to fall into place in my head: He may have had something to do with the Zini frame-up, the break-ins, and even Jack's murder. I felt betrayed to the depth of my soul and I lost control.

Without any warning, I jumped on him and punched him in the face: 'You son of a bitch!'. I pulled him to the floor and straddled his chest, my knees pinning his upper arms to the floor. I held his throat with one hand and with my lips near his ear, I asked him: 'Did you have Jack killed?'. I was pressing my fingers in his trachea and he could not have answered, even if he had wanted to. I was out of my mind with rage, oblivious to my surroundings. Laura was surprised at my outburst; she stood up but did opt not to intervene. I was not a cop, and therefore not hindered by procedures; she wanted to see where this was going. And the excellent noise insulation of the luxury apartments would certainly prevent any problems with the neighbors.

Alex was choking, his eyes bulging. He was trying to throw me off him, but he was no match for my strength and fighting experience. In fact, he had never been, and I was now also mad with rage.

I released the pressure slightly, but kept my fingers on his throat. Alex was cocky and self-assured; he was a psychological bully, but his threshold for physical pain was very low. By now he surely believed I was going to kill him and I was not sure myself whether I wasn't!

I whispered again in his ear: 'Did you have Jack killed?'

He moaned: 'No! No! I swear. I had no idea. I swear'

I started squeezing again: 'Then who? WHO?'

He gurgled. I let go a little. 'I do not know. It could be the Latvian mob. They control everything. I do not know. I swear. I had nothing to do with Jack. I am sorry, Olivier'. He was crying, but I did not know whether it was from pain, shame or fear.

I kept talking into his ear: 'Now listen to me, and listen to me closely. The Feds are on to you and you are going down, no matter what. You can help me to cooperate and get on their good side, or you can let me remember that you and your friends have tried to kill me tonight and that you have ruined my life's dream. What will it be?'

I looked down at him, still holding his throat and lifting my other fist. His left eye was swollen and purple from my first punch. I could see he was scared to death, but was it of me, or of "them"?

I looked up at Laura, and she averted my eyes, in a clear "do what you have to do; I do not want to know". I slammed my right elbow down on his face. A few seconds after the shock of the blow, Alex started to sob. But I was drained of pity, I was thinking of Jack. I went to his ear again: 'Tell me what it is all about. Where is the money coming from? How does the fund make so much money if the system does not work?'

I lifted my elbow again and looked at him. His forehead was bleeding now, and I saw in his eyes that he was broken. And he was ashamed! He started talking and sobbing at the same time: 'I am sorry, so sorry! It started slowly and easy. At first, it was just investing in your fund, then just a little money to be laundered. Then there was more and more. And then it became a Ponzi scheme, a huge Ponzi scheme. I could not stop these people, they are so dangerous and they squeezed more and more. I am so sorry, Olivier, I did not want that!'

'Who? Who are they?'

'The Latvian mob. I do not know names. They forced me Olivier, I had no choice'

'But how can that be. All the accounts stick. There were already several SEC audits. It is impossible'

'Ofer! He wrote a program fabricating false records a few milliseconds after the actual quotes and showing gains based on what really happened in the market'. I must have had an incredulous look on my face, because he kept explaining: ' Ofer wrote a foolproof system that hacks into the exchanges' databases creating false transaction records with dummy counterparties. Anyone looking at the trades would see how we are consistently profitable and the trades are struck at the quoted levels for the given time stamp so there is no inconsistency. In addition, the large amounts of false trades are mixed with an even larger amount of real trades with small notional orders that are executed based on a simple momentum-software he wrote. The software actually breaks-even but at the same time manages to hide away any false trades and patterns by mixing them inside an incalculable number of real ones. The guy is a genius; the outside databases are hacked into and the records are foolproof. The money now comes mostly from new clients; laundering has taken a back seat because the fund attracts so much money. But I just manage the fund, I have nothing to do with the violence. I had no choice, they would have killed me'.

I looked at him with disgust. I wanted to ask how, when and how long, and so many other questions, but I did not trust myself. I did not know how much I could handle without becoming violent again. I stood up slowly, looking at Laura: 'What do we do now?'

Laura was thinking hard. After a few seconds: 'We need the computer data from Manhattan and compare it to Upstate. We should also try to copy the base code with Ofer's program. I think I had better call the guys in'

I countered: 'Please don't. Let me get it, it will help me later in front of the authorities. I can get in easily, it is my company. I want to save myself and what I can from my company. And redeem myself. Please'.

She thought for a moment: 'OK. You deserve the chance, Olivier. And we could wrap it all up tonight. Let us go. But what are we going to do with him? I cannot leave him here; he could bolt or warn his accomplices'

Alex pleads from the floor: 'I won't talk to them, I promise. They'd kill me!'

I shot back: 'And it would serve you well'. It suddenly crossed my mind: 'Who would you call, anyway? Who is your contact?'

He hesitated. I stepped menacingly towards him. 'Jan! It's Jan. He is the go-between'. Alex shouted covering his face with his hands.

'Fuck!' I had suspected that much after we were attacked in Jack's house with Jan's security 'sitting' outside. This was bad news. This was a tough well-connected pro, and with armed people at his boot. 'We take him with us to the company, I get the data, and then we call your people in. OK?'

Laura hesitated: 'I'll get crucified, but I like it. Let's go'

We needed to freshen up first. I took Alex to the Master Bathroom. I had to wash up my fists and elbows from his blood. I had some on my fleece, but I just pulled it off and stayed in my t-shirt. I cleaned Alex's face and stuck a Band-Aid to the cut on his forehead. He still looked bad with one swollen eye and a few contusions. I watched him dress. He looked like a broken man. 'Which cars do you have down in the parking lot?'. Alex always had a few luxury cars around to impress the ladies. He looked dazzled, lost, and it took him time to collect his thoughts: 'There is the Maserati coupe and the Porsche Cayenne'. We are three, so it will have to be the Porsche SUV. 'Keys?'

'On the bedside table'

A few minutes later, we are down in the parking garage. There is a direct lift, so we did not have to show Alex's face to the doorman.

I took the driver's seat. Laura and Alex took the back seats. Laura had now her gun out; to remind Alex we were serious.

I started driving and asked him: 'Did you send the burglars to Caroline? Did you have people trying to shoot me tonight?'

'I had no idea, Olivier. I swear by all that is dear to me. I am just running the financials for these guys. I had no idea it would come to violence or anything of the sort. I am sorry, Olivier'.

He was regaining confidence, slowly, and asked Laura: 'Who are you?'

'Shut up!', Laura and I retorted in chorus.

He sat cowed until we arrived at the company's underground parking space, only a few blocks away. Showdown!

■■

The Rain Fund Offices, Manhattan, New York City

In this building, we had no choice but to go through the lobby to change elevators from the underground parking to the elevators serving the rest of the building. It was a prestigious offices-only building, with tight security and hands-on management. We had hoped to go through the very big marbled lobby unnoticed or at least unchallenged, but it was not to be. The uniformed security guard on duty called us up: 'Mr. Van Dijk, Mr. Prilutski, your guest must sign in'. He was referring to Laura. We had no choice but to approach his desk, blocking our way to the elevators.

'Evening, Joe'. He was a usual, and we knew him well.

I saw immediately that our disheveled state and Alex's beaten face had alarmed him.

'Is everything OK?'. He was standing up from behind his desk.

There was no way we could weasel our way into that and keep everything quiet. So, Laura cut in and showed up pulled out her FBI credentials: 'Joe. This is an FBI matter. I shall not sign in. These gentlemen are fine and helping us with an investigation, you have nothing to worry about. You will not call anybody about this, not now, not ever, or I'll haul your ass in for hindering a federal investigation. Capisce?'

Joe was taken aback. He paled, looked from me to Alex. I nodded to him it was all right, but he still hesitated, clearly torn between procedures and trouble. He finally answered: "OK. Understood. Go ahead'.

We took the lift up to the 33rd floor and I opened the glass main door, simply marked: "The Rain Fund", with my code. Laura asked: 'Where to now?'

'Alex's office has mainframe access', I answered while walking briskly towards the operations side of the floor. The whole floor was lit only by dimmed lights. Alex was following silently, his head down and carefully watched by Laura. He punched his code to open his office's door. The lights lit up automatically as we went in. This was an office comparable to mine in size, but its decoration was typical Alex: crowded with expensive props, art works and a lot of glass and shiny stainless steel. And his pride: a huge handmade Oriental carpet he had custom-made to his precise specifications in Kashmir. Alex went behind the desk and powered his computer. He lifted his eyes while the computer was powering up, and I could see the shame. I remembered the always uplifting friend of mine from our University days in London, and I could believe he was not inherently bad but had slipped slowly and gradually into a situation that would eat him up. I was still angry, but some pity for his predicament was creeping in. I was a sucker for the good in people. Then I remembered that he had dragged me down with him, and that he had swindled our clients. I quickly switched back to very-angry-mode.

'Computer is on. What now?'

Laura took out a weird-looking USB memory stick and went behind the desk: 'Log to the mainframe, and this gizmo will do the rest. I need all the trade history relevant to last weeks' Prometheus data'

Alex crouched on the keypad, clicking. He looked cooperative, but had no choice.

At that moment, the door burst open and Jan Thompson bulged in: 'Alex, what are you doing here at this hour?'. What was he doing here so quickly? He was most likely always on duty and notified of any use of the keypads and entries into the facilities, especially at unconventional hours. Or was it something Alex did? From his tone, and the fact that he did not even bother knock, I realized there was truly no doubt about who the real boss was around here. And it was not me, and not Alex. Jan immediately noticed me and Laura, and stopped in his tracks: 'What are you all doing here? What is the matter?'

I saw Alex turn pale as he looked up: 'Just doing some late work, Jan. No problem'

'What is she doing here? You know she is not vetted for here. He was pointing at Laura, and reverting to his Head-of-security role. He was a bad actor though. 'The data here is highly classified, I suggest you all clear the office, and we'll discuss that in the lounge'

That made no sense; what was he doing? It hit me that he was probably trying to gain time: He was not alone! I closed the door and told him: 'Jan! Remember your place: This is my company and Alex's. This is our responsibility. Sit down a minute and I'll explain the situation to you'. I signaled Laura to stick the USB in, and Jan noticed it.

'Stop what you are doing right now!' Jan did not sit as ordered but instead started to shout. 'I also have responsibilities towards the investors who own half this company. Stop what you are doing right away!'. He was shouting, probably to attract attention, and suddenly, he rushed Laura, circling the table before I could react. She was sticking the USB key into the PC linked now to the mainframe; and she did not have her gun out. He easily knocked her down, taking Alex along with her to the floor. Jan was a fighter with great instincts: He went directly for Laura's gun in her side pocket. After the initial shock, I overcame my inertia and geared to intervene. I was already jumping over the glass desk in a classic *Parkour* move, falling on him as he straightened up with Laura's gun. I caught his wrist with both hands and tried to get him in an arm-lock. Jan was older than me, but an experienced soldier and he resisted. Luckily the safety was on and no shot was fired while we were wrestling for the gun. Laura was back on her feet and tried to help, but as she got close, Jan kicked her in the stomach. She fell back on the floor, writhing with pain. This was Jan's mistake: Not only did it split his attention for a second, but it also made me mad and, in a surge of energy, I succeeded in placing his straightened elbow under my armpit. I pulled up his wrist with both hands while jumping up and falling with my whole body weight on his upper arm. He let the gun go and crashed on the floor face first. But Jan was tough: He succeeded in wrestling his arm out while pivoting on himself 360 degrees. He hit the back of my neck with an elbow strike that stunned me, and then followed up by climbing on me, reaching again for the gun. Everything was taking place before my eyes in slow-motion: Laura was a few meters away, starting to stand up and Jan's hand was a few inches from the gun. That's it, we were done.

At that moment, Alex jumped in and kicked the gun away. Jan looked up in surprise.

Until that moment, I was not sure of the truth behind Alex's penitence. I was even pretty sure he'd turn at the first opportunity. But he had delivered, and he had saved our lives. I was already climbing on Jan's back, and, incredibly, Alex was stomping on Jan's fingers! Alex had never been physically strong and had always avoided fights. This was a surprise. I was pounding Jan's head, and we subdued him easily. Laura handcuffed him, picked up her gun and went back to the computer to stick the USB device in.

Jan was on the floor, on his belly, with his handcuffed hands behind his back. He was groaning: 'You have no idea who you are dealing with. Stop that. Let me go. Let us talk'. And a few other unintelligible short sentences. I nodded thanks to Alex, who looked totally lost. He was probably wondering if he had done the right thing.

I had a look at the screen. There was a flashing window: "Downloading". Laura was smiling with relief.

'This is state-of-the-art techno-stuff', she said, 'It will copy everything opened, and fast. It could take a while though. I'll call my boss now'

At that moment, the blinking window turned red: "Alert! Download interrupted". We were watching the screen intently. And it suddenly turned black.

'What the hell...' Laura hit the keys to no avail.

'This is probably a protection program or something. Your state-of-the-art has been detected. We have to go to the mainframe'. I was surprised: It was Alex, and he was fully on board!

We ran through the door, leaving Jan on the floor, in handcuffs.

Big mistake.

Chapter 20

Be3 Nh5

The Rain Fund Offices, Manhattan, New York City

While we were running towards the IT department, all three of us, I asked Alex: 'Did you lock your office door?'

'Cannot lock from the outside. Anyway, he is handcuffed'.

'He could still be up to something'

'OK. I'll go back, see what I can do', and he turned and sprinted back to his office. It looked like Alex had chosen a side. Conceivably, bad conscience had been festering in him for some time with no way out in sight until we forced him. Or so I rationalized.

At the end of the corridor, Laura turned left towards IT, and suddenly slowed. I was on her heels and crashed into her. There was a security guard in front of the big steel door of the IT department, in a "Rain Fund" uniform. He was not building security, but one of Jan's subordinates, and he was clearly there to block the entrance.

He was big and had a black eye and a band aid on his nose. He looked fierce, but surprised to see us. I overtook Laura and came close: 'Move out of the way, please'.

The guard hesitated one second, clearly unsure of what to do. 'Mr. Thompson asked me to make sure nobody comes into IT'. His eyes twitched a little and he looked very uncomfortable, unable to look me in the eye; and it suddenly dawned on me: This is the burglar I tackled at Jack's house, and his face is my handiwork. And he knew it was me… We did have unfinished business, and I was dying to get it going. I had been an unknowing victim, but not any more.

'I am the owner of this Company, and both you and Jan Thompson work for me, not the other way around. Please move, right now, or you are fired', and I extended my arm, as if to push him aside. I think he then understood that I knew of our common history. But this time I was ready: From the corner of my eye I saw that his right hand, hidden behind his thigh was holding a retractable stick. And it prepared to move. Retractable stick? Fool me once, shame on you, fool me twice …

Movies and traditional competitive fighting sports have made people used to fight standing up, exchanging blows in a set code of rules. Bullies do not expect to be kicked or tackled. Too bad for him! I eye-jabbed him fast and ducked below the trajectory of his stick, "shooting" for his legs. With my shoulders slamming in his hips, I lifted both his legs, twisted when he was airborne and slammed him into the floor, with my whole body weight on top, in a classical wrestling *suplex*. Spectators of the wrestling mania shows of the 80ies and 90ies think that this is no big deal and you can get up unscathed from such a throw, just like they did in those fake shows. In reality, when it is not make-believe theatrics, you are falling from quite high with no possibility of breaking your fall, directly on your back, and generally on your head too: You get all the air thrown out of your lungs and the hard floor will seriously hurt your back, your spine, your kidneys and your skull. I know it is not politically correct, but I must say I was happy that all these bodily damages transpired on this bully all at once. I stood up immediately and asked Laura to take the guard's own cuffs to restrain him. I punched my code in the side pad and stormed inside IT. Laura did not need my help.

The IT room was huge and air conditioned to a freezing temperature. The offices and the control rooms are at the end of the huge room lined by tall purring computer servers and mainframes in cupboards, with an array of blinking lights. I ran to the end of the main room, and only the Head of IT's office was lit up. This was no wonder, as nerdy Ofer had strange habits, and was commonly hanging around at all hours of the day or night. He most likely lived here, somewhere inside a fake computer cupboard, I sometimes wondered.

As expected, Ofer was at his main computer station clicking away. I barged into his office, a very spacious cubicle with plenty of screens on side tables, sticking out through mountains of discarded greasy fast food containers and wraps. He looked up, through his thick nerdy glasses: 'Olivier! What are you doing here? Anyway, I am busy now. Somebody is trying to hack into our system'

'No. No, Ofer. We are trying to copy a few files from Alex's office! This is not a hack!'

'Yes it is! Have a look'. He pointed at his screen, and stood up to let me have a look. Stupid me, I sat and looked, but there were only strings of unintelligible base code. I turned to tell him, when I felt the cold steel of a gun resting against my temple.

'Do not move. Tell me what you are doing, Olivier. Or I shall not hesitate to shoot'

This was the last thing I expected: This little insignificant punk was pointing a gun at me!

I was thinking furiously and then hopelessly tried a big lie: 'We were just copying some files. Relax, Ofer. Alex and Jan agreed, I am in on the whole story!'

'Alex and Jan agree? '

'Yes. They pulled me into the scam. You have to do as they say! Point this gun away'

There was suddenly a sardonic smile on Ofer's face: 'Nice try, Olivier. The thing is that *they* are usually doing as I say, not the other way around. What were you trying to do? This downloading is super hi-tech, where did you get it? Talk!'. He pushed the barrel of the gun into my face.

This whole affair has been a string of surprises. Ofer was running the show in my company? I could not believe it, but I had enough cold steel in my face to be fully convinced. I was sitting in his office chair, on wheels and with all kinds of reclining positions: The worst possible position to move fast from. There was nothing I could do to retake the offensive.

At that moment, I heard Alex's voice from the line of hardware cupboards: 'Ofer! Oh, good, you got him'. Ofer took a step back into his office to be able to cover both of us with his gun; as Alex came into the office. Ofer was hesitant and looked definitely unconvinced by Alex's words.

'He beat both me and Jan up, and then tried to copy files from my computer. The son of a bitch!'

Ofer looked at Alex's beaten up face and relaxed. I was now so glad I beat him up; it gave me a few more minutes to live my life to the fullest. Alex continued: 'We have to clean the records fast before morning, and transfer the money out. Tell the boss that we had no choice but close up: The place will be crawling with cops at daybreak'

My heart sank. Turncoat! Of course, with all records expunged, there would be no proof, which translates, in this great country of ours, into no conviction. Alex was rotten enough to go where the situation took him. Go with the winners. And then I heard Alex's cold voice slicing through my heart: 'We have to get rid of him'

I saw Ofer extending his hand, pointing the gun at my face, and his finger starting to twitch. I would have wanted to die fighting, but I could not jump efficiently from this damned chair. I had to try though, and as I gathered myself, I saw Alex plunging and pushing Ofer's armed hand. The shot resonated in the office and went to lodge itself in the ceiling. Alex was tumbling on the floor, trying to wrestle the gun from Ofer. I jumped on the both of them, when another shot rang out. I felt a jolt in my left shoulder, but kept on fighting. The gun was between them and they were both stunned. I pushed them apart and grabbed the gun. I then hit Ofer hard in the face with it, breaking his ugly glasses, just to make sure. Laura appearing from the lines of computer servers ran into the office. Only then, did I notice the blood on Alex's shirt, around his lower belly: He was lying on his back, unconscious. I tore my shirt off, with my right hand only, making a makeshift dressing and pressing it where I thought the wound was. I was shouting at Laura: 'Call 911, call 911', but she was already on the phone, her gun pointed at Ofer. After she was off the phone, she told me quietly: 'You are wounded too, Olivier', pointing at my shoulder. The one bullet had probably gone through Alex and into me!

'I am fine, we have to save Alex!'

'They are on their way, keep at it'

She went to Ofer's computer and stuck her special USB stick in. After checking the screen, while keeping an eye on him across the floor, she looked satisfied and came to kneel near me. She tried to replace me at pressing Alex's wound, but I did not let go. The blood was seeping through my shirt pressed on against the wound.

I do not know how much time passed, a few minutes or more, but there was a commotion and the floor was suddenly crowded with police and paramedics. I was relieved, I could now let go; I then simply lost consciousness in Laura's arms. Everything went black.

Chapter 21

Kh2 Bd6

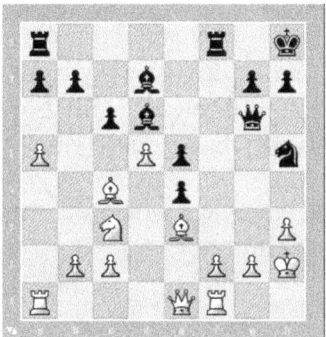

New York Presbyterian Hospital, Manhattan, New York City

I opened my eyes, and closed them back at once. The light sent a searing pain into my brain. I tried again slowly, getting accustomed. Not yet. I felt groggy, and my mouth was parched. I tried to move and I felt that my left arm was immobilized.

'Look who is waking up'. It was Laura's voice, coming from my left.

I turned my head slowly and squinted. She was sitting on a chair, besides my bed; at least I assumed it was her as I began to discern a form. I was trying to remember what had happened and where I was. The smell was distinctive of hospitals: disinfectant clean, but also carrying the indefinable odor of sickness. I was still disoriented, but my memory came back gradually. My first words were: 'Alex?'

'Alex is alive. He was operated upon and is still unconscious. No prognosis yet. I hope he'll be fine, Olivier. I know he has been a close friend for years, but you have to realize that, if he makes it, he'll probably spend all what is left of his life in prison'. She said that in a soothing and caring voice. And then:' How do *you* feel'. She touched my right arm, lightly.

'OK I guess'. I leaned up a little, trying to look for water on my bedside table. Laura understood without a word and brought a small bottle of mineral water to my lips, holding my head. Her touch felt good. After taking in a few very small mouthfuls, I laid back down, feeling a little better. I had a drip into my right arm and my left arm was in a sling, but I thought I felt basically good. On the other hand, I usually want to feel better than I really am.

I gathered that I was in a single room, well appointed, with a large window and a private bathroom.

'So what's the deal with me, then', I asked her.

'The bullet went through Alex's side and ripped your shoulder. You have been rushed into surgery without waking up. You had lost a lot of blood, but the doctors say you'll be fine. You will need some rehabilitation though. You are a tough customer, it seems, more lives than a cat'

'I meant legally, Laura'. My mood and my tone were serious. I had not had the time to dwell on all that had happened, nor on the eventual consequences.

I thought she seemed pained that I saw her first and foremost as the FBI agent she was. But she played it cool: 'Oh! I see! Playing macho!'. She continued: 'If you do not die on me from a hospital infection, you are free to go home. My boss did not fire me, because of the success of our little operation, and he has pulled some strings. It is clear now that you were in the dark about what was going on in the Fund. I will testify and there is now plenty of evidence to that. So you will be investigated, you will undoubtedly be prosecuted for your involuntary part, your negligence and your corporate responsibility. But you will have our support and our public acknowledgement of the risks you took to help to rectify matters. We expect to be able to avoid actual jail, but you understand that there are limits to what we can do, as the executive branch of government. Your company is dead, you are likely to become penniless and you'll probably have to deal with scores of civil suits'

'I love it when you talk dirty'. My twisted way of processing bad news, but she smiled half-heartedly.

'I am sorry this happened to you, Olivier. I think you are a good man'.

'Thanks Laura, I think so too, even if I say so myself. Do you know when they intend to let me out?'

'No idea, but take it easy. You have been shot this time, not just hit with a stick. It is up to the doctors'

After a minute of silence, she continued: 'I understand you are going to be processed by the authorities, and there will be plenty of formalities and paperwork. Your lawyer has already been sitting with my boss, and I have made sure he will support you. Now, I'll be away for a few days. There is a lot of work to do with the Foundation: We cannot leave the patients without care, and we need to organize their future. Luckily, this is a trust and a separate legal entity, and it can go on working on its own for a few more months. I have taken leave from the Bureau to do just that, as soon as all my reports are written. So, get your affairs in order and I'll be back in a few days'.

I am surprised and delighted: 'The foundation keeps working? This is fantastic news'

'I hope you will be able to come and help, Olivier'

'I sure will. I have to do everything in my power to make it right to the patients and to the clients. You are a very special woman, Laura'.

She stood up, embarrassed: 'By the way, we have kept the news about the Fund itself under wraps for a few more days. You know, in the hope we can catch some of the bad guys unaware. There are lots to do with the information in Ofer's computers, about money trails and such. Agents are working twenty four hours a day, before the news break out. So keep it mum, please'

'OK. Tell me Laura. What about Jan and Ofer?'

I saw her face souring: 'Ofer has been arrested, but is already lawyered up. He has a hot-shot counselor and he is not talking. Jan got away; you remember we left him alone, but there is an APB on him. My people think Alex let him go. We'll get him; it is only a question of time. On these bad news, I have to run now'.

She walked to the door. 'Bye, Olivier'. Then she turned back at the door: 'And by the way, it's yes'

'Yes what?'

''Your invitation to dinner', then she disappeared, leaving me looking at the door with a stupid smile on my face; in spite of the load of trouble I was in. The revenge of the Parthians.

I spent the whole day at the hospital being checked and prodded by medical professionals and by law enforcement officers. The former checked my wounds, my vitals and the mobility of my left shoulder. The latter took my statements about Zini's murder, about Jack, about the Fund and about all of the events that had transpired last night. My high-flying lawyer was present most of the time, and I could not help watching the clock and wondering how I was going to pay his bill. At least, this way I was not lying in bed morosely pondering difficult thoughts. By the end of the day I was exhausted. The doctors banished the law enforcement people from the premises and then promised to release me on the morrow morning, after a few more tests. In the meantime, they wanted me to rest. No need to force me, I was feeling weak and had trouble staying awake. I could not think straight any more, not about my situation, not about my future, not about Laura; only time would help me get things into perspective. At 6 p.m. I was already sound asleep.

I woke up with a startle and checked the fluorescent dial of my watch on the bedside table: 1:20 a.m. The hospital was quiet, but only in the way a hospital can be: There is always something going on, muffled sounds and carts rolling in the hallways. I was restless and stood up slowly to try to go to the bathroom on my own. From sitting on the side of the bed, I slowly put some weight on my legs. I walked awkwardly to the bathroom. I felt wheezy but I estimated that it would only take a day or two to get back to normal. I stayed in the dark and took my time. I thought I heard some muffled noise in the room, and I stayed quiet for a moment, straining my ears to make sure; I definitely heard the door of the room close. I left the bathroom slowly, but there was nobody in the room. I already felt better, from stretching my legs and I decided to stroll around and go look for Alex. I took the rolling IV stick from the room, although I was not hooked on it anymore, but simply to help me walk.

I slowly walked, self-conscious of my revealing hospital gown, over to the floor's nurse's station. There was nobody behind the desk. I went behind the counter through a small swinging door and looked at the roster on the desk. I was in room 505, but I knew that already. I saw Alex's name opposite 542 with a note on the side highlighted in yellow: "Police custody. Keep location confidential. No visitors". This was really what was often referred to in French as Polichinelle's secret, referring to *Pulcinella* from the *Commedia dell'Arte*: Everybody knew it, but only Polichinelle still thought it was a secret. But one could not really blame overworked nurses for not behaving like Witness Protection Program Marshals.

I was glad Alex's room was on the same floor; I do not think I would have had the strength to take the elevator for this impromptu visit. I walked slowly to room 542 in the maze of shining clean corridors. It quickly came into view, easy to find: There was a cop sitting on a chair beside the door. Very confidential indeed.... As I approached, clearly heading for him, he stirred: 'No visitors, move on please'. He had his hand on his gun, obviously taking his work seriously. It was a young uniformed New York policeman, with his cap on. I lifted my healthy hand. 'Good Night, officer. I am his partner and I was working with the FBI on that case. I just want to see if he is going to make it. In fact, same bullet!', and I showed him my arm.

'Sorry, Sir. But I have my orders. Only nurses and doctors'. Young professionals usually stick to the rules; they lack the confidence of experience.

'OK, I understand. But do you have any idea if he woke up, or what his status is'

'Dunno. The lady doctor who was just in told me to be quiet and let him sleep'.

That sounded encouraging. I pressed on: 'Can I just have a peek; this is a really close friend, please?'

'Sorry, can't. The guy is both a flight risk and in danger. No exceptions'.

I move away: 'Thank you anyway, good night'.

As I walked away, I mulled over the word danger I just heard. I suddenly realized that I had had no doctor visit, simply because no doctor would do his rounds at 1 a.m. And I remembered the deserted nurse station.

I turned back, as I was already five or six steps away: 'You said there was a doctor in his room a short time ago? Did you check on him since? Or has anyone else checked on him since?'

'No. Why should I?' He looked down at his pad: 'There has not been anyone in since Dr. Menze, fifteen minutes ago. A lady doctor'.'

I was suddenly taken over by a wave of dread, of the type that constricts your heart. I did not give a second glance to the policeman as I walked fast, leaving my IV stick in place. I opened the door and bulged in.

He was lying quietly in his bed, eyes closed, with tubes everywhere, but there was something strange: the electronic equipment beside the bed was silent and off: Screens were blank, no lights were on. The cop was on my heels, shouting, and brandishing his gun. He caught me by my hospital gown as I was reaching to check Alex's pulse at the carotid.

I could not fight back in my weakened state and with only one free arm. I had to let go, but I started shouting: 'Call for help, there is something wrong. Don't you see all monitors are off. Help!'

I fell on the floor on my bared behind, screaming: Help…

This thing was far from over.

Chapter 22

Bb3 Nf4

Olivier Van Dijk's Apartment, Manhattan, New York City

Alex was dead!

There was no doubt that something had been injected through his IV bag, after all monitors had been unplugged. Only chemical checks would give a definite answer, though finding the night-shift Head Nurse unconscious in a broom closet was close enough for a confirmation. I was now wondering about the closing door I had heard from the bathroom. Maybe they had also been after me, and I had been saved by Nature's call. This was scary, I thought this nightmare was over and I could concentrate in doing the right thing. But now the Mob was trying to stop people from talking, or simply settling scores. Either way, they had wasted no time. After my release was approved by the medical staff, with a big supply of pain killers and the solemn promise I would come for weekly checks, the police sent me home under escort and placed a guard in front of my apartment door. They doubled the protective detail around imprisoned Ofer Dobry, who was the prime link to the crime syndicate. Truth be said, he was not cooperating with the authorities.

There probably had been some more accomplices in the company, but the FBI had not been able to check up on all employees yet. They also made the point to tell me that they were actively looking for Jan Thompson.

In spite of all this, the politically-driven Bureau was trumpeting victory: They had captured most of the vast amounts of crime money from this organization from over the whole world; they had the laundering itineraries of all the US operations of the Latvian gangs; and they, not the SEC, had stopped another Wall street Ponzi scheme, although this part was still under wraps. Already, FBI agents and local police were raiding illegal businesses and arresting mobsters under tax and money laundering statutes. This was a huge blow to the Latvian mafia and their associates. Of course, it looked like they were enraged, and that they were doing something about it.

Laura called me from the Foundation. Of course she had heard about Alex. She extended her condolences. She told me they had put out and APB but had no real info on the woman killer, as the security cameras did not have a good picture of her. She told me the assassin was definitely a professional, and she knew how to move around. Even the police guard did not have a good description: He had been looking at her cleavage more than her face, and she wore distinctive designer glasses destined to attract most of the remaining attention. Laura then told me in confidence that her colleagues tried to keep from me that the security cameras showed that the killer did enter my room for a few seconds after killing Alex. That explained the bodyguard I had been granted. She hung up after telling me she was making huge progress and would tell me about it in a few days. She urged me to be careful.

I was moping around my apartment, thinking about Alex, at least about the Alex of the good times. Alex was not of perfect moral fiber, but he would not have willingly gone in bed with murderers, slavers, rapists and drug dealers. I remembered how he had told me many times, when we were last year students in London, that he considered himself ethically as a lawyer: He should be able to work for anybody, without asking questions, his job being making money out of money. The provenance of the money was not supposed to be his problem. That is probably how it started, but Alex did not realize how slippery a slope it was, and that, with some kind of people, there was no way out.

I also took the time to look into my financial situation: The company was as good as dead. I would have colossal lawyers' bills to handle and even larger civil liabilities. The only good thing is that most of the money was dirty money, and it could mitigate the effect on the honest investors who had flocked to the Fund. Or at least, I hoped so. I had money stashed away; I could just disappear and live relatively well in a place like Costa Rica or Ecuador where a million bucks went a long way. It would cost some money to change identities and live hidden away, but it was possible. I had thought about it long and hard. But I had decided that I would do everything in my power to help our legitimate clients. I had some property and cash from before my hook up with Alex, but I would burn through it quickly. I corrected myself: My hook up was not with Alex; it was, unwittingly, with the mob! My God, what a mess! I would probably have to find me a cheaper place to rent. And what would I do for a living? I was certainly unemployable in the Financial Industry, and I could also be barred by the courts from working in this field for years to come. Anyway, my life's dream had collapsed: I was so sure I had discovered the most fantastic of ideas for market charting; but reality proved that it did not even work. When the dust would settle, I could always go away and invest my own money for a living, in the traditional way. In fact, I had been a pretty good trader in my time; the money problem should turn out all right after some hard work.

I snapped out of over-thinking this issue and decided to go to the gym to do some recline biking. Because of my gun wound and all the injuries I had collected these last weeks, I could not really perform my favorite physical activities, no Martial Arts, no *Parkour*; even jogging would be a problem with the shoulder wound and my still-busted-ribs. I took my federal-paid bodyguard with me; I was sure he preferred that to sitting near my door. Tomorrow, after putting some order in my affairs, I would call Laura and visit the Foundation; I was dying to see her again.

***

1982, Kanosta Prison, Liepaja, Latvia

Young Aivars Bertulis was sitting on the bleachers in the small exercise courtyard of the Kanosta Prison. He had been processed and issued smelly gray overalls and plastic shoes, before being shown to the cell he would be sharing with another five inmates for the next few years. But for Isaac, none of his other cell mates had even acknowledged him. Isaac, a mild-mannered forty years old accountant, had shown him the remaining upper bunk closest to the toilet hole, and taken him under his wing.

They were now sitting together on the bleachers, during the one-hour daily fresh-air slot. Aivars was happy to learn that his cell mates were all ethnic Latvians, but less so to understand that they were sitting their time, not for nationalistic activities, but real crimes: There was a serial rapist and a murdering thief among them. Isaac, himself had been convicted for book fraud and corruption; although he maintained he was the scapegoat for the Russian owner of the company. Being Jewish had not helped him in his scapegoat role.

Aivars was telling him: 'I am going to keep to myself and away from all those criminals. There is no way I will let myself be sucked into that'. He was thinking of his mother, and the good education she had tried to give him and his siblings.

'You will not be able to cut yourself off from the rest of the prison population. If you do not fit in, you will be beaten up and even killed. Believe me, young Aivars, this is the world you are in now, rotten and violent'.

They kept on discussing Aivars' future and his convictions. Isaac gave him the lay of the land and the daily time table.

Suddenly, two young and bulky men were sitting on both sides of the talking couple. Isaac looked up, and he looked scared. A third man was standing a few feet away, with a wolfish smile on his lips as he looked at them.

'What do we have here? Fresh and young Latvian meat?'

The man was obviously an ethnic Russian. He was middle-aged, but looked tough, with beefy forearms covered with tattoos.

Isaac answered in a quivering voice:' Illya Stefanovitch, this is just a child. Leave him alone'.

'Isaac, my dear. I am just dying to make his acquaintance. A beautiful young boy like that will be very popular in this place. He will need a protector'.

Aivars was young but not naïve; he understood the innuendo at once and stayed motionless and silent.

Illya Stefanovitch continued, while both his accomplices were squeezing Aivars and Isaac between them: 'Anyway, it is important that he knows who is in charge here, isn't it?'

Isaac answered: 'I'll tell him about everything. Do not worry'

Illya smiled cruelly: 'Of course you will. For now, I just want this little piece of Latvian shit to kneel before his master'.

Aivars was thunderstruck. He had thought he could stay away and do his time. But even here inside, the Russians were oppressing his people. Aivars was thin and wiry; his strength was no match for the bulky adults around him. But Aivars was also fanatical about his Latvian nationalism and was stubbornly single-minded, which gave him power and endurance far above his physical frame. When Illya nodded to his acolytes, and they reached for him, Aivars was instinctively ready. He was honest, but the hard life of Riga had given him street-smart. He was no match for the two hulks who caught him from both shoulders, pushing him forward. They were obviously trying to make him kneel in front of Illya. Aivars twisted and jumped up; there was no way he would kneel before a Russian

*thug! He writhed around, kicking his assailants, and succeeded in
freeing one of his arms. He punched the bully on his right, and then
attached himself to him, scratching, biting and kneeing. His rage,
his fanaticism and single- mindedness made him a formidable
opponent, far beyond his relative weight. But he was no match. The
two prisoners, together, started beating him up. Aivars, punched and
kicked all over, did not relent. He was half-conscious, but kept
fighting back. They tried again to make him kneel, but with no
success. Even Illya deigned to sully his hands and punched him
several times. The guards, fellow Russians who had been looking
away of course, did finally intervene, sending Illya and his friends
away with a conniving look. Today's intermission was over, and
they did not want the paperwork. They charged Isaac to carry
Aivars to the rudimentary infirmary, hoping he would make it.*

This single incident would have immeasurable consequences.

Chapter 23

Bxf4 exf4

The Prometheus Foundation, Washington County, New York State

I was riding shotgun in my own car, deep in thought, on my way towards Greenwich. I did not have to check whether I was followed any more. My day-bodyguard was driving; a nice young marshal named Frank, with a Marine haircut and a Southern drawl, though he did not do much talking.

I had woken up early, eager to be active instead of being walloped into demoralizing melancholy. I had tried to do some light exercise, but it was still near impossible, and I quickly gave up. I did some memory exercises instead and then solved a few hard Sudoku puzzles. The brain must be trained too, doesn't it? I had prepared a very strong brew of my best Arabica for me and my body guard, and then sat down to put some order through my affairs. I fired the cleaning lady, cancelled my membership in a score of clubs, and consolidated my American bank accounts into one. I took a few cost-saving decisions, and then I finally called Laura. She sounded genuinely happy to hear my voice and my intention to visit, and promised me a surprise, in a happy cheer, just before hanging up. My curiosity was piqued, but I had no time to wonder: Dave Freeman had called me a few minutes later to tell me about Alex's funeral arrangements. He had already told me that, for security reasons, I would not be allowed to attend; but he now informed me that Alex's will requested a burial in Israel. His corpse would be flown out for a small family ceremony there, where he had a sister. I truly wanted to go and see the body to pay my respects, but the casket was already on its way to the Airport.

As we approached the Foundation's gates, I saw that it was guarded by a twin brother of my bodyguard, signaling us to stop. He obviously knew Frank, and whisked us in after a nod. Not very talkative those marshal types; it had probably something to do with their haircut. I was glad to see that my reserved space was still free, in spite of my obvious problems. Anna, the receptionist was at her post, and behaving as if nothing had happened; as if the place was not under FBI tutelage. I was grateful for that too.

I went directly for Laura's office, and Frank stayed in the lobby. From the mezzanine gangway, I saw Laura in the big room with two technicians around Number 3's workstation. Tom, our new Number 5, was typing away at his desk, and Number 2 was also around, not working, but in a cleaning-his-glasses repetitive behavior. I saw only one member of the Nursing team, and I assumed there had been some cost-cutting. I took my time, looking at Laura directing the technicians. Today, she was dressed in elegant slacks, under her ubiquitous white doctor coat. Suddenly she looked up and saw me up the stairs. I waved self-consciously and she waved back, signaling she would be up in a moment. I went to her office and she arrived after a few minutes. She surprised me by hugging me, carefully, on account of my left arm in a sling. I still winced from rib pain, but I was elated by her warmth. Is that the meaning of "No pain, no gain"? After a few pleasantries and reiterated condolences, we sat in her office with a bad cup of coffee each.

I cut to the chase: 'I have been dying to know what the surprise you told me about was?'

'Olivier dear', she was taking her time, on purpose quite likely,' there are news, and there are good news. Which do you want first?'. She was smiling mischievously.

'Laura, please, get on with it. I am injured, remember'

'OK. The news first: We are doing a supervised "beast" trial later today with Number 3 and Number 5. I do not know if you are aware of the fact that Tom is a computer genius as well as a mathematical one, though the two capacities are related. His dad told me, in confidence, that he had been part of the international group LulzSec that hacked into the FBI and Scotland Yard computers in 2011.He intervened before Tom could get in trouble, but there was another Asperger-diagnosed young man who was arrested, from Essex in England'

I was interested, but how important was that now, given that we knew that that the whole set-up was a fraud and that it basically did not work better than random guesses? But I stayed silent.

'I hope it will give us some answers and that you'll stay to help us'. She looked a bit disappointed in my lack of enthusiasm. What was I expecting? A Presidential pardon? She continued: 'This facility will still be functioning for at least a few months and we shall keep the patients busy and try to help them learn to function better'.

'OK, Laura, it really is fantastic, and I'll do anything to help. And the good news now?' I sounded as impatient as I really was.

She was smiling like a cat that ate the canary: 'You are not going to believe that! Good that you are sitting'

'Come on, Laura'

'The short version is that the predictive trending by our patients actually works, Olivier. You were right from the beginning'

I was not sure I understood. I had heard her, but the meaning did not register fully. My heart was beating fast though. She was smiling at my discomfiture and decided to put me out of my misery by giving me the longer version.

'What disturbed me is that the basic data collected by Jack at the beginning of the Fund showed clearly that the logic behind the technique was sound and that it should and would work. So, I did some data mining on the correlation figures and I discovered that if you restricted the results to just two of the patients and only to certain areas that you could consider areas of expertise, it works even much better than expected. We forgot that these people, just like "normal" people, have their strengths and weaknesses. Their minds see things in a different way, colors and forms some say, and they express it in different ways too. To cut a long story short, with a little tweaking of the mathematical models and having each of the patients work on his areas of expertise, we have achieved incredible levels of pattern prediction'.

This blew my mind away. I was already thinking ahead of all the consequences. 'This is fantastic. I cannot believe it' I exclaimed, duly excited. I stood up and went around the desk. Laura stood up, and I embraced her with my good arm and kissed her on both cheeks. She looked surprised, but happy. She looked at me, without trying to release herself from my hug, and held my gaze. I kissed her lips gently, and let go. This was neither the time nor the place, so I went back to my seat, with a spring in my stride.

'Laura, you are a fantastic woman. I would like to take you out, once things here settle down. And let me remind you that you already agreed'

'Of course, I will'. She smiled:' Now that you are not my boss anymore'.

'By then, you will probably be dating a felon, but is Friday night OK?'

'Deal. And I'll take my handcuffs, just in case. Now back to business'

'Now that I have a date, anything you want'

We discussed the data and the implications of her discovery. And then Laura started to talk about plans, as if it was clear that we were partners in a future venture. Her eyes were shining and she was getting enthusiastic. And she looked even more beautiful to me. The Rain Fund was as good as dead, but a new company could be created to use these findings to make money and take care of autistic workers. Laura was speaking of leaving the Bureau, and expanding the care to autistic persons without mathematical abilities. I was taken in by her vision, but I had to remind her gently that I was in a delicate situation. We agreed that I would take the data collected during the last two days and analyze its financial implications in detail. We would also give some thought to her plans and discuss them further.

Laura had work to do, mostly preparing the base code-reading experiment for later. I left for what was still formally my office, to work on the recent data and her notes on the tweaked models.

I went through the reception area to let my taxpayer-paid bodyguard know that I would be staying late, and maybe would even stay the night. I suggested that he could go home, as we had another two marshals on the property, but he declined. He had coffee and munchies, and was perfectly fine with the waiting to which he was professionally used to.

I was disappointed to see there were no fresh flowers in my office today, but of course, my faithful assistant from Manhattan was, for now, out of a job. I made a mental note to talk to her and check what could be done for her. The room was stuffy, and I missed the smell of flowers; I opened, for fresh air, the same window I had fled from a few days ago. It had me thinking about how fragile the fabric of life can be: How different was my world today, compared to what it was only a few weeks ago.

I went to my coffee machine and selected one of my favorite single-origin espresso coffees: beans from the "Las Chiquitas Del Café" farm in Nicaragua. This coffee was giving a strong taste of complex berry accompanied by nut undertones, and it was a decisive argument against connoisseurs who argued that only blended coffees gave a well-balanced taste.

There was nothing like a good-quality espresso to kick-start me into working mode. I switched on my desktop PC and played three chess moves against my worldwide opponents; the Chinese guy was having me in a tier, but I could see a way out.

Then I opened Laura's files. After about two hours, I lifted my head and stretched. I had not stopped for a second, and adrenalin was pumping through my veins. This was incredible: Not only did the modified system work; it also eclipsed anything that had ever been done before. The predictions were extremely reliable, and if the trades suggested by the models had been executed, the yields would have been consistent at about 68% on an annual basis, in line with performances peaks of the bests of hedge funds in history. And there was no doubt from my analysis that the system could still be improved by a better fit to the specific working patient. I felt vindicated that my basic idea was in fact sound. Of course, it was such a pity that it had happened only after the total annihilation of my company, but Laura's discovery opened a wide range of opportunities. And she had done all that in a few days only. She was truly extraordinary.

I stood up to stretch my legs, went to the bathroom, prepared another cup of espresso, and sat back at my desk. I drank the coffee in my favorite position, feet up on the desk, and started planning. All those simple activities were harder with only one functioning arm. It is funny the small things we all take for granted.

After a few minutes, I sat normally and opened Laura's file containing the results of the last two days projections as achieved with the tweaked protocol. I simply extrapolated the most lucrative trades that such predictions would point to, and after half-an-hour, I had a short list of 8 trades that were still relevant. I memorized the list, -easy for an USM practitioner-, and destroyed it.

I did not hesitate,-my mind was set-, and just like when I played chess, I could see the rough outline of where my actions would take me under several probable scenarios. I opened my locked desk drawer and took out one of the throw-away phones I kept there just in case. I switched it on and dialed a number in London, United Kingdom. The London number was not really a residence, nor was it an office, but a sophisticated relay station that would make it impossible to trace the call. Any future check would show that a call was made to someone in England, but the phone that finally rang was in the much closer Fiscal Paradise Islands of Turks and Caicos.

'Yes'

'May I speak to George, please. My number is 67523'

'And the corresponding name, please Sir'

'Enigma'

'Just a moment, please'

After about a minute and a few clicks, a booming voice came on the phone, with a typical exaggerated British accent: 'Olivier, old boy, is that you?'

'How are you George? And you can cut the fake accent'

'Long time, Olivier. I am great. What could be bad? I am making tons of money in a tropical paradise, wearing shorts and sandals all day. Beats the hell out of commuting to the City in the wretched tube and watch the rain on the window panes during the week-ends'.

George Baker was another friend of mine from the University days. He was English, from a family of old money, and after his required stint as an intern in a London hedge fund, he had left to found a bank, no less, for wealthy tax-dodgers. We had kept in touch over the years, and, although I was small potatoes for his operation, he was the keeper of my hidden nest egg.

'I would like to chat, governor, but I am in quite a hurry. I promise I'll come to visit you as soon as I clean up here'

'And what could the famous founder of the most successful hedge fund on earth possibly want from a small operator like me?'. He had obviously read the Business Weekly article.

'Cut the crap, George. This is serious'

'Sorry, mate. Go ahead'

'I need you to realize all that I have in your bank, to give me your maximum margin possible, and then to divide everything into eight trades that I will email you from a web account as soon as I hang up. I need that done immediately'.

'Ok. That is easy. You know we do not do margin, we are not that kind of bank, but for the Rain Fund owner, we can make an exception'.

'Since when do you use the Majestic We? You forget you are talking to Olivier who used to put you to bed when you were too drunk to know your own name. I know you are the bank, not 'we'. And please, George, on a serious note, if you give me margin, do it for your old friend Olivier, and not for the Rain Fund guy'.

George was intrigued, but did not push: 'I see this is serious. OK. The 'We' is force of habit, talking to clients and all. I'll give you 20% margin, and will execute the trades at once. It is 20% on top of about 3 million dollars. Just send the instructions over. What is the stress? Are you in some kind of trouble?'

'For your ears only, George, yes. And you will probably hear about it soon. I promise I will tell all as soon as I can'.

'Sorry to hear that, mate. Anything else I can do, just let me know'

'Thanks'

'And one last thing: You have no problems that I piggyback on your trades?'

'Of course not, George. You are the only guy I know who would ask for permission, but you realize it is at your own risk. This is no recommendation'

'Of course, of course. Cheerio, governor. Send the trades over'. The clown was back with his accent.

I could not help smiling; this all brought back fond memories of simpler days: 'Bye George, I'll be in touch'.

After hanging up, I took out the SIM card, broke it and put it in my pocket for future disposal. I put the phone itself in the sink of my private bathroom, and let it soak.

I then used my computer through an IP masking service to send the eight famous trades from memory from a newly created g-mail account directly to George's private email address, also web-based. After erasing the history, of my web browser, using a program Alex once installed on my PC, I pondered my next move.

I was a banker, not a saint. I had no bad conscience about having built myself a nest-egg away from the scrutiny of the IRS. All the money I had stashed there over the years came from my hard work and risky investments; I had not stolen from anyone or skimmed anything from other people. The only wronged party, in my eyes, was the Internal Revenue Service, and I did not like them. Like most Americans, I thought I was paying more than enough taxes that were subsequently squandered by narcissistic, but yet elected, bleached-teeth politicians. I felt a little guilty for doing this behind Laura's back, but I did not know how she would. I was hoping that in the end, she would approve of the overall plan I was setting in motion.

I took my regular phone to call her: 'Hi Laura, it's Olivier. Are you in your office?'

'Yes, but I am going downstairs in a few minutes. We will start the experiment soon. You are coming I hope?'

'Yes, I'll be there. I just wanted to ask you to keep the patients working on the actual up-to-date trends, just as before. I have analyzed the data and we are really on to something. I need more data for confirmation'

'Of course. That was my intention anyway. I want to keep them busy doing productive work and maintaining their previous routines as much as possible. I know there is nowhere to send the data any more, but we shall keep things as they were. I'll have the data sent to you directly in real time, that will be easier'

'Thank you. I'll be around soon for the experiment'

'We aim to start in about fifteen minutes. See you then'

'Bye'

After I cut-off, I felt even guiltier. Lying is not a great way to start a relationship, but everybody has his little secrets, I rationalized. And our situation was far from normal.

Laura being Laura, my computer emitted a light gong sound and today's trending charts were already in my inbox. As I had another fifteen minutes, I opened them for perusal. I would complete the actionable analysis later in the night, but it was fascinating. One of my trades would have to be rolled over in a day or two, but the rest were on track.

After twenty minutes, I hurried to the big room. From the gallery, I saw that they had not started yet, but that the area was bustling with activity. I could see Laura, in the middle, getting things set-up. There were video cameras on tripods near the work stations of Number 3 and Number 5, there were four nurses from the original team on the ready, our local IT technician, and another two persons I had never seen before but who also looked like IT. Unsightly cables were running from the computers of stations 3 and 5, and there were several monitors on folding tables. This was quite a set-up. There were only two patients around, Number 3 and Number 5 of course, and Tom's dad was present, talking quietly to his son on the couch of his area.

I climbed down the stairs and went to shake hands with Joshua. The noise was such that we could not exchange any words, just nods. I went to sit quietly in the back on a simple folding chair. Laura was getting everybody in place, and raised her voice to ask for silence. Joshua led Tom to his workstation. Number 3 was already sitting in front of his screen with his man-nurse. Both computers were connected to a monitor and started scrolling the base code. Both patients were looking and were being filmed. Tom, being highly functional, had been informed about the purpose of the experiment by his father, in the hope he could help verbalize the findings if there were any. I was impressed by the set-up; Laura was an organized and headstrong woman.

There was not much happening, and my attention drifted. So did that of both patients who had to be prodded from time to time, to get their attention back to the screens. For some portions, they both looked interested; through other portions they both seemed bored. To me, all bits were boring and I think I dozed off.

I was startled out of my impromptu nap, by the start of the expected riot. It had worked, and the problem was in the base code. Number 3 was shouting again, and was being removed gently from his work station by two nurses. Everybody else was talking at once. The technicians froze Number 3's computer, and everyone was now looking at Tom.

Laura asked the technician to stop the scrolling of Tom's screen, and approached him. She asked him if he had seen something, but received no reply. Tom was looking intently at his screen, covered with lines of program language. Joshua prodded him gently: "Tom. Do you know what made Tim upset? Is there something wrong with the program?'

Tom answered without looking away from the screen: 'There is a hidden virus in the machine that can take over the whole computer if activated. I do not know why Tim is upset'.

Joshua continued: 'Which kind of virus is it, Tom? Can you clean the computers?'

Tom did not reply, but kept looking at the screen.

'Please Tom, it is important, you know'

'I cannot clean it, dad; It is not in the program, it is in the machine'. Tom sounded irritated.

There was silence, and then again, everybody was talking at the same time. Laura decided to clear the room, but for Tom, Joshua, myself and the IT technician. She asked the latter if he saw something in the code and if it was possible at all.

'There is nothing wrong with what I see, and our firewalls and antivirus programs are the best in the market. I really do not see anything. And we have run a diagnostic before the experiment'.

Joshua went back to Tom: 'Tommy. Can you show us the virus?'

This time Tom answered immediately, but with rising tones. He was becoming upset: 'The code shows that there is a Trojan in the hardware waiting to be activated. I cannot show it. We must open the box and look. It is disturbing my numbers. I do not like it. We have to take it out'.

'OK, Tom. Do not worry. I believe you, and we shall leave it at that for today. You have been very helpful. Take a break'.

Tom's caretaker led him away back to his flat, and we all sat together in Tom's lounge.

Laura said: 'We now have a lead, and there is definitely something there'. She addressed the technician directly: 'You tell me the software is clean, and a genius tells me there is a hardware virus in our computers. What can we do to verify this?'

'I can only re-check the whole system, and then maybe re-boot it. But I have never heard of such a thing as a hardware virus'

I cut in: 'I remember reading something about hardware virus in a popular scientific magazine. The article explained that computers are designed and built with thousands of components coming from hundreds of outsourced designers and sub-manufacturers the world over; and that therefore it would be easy to introduce a Trojan design. I remember that the article concluded that actual cyber-security was powerless to screen all possibilities; it is virtually undetectable until triggered, because the number of possible trigger mechanisms is infinite. It could be a very big thing we have just stumbled upon'.

Joshua asked: 'Do you think that would have anything to do with the mob operation that took over your Fund?'

'I really do not see why they would rig the patient's computers, it does not make sense'.

Laura suggested we let it rest for the night, and take it up again with Tom in the morning. She dismissed our IT guy who was clearly in over his head.

As we stood up, Laura made a point to thank Joshua: 'Tom was fantastic; this has been of great help, Joshua. Thank you very much'

Joshua was beaming, and his smile was stretching his facial scar in a way that nearly made it attractive. 'You are welcome. I am very proud of him. He is calm now, but he does not like when people doubt what he says'. He became serious:' Listen you two. I had an idea. I have a friend from the army who has set up a cyber-security company in Washington, top-of-the-line. He is doing consultancy work for the Pentagon and Homeland Security. If I ask him, he'll come and check it up, perhaps even together alongside Tom. Are you interested?'

I agreed; naturally taking charge, as if I was still the boss: 'Of course. But are you sure he will have time for this?'.

'Sure. He owes me. Besides, ex-SEALS are always available for their buddies. You'll see. He is a great guy'

Laura intervened: 'OK, then, Joshua. Set it up. Great idea'.

With this agreed, we all went our own ways. Joshua left to check up on Tom, Laura wanted to finish up her reports upstairs, and I hurried to my office: I had data to analyze and trading orders to place.

On my way there, I stopped to let bored Frank-the-Marshal know that I would be ready to drive back to Manhattan in about half an hour. He looked happy to let me know, that he had just been informed that, from tomorrow, I would be on my own again: my police protection was cancelled based on a situation assessment, other priorities and budget constraints. Uncle Sam did not give a damn if I was murdered or not; I now felt lighter of having kept secrets from the IRS.

But I still felt apprehensive.

Chapter 24

Qxe4 f3+

Olivier Van Dijk's apartment, Manhattan, New York City

Now was the time to become both careful and proactive. I was in grave danger and I had work to do.

I woke up around 6 a.m., like most days. Although I had arrived home only around 1:00 the night before, after saying my goodbyes to my short-time marshal friend. I was still tired, and my injuries were still sore, but I forced myself out of bed to do some light training. Slow kicking and isometric contractions in the bedroom were hard but slow exercises compatible with my current diminished physical state. After twenty minutes, I was covered in sweat and Endorphin release made me feel real better. After ten minutes of careful yoga stretches that could be performed one-armed, I entered the bathroom.

Fresh, dressed up in jeans and a Polo shirt, and with a cup of my special mix for filter coffee, I sat down in my home office to start the day's work. My first call was to my friend and Ju-jitsu trainer Rui, whom I had helped to legally set up business in America and whom I told nearly everything. We were very close, and I was even his daughter's Godfather, a role I always took very seriously.

'Allo Rui. Olivier here. How are you?'

Rui was panting. I probably had caught him on his morning jog: 'Olivier. Good to hear from you. Are you feeling better? Do you want to schedule training sessions?'

'No Rui. In fact, I am much worse than when I cancelled, I have an additional shoulder injury. And I call to ask for your help'

'Anything. You know that'. It has always struck me that it is the people who look simple and unsophisticated that you can count on. Not the hypocritical so-called elite.

'Thanks, Rui. I'll tell you the whole story face to face, but just know that my friend Jack's death was not accidental and things have gotten even worse around me since'. Rui was breathing hard, and waiting for me to continue. 'Could you organize a guy or two looking out for my safety, something like discreet bodyguards? You know, just making sure nobody is following me around or trying to hurt me'

Rui had once been a gang member in the *favelas* of Rio. He was totally reformed and honest today, but still had contacts with more borderline characters. He also had scores of Martial Arts students, always looking to do some security work for extra money.

'That should be no problem. I'll set it up. Give me two hours, and there will be at least two people covering you 24/7. Are you at home now?'

'Yes'

'OK. Do not leave before 9:30, and leave it to me. I'll take care of their fees, and we'll settle later. Is this serious trouble? Anything else I can do?'

'That is more than enough for now. Thanks, buddy. We'll meet as soon as I can free myself, and I'll tell you everything'

I rang off, warm-hearted by good friends you can count on when the odds are down.

After refilling my cup with fresh coffee, I switched on my computer and checked the world markets in the general context of the trades I had placed the day before. Everything looked on track. I ran a few models, just to make sure, and was smiling from ear to ear. In this good mood, I did my chess moves, among them a daring escape from my Chinese opponent. Things were looking up.

I checked the time: 8:06. This was not an ungodly hour anymore, and honest people should be up already. I called my lawyer, Eli Rosenthal, on his cell. He answered on the second ring. Of course, when you charge that much per hour, you would want to be awake a lot!

'Mr. Van Dijk. Good morning. I was just about to call you. In fact, I was waiting for 8:30, just in case you were a late sleeper'

8:30, a late sleeper? Is this guy for real?

'Good morning. But I have been up for two hours. I did not want to call earlier myself'

'This is an amusing coincidence, Mr Van Dijk. But you succeeded in calling first, so please advise me first of what was it you wanted'

'Oh. I just wanted to check up on the situation regarding the Fund and my personal legal situation. I understand you have been sitting with the cops, the FBI, the DA, the SEC and probably a few other governmental acronyms I do not know about'

'Yes. In fact I have done little else these last few days, and I have assigned three of my associates to work on it. We are attempting to link everything together for a comprehensive deal closing all cases related to you personally. This is very complex and will take some time, as you surely realize, but I shall fill you in on the status when we meet. In fact I was about to call you to invite you to our offices'

'Eli. Could you fill me in over the phone? I have a busy day. I have a medical check, some physiotherapy in the Hospital, and a few other engagements'

'Oh. I am terribly sorry I did not make myself clear. Of course, I could fill you in over the phone, but I need to see you in person regarding another matter. I have something of importance I am bound to give you in person'

'What is it?'

'I am afraid I would rather not mention it over the phone. But it is definitely important'

I was intrigued. Or rather, extremely curious. I could swing by Eli's offices, take whatever he needed to give me, and still be on time in the Presbyterian Hospital for my scheduled check-up.

'Ok. Not even a hint?'

'I am afraid it is not advisable'. Eli was not a very funny guy. He was brilliant and affected, but had no sense of humor.

'OK. I'll swing by your office around 9:45, but I'll have to run to the Hospital from there. Just give me the stuff, and you'll fill me in about the case by phone later on'

'I shall be awaiting you, Mr. Van Dijk. See you soon'.

After I rang off, I racked my brains for a few minutes, trying to figure out what this last twist was about, but to no avail. After another refill of my cup, I called Laura

'Good morning, Laura. How are you?

'Good morning Olivier. Fine, thank you. And yourself, feeling better?'

'Slowly, slowly, thank you. As a matter of fact I have the doctors checking me up today. What a day was yesterday, wasn't it?'

'You can say that'

'I was calling to check if Joshua came through with his computer friend'

'No, not yet. But it is still very early. I'll call you as soon as I have something. Have you given some thought on what we discussed yesterday?

'You mean our date?' I said playfully.

'Of course not, stupid. The Foundation and where to go from here'

'Ah! That', I continued in my disappointed voice

'Be serious now'

'Of course, I have given it some thought. In fact, I have not been thinking of anything else. We'll have to discuss it more in depth, soon. Maybe… when we meet for a date'

'OK, OK. I give up. I'll let you know when I have news from Joshua'

'You are not trying to weasel out of our date, are you?'

'Bye, Olivier'

Then she cut off. Still, I was pretty happy with myself. Things were definitely looking up.

I made a few more calls. Among them, I spoke to my very emotional former assistant of six years. She was more worried about me than about her future; I reassured her and promised her I would do everything to help her with another job; and I meant it.

At 9:30 sharp, I left my apartment and hailed a cab in front of the building. I made a point to do it myself, not with the concierge's help, in order to be noticed by Rui's friends. Or at least I hoped so. Driving myself would still have been a problem anyway, but taxi hopping would make it easier for my guardian angels. I tried hard to find out who they were, but I did not notice anything special. I trusted Rui implicitly, and it was quite literal to say: with my life. No imagery there.

I asked the cab driver, in French since he was obviously Haitian, to wait for me in front of the entrance to the building hosting the offices of Rosenthal, Feldman & Partners. I would definitely have to wrap it up in 15 minutes or less, in order to make my hospital appointment.

The sumptuous offices of the law firm occupied the entire twelfth and thirteenth floor, but the entrance was restricted to the twelfth. Anyway, who would want to take the lift to floor 13? The spectacled blonde receptionist had been warned of my upcoming visit, and had Eli's secretary come to fetch me at once. Inside stairs took me to the dreaded thirteenth floor, although one could argue that it was not really floor 13, but more of a duplex number 12. Upon arrival, Eli's office was everything you would expect from a first-line attorney: Plenty of wood and leather, impressive antique book collections, green desk lamps, diplomas on the walls and pictures with celebrities and politicians. Eli stood up to greet me as his assistant left the room.

'Mr. Van Dijk, good morning to you. Thank you for coming'

'Good morning, Eli. You really piqued my curiosity'

We shook hands and he went back behind his desk as I sat down in the comfortable leather armchair.

'I understand that you are in quite a hurry, so I shall go directly to the heart of the matter. Just know that we are making progress with the predicament of the Rain Fund, and I expect to have a general outline ready for your perusal in about ten days. Now to the matter at hand'

Eli Rosenthal suddenly takes a grave expression. 'I expect this to be somewhat painful to you, and I first want to reiterate my condolences for the tragic fate of your friend and partner, Mr. Prilutski'

'Thank you, Eli'. I started wondering where this was heading.

'Mr. Prilutski instructed me to deliver a sealed envelope to you, in total confidence, in the event of his untimely demise. I now have the sad duty to execute his wishes'

My heart missed a beat. I was surprised and saddened by the memory of Alex, but stayed as impassable as possible. Eli opened his desk drawer with a key from a huge key-holder that carried dozens of them more. He took out a simple white envelope and a document he asked me to sign. This was just an acknowledgement of receiving the envelope as per Alex Prilutski's wishes; I duly signed with a trembling hand holding Eli's Tibaldi Constantinian gold fountain pen. After placing the document in a folder and back into the drawer, Eli pushed the envelope towards me, across the large green blotter paper covering the desk. The envelope was plain white, of thick premium quality paper, but not embossed. On its facing side, a simple word was written in Alex's typical calligraphic handwriting: "Olivier".

Eli added quietly: 'I have been appraised by Mr. Prilutski that the content is of a sensitive nature and that it would be best if you would open and read it in private. I suggest you use the adjoining meeting room. When you are finished, you can let yourself out on your own, unless the content raises any question you would like to ask me'.

'I'll do that. Thank you, Eli. And I think I'll leave immediately after because I am in a hurry. If I have any questions, I'll come back'

'You are welcome. Thank you for coming, and I shall contact you shortly regarding the other matter. Follow me, please'

Eli led me to the meeting room next door, with a mammoth mahogany table seating fourteen, and the wall covered by old but perfectly dusted leather-bound law books. After saying my goodbyes to which he replied gravely in kind, I closed the heavy padded door and looked at the envelope. I was too nervous to sit; so, I tore the missive open with my finger where I stood. It contained just two handwritten pages, and there was no doubt it was Alex's handwriting that I had known since college: ornately calligraphic in an old-European kind of way that he liked to affect, as though he was a long lost descendant of the old czar family. My emotions were conflicted: I was still mad at Alex's betrayal, but he had tried to redeem himself in the end; above all I missed my old friend. He did not deserve to die.

I started to read, slowly and silently:

Dear Olivier

If you are reading these lines, I am probably dead and not from natural causes. I write this letter in shame and I am not asking for a forgiveness I do not deserve. I owe you the truth though, so that you can act to protect yourself. I will always see myself as your friend but I have been weak and stupid and I have brought both of us into an impossible situation.

When we went our separate ways after University, I started managing private money for a friend of my father, a Latvian oligarch, and a few of his associates. It was clear to me that the money was only border-line clean, but I was young and did not care. I slowly became more and more involved, until it was made clear to me that there was no way out. I was then asked to buy up an investment fund for money laundering purposes. Your fund was perfect and I sacrificed our friendship on the altar of greed and fear. Of course the money for the buyout came from the Mafya *and they also stuck me with Ofer Dobry. He had written an incredible program capable of mimicking trades that had not happened and alter the public records, at the same time-legitimizing the trades for auditing purposes or other types of oversight. The fake profits could be used to launder mob money shiny white. I am sorry to have to tell you that your savants' results are not more than market average, and that we did not use their input for our trades. Nevertheless, with the apparent success of our Fund, people came knocking at the door and it would have looked suspicious to reject them all. That is how our Fund became a gigantic Ponzi scheme on top of being a mob launderette. In view of the huge amounts of money we are making, the organized crime behind this is becoming more and more greedy and aggressive. These people are really rotten and violent. Please note that Jan Thompson and all members of his team are reporting directly to the Head of the Organization, a Latvian named Aivars Bartulis. I gather that there are a few more workers scattered*

*among the company staff who are spying on us. I do not know what
you can do with this information, but use it extremely carefully. If
you read this, they must have murdered me.*

*I am truly sorry, and the only way I can think of to partly make it up
to you, is to make you the recipient of the money I have skimmed
from the Fund operations over the years in preparation for the
getaway I was dreaming of. I have amassed over ninety million
dollars, and my conscience is clean because it was stolen from
bandits and murderers. You have irreversible power of attorney on
this account, and the password is the name of the pub we used to
haunt in London. The account number is 5432765 at the Royal
George Town Bank and Trust, in George Town, Grand Cayman.*

*I know this cannot erase what I have done to you, but it is the best I
can do.*

I have always admired you and loved you like a brother,

Have a great life,

Alex

My eyes watered a bit on reading the closing. This was the real
Alex, deep below the coarse exterior. I noticed that this letter had
been written over 7 months ago. I placed the letter back into the
envelope, folded it and put it deep in my blazer's pocket. I ran out of
the office to avoid being late for my hospital appointment. My mind
was whirling with the contents of Alex's letter and what my next
steps should be. I hurried into my waiting taxi and sent it on its way
to the hospital. I then made a first inventory of my situation: I now
had about one hundred million dollars, off-shore, and the names of
the main culprits in the murder of my two best friends in the world. I
could disappear and live off Alex's money, it would now be much
easier. Or I could use it to rebuild myself and a new Fund. Or, I
could try to compensate the honest people who had lost money in
the Ponzi scheme. And I could try to avenge Jack's and Alex's death.

Should I turn the money in to the Authorities and have the FBI go after the murderers? I was juggling with dilemmas.

I decided to put all this aside to brew for a few hours. I switched on my cell phone, which I had turned off in Eli's offices, and it went crazy with message ringtones. I looked at the screen to discover that I had seventy-two messages, voice and text. I chose to open the second voice message which was from Laura: 'Hi Olivier. Laura. Your phone is off. So, two things: The news about the Rain Fund Ponzi scheme are out, so beware. The Fund story is opening the News on all channels. Reporters are going to hunt you down. And second, Joshua's friend will be in early on Monday morning to check the computers. Call me when you can. Laura'.

So the brown stuff had finally hit the fan. I erased all messages without bothering to check them, and I switched off the phone, just as it started ringing again. I would have to get myself a new number, and I probably needed to move into one of the flats at the Foundation. I decided to call Laura later. The journalists and paparazzi were going to do everything in their power to obtain a comment or a picture.

As I exited the taxi in front of the hospital, I decided to put everything out of my mind for a few hours. I was glad to see no journalists when I ran in.

***

It was late afternoon when I was back in my apartment. I had to sneak in through the underground parking on account of the reporters and photographers waiting for me at the front of the building. Thank God, I did not have a land-line in the apartment, only broadband access. On the way from the hospital I had stopped for a new cell phone: I now had a brand new Samsung Galaxy to which I had transferred my old list of contacts.

I had sent my new number to all those I could count on to keep it to themselves, and was now throwing a few necessities in an overnight bag. I had to get away from the media vultures until the storm abated; and the Foundation was the perfect place to go to. The fact that Laura was around there also had crossed my mind, I admit.

My new cell rang; it was Rui.

'Hi Olivier. I have seen the news, sorry for you. I know you are in your apartment. Do you intend to leave?'

'Yes, I am throwing a few things together and I go to the Foundation. Why?'

'I need to show you something. Stay. I'll be there in half an hour'

'OK. I'll tell the concierge to let you up'

After I rang off, I finished packing my bag, and then called Laura: 'Hi Laura. Got your message, thanks for trying to warn me'

'How are you holding up?'

'OK, I guess. I have seen the news on the hospital TV's. It sounds bad, and now every journalist in the city is trying to interview me'

'In a few days, you'll be yesterday's news. You'll miss the celeb feeling'

'Keep making fun of me. I just wanted to let you know that I'll be bunking temporarily at the Foundation, so I'll see you around, later tonight or tomorrow'

'Great. We can continue our discussions then. And I suppose you'll be around on Monday?'

'Of course, Laura. Wouldn't miss it. I'll be in touch when I get there'

I wanted to talk to Dave freeman at the FBI about the investigation, but I decided to first check today's patients' trending work. I just had enough time before Rui would get here. The market was definitely going my way, and today's work was pointing at a few possible ameliorations to be made. I would have to do the math later tonight and place a few orders, but there was no need to start now only to be interrupted.

While waiting, I went back to consider my options regarding Alex's money. I was starting to see how to integrate it in a general, but still vague, life plan. My train of thought was interrupted by the intercom. The screen was showing Rui's face and the concierge voice asked if I could confirm that it was the expected Mr. Monteiro. I would have to tip the lobby employees, because they must be working hard at keeping the media people at bay.

After a few minutes, Rui was at the door. He had brought pizza; I really loved this guy. He came in and hugged me, the Southern European way, with big slaps on the back. He went into the apartment with long strides, calling me in: 'Come with me'. He threw the pizza box on the lounge table and kept going. I followed him as he went to my room, and finally entered the Master bathroom. That was a surprise! He went for the shower and opened the tap, and then he went for the bath and put the cold water on. He sat on the side of the bath and indicated the toilet in a clear gesture to invite me to sit on it. I started to understand where this was going, and I lowered the lid before I sat. Rui was never one to mince his words or loose precious time on inane niceties. He took out a manila envelope from his shoulder bag, and extracted a grainy photograph.

'Do you know this man?'

The photograph was of Jan Thompson, no doubt about it, in spite of a cap and a new beard, probably dyed black. The graininess showed that it had been taken from far away, and the whole impression from the picture was one of furtiveness and concealment.

'This is Jan Thompson, one of those who could mean me harm. Where did you get this?'

'This man has been following you since you left the lawyers' office. Who knew you were going there today?'

'Only the lawyer, Eli Rosenthal. And it was sort of a last minute thing: He called me at 8, and I was there at 9:45. The receptionist, and maybe his assistant were aware of my coming, but that is it'

'That is what I expected. That is why you cannot rule out that your flat or your phone, or both, are bugged. That is why you are sitting on the … *vaso sanitario,* how do you say in English, …throne right now'

'Yeah. Thanks for that. But, if they have bugged my apartment, why not follow me from here, as a routine?'

'It could be because of what you went to do at the lawyer's office. Or they just started following you around. Could this man be a killer?'

'This man is an ex- Special Forces soldier from South Africa; he is working for organized crime, and he could be a killer; definitely'

'But in the meantime, he has been only following you. Anyway, my guys are on the look-out for him, and they will protect you'

You know, it could be that it has something to do with the lawyer visit, and it kind of falls into place now. I have an idea, but it could be dangerous, and I need your help, Rui'

'You know you can count on me, Olivier. But tell me, what is it all about?'

I started to tell him my story in broad lines, from the beginning: Jack, Alex's betrayal, the Fund, the mob, the Ponzi scheme, Laura, the murders, and all that was in between. During that time, the water was running around us, hopefully covering our conversation. I left out the facts that the methodology now worked better than even expected in our rosiest dreams, and that I had huge amounts of money in off-shore accounts.

'Meu Deus! Quite a story you got here, Olivier. What do you want to do now?'

'I want the bastards who killed my friends and destroyed my company to pay. I went to the lawyer for a posthumous letter from Alex with the names of the people responsible. I want to use it to lure them in and then get them'

'Why don't you simply give the letter to the police?'

'Because they will not do anything, and they need all kinds of proofs and due process. Besides the head guy is a Latvian, probably living in Europe'

'Let us say that you succeed in getting him here, what will you do? Kill him?'

'I would rather try to have him arrested if I am sure he can be connected to some wrong doings. But, if I have to, yes, I would kill him without any remorse. I would just have to think of Jack and his family. Although there are also Alex, the journalist, and probably many more'

Rui did not flinch. He knew, only too well, about vengeance, violence and vigilantism.

'So what do you want to do?'

'First, if they know about the letter, I'll make a fake letter to lure them in, and I'll make sure they hear about it and look for it. When they come for me, your guys will warn me and we shall catch them. We'll play it by ear from there'

'This is like you make yourself into a goat to attract the lion?'

'Yes. A bait. I did not know you had lions in Brazil. But I'll be a fake goat and forewarned, with lion friends around'

Rui was pensive. 'You'll have to be very very careful. You understand that there are no guarantees. Criminals are dangerous and do unexpected things'

'I understand, but I have to do it. If I do not do it, they will go on with their lives, unpunished, while my friends' bodies are eaten by worms. And anyway, I'll have to live in fear of being another victim. No way'

'OK. I will need to have more people around you'

'Do it, Rui. Money is no object. I'll transfer you a fat advance tomorrow morning. Now, I need something else. I'll be leaving this place for Upstate. Let your guys know. Did you come by car?'

'Yes, my old Buick LeSabre. Why?'

'Let us switch cars, take mine and have the journalists follow you. I still have trouble with my left shoulder, but, I can drive your car with one hand. Rush out with my Toyota to make it obvious I am trying to shake them. I'll use the diversion to run to yours and disappear'

Rui was smiling. 'Can I keep your car later? You can have mine, it is probably a collectible. A 1970 LeSabre I bought at a Police auction'

'After all this is over, I'll buy you a new one. Now, I'll go and prepare the fake letter to leave in my office, and I'll tell you about it in the living room for the microphones. I'll also call you later on my old cell to tell you about it'.

We left the now very humid bathroom; I went to my home office and Rui switched the bedroom TV on. While he watched UFC fights on ESPN, I typed a copy of Alex's letter with a few changes: I changed the numbers from ninety to forty five millions, and I changed the bank details. I printed the letter and erased all traces from my computer. After folding it several times, I placed the letter in the original envelope and in my office safe, a very simple and basic safe box bought at a DYI shop. No need to make it too difficult.

Of course I took the original letter with me. I dressed in a well-used dark blue track suit, black sneakers, and a black woolen cap. I then exchanged keys with Rui and we sat in the living room.

I started by thanking him for the medical massage he gave me, in order to avert suspicion away from the long period of silence that anyone listening-in would have experienced; afterwards we started eating the now-cold pizza. I then told him in a clear voice that I had received a letter from Alex's lawyer, and that he had at least managed to screw-over his killers. We finished the pizza while exchanging platitudes and talking about sports, then we said our goodbyes. I took my overnight bag and we left for the underground parking where we climbed in my car, with Rui in the driver seat. He let me off just before the gate, where I glued myself to the left wall. Rui pressed the remote to open the heavy sliding gate, and drove hesitantly towards the street, in order to be noticed. A crowd of photographers made him immediately and ran towards the car, at which point Rui roared forward in a screech and turned right into the traffic. There were honks from the surprised drivers and all the paparazzi's started running after the Toyota. Some climbed on motorcycles whilst others ran to their waiting cars. I took advantage of the commotion to walk briskly, but without running, turning to the left as I got on to the pavement. The gate was already closing back. I had my collar turned up and my woolen cap deep down; nobody noticed me. I walked to Rui's old Buick, two streets away, and off I was journeying towards the Foundation.

I was basically driving with one hand, my shoulder being still very sore, and therefore, I could not talk on the phone. I used the drive to relax and think about the overall plan I had just put into motion. It was pretty reckless, but I felt I had no choice: It was time to take the initiative and fight back.

Vengeance wrapped in a pre-emptive strike. Or so I thought.

***

Alyssa Olrov, a.k.a Dr. Menze and a whole list of other fake identities, was standing in the rain in front of Van Dijk's apartment building. She was together with the journalists trying to ambush him, but always slightly outside the group. She looked the part though, holding what looked like a camera bag and beating the pavement like the others. She was alert though, scouring her surroundings at all times.

Unlike her momentary colleagues around, she had been advised that Olivier was in his apartment right now, and not alone. His having a visitor prevented her from even trying to gain access to the premises and do her job; but, anyway, scrutiny of the security guards was such right now that it would have been problematic in any scenario. The circus camping in front of the entrance meant that, sooner or later, Olivier Van Dijk would have to use the parking entrance to leave the building, and probably go somewhere else for some time. It could take long, but as a hunter of men, she had the patience required. She kept an eye on the parking exit at all times, unobtrusively.

She discerned movement inside well before a car approached the rolling iron gate, and she positioned herself for optimal observation. Suddenly the gate started to roll open and a big Toyota 4 by 4, Olivier's car, positioned itself for a swift exit. She smiled at the amateurish behavior of the driver, doing too much to make himself noticed; he was even revving the engine like at the start of a F1 race. There was no doubt in her mind that this was Olivier's visitor, readying to lure all journalists and paparazzi's behind him and away from their real quarry. As soon as the rolling gate afforded it, the car rushed into the traffic in a screeching of tires, creating some havoc. Unlike all her so-called colleagues, she did not let her eyes off the parking entrance, and, as she expected, here came Olivier, squeezing himself out, by foot, just as the gate was closing back. There was no doubt in her mind that it was Olivier: His demeanor, his walk, his immobilized left arm, all pointed to him, under the cap and rolled-up collar. She was still impressed though: He was not running; he was keeping a fast but normal pace and was not looking suspicious at all. He could have left with another car from the parking garage, and that would have caused her a temporary problem. But this was going to prove much easier. She started behind Olivier, from the other side of the street, going fast and silently in her light sneakers. Her hand, into the camera bag, was already holding a silenced handgun with the first bullet chambered.

She crossed the street diagonally as Olivier crossed one side street, and she was about ten paces behind him when he stopped besides a big car past its prime. She slowed down and looked around: There were a few people on both sides going around their business, but not many and it was dark enough to get it over with.

Olivier was fuddling with a key set and bending to unlock the car; this was the best moment. But her cell phone suddenly came awake and vibrated in her pocket. Only her employer had this number and she hesitated for a second, before retreating a step or two to take the call.

'Da?'

'The Van Dijk assignment is to be put on hold until further notice. Please acknowledge'

'OK. Van Dijk on hold. It was close though'

'Believe me, I wish you had done it before I caught you. But something has come up'

'OK. I still keep half the fee anyway'

'I know that. We'll be in touch'

She hung up as she saw Olivier's strange car ease into traffic. This guy had more lives than a cat. First he was out of bed when she visited him in the hospital. And now, he was literally saved by the gong. But three is a charm, is it not?

***

All these strange goings and comings were observed from the shadows. A man in a long black trench-coat with a large-brimmed hat, vaguely reminiscent of world war two Nazis, had been lurking in front of the garage entrance while keeping an eye on the journalists grouped at the main entrance. He had not been fooled by the diversion and had observed Olivier sneaking out and walking away. The move and the disguise had been pathetically transparent. Maybe not to the press hyenas, but certainly to him.

He started following Olivier from afar; today, he was just observing. There was the obvious body guard who had been around on a motorbike all day, but he was staying in place, probably forewarned of the destination. But he observed that, surprisingly, he was not the only one actively following. It was probably one of the smarter journalists. But something felt wrong. He increased his pace to keep them both in view. There was definitely something wrong: As Olivier stopped to a parked clunker of a car, the woman behind him placed her hand in her pocket. It was unmistakable: She was going for a weapon. His heart quickened. What was going on?

Suddenly, the woman retreated slightly, and, after a minute, she turned around and walked away. Definitely not a journalist then, but a very strange character. The man in the trench-coat retreated in the shadows, pensive. He would have to be extra careful with this one. But he would still do it. The news had just named him as a huge Ponzi-schemer, ruining regular people's lives. Just like his. He watched Olivier's car driving away. His hand in the coat pocket was fiddling with a deck of playing cards.

Chapter 25

g3 Bf5

The Prometheus Foundation, Washington County, New York State

It was late when I finally arrived at the Foundation, with still plenty to do. The Buick LeSabre might have been a great car a couple of decades before the end of the millennium, but now, it was a noisy clunker drive. But beggars cannot be choosers, can they? I had to identify myself to gain access to the compound, as the marshals were still around. I assumed that it was just me personally that had been dropped for budgetary reasons. I was happy to be free of my escort, especially as I knew I had other guardian angels around, but still, it was difficult not to take it personally.

I had a look in the big room mezzanine, and I observed all lights were off. I assumed Laura was already in her flat or home, so I went directly to my office. I freshened up in the adjacent bathroom, prepared myself a cup of decaffeinated Blue Mountain blend, and sat at my desk.

My first call was to Dave Freeman of the FBI. I knew it was late, but I did not care. 'Agent Freeman?

'Yeah. Who is it?'

'Olivier Van Dijk. Good night, Dave. Sorry to call so late'

'What is wrong Mr. Van Dijk?'

'Nothing wrong, …yet. Now that you have dropped my protection, I am somewhat anxious, and I wanted to know if you have made progress in rounding up the bad guys'

'Sorry about that, but we had no choice. Just keep your eyes open, we have assessed that you are not a target, as you knew nothing of the scam'

'Have you caught Jan Thompson?'

'No, not yet. But we'll catch him. Do not worry. He is concentrating on hiding from us, not looking for you'

I had a picture shouting the opposite, but I was not going to tell him that.

'Were there other employees of mine involved, Dave? I need to know'

'Yes there were, but they were small fry and more on the computer side. Three guys from the IT department disappeared, and all of Thompson's employees. But that is it. One of the IT guys was found dead, floating in the Hudson, yesterday; but again, these people knew too much. Unlike you. We do not think you have anything to worry about'

These people were either dense, or really did not give a fig about me, or for anything else other than their careers. Thompson was in plain sight tailing me, all the bad guys, but Ofer and the guard I had collared were scott-free, and various accomplices were being murdered. Nothing to worry about, really.

I closed off: 'If it is the Hudson, it's OK. Thank you, Dave. I'll just sleep with one eye open, no problem'

'Yeah. Just do that. Good night'. These guys do not even grasp sarcasm.

I was now completely convinced that I had to take care of myself and go forward with my crazy plan. It was better than wait for a bullet in the head and a swim in the Hudson.

I took my old phone, switched it on and called Rui. While I was calling, messages were piling up in the memory. The incredible persistence of journalists and gossip-hungry acquaintances.

'Everything OK?'

'Yes. They have been running after me for hours'

'Just to ask you to keep what I told you about Alex's letter secret. Just between the two of us. I do not want people to hear about it and the money'

'No problem. Your secret is safe with me'

'OK thank you again for everything'

'Take care'

After this call, if either my cell or my flat were bugged, the opposition would know about Alex's letter. Or rather, the fake one. I switched off my old phone, still piling up messages in its memory, and put it aside.

Money is the sinews of war, say the French, and I was facing a serious one. Now it was time to finish my trading analysis and prepare a few orders. This took me another 45 minutes, after which I was ready with a list of orders. I took out another one of my disposable phones from the desk's locked drawer, and I endeavored to wake up my friend George using the same phone routing system as before. It took twelve rings and I heard a not-so sleepy voice; 'Allo? I hope it is important'

'Hi George. Just checking if you were sleeping'

'Is it not the man in the news? I was dozing off, but I'll make an effort just for the gossip. Sorry to hear about your troubles. And my sincere condolences for Alex. He never was my cup of tea, but I know you two were close'

'Thank you, George. I appreciate it. I am sorry that I'll have to be brief again, but I promise I'll hop over soon to tell you everything in greater detail. Just know that I had no idea of what was going on, that Alex was in on it but against his will, and that he was murdered in his hospital room after fighting the bad guys to make things right'

'Great Scott!', he exclaimed using our common favorite line from the all-time great "Back to the future" movie. 'That sounds like a movie script. I am dying to hear the details, but as you hinted, it is quite late'

'If you think it sounded like a movie, wait for what I need now. You still have my irrevocable power of attorney, do you?

'Yes, of course'

'OK. I need you to contact the Royal George Town Bank and Trust, in George Town, Grand Cayman. I'll send you the details and numbers in three separate emails. Use the usual decoding system to get the real numbers. This is an account in Alex's name to which I have the signature. By the way, I heard about it today for the first time. Close the account in Grand Cayman, transfer out and place half the money in my account with you, and the other half in a new account in your bank, but under Alex's name, in the same form as it was down there. I'll send you the details in a fourth email. Up to here OK?'

'Yes'

'Once the money is in my account, I need you to rebalance the total as per the eight trading methodologies I have sent you. I'll update them slightly later and send it through the system'

'By the way, those were great. You have made yourself, and me, a lot of money in just a few days. Quite extraordinary. If you keep this up, you'll double your money in a month'

'I hope so, George, I hope so. I'll let you go back to sleep now. Just make all this A.S.A.P, please. First thing in the morning. I'll send you the details and I'll upload the trades right now. Thanks and I'll call you soon'

'Cheerio'

I rang off and proceeded with the mailing. It was now nearly three in the morning; I was tired and my shoulder hurt. Instead of checking into one of the flats, I just took off my shoes, switched off the lights and went to lie down on the couch. I closed my eyes and was fast asleep within a few minutes.

Chapter 26

Qh4 Rae8

Riga suburbs, Latvia

Aivars Bartulis was an angry man.

He was unapproachable since the fiasco at the Rain Fund. He had been even snapping at his wife of thirty years, an event that rarely happened; cruel and implacable Aivars was usually a gentle bear with his own family.

He was brooding, watching through the huge French windows of his palatial villa: He could see a deer tentatively coming out of the woods bordering his garden, looking around for food. Winter had come early and there were patches of frozen snow here and there. If Aivars had had his gun at that moment, he would have shot the animal on the spot, just to calm his nerves. The Rain Fund Ponzi scheme had been a huge money maker, and now, all this money was lost. On top of that, all the money laundering in the US needed to be outsourced, not that there was that much left to launder. The authorities had started to follow the money tracks and disrupt many ongoing operations. A few scores of gang members had been arrested, with more who simply had disappeared and ceased operations. This was a serious hit.

Aivars was an intelligent man. He realized that all had been set in motion with Jack's murder and all the ensuing strongman tactics. However, he knew that it was the only way to lead a crime organization: Show even a hint of weakness, and your people will turn on you. The fiasco had proved unavoidable the minute that the shrink had uncovered that trading orders had nothing to do with his idiots' work.

Not that Aivars was having any money problems. As one of his country leading oligarchs, he possessed so much money that he could do anything that pleased him. In fact he had no idea of the precise amount, just the fact that it was denominated in Billions. Irrespectively, Aivars hated to lose. This was all about face, about honor. All people involved would have to die.

Aivars was day-dreaming about the way he had really been sucked into a life of crime. When arrested at 19 for painting nationalistic anti-Soviet slogans on the walls of government buildings, he was thrown in jail where hardened criminals were mixing with political prisoners. The hilarious thing about it is that this same Soviet jail, Kanosta in Liepaja, was today a hotel where crazy tourists were paying to experience, -as if-, the life endured by prisoners of the Soviets. Some people are really crazy, and there always were keen entrepreneurs ready to take advantage of that! Anyway, their touristic experience had really nothing in common with a real Soviet jail. Aivars remembered how he was badly beaten up on the first day for refusing to kneel in front of the ethnic Russian thug who was running the show inside and terrorizing all inmates, but especially the Latvians. Aivars had known already then, instinctively, that retribution had to come fast and ruthlessly; if not, his life would become a living hell. Then thin as a wire, he had skipped out of the infirmary during call-over and hidden in the Russian's cell, in his cot, but invisibly rolled on the side of the bed into the covers. Aivars was now smiling thinly as he remembered waiting patiently for the "king of the prison" to come back to his cell. He even remembered his name: Illya Stefanovitch. As Illya had sat on the bed after having dismissed his bodyguards, Aivars had sprung out and stuck a pair of small scissors stolen in the infirmary into his right eye, all the way in, and then proceeded to stab him repeatedly in the throat, puncturing the trachea and the carotids. Aivars had then taken the time to carve out the tattooed flesh of Illya's knees and arrange the body on those same mutilated knees, supported by the side of the bed. This was a clear message: No more kneeling for ethnic Latvians. Aivars had become an instant hero in the prison, and had earned his first underworld tattoos, painfully designed with ink made from soot of burnt shoe soles mixed with urine. But he was proudly showing off stars on the knees, symbolizing that he would not kneel before any man, and a spider web on the left elbow, symbolizing the dangerous predator he was. At his very young age, he was already a leader of men, and naturally started to enforce gang discipline within the prison's walls. His role had caused him many troubles, and he used to spend long stretches of times in solitary confinement, where he took up playing chess in his mind.

He was shaken out of his reverie by the ringtone of his secure phone, fittingly the theme from "The Godfather" movie.

'Ja'

'Jan, here. Prilutski left a letter to Van Dijk through his lawyer'

Aivars switched to English: 'And what does it say?'

'I do not know. It sounds like there is money involved'

'How do you know?'

'We had his place bugged and phone hacked'

'Get the letter. And do not harm him before we know what it says'

'OK'

Aivars switched off. At least, something was moving, and some action could be taken. Already in a better mood, he stood up and went to his top of the line chess computer. That would relax him, and should he lose, he would not have to kill the computer.

Chapter 27

Rae1 Be5

The Prometheus Foundation, Washington County, New York State

I woke up and checked my watch: 7:30, startled. This rarely ever happened; I usually woke up at 6:30, no matter what. I must have been really tired, or maybe it was the antibiotics I had been taking since the operation. My office couch was wide, deep and comfortable, but I still felt sore. My shoulder was especially stiff. I stood up carefully and stretched lightly. First thing I would do, was to commandeer one of the serviced flats.

I used the office bathroom to freshen up and brush my teeth. Then, of course, a double espresso of my favorite single-origin Nicaraguan beans, followed by a glass of water, the Italian way. In my crumpled trainers, I went to look for a free flat on the second floor.

I used my master key to open the door of the last one in the hallway, thinking it was the one most likely to be free. It was. I unpacked quickly, and decided to do some exercise before showering. The Foundation gym was on the same floor, but on the other aisle; as I was crossing, I could hear noises of the building waking up, much like a hotel: clonks from the kitchen, doors opening and water flowing through the pipes. The Foundation gym was well stacked: there were treadmills, steppers, elliptic machines, weight machines and free weights. With my shoulder still sore, I opted for the strenuous but less jerky stepper. I started the climbing motion and kept it up for half an hour. I was definitely out of shape, but felt much better than a few days ago. I did 500 sit ups before calling it quits, but while doing them, I formed the resolution to come back to a strict training routine within two or three days, as much as my injuries would allow. I was tempted to do a short wet sauna, but I was too anxious to check my e-mails; perhaps tomorrow. As I was leaving the gym to go and shower in my room, Laura came in.

We exchanged pleasantries and agreed to meet in the cafeteria in an hour. Eating breakfast with a woman you truly love, life does not get better than that.

After a revitalizing shower and fresh clothes, I went to my office and checked my inbox and phone messages. All my requests from George had been executed. My plan was rolling along- so far so good.

The cafeteria was situated on the ground floor; in the aisle opposite the *Big Room*, as its name had been set by the staff here. In fact, it was below my office suite. It was served by the same kitchen preparing food for the patients; though being reclusive in general, they preferred eating in their apartments. The staff in place was taking their meals there when on duty. When I arrived to the cafeteria, I noticed Laura was already sitting at one of the tables. Two other tables were occupied, one by two nurses and one IT employee, the other by Patient Number 2 and his caretaker.

I asked Laura if she wanted me to bring her anything additional to the granola yogurt, the fruits and the salad in front of her. She declined, so I went to the buffet table and loaded a plate with greasy bacon, fried tomatoes and mushrooms, beans and potatoes. I also entered the adjoining kitchen, and asked the cook for a cheese omelet. I put down my plate in front of Laura, and went to fill another one with blueberry pancakes and croissants. She gave me a seriously disapproving look, very much like the one I had given her celery sticks.

'You know what this is doing to your arteries, do you?'

'What do you care? We are not even dating yet'

'It is a very unhealthy way to remind me that we have a date tonight'

I smiled: 'Mission accomplished. I'll burn it off later'

We talked a bit about the patients, especially Tom's high social skills, and overall, it was an enjoyable breakfast. I suggested we followed it up with a much better coffee in my office, so that we could discuss sensitive matters. Laura agreed to come up after getting the day started in the big room. We set our dirty trays on the appropriate carriages, and went our separate ways.

As I was climbing the stairs towards my office, my phone rang. It was Rui.

'Hi. People have been sniffing around the Foundation. Your Thompson guy with a few of his friends. A Chinese guy probably working for them has been asking questions in the pub down the main road. My people are around, no worries. But just so you know'

'Thanks. Anything in Manhattan?'

'No news there. Yet. Ciao'

Forty five minutes later, Laura was at my office door, in her eternal doctor's coat, begging for real coffee. I poured water that had stopped boiling for about two minutes, into my press-coffee glass device, and brought it to the coffee table of the office lounge. Cups, cream and sugar were already set up in preparation.

'With service like that, we could skip the date; I'll marry you at once'

'I hope you didn't notice the look of sheer panic that my eyes might have given away, did you?'

As she smiled, I continued: 'A propos the date, Shall I pick you up from the lobby at eight? '

'OK. Where are you taking me?'

'Surprise. It is a bit inappropriate given that we are already living under the same roof, but I'll pick you up as if this was your parents' house. Do not worry, I did not intend to take you to the cafeteria'.

She became serious. 'OK. To business now. I have to tell you that no progress has been made regarding Jan Thompson and his accomplices. Some of your former employees from the Security and the IT department have disappeared and one IT guy was fished out of the Hudson. Ofer Dobry is not talking and his ass is covered by an army of expensive lawyers'

I pressed the plunger in the coffee device and poured it into both our cups. Nothing like the smell of fresh coffee for ambiance: 'So I guess, the killers of my friends are running free, and will probably get away with it'

She added a smidge of milk to her coffee. 'It looks that way. And it also looks as though you should take precautions and be very careful. You do not know anything that endangers them, but they could still want to kill you out of spite, or just in case they suspect Alex might have told you things'

'Hence the removal of my protection detail ...'

'Yes, sorry about that, but there is nothing I can do. I gave a mouthful to my boss, but nothing doing. It appears that my influence at the Bureau is waning, due to my being on leave right now, and also generally insubordinate. Nevertheless, I have had wind that things will go quite easy for you, because of your heroics and good will. There is a two days full staff meeting next week in Manhattan about the case, with my boss and the D.A. and a few other agencies, and it should be critical'.

'About the Bureau… You told me you wanted to be a profiler. What about that?'

'Let us say I have evolved. It was a dream I had, probably from TV series or a similar influence. But, I have seen FBI bureaucracy from close up, and I have found something much more fascinating and rewarding: this work with the gifted autistics. A propos, have you given some thoughts to what we discussed'

'Have I? This is just what I wanted to talk to you about, because, no shop talk during dates'

She lifted her eyes, exasperated. I continued: 'Prometheus is a service supplier and belongs to me. With no fees from the Rain Fund, it has no income, with only this House as an asset. I'll take you in as an equal partner for one dollar. Of course you should leave the Bureau ASAP. Then we would have to set up a financial company, just like the defunct fund. Formally, I do not know if I will be allowed to be an owner or a director anymore, but there are ways around it. We would start with our own money, and then sell our success. We should agree in advance that 50% of my part of the profits should go, first to repay the victims of Alex's scheme, and thereafter to charities linked to autism'

'But we would need money to start'

'I can whip up enough to start. In fact, we should start immediately. I have been checking the trending results, and they are simply incredible. How much savings do you have that you would consider investing in our project?'

'I have some family money, but, remember that I am fresh out of college. I would say, eighty or ninety thousand dollars overall'

'Fine, Laura. Believe me it is enough to start working. I'll advance you two hundred grand, and then put my half in. It means that we have Six Hundred thousand dollars and a winning methodology. Furthermore, I can get supplementary capital in the future. Most importantly, let us get this thing rolling as soon as possible if for no other reason that so, patient care can flow uninterrupted by financial problems'

'How would we split the work?'

'Simple. You do what you do best, handle the patients, look for more and take care of the charities. I do the trading part. The weakness of our previous system was that it relied too much on computer models. I personally did the interpretation of the trending results from the patients, and the resulting trades were out of the charts. So plenty of work and research to be done. The only thing we will need in the future, is professional corporate marketing to get outside clients, but we could hire an expert for that or simply sub-contract'

Laura hesitated for a second. 'I think I have a better idea'. She seemed slightly embarrassed. 'What about Joshua? What if we tried to take him on as a partner and let him handle the marketing? He is very successful, and obviously honest'

That felt like a punch in the gut. She obviously had given it some thought before. She noticed my surprised unease, and continued stating her case: 'And we owe him a lot. Tom is a very special patient, and it would be an asset to have him on board'

I stayed silent, munching over that. She was right of course. Pros: the guy is honest and ethical; if not he would not have cooperated with the FBI in the first place. He is a successful businessman. He probably has money to invest. We could tie in his very special son this way. I like the guy. If it does not work, I have enough money to walk away anyway. Cons: He is likeable and I do not want him around Laura, but I cannot tell her that, can I? Another con: in a three-way partnership, two sides can gang up on the third. This would not be my fund anymore, but only a partnership where I could be voted down.

I made a snap decision, probably influenced by my infatuation: 'It makes sense. Have you talked to him about this, at all?'. And I was really thinking: Who knows, maybe he would have no interest in this anyway?

'No, it just came to me yesterday night when I was talking to Tom'

'OK, then. I'll talk to him. And I'll have my lawyer draw up some papers, whether Joshua is in or not. I want to start trading our money with the new models as soon as possible'. I felt guilty saying that; I was already making bundles as we were speaking, but I had the intention of coming clean gradually in the future.

She finished her cup and stood up: 'Great. Get on it. I have plenty to do. I guess I'll see you at eight'

'You betcha'

As she left my office, I went online to book myself a flight for Turk and Caicos. I had things to discuss with old boy George.

***

At eight o'clock I was in the foyer, waiting for Laura. I had made a point to make it a real date and changed into suede moccasins, white trousers, a real white shirt with buttons and a blue marine blazer. I was quite proud of myself. Nonetheless, when Laura descended the grand stairs a few minutes later, she took my breath away, and I felt inadequate. She was wearing a simple short black dress and black stiletto shoes, showing off her magnificent legs. Her hair was done and she had a hint of make-up emphasizing her cheekbones. She was also wearing a simple pearls necklace. She was carrying a black coat on her arm and holding a small purse.

I was glad that the receptionist was already gone, because my amazement was difficult to conceal. How was such a fantastic woman still free?

'Where have you been my whole life?'

'Flattery will get you nowhere; let's go shall we, Olivier'. I was glad I had succeeded in slightly embarrassing her. Never let a good compliment go to waste. But I had no doubt right now that I was really falling for her, and it was quite a new feeling for me.

I took her to Rui's old Buick, to her surprise: 'We are not yet in business, and you are already broke?'

I opened the passenger door for her: 'No business talk tonight, please. Anyway it is a long story. I had to escape the paparazzi, and it seemed a good idea at the time. Sorry'

'Just kidding. It is probably more comfortable than my Honda'

As I climbed in the driver seat, she asked: 'Where are you taking me?'

'Not that far, since I can only use one hand to drive'. I did not wear the sling any more, but kept my arm carefully close to the body and refrained from unnecessary stimuli. 'I hear there is a great Pizza Hut around the corner'

I could see she was not completely sure whether I was joking, so I left it at that; nothing like a surprise to enchant a damsel. The drive was uneventful; we discussed lightly, anything but work, or business, or police matters. It was refreshing to find out how relaxed Laura could be, as opposed to her intensity in work-related matters, be it psychiatry or police work.

I took her to Greenwich's best French restaurant, '*Chez Jean-Jacques'*, not the most pretentious, but the best cuisine. When I stopped the Buick in front of the valet, he looked at it as if I had mistaken his cul-de-sac for a Mac Donald's drive–through. To his credit, it must be said that he did not voice what he clearly felt, and he swiftly drove to park the car as soon as I had managed to crank open Laura's difficult door to let her climb out. I did notice that he parked on the furthest corner of the lot, most inconspicuous.

I had made reservations under Laura's name on account of my temporary celebrity status; the maître d' that I have known for years did not comment and simply took us directly to the booth I had requested. It did not take more than three minutes though, before a thinly mustached rotund small man appeared, dressed in perfect white cooking attire including the distinctive high *toque*.

'Olivier, mon vieux. Quelle surprise'

'Jean-Jacques, comment-vas-tu?'

As he noticed Laura, Jean-Jacques switched to English: 'Good evening, Mademoiselle. Welcome to my humble restaurant', as he took Laura's extended hand to kiss it lightly. 'What is a beautiful lady like yourself doing with a rascal like Olivier?'

As Laura smiled at this display of Old World charm, I cut in: 'Jean-Jacques is the best French cook I know on this side of the Atlantic, but he is a jealous womanizer. On top of that, he is not even French. I come here because he is from Belgium, like me, and knows what really good food should taste like'.

'Will it be the usual then, Olivier?'

'Of course. I need comfort food, I have experienced a challenging few weeks to say the least'

'So I have heard. *Alors*, it will be *Fondus au Parmesan, Americain* and *Mousse au chocolat'*

'Exactly, my comfort foods. And please make sure Laura will never forget this meal'

'She will probably forget you, but not this meal, Olivier. Are you a meat or fish person, Laura? I would venture a guess and say fish'

'You are right, Jean-Jacques. Fish or sea food'

'I would strongly suggest our *Sole Meuniere,* Dover Sole fish in butter sauce. And maybe, for the *hors d'oeuvre*, I would suggest shrimp croquettes that would go well with Olivier's *Fondus. Et*, of course, there is no way you are leaving my establishment without tasting my very special interpretation of the Chocolate Mousse au Grand Marnier'

Laura was smiling at the exuberance of our host, and she readily agreed to his suggestions. I let Jean-Jacques decide himself the best wines to go with all that, of course White for Laura and Red for me.

As Jean-Jacques retreated to his kitchen, Laura said: 'Quite a character, your friend'

'Only the French and Belgians are so passionate about their food. I wanted to take you out to something special, special to me at least'

'If it tastes as good as it sounds, I should enjoy it. What was this *Americain* you ordered as main course, it means American, I guess'

'This is my favorite comfort food. In Belgium, it is the way we call what is known elsewhere as *Steak Tartare,* basically raw minced meat. In addition, it is mixed with raw egg and various condiments, but it still is raw meat'

'Thank you for not ordering that for me'

'I agree it is an acquired taste, or something very ethnic in American eyes. But you should try it sometime. This is the only place outside Belgium I would eat it, so each time I come…'

'Thank you, Olivier. I'll stick with the fish'

The evening passed quickly. We enjoyed each other's company, the good food and the wine; and we forgot for a few hours the world around us with all its problems. Laura was relaxed and enchanting. We discussed our early lives and backgrounds, her growing up in Los Angeles' Valley, with her Irish father, Korean mother and autistic little brother. Her father was now a retired, general practitioner, and her mother a retired nurse, taking care of her brother by themselves. I told her about my younger years centered around Belgium, but extended all over the world where my late father's banking job would take him. I told her about the schools I attended in Hong Kong and England. The wine flew freely, and she loved Jean-Jacques's *mousse au chocolat* so much that she ordered seconds while promising herself extra gym time.

At the end of the meal, Jean-Jacques came to receive his well-deserved compliments. After a few pleasantries, he switched to fast and Belgian-accented French: 'Do not look right now, but there is a guy sitting alone at the corner table, out of place. He has been checking you out suspiciously all evening'

'Thank you Jean-Jacques. I shall handle it. Send the check, and I hope to be back soon. It was excellent, as usual'

This sobered me up fast, back to reality. Laura saw my change of demeanor, and asked: 'What happened? Something wrong?'

'I hope not, but Jean-Jacques tells me someone has been watching us. It could be nothing, or simply a journalist. Either way, we should be careful'. I paid the bill, and left, as usual, a generous tip. We stood up and I took Laura's arm to escort her outside. While the valet went to fetch our ride, I called Rui on my cell phone: 'Is one of your guys, bald with a red-striped shirt and black pants'

'No. That would be the guy who has been following you and was sitting in the restaurant. Do not worry, we have your back, my people are watching this guy like hawks. Do you want to shake him?'

'No. I am going back to the Foundation anyway. But tomorrow, I want them to stop him, or anybody else, from following me when I leave in the morning'

'OK. In the meantime, they will make sure nothing bad happens'

'Thanks'

'By the way, you had visitors in Manhattan. I have it all on tape'

'They were in the safe?'

'As planned. Be very careful now, Olivier'

'I will. I owe you. Bye'.

As I rang off, Laura looked at me curiously. I saw her hand was in her purse.

'You've got your gun?'

'Just in case. You know that some of the Rain Fund bad guys are still running around'

'As you gathered from my call, I have people watching over us. And I hope the gun is not your routine set up in case the date does not go well'

The mood was definitely ruined, but she smiled. We climbed in the Buick and drove back to the Foundation, checking regularly the road behind us. We tried to forget this ugly reminder of unresolved issues, but Laura was wondering whether to do something about it, have the Bureau check our tail, or even confront him. But as we did not notice anybody following us, we decided to let it lie. With the mood broken, we went back to talk shop.

When we reached the Foundation, I escorted her to her flat's door, as the perfect gentleman I was. I told her I had a wonderful time.

'I had a great time too, Olivier. We should do that again, soon'

I kissed her lightly on the lips: 'Good night, Laura'

She went in smiling: 'Good night, Olivier'. And closed the door.

I was still standing there, unsure, when the door opened again after a few seconds: 'Come in, you stupid. Do I have to do everything?'

I smiled back: 'But you had a gun'.

My life was changing, forever.

Chapter 28

Qb4 Qh6

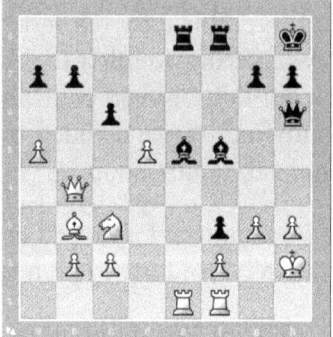

The Prometheus Foundation, Washington County, New York State

I woke up around 4:30, thanks to the alarm of my Rolex
Submariner. In Laura's bed, though a gentleman should not
tell…This was going to be a busy day.

I needed to leave, and I did not know if I should wake her up or just
leave a note. I was a little bit out of my depth here, and finally
decided that a note, in these circumstances, would be callous. I
touched her lightly, and she opened her eyes, just a little

'Hi Laura dear. Keep sleeping, but I have to go. I'll be away until
Monday morning, something to do with funding our project. I'll try
to call you'.

I kissed her forehead, and she groaned and rolled over to try to keep
sleeping in. I dressed silently and left the flat. I went to mine, just a
few doors away, to pack up. The hallways were empty and silent.
With a very light overnight bag, I went through my office to pick up
my laptop, my phone charger and my passport. Before going down,

I dialed Rui. A stranger's voice greeted me, with a very thick Brazilian accent: 'Olivier. Joao here. Rui is in training, but he told me to await your call. You need the people following you neutralized?'

'Exactly'

'OK. Wait for five minutes, then go'

I checked my messages, nothing. I left a message to Laura, just in case she was too deeply asleep to remember what I told her. I went down to Rui's Buick, and waited another three minutes just to be on the safe side.

I drove directly to JFK. After I found a parking place, I called Rui to tell him where, so that he could come and pick up the car. I sincerely hoped I would never see it again.

The American Airlines flight to Provinciales took about 3 and half hours, and I was thankful it was a small Jet, and not a propeller plane, like the ones I had to use in the past. There was no other class than coach though, hence I felt cramped and uncomfortable like everyone else. I was in an aisle seat, but the plane was full, as was the usual for week-ends and there was very little elbow room. I took out my laptop to do some work and managed to complete the full analysis of the trending our patients had produced on Friday. I was so engrossed in those fascinating reports that I hardly felt the light turbulence and that I was even more surprised to hear the pilot's "fifteen minutes to landing" announcement.

As soon as you leave the plane in Turks and Caicos, you feel the warmth, the humidity and the sea's pervasive smell. It is a long cry from New York in autumn. The smiling clerks of immigration are also a far cry from the sternness of US Airport Security and Border Control employees. It is as if you feel immediately on vacation as soon as you land. I think that border police should wear Hawaiian flowery shirts. I used my Belgian passport, as I usually do as soon as I leave the US. Belgium is such an insignificant country, besides for waffles and chocolate, that it does not cause any enmity or raises any questions.

I took an air-conditioned taxi to George's bank. All those cars driving on the left side of the road reminded me of the time I spent in London at University. Insouciant times if there ever were; I had come a long way. These Islands of only 200 square miles, are home to no more than 50 thousand inhabitants. The funny thing is that the currency is the US dollar, but the people are still subjects of the Queen of England and drive on the wrong side of the road. Land of contrasts.

Driving around the island, you definitely get a feel as to why so many American tourists come here to relax, sail and fish. The whole atmosphere, wherever you look, is that of an Island Paradise. Of course, I was here for the second biggest industry of the Islands: off-shore banking. The taxi left me on the pavement in front of the very quaint-looking building of the "Providenciales Royal Trust". It was basically a big villa with its back to the sea, and a small but lush tropical garden in front. The path to the main door was lined with coconut trees and trimmed bougainvillea's bushes. It looked more like a hotel than a bank. Typical George. I took out my phone to call George out.

'Welcome, Olivier. You cannot wait to have your ass thrashed can you? Out in a sec'

A few minutes later, George was out the main door, carrying a small sport bag. He was wearing chinos, sandals and actually the ubiquitous flowery tourist shirt. This was a far cry from a London City banker, and definitely more enjoyable. We hugged. George was a thin balding man, of about my height, always infectiously optimistic. His island tan made him look very healthy.

'Are you really handling clients in this attire?'

George was smiling from ear to ear: 'Is it not great? Banking here is about tax evasion and secrecy. Who cares how you dress, so long as you keep their money safe and moving around. Besides, Linda and the children love it here. It is like being on holidays all year round'

In front of George's bank, there is a park where we used to meet when he was only setting up shop. There was a fountain, landscaped gardens and benches. In one corner, there were a few public stone chess tables. We had made it a habit to do a fast match each time we met. Like most mathematical economists that we were, chess was like a normal pastime, and we always used to argue with our bosses that it was work-related.

We were alone in this part of the park, possibly something to do with today's iPads and video games crushing away good old-fashioned board games. George took out the chess clocks and wooden pieces, and more importantly, a six-pack of Fuller's, his favorite English beer.

We were both good chess players, and we eased into the game while I recounted the whole of my story. He did not interrupt me; he just listened as we drank and played. I was obviously not concentrating, and my game was in dire straits, but it felt good to unload my story onto somebody trustful. As I finished, he looked at me, and simply asked: 'Unlucky *tosser*. That's what you are. What can I do to help?'

'You have already done most of it. You have transferred Alex's money to your bank, and placed half of it in an account under his name. I need you to make his account look just as it looked in Grand Cayman: transferrable only to me and in person. The account should look as though it was always at your bank and no money was ever taken out'

'OK. Done. But now can you explain the Why?'

'Because, I shall be coming to you, one of those days, together with the mobster who created this mess, and I intend to hand over this account to him'

'Why in Heaven would you do that?'

'Because he'll take it anyway. This way, I can both remove his reason to be pissed at me, and have you get as much identification from him as possible. And also, I can ask you to tag this money, so that it can be traced in the future through the financial system'

'Wow. Not asking much, are you mate? Betraying the banking secrecy that is the basis of my livelihood, falsify documents, and by the way: Checkmate'

'I know I am asking a lot. But I really need this, and you are my only hope. Moreover, I did let you win. So what will it be?'

George was not smiling anymore, which meant it was not an easy decision.

'I'll do it. It looks like this bugger really has it coming. Anyway, I owe you for those trades you gave me. They are dynamite'

I let out a sigh: 'Thank you, George. And *a propos* the trades, they really rock, don't they? I have more with me here, and I am curious to see my balance'.

With the game over, we just stretched back and finished sipping the last remaining cans.

'If you are really setting up a new Fund with that kind of mojo, I want in'

'Ownership of the Fund is closed, but I'll be glad to invest your own money. Your clients' money is more of a problem, as they want it to stay away from those shores. Maybe you can bundle some of it in a fund of your own that would buy some. Anyhow, where there is a will, there is a way'

'In the meantime, I am just piggybacking you, and making bundles. Now that we are properly hydrated, let's go in and do some real work'

'OK. Next time I am in town, I'll concentrate on the game and give you the drubbing you deserve'.

We picked up our things and went into the bank. There was a sleepy security guard in the lobby, and a few beautiful receptionists. Not much security, but, as George always said, not much to steal here, apart from faxes and computers. Cash deposits were done in the secure clearinghouses of the larger banks. We sat in George's office, a testament to island decoration, with typical rattan furniture, plants, and bright-colored paintings of birds and vegetation, all the way to ceiling fans, in spite of the perfect air conditioning. I stopped drinking beer, unlike George, and switched to tonic water, as we started reviewing the paperwork around Alex's fake account. This took about twenty minutes, and George finally unveiled the state of my own account: Fifty seven million dollars and change! Nine million dollars in a few days, was a lot of dough. I supposed this kind of growth was unsustainable, a bit of beginner's luck, but it still exemplified how good the trending data from Prometheus could be. I modified the trades that needed tweaking on the basis of Fridays trending, and I added a trade. After redistributing the whole contents of the account, we called it a day.

George insisted we had dinner at his place, with the "*wifey*" and "*heirs*", and it was really a pleasure to sit with a loving family and reminisce about the good times we shared. He took me to the Airport Inn where I had a reservation. I would take the next flight out in the afternoon, after some beach bumming, back to Upstate New York.

The dice was rolling and there was no way back anymore. This was going to be a very dangerous game, but I felt I had no choice.

Chapter 29

g4 h5

JFK Airport, Queens, New York City

Rui came to fetch me at the airport, with my car this time, and was I glad to see them both! I had used the time left in Turks and Caicos to do some catching up on my training and to enjoy the invigorating sea air. I had called Laura to exchange a few words; she had not asked about my whereabouts and we limited ourselves to pleasantries. We also agreed to keep our relationship discreet for the time being. According to our respective plans, it looked as though we would not meet before Monday, at work. Taking it easy was fine with me; I was still trying to figure out what the word relationship really meant, though I felt good about it. This was one of the things I was discussing with Rui, as he was driving from JFK to my Manhattan apartment. But who was I asking? The guy was married and had a beautiful little daughter, so it was clear his views would be biased by this blatant success, wouldn't they?

We stopped at my apartment, just long enough to pack up the few things I needed. Rui had one friend staking the place, and who gave us the green light: nobody was going to ambush me there and I felt somewhat surprised when coming inside: the place was just as I had left it. Although I had been informed of everything which had happened and how the burglars were careful to put everything back in place, I was still expecting everything to be upside down and the safe to be torn out of the wall. Rui had promised to show me the tape of their burglary later. We kept silent as I packed up, if only for the eventual mikes, and we left immediately after.

We stopped at Rui's place, a small apartment in Queens, on the second floor of a nice four-floors building. His wife and daughter were out of town with family. He showed me the video of the break-in on his desktop computer: It was Jan and one of the men who had worked under him at the Fund. I wanted them to do it, but it still brought my blood to a boiling point. They wore gloves but, unsuspecting, they had not covered their faces; they simply picked the lock, came in and checked the desk drawers, before turning their attention to the safe. The small hobby electronic safe resisted the assault of a little gizmo they brought for merely a minute before yielding open. The use of the name "safe" for these devices should be outlawed. They scanned Alex's letter with a hand-held device, and placed everything back in the safe, not even touching the cash that lay in there for the taking. They closed it, and straightened everything they had put their hands on, making sure the apartment looked untouched. They then left the same way they came in.

I now possessed further proof of criminal behavior from Jan and associates, and more importantly, I had them hooked. My plan was still half-baked, but the bait was successfully swallowed. I discussed with Rui the need for tighter security around me and how to get organized for the show-down, which would most likely occur in Turk and Caicos. We agreed that two of his associates would already fly out and get acquainted with the place and the lay of the land.

After having tried to check and discuss all possible options, Rui forced me to accompany him to his nearby gym for a training session he decided I badly needed. We met up there with two of his students, and used a studio for some Mixed Martial Arts training. Rui had everybody's left arm put in a sling and tied to their body, to simulate a shoulder injury like mine. An injured fighter should keep on fighting, was today's motto. After a short warm-up, he started drilling us like army recruits, pushing us as close as possible to exhaustion. He showed us various one-arm techniques and legs-only maneuvers, and how to set them up. After forty five minutes of those, he had us free-fight one another, lightly in my case because of my real injury. Pushing yourself physically to the limit was exhilarating; not only did your mind forget all tormenting thoughts during the effort, but the endorphin released was giving you a real high. After such a work-out, you would always feel tired and sore, but good in a way which is difficult to define.

That is exactly how I felt after a long hot shower, good, but still too tired to consider the night drive to Upstate New York. I crashed on his Rui's couch, ready to drive in the morning. Close friendship gives you a much needed safety net in life, and a good feeling about life. George and Rui were the real thing and I was glad to have them in my life. I still did not know how much.

Chapter 30

Rh1 gxh4

The Prometheus Foundation, Washington County, New York State

When I arrived at the Foundation, Monday morning, there were several unknown cars parked close to the entrance, one of them in my reserved spot. This usually drove me mad, but today, I took it in stride. These were probably Joshua's friends, and they were basically here to help us. The traffic out of Manhattan was heavier than anticipated, and I gathered I was late to the show; it was already 9:30. I left my bag in the car and climbed the grand stairs two at a time.

I hurried to the big room, nodding at Anna behind her desk at reception. The sight, from the mezzanine gallery was pure chaos: there were at least ten unknown people running around, and the box of computer number 5 was opened up, with all kinds of cables leading out to strange diagnostic machines. There were toolboxes scattered across the various working spaces, and two desks had been pulled from around the room to area five. I saw that only Number 1 was at his station, working with his care-taker, as though there was no brouhaha around. All other patients were probably in their flats, but for Number 5, Tom, well in the middle of things; he was poking around his opened computer box, with his father at his side. I saw Laura running around and the cook marching in with a tray stacked with sandwiches destined for the coffee table in Area Four. I felt glad I was late.

I climbed down the stairs and passed by two technicians I did not know, and who did not give me a second glance. I went straight to Laura who noticed me approaching.

She was back into serious working-Laura-mode. Her eyes squinted a little: 'You look tanned. Enjoyed your working week-end?'

She was either jealous,-good-, or she thought I made up the work part to go playing golf or another male-only leisure outdoor activity. 'Yes, I did. So what is up here?'. Do not give unrequested explanations, it makes you look guilty.

'Come. I'll introduce you to Steve. They are tearing the computer apart, and they are confident there is something wrong'.

She took me to a short athletic Caucasian man, in a T-shirt and jeans, with bulging biceps. "Steve. This is Olivier Van Dijk, the owner of the Foundation and this is Steve Gold, cyber-security expert and Joshua's friend'.

We shook hands, and I regretted it immediately; he had a crushing handshake that would verbally translate to: I mean business and I am stronger than you. Steve had a full head of brown hair, some of it graying at the temples, and he looked like the tough ex-soldier he was, doubtlessly cultivating the look, all the way to the very short sleeves. I suppose it was good for business to look the part when you are trying to subcontract for the defense establishment.

'Thank you for coming in to check this, Steve'

'Joshua asked, that is enough. But this is one of the most interesting things I have seen in a long time. There is definitely something wrong here, and Joshua's boy is like an instrument we have never had. He is seeing things we cannot fathom, and he turns up right, every time. We are checking the hardware piece by piece, and having Tom verify our work each time, it is going to take time. The problem with this type of hardware-hacking is that you need to activate a trigger to get it in the open, so to say. And the number of circuits to check is vast. We are proceeding by elimination, and we have designed a plan on the basis of the ease of putting a compromised component into the machine in the first place. We'll get there, do not worry'.

Steve went back to work; he looked like he knew what he was doing. I was left alone with Laura, and asked her in a low voice: 'Good to see you. Can we meet tonight?'

She looked happy to send me packing, probably on account of my tanned face from the week end: 'I am spending the night in Manhattan; I have a two-day conference about the case with all agencies and the DA'. She then continued with a wicked smile: 'Your fate will probably be decided there'.

'Pity. I have missed you'

She softened a bit: 'Me too. But it is going to be a hectic three days. We'll catch up later'

'OK. What about the trending work with all the riot here'

'Not easy, but as you have seen, Number one is impervious to the noise. We have Number three working on two laptops. The other ones are just out for the duration. I'll take the opportunity to do some catching up on their sessions'.

Laura is really an effective manager; I am even more impressed than I was before. She continued, relentlessly: 'What about you? Have you made some progress? Besides tanning, I mean'

Remember: No need for justifications: 'In fact I have. I refined the trading model, and I have basically organized the funding for our enterprise. Only then, I went sunbathing'. I smiled, but she did not, as the hard–nut-to-crack she was. I continued: ' I want to catch Joshua now, and then we'll be set. I suppose we'll be in a position to finalize after your conference'

I went directly for Joshua, who was standing near Tom, at a desk with several laptops linked by cables to strange-looking electronic boxes. Steve was asking Tom if he was seeing something and Joshua was gently prodding him. I waited silently for a lull in the exchange to touch Joshua's elbow.

We shook hands. 'Could you spare me half-an-hour. There is something I would like to talk to you about'

'I am afraid not, Olivier. Sorry. I am already running late. I have viewings all day. What about tomorrow? I'll be checking up on Tom in the morning'.

'Great. What time is convenient for you? '

'I'll stay with Tom up to nine. Is nine o'clock OK?'

'Fine. Can you come to my office? Just ask Anna downstairs'

'No problem. See you tomorrow. Gotta run now'. He kissed the top of Tom's head and jogged away. Laura had watched the exchange and I gave her a thumb-up. She mellowed a little and smiled back. I mingled with the technicians hard at work, but it was all both boring and well above my technical skills. I left and went to recover my bag from the car. Time for a good coffee in my office.

I did serious work on the optimization of my personal trading model for the trending analysis; it was fascinating work. With the success of the Rain Fund, I had slowly drifted away from my responsibilities and from the mathematical analysis I was so fond of in my early professional years. I forgot how fulfilling it could be. Time passed quickly, and it was a call from Laura that reminded me of the hour, more precisely lunch time. We met in the cafeteria a few minutes later, to have, respectively a salad and a hamburger. The place was half-full, so we had a table for ourselves. Laura was back to her agreeable self and I told her about meeting Joshua tomorrow. She told me about the sessions she had conducted with patients today. Her phone's ringtone interrupted us. She looked at me, then sadly at her salad: 'They have found the virus. Let's go'.

That was great news, but still, was it worth half a decent hamburger? Probably. As we left the cafeteria, I grabbed two apples from the counter.

All our visitors were huddled around the opened box of computer number 5, and Tom was seated, together with his caretaker, at the desk with all the laptops. We immediately approached Steve, and Laura told him: 'Steve. Congratulations'. He looked up.

'It is not me; it is Tom you should congratulate. This boy is fantastic'

We turned to Tom and warmly congratulated him, but he stayed impassible.

Steve showed us a small wafer, or whatever these electronic chips are called, on the desk with his small screwdriver. The tiny electronic part had been removed from the box with many others, but kept linked with appropriate thin wires.

'This is one of the simplest and most common units used in nearly all computer drivers the world over. We would not have found anything wrong with it without Joshua's boy. He is simply extraordinary: he sees the inside of computers as colorful forms that translate what the hardware does. It is impossible to understand for us, but it simply works. By looking at the flow of electricity in the different parts and the changes in the base code, he instinctively knew how to activate the Trojan virus set in the hardware. We have not decoded the password he used yet and how to deliver it, but what Tom did caused this tiny thing to completely get control of the computer from the outside. This is the perfect virus, as it is totally undetectable yet truly powerful, and it is the first time I see one outside of a Research Laboratory'

'What does it mean? Someone has been targeting us through the equipment?'

'I have no idea who or what or why. It is much too early to say. But, at first glance, it looks like it could be a more general problem. This is a very common part of many computers'.

'What do we do from here then?' Laura asked.

'What I think I would like to do, after we have Tom help us to translate what he did into practical terms for us, is to have your permission to take this whole computer, and another one from your set-up, back with us to Washington for further analysis in our labs. What do you say?'

I answered: ' Of course, take them and do what you have to do. Just keep us posted. You have come to help us, and we are very grateful. Anything we can do, just let us know'

'Thanks, folks. I do not know yet, but you could have stumbled on something very big here. Maybe even National Security. We'll try to wrap it up here and finish the work in our Company's laboratories'.

'Have you told Joshua, by the way?' asked Laura

'Of course. First phone call. He was proud of his kid, and rightly so'

We left him at his work. Both Laura and I were flustered; we did not know what to make of this new finding. The only sure thing was that Tom was even more of an asset than what we estimated before. I was now convinced that having Joshua as a partner was the right thing to do, in spite of my personal reservations.

We both went back to work until Steve called us to take his leave; it was already 5 p.m. He was waiting in the lobby, with two of his assistants. The rest of the crew was loading up their gear, and two of our computers, into their car fleet. I tried to avoid shaking hands, but did not succeed; it would have been rude. So, with crushed fingers, I thanked him and asked for his discretion with any findings that may result. He agreed that we would discuss between ourselves before any action should be taken, if relevant at all. I was surprised not to see Laura wince when she shook his hand, and I surmised that his alpha-male habit was not extended to the fair sex.

After they left, I went to help Laura with the re-organization of the big room, substituting new computers and placing everything back in place. I accompanied her to her room to fetch her overnight things and bring them to her dented Honda remembering that one of the dents had saved my life. After a passionate kiss, she proceeded to drive back to the city, while I went back to some more mathematical modeling. I definitely preferred kissing. I would have done more of it if I had known what was coming.

Chapter 31

Kg1 h3

PLA Military Intelligence, Second Directorate, Cyberwarfare Unit, Guangzhou, China

Colonel Jeung was sitting in his small but modern office, reviewing reports about the different projects run by his unit. His work was made more difficult due to the recent public admission by the Army that confirmed their development of such a cyber-warfare Unit, although the army paper which revealed it was underlining the defensive tasks at hand. The only good thing about the publication, from Jeung's point of view, had been seeing the apoplectic General Wong foaming at the mouth while cursing all politicians and telling whoever was forced to listen that this would have never happened in "his times". Jeung had lost his respect for the General; he still experienced trouble sleeping; the senseless massacre of the Sin Kiang base engineers was haunting him fiercely.

Colonel Jeung was a patriot, and he thought he was doing a good job. He was happy to be away from the now completely destroyed base in the Gobi desert, and was trying to put the ghastly images of the past behind him. He was, at present, one of the two joint commanders of the important cyber-warfare unit. He had understood a long time ago that this area would be a key to victory in any future conflict, and he had worked accordingly to make the brass understand it. There was no doubt that a good cyber-attack could bring any modern country on its knees nearly instantly without having to fire a single bullet: China needed to be at the forefront of the field while preparing an impervious defense to a similar attack. The Colonel was managing all kinds of relevant projects: he was hacking into sensitive computer nets to assess the degrees of security, he was building a network emergency firewalls aptly named "The Great China Wall", he was perfecting small and big Electromagnetic Pulse bombs and developing countermeasures, he was developing new virus types and trying to have backdoors included in world renowned software programs, and the list was growing daily. But the prized project, the top-secret one which would give them literally world supremacy in case of conflict, was code-named project *Peng*, after a Chinese mythological bird. It was the undetectable back door to virtually any computer in the world China would want to read in or to take over. It had been his idea, but he did not know then that it would cost the lives of 183 Chinese technicians, and the later suicide of one of the executing soldiers.

When the phone on his desk rang, Colonel Jeung did not think for a second that it would concern the dormant *Peng* project.

'Colonel Jeung. This is Corporal Ma. We have received an unscheduled *Peng* activation in the USA'

'What! Are you sure? This cannot be'. Colonel Jeung felt his heart constrict; this was a huge problem.

'We have rechecked the data, Colonel and there is no doubt'

'This is a catastrophe. Print all the data available and meet me directly in General Wong's office. Now'

The colonel cut off and dialed General Wong's extension. He did not greet him but just said: "General, this is colonel Jeung. We have an emergency. I'll be in your office in a few minutes, together with Corporal Ma'

'Ma? It is something about *Peng*?'

'I am afraid so, General'

'I'll be waiting, make haste'

The Military Intelligence Headquarters in Guangzhou was a group of several buildings in the government complex, all linked by underground tunnels. After a few minutes, the Colonel and the Corporal arrived together in front of General Wong's antechamber. General Wong's Guangzhou office was very different from the Spartan quarters he had occupied in San Kiang. It was high-ceiling and ornate, in a Fifties' Stalinist way. That had nothing to do with creature comforts: General Wong believed that Communist Pomp was important to impress and awe.

Jeung and Ma knocked and entered, and Wong signaled them to sit down in front of his desk.

Corporal Ma opened his file: 'There has been an activation of the hardware virus on a computer in New York, USA. The internet connection was active for about an hour, and then disappeared. We do not know if the hardware was destroyed or if the connection was switched off. We have the IP address and can identify the computer. That is all we have at this moment in time, General'

'Does it mean that we have been detected?'

Colonel Jeung answered: 'Not necessarily, General. First, it could be a fluke or a technical problem that nobody had planned for. There would be no reason to notice it. The activation could have been random or linked to a shock to the computer, like it being destroyed or damaged'

Ma completed: 'The probability of deliberate triggering is very low. And so is the probability of anyone detecting that the computer could be controlled from afar. Let me remind you that the computer in question is not controlled or interfered with in any way, thus detecting *Peng* is impossible'.

General Wong asked pointedly: 'But we should still check what happened. This project is of critical importance and must be safeguarded at all costs. I repeat: At all costs. Did I make myself clear?'.

'Of course. We need an answer fast. We have no choice but to use one of our American moles. This is too important, and we shall have to take the risk of having him exposed'. Jeung signaled Corporal Ma to go and wait outside. As the door closed, he continued: 'It is dangerous to use a key asset for tasks other than their usual cover role, but this needs to be checked fast and thoroughly. And dealt with if action is warranted. I want to use "*Phoenix*". Do you concur, General'

The general acquiesced: 'Use him. We have no choice, this is critical. Go, Colonel. Take care of this, fast, and report back immediately'

Colonel Jeung hurried to his office, he had work to do. The project must be safeguarded at all costs.

Chapter 32

dxc6 bxc6

The Prometheus Foundation, Washington County, New York State

I was in my office degusting a Kona blend brewed in a big French press *Cafetiere* as Joshua showed up right on time. Punctuality is the mother of all virtues, my mother used to say.

'Please sit down', as I poured him a cup I had readied: 'How do you drink your coffee? Milk and sugar?'

'Just a cloud of milk, please. Thank you. It smells better than the coffee from the Big Room machine'

'Welcome. I agree with you about the machine. First order of business: We shall do something about it'

He smiled, but of course did not get my pun. Yet. 'What did you want to see me about, Olivier? I suppose it is about Tom's future'

'In a way, it is. But not entirely. I'll go straight to the point: Laura and myself are going into business together, and we would like you as a partner'.

Joshua did not flinch. Tough crowd. 'You will have to elaborate'. Joshua was a consummate businessman, if his reaction, or lack off, was any guide; and probably also a great poker player.

'We are setting up a new fund based on the savant's methodology. The improved model, coupled with the way the trending is implemented into trading, is working far better than the rosiest expectations. We have been back testing it, and I have been checking forward trades for a few days. To be honest, Tom has a big part in what allowed for the debugging of the previous model'

'You realize, Olivier, and I mean no offense, that your history is not very conducive to finding partners. And a few days data is no Holy Grail'

I winced at the deserved comments: 'You know I had nothing to do with what happened at the Rain Fund. And I hope you are not suggesting I have blinded Laura with tweaked data and promises of riches. Not only is she dear to me, but she is also an extremely intelligent woman. In fact, she was the first one to find the flaw of the original model'

'OK. I am not trying to push your buttons, just putting everything out in the open. Let us assume that the data keeps coming in as extraordinary. What do you need me for?'

'Neither Laura or myself are good salespeople or business managers. You are a successful business owner, we know you are straightforward and honest, and we would need a marketing manager, preferably a partner and not an employee. And full disclosure, Tom is definitely the best-suited savant we have ever seen, for such a business, and you come as a package'

'At least, you are honest. You want me in, but it is to ensure Tom's talents'

I now remembered my reservations. Joshua was a headstrong man, and in a three-way partnership, things would not always go my way. He was now irritating me more than a little. 'You want honest, I'll give you honest. Yes, I think it would be a great way to make sure

Tom stays with us. And it was Laura's idea to ask you in, not mine. I did not want to. I can see the benefits, but we can also do without you. Yes, you would probably be a great face to the company, a good business manager and sales executive. Yes, you obviously are honest and hard-working and you would be an asset to any business you would be a partner in. Yes, Tom is fantastic and it would be great to have him *ad vitam eternam*. But no, we do not need your investment money. No, we are not dependent on Tom's talents alone. On the other hand, yes, it would also be fantastic for Tom to have a secure place where he would be taken care of and where he would be a productive member of society. And no, you are not the only solution to our management needs. And no, you are not straightforward. You are simply rude. If you are not interested, just say so'

Joshua lifted his hands in mock surrender. He had a hint of that irritating smile on his lips: 'Sorry. Truce. I apologize. This is a very big thing you have laid on me, and this is my way to get the feel of people's intentions. I did push you around on purpose. Please accept my apologies. It is an army thing: Shake the tree and see what falls down'

I mellowed a little, but was still rattled: "Apology accepted. Do you have any relevant questions about what we are proposing?'

'Why isn't Laura sitting in on this?

'She has FBI meetings in town for two days, and she wanted me to approach you first, on account of my being less enthusiastic than her'

'Let us say I am interested in principle. Of course, I would want to see the data you referred to. But what would exactly be the terms of this partnership?'

'I have the data here, and I'll show you after we discuss terms. We are talking about an equal thirds-split partnership, no preferred shares or rights or executive positions. I would sell the Prometheus Foundation, assets and working company, to the new company for one dollar, and I do not want any special rights for it. We would start with our own money, a modest three hundred thou each at the beginning. The only irrevocable caveat is that fifty per cent of profits would be going to compensate the Rain Fund honest victims, and when all is settled, these fifty per cent will still be set aside to be given away to charities dealing with autism. We would consider using part of it to care for a few non-savant patients by ourselves here in at the Foundation'.

I could see on his face that he liked the pitch. But still: 'What about my business?'

'This is only my opinion, but I firmly believe that you could ease out of the day to day management of your agency. As we would start with our own money, there would not be much to do in terms of outside marketing at the start. That would give you time to find and train a good manager. You do not need to go and run by yourself to all these viewings, do you? And you could still keep a very close eye on your company while working here, once you have found the right manager, of course. Let me remind you that even half the projected profits of this endeavor are at least one order of magnitude above your current turn-over'. I looked at him expectantly. I had made my pitch, though frankly, I did not care one way or another, if he took it or not.

Joshua took his time. 'OK. I am interested, in principle and if the numbers click. And of course, pending my lawyer's checking the incorporation contract. To tell you the truth, the main reason tipping me over is Tom's care. This place has done wonders for him'

'It is perfectly legitimate. I'll show you the numbers, and you can take them for verification. No need to impress upon you the importance of secrecy on how they were obtained?'

'Got it. Silent as a tomb, do not worry. Show me numbers, please. I have a viewing later on, so take me through the salient points first'

I took out my file, refreshed the coffee cups, and we went to sit on the office couch. Joshua was very down to earth, and I was surprised at his healthy grasp of financial matters. He did not use the fancy words, but always asked the bottom line questions. We would probably never be best friends, but I could see he would be a good business partner. I was glad he looked impressed with the results I was showing him.

We were only ten minutes into the discussion, when my cell phone rang. I excused myself and checked the dial: It was Laura. 'Hi Laura. I am just sitting with Joshua about …'.

A male voice, with a very thick East European accent, cut in: 'This is not Laura, Mr. Van Dijk, as you can obviously deduce. My name is Aivars, and I am afraid you have something that belongs to me'

I blanched. Joshua looked at me alarmingly.

Chapter 33

Qc5 Qg7

Downtown District, Washington D.C.

John Kwan was sitting in his office, at the back of his travel agency on 7th Street. The agency was of top-of-the-line design, ultra-modern in style and mostly catering to businesses and government agencies. He just returned from a long lunch, and there were three employees still manning the customers' stations, all attractive young women; and the middle-aged Chinese agency manager in her cubicle.

Today, John was concentrating on agency business, checking accounts and customers' lists. His agency was a very successful business in its own right, although it had been started and put on tracks by Chinese government monies.

His private line rang. Only family and very close friends knew of this number.

'Good afternoon. Mister Kwan?'. The voice was slightly accented.

'Yes. Who's calling, please'.

'This is Samuel Wong, from the Far East Tourism board. I have just sent you by email the quotation that you requested, and I just wanted to ensure that you received it fine'.

John was suddenly nervous, although nothing in his voice or demeanor would show it; he recognized code words for an emergency meeting. Emergency is never good, is it? Was his cover jeopardized?

'Let me check, please'. He opened his inbox with Microsoft Outlook and found the email. 'Yes, of course. Here it is. I'll check it up today. Thank you very much'.

'You are welcome, Mr. Kwan. I look forward to doing business with your company. Goodbye'.

John hung up slowly; he was already checking the email and translating the cues, scattered innocuously into the text, into the place and time for the meeting. After a few minutes of deciphering, it read: Ming's Gardens, Chinatown, 20:00, Ming's private booth.

Wondering what it could be, John called home and told his wife distractedly that he would be back late, due to a business dinner.

***

John had taken forty-five minutes to run around in the metro and in and out of businesses to shake any possible tail. At 7:50, he was passing under the Chinese Gate of H Street, marking the entrance of Washington's small historical Chinatown. John knew that most of the historic Chinese population had moved out of here a long time ago, and that the neighborhood was just a kind of tourist make-believe. What is in a name? And most visitors did not know that the neighborhood was originally built and occupied by German immigrants.

John entered the Ming's Gardens restaurant and asked the traditionally-dressed hostess for Ming's private booth. He was led to the back of the restaurant, through a narrow hallway, to a small room with a six-seat table. The décor was kitsch Chinese, for tourists or for Americans who never left the Country. A small, bespectacled man, was sitting at the table alone, and addressed John in Mandarin Chinese, as soon as the door closed behind the hostess.

'Greetings'. Names were unnecessary. 'I assume you have made sure you were not followed'

The unnamed man invited John to sit with a large hand gesture; the table was already laden with an assortment of dishes.

'You have greetings from Jeung. Let us eat while we talk'.

Jeung's name was the identification password; everything was safe and clear. Once their plates were covered with the excellent fare of the restaurant, the diminutive bespectacled man started to talk, while chewing.

'We need you for a matter of the greatest importance and urgency. Important enough to justify this meeting and also use you outside of your deep mole position. It is regrettable, but we have no choice. This place is completely bug- and sound-proof, which is necessary as I have to appraise you of one of the most important ultra-secret projects we are handling'.

John just nodded, pushing food into his mouth with his chopsticks.

'We have succeeded in introducing a hardware Trojan virus into most of the world's computers, through a small component bought by most manufacturers from a specialized Taiwanese company. This is the most potent weapon ever designed, and it must be kept secret at all costs'.

John stopped eating, thunderstruck by the news. Only the great Chinese people could have come up with such an ingenious strategy; he was proud by association.

The Chinese spy continued: 'The device needs to be activated by us with a special procedure through the internet or via a radio wave coded transmission. For reasons we do not understand, one such device was activated somewhere in New York State, in a secretive compound. It is imperative that we discover the identities of the individuals behind the activation, that we find out how much they know precisely, and then that we eliminate anybody who knows anything of significance. The activated computer must be retrieved or destroyed. You understand the importance of making sure there are no traces and that this project stays a guarded secret'.

John thought for a moment, and then answered: 'Let me be sure I have understood. You want me to travel to New York, check whether the location where the chip was activated is government-linked, find out whether anybody outside the place knows about the virus, and then destroy the place and kill everybody who knows?'

The small man smiled thinly. 'Put crudely. But exactly right'.

John took another moment to think. 'I have no compunction about killing and you have trained me well to do that if necessary. Destroying the place with the people should be done by fire, I suppose. But it is not something I can do on my own. We also have no idea how many people are in the place and if it is protected'

'You are right, of course. Together with the details of the place and the computer IP, I will now give you the phone number of a man who will organize the muscle for you. This man is a Triad boss with whom we have a special relationship; although we do not condone his behavior, we have leverage on him and we can use him when needed. Let us say that with the kind of leverage we have, he can be trusted implicitly. He will give you as many men, weapons and support as you need, and his people will obey your orders to the letter. We shall pay for all expenses of course, directly. Needless to say, you should not give him or his men any information they do not need to know. We are using a Triad to ensure no connection is made with the state. Is everything clear?'.

John pondered the task for a moment. 'I think I got the picture. Can I contact you if I need more precisions?'

'No, you cannot. In fact, we shall never speak again. All the data we have is on this sheet of paper, and you have understood your task perfectly. I repeat: do whatever is necessary to make sure the project is safe. When it is over, just post a job opening on your website, and somebody will contact you for a debrief. After the operation, do not contact the Triad boss ever again either, OK?'

'OK'

'Good. Let us enjoy this fine cuisine then, and off you go to your assignment. Good luck, we are counting on you, -your country's fate and future literally depend on it'.

Chapter 34

Kh2 Qf6

The Prometheus Foundation, Washington County, New York State

My knuckles were white from the crushing grip I unconsciously applied to the cell phone: 'Where is Laura? What do you want?'

'I am afraid Miss Wheelan cannot come to the phone right now. She is indisposed. And you know what I want. You know who I am and I want what is rightfully mine. If you really care for Miss Wheelan, I suggest you come to the Islands where we'll contact you for a fair exchange'

I tried to cut in, but Aivars did not let me: 'I'll call you back in two days. You'd better be there and keep this from the authorities'.

He rang off. I looked at the phone, completely lost. I heard Joshua asking about what had happened, but I was in a trance. I frantically tried to call Laura's phone back, but it was turned off. This was bad. How stupid had I been? I caused this. I wanted the mob's attention to try to exact my revenge, and I had planned on making myself the bait. I had not thought they would try to kidnap Laura instead of getting me. I completely and naively overlooked the mob's option of kidnapping someone close to me rather than myself. How did they know we were close? The date, of course; the man who was following us.

I glanced towards Joshua, who looked very worried: 'Anything happened to Laura?'

I had to tell him, he had heard enough not to be easily brushed off. And I needed to tell someone.

'Laura has been kidnapped by the mobsters who have destroyed the Rain Fund'

'What? What do they want?'

'Money of course. Money that Alex skimmed. I would have given it to them anyway. Just let Laura be safe'

'We have to call the FBI'

'No. No. They said no police. They would kill her with no compunction. I have to do it myself'

'How can I help?' said Joshua.

I was gathering my wits and thought about it for a moment. I had no other option. I had to go through with my plan as if it was me in their clutches. I would just have to be extra careful, and do nothing to endanger Laura. At the first hint of a problem, I would drop everything just to save her. The old Olivier would have had to think about it, checking what was in it for him. Not the new one! I would sacrifice everything for Laura, money, myself, everything... I could use all the help I could get though.

'You were a Navy SEAL, right?'

'Yes'. He answered simply.

'The exchange will have to happen on the island of Turks and Caicos. Could you come with me there? I'll have a few more friends who'll be coming; they will obtain some weapons locally if needed. Would you use a weapon if necessary?'

'If it is to save Laura's life, certainly. And I can most likely get better ordinance than you down there. I have an old friend from the Unit who is bumming in those waters, and he can get me anything I need. What would you have in mind?'

I know exactly where the exchange will take place, and I fully intend to give them everything they want. All the money, I don't care. The only thing I need, is to make sure nothing happens to Laura, and that they do not try to kill her, and me, as soon as I have signed the money over to them'

I barely knew Joshua, but he was all business. 'Where and how would it happen?'

'I have to sign the account personally over to the mob guy. That would be in the bank itself. I would not do it if I had not seen Laura around and made sure she was OK. He will definitely not come alone. So I suppose we would have to have several people making sure she stays around and is not harmed while I am inside. The tricky part will probably be as we exit and he has control of the account. We would have to make sure that the bad guys are under threat until Laura is safe'

'How does the place look?'

I started drawing a sky view of the bank's surroundings. Joshua was asking pointed questions and basically taking charge. After a few minutes, he concluded: 'You'll have to be firm. No going into the bank without Laura in the park, under our eyes. No discussions, even if they make her shriek into the phone. Hostage situations are the trickiest. How many people can you have to help, and what kind of training do they have?'

'I would say four or five, but they are not soldiers. They are martial arts athletes with some bodyguard background, no more. And probably a bit closer to the criminal world than you and me, though the length of my rap-sheet has increased exponentially these last few months'

'Good enough. I can have one or two ex-SEAL friends to help, for a fee. Can you make sure everybody understands that I am in charge of the operation? You are emotionally involved and there is no better way to botch an operation than a blurred line of command'

'OK. Done. I'll talk to them. And, Joshua, money is no problem. Spend as much as needed'

'I'll call my secretary to cancel everything. Let's get there as soon as possible. Get your people flown there, and I'll get the equipment. Please print a few Google maps of the area, to study on the flight'

He was going out, half-running. I called after him: 'Thanks, Joshua'

'Thank me when this is over'. He then stopped at the door and turned back: 'And I am doing this for Laura. But please call one of her colleagues at the FBI meeting to check that it is not a hoax. Just make sure you behave innocently so that you don't alert the FBI, OK?'

'You are right. Good idea'. At least Joshua was thinking clearly, unlike me.

As Joshua disappeared, I grabbed my phone with a trembling hand to call Rui.

Chapter 35

Qxa7 Bd4

Neptune Motel, Provinciales, Turks and Caicos

Room 116 of the Neptune Motel, in Provinciales, was transformed into a war room. I was the only one not residing there. Although I had booked four rooms at the motel, I, myself, was sleeping at the Airport Inn. I had taken all precautions possible to arrive here undetected, and only after getting Rui's all clear that I was not followed. The room was for planning purposes only: the curtains were drawn and there was a "Do not disturb" sign on the door. There was always someone inside to make sure no cleaning staff would gain access. The room, with two beds, was quite spacious and sported a desk as well as a small dining table. The Neptune Motel was not a five stars establishment, but it was clean and modern.

All Rui's friends and one of Joshua's were staying in the other rooms of the motel. Joshua was staying on his friend's boat, with all the equipment. Assembling this group of people and the necessary tools, in such a short time frame, had been a *tour de force*. It would not have been possible without Joshua and his friends.

We had just completed a final briefing directed by Joshua. All participants were in attendance, sitting on chairs and the beds. Rui's group consisted of another four of his martial arts-trained security guards, all Brazilian: one of them, Joao, I already knew; I now had made the acquaintance of Ze, Zeca and Manuel. These were Rui's friends and students, and I trusted them implicitly. Joshua had brought two ex-SEALS, the island-hopping boat owner, Matt, and a tough-looking, muscle-bulging, scars-covered African American from Miami named Sam. Matt had brought in his boat top of the line communication equipment, tasers, handguns and a sniper rifle.

Joshua made it very clear that the weapons were only there as a last resort. The only mission was to bring Laura and myself to safety, not to assassinate anybody or take revenge. He was looking at me directly when he said that. A successful mission would be one in which no shots were fired. Each one received his position and role in the mission, and then left, in small groups, to reconnoiter the terrain. Everything was as ready as possible, and we were now waiting for the kidnappers to contact me.

Joshua did not approach the situation only in a passive way. He had requested Matt to use his island contacts to check the arrival of private jets which could have brought Laura in. This was the only way she could have been brought to Turks and Caicos fast without alerting the authorities. However, the task proved daunting: the fiscal paradise was buzzing with rich people flying in and out, and the number of private planes on the several airports was in the dozens, with no possible way to distinguish between them. More than half of them came directly from the US.

It was late at night, and Joshua was betting they would only call me in the morning and rush me to the bank at the last minute. He expected they would have had time to prepare the terrain, and keep me off-balance. It was agreed that everybody would be in place at six a.m., whether I had been contacted or not.

I hugged each one of these men, who were going to risk their lives for me and Laura, before I left for my hotel, on foot. It was a thirty minutes' walk, but I wanted the fresh air and the light exercise.

Joshua was wrong. On my way to the hotel, my cell phone rang; it was not Laura's cell this time, but a local one.

'Tomorrow, be at the bank at 8:30'. It was Aivars.

I immediately started: 'I won't go in if Laura is not there'.

Aivars had cut me off before I finished the sentence. This was not starting well.

***

It was only 8:10 in the morning, and I was already approaching the park from a side street. I was dressed in tracksuit and trainers, just in case I had to move fast, or fight. I had no weapons with me, as they would surely pat me down. Just before the corner, I took out my cell phone and called Joshua. I was wired and they could hear everything around me, but I was deaf: an earphone or earplug of any sort would have been too blatant.

'I am going in'

'They are already there, waiting for you. Listen carefully. We have spotted a sniper on the roof of the building opposite the bank. We shall neutralize him exactly 15 minutes after you have entered the bank. Do not, under any circumstances, leave the bank or let him leave the bank before those 15 minutes have elapsed. As soon as you come out, we'll start neutralizing their perimeter, and you start warning him off as we agreed'

'OK'

'They have several people around, so you will not see any of ours. Do not worry; I shall have them put in place after you enter the bank. Remember: Do not enter the bank under any scenario, without having Laura sitting in the open. We have discussed this. Even if they hurt her! If she is not out there, she is as good as dead. Go now. Good luck'

I pocketed the phone and turned the corner. This park was so tranquil and picturesque, with its gurgling water fountain and tropical vegetation, that just catching a glimpse of it relaxed me, albeit only a fraction. I needed that; I had found myself unable to sleep even a minute the night before. I was so worried about Laura... I saw a few people in the park, but the only one sticking out was an obese man sitting at one of the public chess tables. He was nearly bald, sweating in spite of the shade, and carried an aura of strong malevolence exuding from his entire demeanor. He was dressed as a tourist in light chinos and a colorful cotton shirt, with big sunglasses covering most of his face; but the hulk of a man in a suit standing a few paces behind him told the whole story: a mob boss and his bodyguard. As Joshua had informed me, there must be more of his acolytes scattered about. I was psyched up, but not afraid any more. I was a regular Joe, but I had been pushed to the edge by rotten people. And I would do what I had to do. I approached slowly, in a purposely non-menacing manner; the obese man signaled me to come closer with a flick of a hand glittering with gold. There was no doubt this was the Aivars Bartulis mentioned in Alex's letter, the man ultimately responsible for the death of Jack, Alex and Zini. And now Laura's kidnapping. I felt a surge of hate and an impulse to throw myself at his throat, but controlled myself. Anger would prove futile at this junction. His bodyguard came around and patted me down quickly and rather discreetly for weapons, as I expected. I kept my cell phone in my hand.

Aivars signaled for me to sit in front of him: 'Mr. Van Dijk. I knew you would be early. Please sit down'. There were huge gold rings on three of his fingers, on both hands, and a gold Rolex glittering with diamonds on his left wrist. The effect was ridiculous. He carried a thin sadistic smile on his lips, obviously enjoying the situation.

I noticed that there were stone chess figurines on the table.

'Where is Laura?'

'Relax, Mr. Van Dijk, be calm. You have my word: Laura against the money, nothing to worry about. The bank does not open before 8:30, so we have time to unwind. Let us have a game of chess'.

'I shall not play with you and I shall not enter this bank, if I do not see Laura sitting here in this park, in good health'.

I could not see Aivars's eyes, but I was imagining them, as I heard the steel in his voice: 'You will do as you are told, if you do not want her to be hurt'.

'If she is not brought here at once, there will be no deal. It means she is going to be killed anyway, or probably is already. So no money for you', and I stood up. At that moment, I was ready to leave; it was no show.

Aivars looked at me, probably gauging me. I suppose that my body language was unequivocal though, because he blurted, as I was starting to turn away: 'Sit down. I'll bring her'.

I kept standing, looking at him, unwavering. He sighed, and talked in a normal voice, in English: 'Bring the girl'. He was geared up with sophisticated communication equipment; I could see now the very discreet ear-plug. I had to be very careful not to underestimate him.

I looked around. At the opposite side of the park, I noticed the back door of a parked black stretched limo opening. As I watched intently, I saw a big muscular man, come out. He looked like the twin brother of Aivars's bodyguard. He pulled someone from the back seat, and there was no doubt it was Laura. My heart missed a beat, but I tried to stay impassible. As she stumbled out, held under one arm by the Schwarzenegger look-alike, the other back door opened. I focused all my hatred on the person I immediately recognized as Jan Thompson. He came around the car to fetch Laura, and half lead her, half carried her towards us.

Laura looked pale and weak, probably drugged. She was dressed in a crumpled cheap tracksuit, and flip-flops. She was stumbling every few steps, but as she approached, I saw an undefeated look in her eyes. They stopped a few tables away from us, and Aivars signaled

Jan to sit. Jan was looking at me with a mocking smile on his lips, but did not say a word. He made Laura sit on the stone bench, and sat himself beside her. His hand was inside his small shoulder bag, making sure I understood that it was concealing a weapon.

It was Aivars who broke the silence: 'You see that I am a man of my word. Now, sit down'.

I sat down, and looked back at him, unflinchingly. I had so much hate in me right now.

He continued, in a lower voice: 'I promised her life against my money, and I keep my word. But I did not promise not to kill you. You have disrespected me, Mr. Van Dijk, and I cannot let this pass'.

I kept looking at him, without letting myself be goaded or show any emotion. But my hatred kept growing; I wanted to kill this monster here and now.

He leaned back smiling: 'But I am in a good mood today. I'll make you a deal. Let us play this match: If you win, I'll let you live'.

And without further talk, he simply pushed his white soldier forward to e4.

I did not answer. I was a good chess player, but not great. I have memorized close to 300 of the most famous chess matches ever played, both as a training exercise on the Ultimate Study Method course, as well as a personal hobby; this usually gave me an edge over most players that were tactically better than me. But I had no idea how good Aivars was. On the other hand, why would it matter? He would probably try to have me killed either way, if I let him. I started playing, with my mind focused by the adrenalin-charged situation. I made my moves in a nearly second state, letting my mind work on intuition, weighing every move based on all the games I had ever memorized, as well as played. After a few moves, Aivars remarked: ' A Latvian Gambit, how appropriate'

If he knew that, he was good. The Latvian Gambit is a very aggressive opening defense for black against one of the most common openings for white. This opening is relatively surprising, as most masters refuse to give up pieces early on in a game. The great Bobby Fisher was once beaten by a neophyte as a result of this opening.

I did not reply; I just kept playing. Aivars was a very good player; but, today, I was focused like I had never been before. It was already 8:40, but he was intent on winning, oblivious. He had taken off his sunglasses, and was wiping the sweat off his forehead with a white monogrammed handkerchief. He had small, very blue eyes, but porcine in aspect because of his obesity. Suddenly those very clear blue eyes clouded, and I saw in them the shocking realization that he was about to be checkmated. I had played from memory a variation of the Latvian Gambit games I had memorized, and he had fallen for all the typical mistakes of great players.

He stood up, looking at his watch: 'I am afraid we shall have to finish this game later. We are on a schedule'. Aivars would never admit defeat, certainly not in public.

'But we are close, just a few more moves. We are playing for my life after all, aren't we'.

'Indeed, we are. But we can finish this later, or even by correspondence. You are in no hurry to die, are you?'.

I took another long look at the check board, committing it to memory. 'OK, we'll finish the game though. You are a man of your word'. I stood up slowly, and followed Aivars towards the bank. He was bulky, but moved surprisingly fast, a little like those Sumo wrestlers who are fat, but still consummate athletes. He was definitely not to be underestimated.

I saw Jan standing up and trying to pull Laura up. He stopped as I yelled at him: 'You do not move from here. I have a friend around. If Laura moves, disappears, gets in a car or is hurt, I am called at once and the deal is cancelled'.

I turned to Aivars: 'Let us get this thing done easy and fair; it will be better for everyone involved. You get the money and I need assurances that Laura stays OK'.

Aivars smiled condescendingly and signaled Jan to sit down. I could see that Jan did not like this one bit; he wanted to say something, but Aivars motioned him again. He was so sure of his sniper and his other foot soldiers around that he was probably looking forward to crush me after giving me this sliver of hope. I took out my cell phone, just to emphasize the point and I fell in step with him as we crossed the road and climbed the steps to the bank's gates. The two bodybuilder hulks were a few yards behind us, but stayed on the steps as we entered the bank. I checked my watch, starting to count fifteen minutes. The old security guard was at his post, and he just let us through the magnetometer portal, without standing up. I asked one of the attractive ladies at reception to let the manager know that a client was here to see him.

Not more than a minute later, George came in from a side door, looking nervous. He was anxious to get this over with; he was doing me a huge favor and not liking it one bit. I did a show of introducing myself, and Aivars just shook hands with him, looking him up and down, clearly surprised by the dress code. I hoped I was not overdoing it. George invited us to a conference room, behind another door of the lobby. It was a small room with a 6-seat glass table, chairs, two computers and a magnificent sea-view from a window spread across the entire back wall.

George sat behind one of the computer terminals that he activated, and asked: 'What can I do for you, gentlemen'.

'Simple. I am here to transfer the account left to my care by Alex Prilutski, to this man here'

George, as the consummate banker, stayed impassible. 'I need to see some identification, as well as some data. If we did have a Mr. Prilutski as a client, I assume you would be in possession of account numbers and passwords'

I took out my passport from my shirt pocket, and pushed it towards George. On its first page, there was a folded piece of paper with the account details. George had a look and scanned the passport in the scanner on his side of the table.

'That looks in order, Mr. Van Dijk. And you wish to sign off the account to this gentleman here?'

'Yes I do'

He turned to Aivars: 'I would need all your details, Sir, as well as a government- issued ID'.

Half-standing in his chair, and that was no easy task, Aivars took out his burgundy red Latvian passport and a small USB key from his trousers' right pocket. This required quite an effort. The cover of the passport had embossed in it the words: "EIROPAS SAVIENĪBA", obviously meaning European Union, and it made my stomach turn. 'My details are on the USB. But before you proceed, I want to know the amount of credit in the account'.

George looked at me: 'This is still your account, Mr. Van Dijk, do you mind?'

I nodded no, and George struck a few keys on his keyboard. 'Forty seven million two hundred and fifty three seven hundred and twenty two dollars US'.

Aivars did not show any emotion and simply said: 'OK, go ahead'.

George scanned the passport and gave it back, and then stuck the USB key into the computer below the table. After a few minutes of keyboard clicks, the printer on the side table whirred and threw out printed pages. How simple are things outside the regulated banking system. When I think how many trees had been felled just for the paperwork of my opening a checking account at my bank in New York… George stood up and brought the pages, three sets of three, to the table, asking Aivars to sign first, on all pages. After reading them all quickly, he signed all of them and pushed them towards me. I made a show of taking out my phone, again, and checking that no messages or calls had been made to it. I checked out the time, twenty minutes had passed. Surprisingly, Aivars did not comment or show any irritation. I then signed all the papers and handed them over to George, who signed and stamped them noisily. He looked at us, handed each one of a set of documents, and asked: 'The account is now Mr. Bertulis', exclusively. Anything else I can do for you, gentlemen?'

Aivars stood up: 'No thank you. We shall take our leave now. I'll be in touch to transfer the money'. He just turned and walked through the door into the lobby. I shook hands with George, saying Goodbye, and jogged after Aivars, while stuffing the papers in my pocket. I made sure I got to the bank gates before him, not a major challenge considering his bulk. As I stepped outside, the two bodyguards, still on the stairs looked up. I moved aside to let Aivars out, who did not look at me, muttering something in Latvian; for his microphone, I assumed. I looked in the distance and saw Laura sitting, with Jan one stone seat away, just as we left them.

I called out to Aivars, who was already taking a step down: 'Stop. Stay right where you are, Bartulis'. He turned slowly, his small eyes mere slits, astonished at my insolence. I continued: 'There is a sniper rifle aimed at you. If you move or retreat before Laura is safe, it will fire. If Jan moves towards her, it will shoot, both of you,- with you first. If your bodyguards move, you take the heat'.

Aivars looked up at me incredulously; how dared I threaten him? Everybody froze. He barked something in Latvian, probably along the lines of "take him out".

'As you can see, your sniper is out of commission. However, all of mine are not'.

Aivars started to run down the stairs, but stopped suddenly as a bullet struck the step below, making an audible thud and sending a rain of stone debris around, including onto Aivars's shinbones. The shot had been suppressed, usually difficult with sniper rifles, but not for SEALS experts and at this relatively short distance. Joshua was a professional, the kind only the SEALS can produce. The bodyguards were moving towards him and he shouted something in Latvian to stop them. He turned and glared at me: 'What do you want?'. I supposed he was still hoping his men from the outside perimeter would intervene. His hopes were dashed when he saw the turmoil around Laura.

Jan had edged closer to Laura as we exited the bank, and he turned his head sharply at the sound of the suppressed round. He was a soldier himself and recognized a sniper warning shot when he heard one. Although we were supposed to handle it through Aivars, Joao saw the opportunity and took it. He jumped out of the bushes around the chess corner of the park, and with two long strides he landed on top of Jan, controlling the hand holding the concealed gun. His friend Ze, disguised as a local gardener on account of his very dark skin, was on his heels to lift Laura and whisk her away. Merely a second later, another body crashed violently into the now struggling Jan.

I told Aivars: 'Tell your men not to intervene, if there are any left. We just want Laura safe'.

Aivars shouted in English: 'Stop everything, leave them alone. It is an order'.

I was watching Laura being carried away, by two men, towards a parked pick-up truck. Jan Thompson was lying on the floor, obviously disarmed, and no match for the young Brazilian street fighters. There was a passer-by looking on curiously and a lady sitting on a bench who did not seem to have noticed anything out of the ordinary.

'I do not want anything from you, Mr Bartulis, except for what we agreed. We have Laura, you can keep the money and go. Leave us alone. Tell all your people to retreat and walk slowly towards your limo. Then you can drive away and all is well'.

Aivars climbed down the stairs slowly, talking in his mike and followed by his two guards. Jan was up and limping towards the limo, and so were two other men from different sides of the park that must have been neutralized by Rui's team earlier on.

As Aivars reached the bottom of the stairs, he turned and looked at me, exuding malevolence; 'You realize this is not over?'. I did not answer.

A few minutes later, the limo drove away. I could not see through the tinted windows, but I had no friends in there and I thought I could feel the cold blue eyes staring through and plotting revenge. I sighed, weak at the knees. It was over.

The elegantly dressed lady, who had calmly sat reading on a wooden bench in the far side of the park during the entire affair, now stood up to leave. I had no idea that she was the one supposed to terminate Laura after the exchange. She was known by many names, including Alyssa Orlov.

Chapter 36

Qc7 Bxf2

Neptune Motel, Provinciales, Turks and Caicos

It was night already, and we were all back in the situation room, but for Joao, who was sitting in Laura's room to guard her as she slept her ordeal off; and but for Matt who was already on his way out of territorial waters, spiriting away the illegal ordinance. There was a reason why the SEALS were the best Special Forces in the world, and much of it was probably due to painstaking planning. Joshua had prepared this operation to the finest detail, and hence the resounding success. Matt had followed the limo from the park to the airfield from which Aivars, and his retinue, left in a private jet a few hours later.

No doubt Aivars was seething with anger, the loss of face being much more important to him than the money gained. I knew he had the money for which he came, but we still needed to be very careful. He had underestimated me, planning for, perhaps, an amateur friend or two to help me, but not for a small SEALS unit and five fighting-fit athletes. Aivars would definitely seek revenge, and he would not underestimate me ever again. I had gone back to the Airport Inn to pay my bill and fetch my bags, and then checked in with the team. When I arrived, Laura was already asleep, exhausted by her ordeal. After a fast food meal, she had been checked by a local doctor brought in by Rui, and cleared as healthy apart from a few bruises and the grogginess of having been drugged for a few days. The doctor had simply advised for a high intake of fluids, and maybe a saline drip while she slept, that she had refused.

Joshua insisted on debriefing everybody, as the veteran soldier he was, to verify that he had not overlooked anything. We were doing just that, but in a good-natured way; everybody had a beer can in hand.

We were planning to leave tomorrow, in two groups and on two different flights. One of Matt's contacts organized a fake landing card for Laura; it would have been difficult to explain to immigration on our way out how she managed to enter the country without them noticing. There was no way for us to come clean with regards to the events that transpired, even with the easy-going islanders. That is also the reason why Joshua had set the sniper and the two other incapacitated accomplices free after everything had gone down. He considered leaving them trussed up to be discovered with their decommissioned weapons by the local police, but decided against it to avoid extra general scrutiny at the airport.

It was time to relieve Joao, and I joined Ze for the walk; I was hoping to find Laura awake. Leaving the air-conditioned room, we were assailed by the warm and fragrant sea breeze; this closeness to Nature always gives you a feeling of well-being. No wonder the Caribbean was such a hot tourist attraction. Laura's room was around the corner. I was in a hurry to see her and maybe catch her awake and I walked in front. Just as I passed the corner, I noticed a cleaning cart in front of Laura's room and the door just closing. Alarm bells rang in my brain: There was something terribly wrong. There was no evening turn-down service in these cheap motels, no reason to come to clean at night, and certainly no reason for Joao to let anyone in. I broke in a run and turned the door handle. It was not locked, and I pushed the door open. It stopped at mid-way because a body on the floor was jamming it. I could still wiggle through, while peering inside. My heart again missed a beat: A woman in cleaning staff uniform was nearing Laura's bed, one hand extended towards Laura and the other reaching inside her pocket; Laura was waking up and attempting to sit up in her bed, startled by the commotion. The scene before me began unfolding in slow motion. I jumped into the room; the intruder heard the door and started turning back while extracting a syringe from her coat pocket; Laura opened her mouth to scream. To have come all this way to have Laura snatched from me again? No way!

The intruder pushed Laura back onto the bed while lifting her syringe, but I managed to jump her from behind. The best way to help somebody being aggressed, if you manage to creep behind the assailant, is to stomp on the back of his knee: He will buckle back and also momentarily lose control of his upper body movements because of the shift in balance. This had been drilled in me by Rui countless times, so I did not go for the syringe arm as instincts would normally dictate, at least not at first. I jumped, and in one leap from a few steps away, I was landing in a stomping kick to the back of this woman's knee. This had been the longest flying kick of my life. And the most important. The assailant was now on her knees, one of them crushed by my foot, with her upper body bent backwards and her arms flailing in the air. I caught the wrist of the hand holding the syringe, but she flexed her joint to stab me instead. I did not let go and I was pricked, but she could not push the plunger from this position. I was scared to death of this needle and the contents it was about to deliver, but I was more scared for Laura than myself. I did not let go. It was then that Laura sat up and caught the hand holding the syringe with both hands. She shook it, and then, in one move pushed the needle into the intruder's chest and pressed the plunger. For a moment, we stayed immobile in this position, the three of us, like a mythological sculpture. I could not see the intruder's eyes round in surprise and desperation, but I saw Laura's eyes, full of rage and shouting away something like: 'Enough'. What goes around comes around, doesn't it?

The woman shuddered and tensed, and let out a muffled cry. She went limp and I pushed her to the floor, looking around me. Ze who had followed me in, was bent over Joao's body. There was no other threat around. I checked the female assassin's pulse and found none, but, as overkill, I checked her for weapons. I found a stiletto in her pocket and an empty shoulder holster. Laura was getting up to go and check on Joao, but I restrained her gently: 'Stay back, just in case'. I went to Joao with a constricted heart, but I saw Ze's smile. I then noticed the taser gun lying on the floor by the door. Thank God, Joao was not shot, but shocked with a minor taser jolt. The assassin must have shot the darts as Joao opened the door and subsequently let go of the gun to administer the poison in a hurry. I heard Ze chuckling in Portuguese and I gathered the general meaning, something not politically correct about sissies being put down by women. I locked the door and went back to Laura; I had to take her in my arms. We hugged in silence, but clutching strongly to one another. I was extatic to hold her safe; there was no doubt I was head-over-heels in love with that woman. After a few minutes, we let go and looked down at the would-be assassin.

'There is no doubt that this is Alex's killer' she said.

'And probably Jack's'. I do not know what went over me, but I spat on the corpse. And it made me feel better. I stood up and kicked the corpse: 'And many others. May she rot in hell! She will be no weight on my conscience'.

Laura limped to Joao who was standing up on wobbly legs. I took out my phone to call Joshua, who appeared at the door a few second later. He surveyed the room.

'We have to get out of here. They know where we are. And we have to get rid of this body; we are in no position to submit ourselves to a police investigation right now, even if it was blatant self-defense. I do not know what the United Kingdom's position is on vigilantism, but I do not expect it to be favorable'

Laura said: 'She died of the heart attack she wanted to give me. We could just place her in her hotel room'

I intervened: 'I already checked. She has no identification on her, no hotel key, nothing'

Joshua settled it: 'We can just drop her somewhere on a quiet beach. It will just look like a heart attack while sunbathing or something. We'll leave the syringe around to make it look like drugs, just in case. I hope they will not notice the busted knee. Anyway, we should be long gone before all checks are made. Laura you go and buy her a bikini at the all-night tourist shops on the promenade. You'll go with three men around, they will help you. The others will pack up and check out. We'll drive around until morning and fly out as early as possible'.

Chapter 37

Rxe8 Rxe8

The Prometheus Foundation, Washington County, New York State

Two days later, I was lying in Laura's bed. I was wide awake, and looking at the ceiling in the growing light of the dawn creeping through the curtains. We did not encounter any more problems since the attack. The lady killer-for-hire was dumped on a deserted beach, in bikini and lying on a big beach towel, with sunglasses and a hat on her face. The empty syringe was left under the towel. Hopefully, they would make the link with the missing tourist in one of the hotels, unless she had arrived with Aivars on the private jet. After driving around, stopping occasionally for drinks and enjoying the sea air, we arrived at the airport early and returned the two rented SUV's. After a hearty breakfast, we were ready to fly back home. At the airport, we took leave from one another with the effusive goodbyes of people who had been through a life changing experience together. Back on the continent, we still had Rui's people looking out for us discreetly, and we now had increased their shifts to include Laura. In other news, Joao's nickname was now the

Brazilian equivalent of "pussy-whipped", and, for that reason alone, I was inclined to pay him a special bonus.

Laura handed her notice to the Bureau. She was reprimanded for disappearing and not showing up for the all-important bureaucratic meetings. Of course, she was unable to divulge information about the kidnapping ordeal because of the way we had handled it: She would have had to give names and questions would have ensued about the money for the exchange, the weapons, the falsification of immigration papers and more. So Laura invoked a crippling breakdown, which naturally led to the conclusion that she was not fit for this job. Laura had liked the idea of law enforcement, but the reality of it was far from her idealistic aspirations. She was happy to have found her way with autism care, and was looking forward to the set-up of our venture. She was still formally an FBI agent for another 2 months, but on leave; she was therefore still plugged in on the case.

I crossed my fingers behind my neck, stretching. We would have to be careful. There was no doubt that Aivars Bartulis was a rotten and vindictive man. He had his money, but he would want revenge, not only for Turks and Caicos, but also for the destruction of his financial empire. I had been naïve in thinking I could buy him off with Alex's money. At least, I now had his personal details, and I would endeavor to neutralize him if I found a way. I had financial resources at my disposal and so I began considering a whole range of options, all the way to hired killers.

Joshua Applebee was keeping his son company ever since we came back. He had delightfully informed us that he was in with us in our venture, pending legal review. After last week, I was definitely happy to have him on board. I had been jealous of having him around Laura, but he was a resourceful and deeply moral man. He had dropped by my office yesterday with news from his cyber-security friend. He explained that they definitely found hacked hardware, but that it was difficult to retro-engineer. The design was at modern science's edge, certainly not a prank by an amateur hacker nor a backdoor designed by the manufacturer. And the special chip design had been found in a few random top-of-the-line computers.

We were urged to keep quiet about it until the facts became clearer, but it looked like his son, autistic Tom, had cracked open a matter of National Security.

I yawned, and looked at Laura still sleeping. She had taken back a few of the pounds lost since her ordeal. She looked fine, but I had no idea about the psychological effects of a kidnapping. She was a strong woman and I hoped for the best. I loved her with all my heart.

Today, I had to drive in the City to meet Eli Rosenthal about my legal woes. I intended to get the new company rolling in the same meeting. I also needed to check up on my trades, and would most likely need to rebalance my positions. I slipped quietly out of bed to go to shower.

Once refreshed and dressed, I re-entered the room silently. Laura was waking up.

'Where did you go, handsome? I thought you left me'.

I went to the bed to kiss her.

'The thought crossed my mind, but I owe you my life'

'So do I'

'We are even then? I can go?'

'Do not even try'

'OK. I am driving to the lawyers today, but I promise I'll be back'. I kissed her again, and it became difficult to detangle myself. I had to push her away.

'Jezebel! You also have work to do. Get up. See you tonight'.

Twenty minutes later, I was driving away, with a big thermal flask full of coffee I had brewed quickly in my office. I had also grabbed and wolfed a croissant from the cafeteria. I would have to stop for a real breakfast when I got to the city. My cell rang, interrupting my prandial fantasies; it was Rui.

'Good morning my good friend'

'Bom dia, Olivier. You are still, or again, being followed. This time, it is the guy with the broken nose who was with Jan Thompson in your flat. What do you want to do?'

'Which car does he drive and how far behind me is he?' So, they were already back on our case. That had not taken long; I was hoping for more time to complete my plan.

'Always three or four cars behind. It is a white Volkswagen Passat. Connecticut plates'. He gave me the number which I committed to memory.

'OK. I'll have the cops pick him up'. That will dilute their ranks and maybe cause the FBI to rethink our protection; but it was worrying nonetheless. Aivars was already whipping something up.

I signed off and immediately scrolled down for Agent Dave Freeman's number. He picked up on the second ring.

'Hi Dave. Olivier Van Dijk here. I have one of the suspects, whom you are hard-at-work looking for, tailing me right now. This is one of Jan Thompson accomplices; you know, the ones that you told me are too busy hiding to threaten me. This guy was working in the security section of the Fund. I do not recall his name, but he has a boxer's nose that is hard to miss'

'Are you certain?'

I was thinking: 'You bureaucratic idiot', but instead I answered calmly: 'I am positive. He is driving a white Volkswagen Passat, a few cars behind me. Plates: 972-PRZ. I am just south of Greenwich on the I95. Thank you for letting me know when you have arrested him'.

And I cut off, for fear of letting myself become more than just impolite. I am not a great supporter of big government, but, I had to admit that Mr. Dave Freeman could be better than the average bureaucrat. Less than fifteen minutes later, I heard a police siren a few cars behind me, for what looked like a routine stop. I slowed down to let the cars behind me overtake, and then I saw a white Passat stopping on the embankment. I pulled over to the shoulder, in order to watch the events in my rear view mirror. The two cops, very careful and alert, had him step out of the vehicle. It was definitely the bastard. They made him lean with his hands against the car, frisked him, found a gun in a side holster, handcuffed him, and then whisked him away. Curious drivers were slowing down to have a look. For them, it was a show; for me: a one down on the scoreboard. I thoroughly enjoyed seeing him being assisted into the back of the police cruiser, in that typical "mind-your-head-please-sir"- move. I gave the finger to the bastard as the police car drove by, sirens blaring. The cop at the wheel shot me a dark look.

I was glad to have been proactive, but this meant that we were far from safe. It was a chilling thought I entertained while easing back into the traffic towards Manhattan.

***

It was already nine p.m. and I was on my way back to the Foundation. I had spent the whole day with lawyers, and I could not think of anything more taxing, -quite literally. Eli's team had done a great job, I must admit, but why did I have to hear about every little detail. It looked like I would be able to avoid prison, for an agreed suspended sentence and community service. It also appeared I could keep working in my profession. Of course, there were huge fines, back taxes, retributions; and did I mention lawyers' fees? I had readily agreed to the settlement, provided reasonable installments could be agreed upon. I was now much more confident that I would be able to handle the legal and financial sides of my ordeal.

I used the lawyers' lunch break to do some trading analysis in one of their conference rooms, and things were really looking up. I also called workaholic Laura to tell her about the morning incident. She promised to call her still-but-not-for-much-longer-colleagues at the Bureau to again request better protection. I also had Eli draft contracts for our new venture, which I immediately e-mailed to Laura and to Joshua. Eli was impressed with my resilience and enquired about investing with us. Quite a vote of confidence, from a conservative guy like Eli!

I was now on the phone with Rui, checking about increased protection, in view of the fact that our enemies were still sniffing around. He told me that he had Joao and Zeca around the compound tonight, and Ze joining them up in the morning. We still had one marshal at the gate in permanence and two security guards hired from an outside company. Rui mentioned that we would soon have to find a more permanent solution to our security woes, and I knew that what he meant could not be discussed over the phone. We had started discussing contracting some of his old Brazilian Underworld contacts, but I had big problems with going down that road.

At the entrance to the compound, I was stopped by the marshal. It was a new officer, pretty young, who asked me for identification and went all formal on me. He was only doing his job but that, together with his Hollywood actor's good looks, made me irritable. I passed another guard, private security this time, at Anna's reception desk. Was this going to be my life from now on, surrounded by a private army?

Laura was still in her office, wearing her doctor coat and clicking away as though there was no tomorrow. Did I mention workaholic? I still had some trading work to complete, so we agreed to meet upstairs forty five minutes later. We both wanted an early night, so we decided against eating out. I would bring up a few snacks and we would have a night cap during which I would tell her about the fruits of my day.

By twelve o'clock we were sound asleep, with the worries of survival pushed aside to the start of a fresh new day.

How wrong!

Chapter 38

Rf1 Bd4

The Prometheus Foundation, Washington County, New York State

Joao was jogging around the compound, making use of this surveillance assignment to work on his stamina. He was in phone contact with Zeca, sitting on his bike with a clear view of the gate. It was 2:30 a.m. He got a call from Zeca about some activity on the north east perimeter of the compound; it looked like a car coming from the North had stopped in the vicinity. Joao asked him to stay in place with full view of the Foundation gates. He estimated he was about five to ten minutes away from the area; he ended the call and increased his running pace.

Zeca had been right. After about five minutes, Joao started slowing down while looking very carefully around the perimeter. He saw a big 4x4 parked deep into the side of the road, under trees, and he would have missed it if he had not been looking for it really hard. The owner had even placed a few leafed branches and shrubs on it for very primitive dissimulation. Joao approached carefully and made sure there was nobody inside the car, a black Range Rover. The car was empty, but Joao did not dare check if it was locked, lest it triggered the alarm system. He took out his knife and punctured all 4 tires, just in case. He then ran towards the compound wall opposite the car and checked the ground for tracks. He found them, not exactly opposite the car, but a little further North; it was clear that the weeds had been trampled and a ladder had been set against the wall. The events that the tracks implied were ominous. Joao took out his cell phone. He first dialed Zeca: 'There are intruders over the wall. Stay in place for coordination, call Rui for reinforcements and be careful'.

He then dialed Olivier.

***

My cell phone resting on the nightstand rang twice. I extended my hand to take the phone, but by the time I reached it, it already had stopped ringing. I looked at Laura; she stirred, changed position, but kept sleeping. I looked at the digital clock of the Sony Dream Machine on Laura's nightstand; it was 2:41 am. I was instantly fully awake: A call at his hour could only mean trouble. The screen showed a missed call from Joao. I remembered that Joao was on duty around the Foundation today; this smelled like a problem. The portentous eerie stillness signaled ill-boding events were about to unfold. I stood up while hitting the "call back" button, but nothing happened. I checked the phone, and I noticed that there were no signal bars, absolutely none, which was very strange. The coverage in this area was very good, with an antenna not far away. Throughout the years I have spent out here, I do not recall anytime at which there was zero cell coverage- not even once. I ran out of the flat, dressed in my bed clothes: boxers and a T-shirt, and went for the stairs. As I passed the first floor's glass doors, I saw lights in the big room and, on impulse, ran in. From the gallery, I could see that Tom was at his computer, and his caretaker was sleeping on the couch behind him. Tom was a night owl, and this was not unusual. I climbed down the stairs and approached him.

***

Zeca was watching the gates with his binoculars, trying hard to see if anything was going awry there, but with no success. The guard was in his booth, watching TV, and there did not seem to be any activity around the building itself. Zeca had called Rui, awakened him and told him about the intruders, but the call had been interrupted in mid-sentence. Since then, he had not been able to get any cellular service. Communications were down. Zeca was worried, but he was torn between staying at his post as ordered by Joao, and taking some action. Something was definitely wrong, intruders and cell phone jamming all together, that could not be a coincidence. He decided to go in and check things out. He went for the dirt bike parked down the hill he had, moments ago, used as an observation spot, and ruffled into the back side-bags. He found what he was looking for after a few seconds. But as his fingers closed on the handle of his Colt 45, he heard a noise behind him and instinctively started turning around. His head exploded before he completed half a turn. The damage of a hollow point bullet at close range was horrifying: pieces of skull and brain covered his bike as a nearly headless Zeca crumbled to the floor. The shot had been suppressed, so no-one heard a sound, except for the muffled pop savored by the killer alone.

A minute or two later, a black GMC van stopped in front of the Foundation gates. The young marshal opened the booth window and asked the driver to identify himself. The driver, an Asian man, left the vehicle with an unfolded map in his hand, clearly at a loss for directions. 'Could you help me to find the way to Greenwich, Sir?'

He approached the window.

'Easy, sir. No need for the map'

But the hand behind the map held a silenced Glock 17 pistol, and the helpful young marshal was dead before he realized something was wrong. A few minutes later, two vans were in the driveway, while the main gate was being locked with the heavy rolling barrier. Lights in the guard booth were switched off. For all intents and purposes, the property was now cut off from the outside world.

Chapter 39

Rxf3 Bxc3

The Prometheus Foundation, Washington County, New York State

I came over to Tom and asked him gently: 'Can you display the feed from the security cameras on the screen?'. Tom did not look at me, but after a few clicks, I could see the screen divided into sixteen images. I looked at the screen intently, as did Tom. In the lower row of images, I could see four people at the services and deliveries side door, fumbling with the lock. That was it! I was now sure we were under attack. Again; so soon… I put my hand on Tom's shoulder and told him: 'These are bad people. We have to go. Come with me'. Instead of standing up, he pointed with his finger at an image in the top row. This was the entrance lobby and it was suddenly crawling with people. I counted eight men, all clad in black, with balaclavas, and holding weapons. On top of everything, the security guard behind the reception desk looked as if he was greeting them rather than being alarmed. Eight and four makes twelve. A situation already dire was getting worse. I saw the guard fumble with the contacts behind the desk, and suddenly the screen went blank. He was definitely in league with the intruders and had cut off the security cameras' feed.

I took Tom by the arm and pulled him up; all the while I checked my cell phone and found that there was still no service. There were landline phones in the offices, but we needed to stay hidden. I decided to try and reach the patient's quarters. I told Tom, and his now fully awakened caretaker to follow me to his flat. From what I had seen on the security cameras, the way should be clear. Once we arrived safely to Tom's flat, I locked the door and went for the phone. To my desperation, the line was dead. Of course, they would not go through all this trouble of cell phone jamming and forget to cut the land lines. I slammed the phone down and asked Tom, who was now sitting on his bed, with the frightened caretaker besides him: 'No phone lines, no cellular service. Anyway you could contact your dad through all these computers, Tom?'. This boy was a wizard with anything electronic.

Tom looked at me and responded with a laconic: 'Yes'. He stood up, took a laptop and a cable from his room work desk, cluttered with another two laptops and several blinking boxes and gizmos. He went directly for the flat's door, with the caretaker and myself following behind. He turned right into the hallway; that was good because it was away from the access area; though I kept looking behind us, just in case. Three doors from his flat, there was a utility room, used for storing cleaning materials, equipment, supplies, trolleys and the like. We followed Tom inside and locked the door. At the back of the room, there were bunches of cables and pipes passing through, all annotated and marked using a non-trivial indexing system. Tom did not hesitate; he simply opened a side box, and plugged his computer cable in. After a few clicks, I heard Joshua's concerned voice on the computer: 'What happened? Is that you Tom?'.

Tom answered: 'It is Tom'.

I cut in, talking in the general direction of the laptop: 'Joshua. It's Olivier. We are in trouble at the Foundation. We are under attack by thirteen people on the last count. Phones and cells are down. Tom is safe, but we need help'

'I am on my way. Tom, get me the security cams feed through to my laptop. And Olivier…'

'Yes'

'Please keep Tom safe'

'Will do. Hurry and call the Brazilians, some of them should be around here at the compound'.

Tom had heard us, and already displayed the previously cut security feed on his screen. I had no idea how he could do that; most likely he tapped into the original feed before the point at which it reached the guard's control room. But for Tom, electronic maps were like a children book for us. This young man was a regular Merlin. From browsing through the pictures, the situation looked calamitous. The group of eight ninja look-alikes was fanning out into several rooms of the ground floor, including the big room. The four intruders from the side door were now in, and were separating into two groups. They were communicating with signs and were now standing in clear view of the security camera. They were hoodless and one of them was in fact my new-found nemesis, Jan Thompson. There was now no doubt that this was an assassination attempt. From the hand moves, I understood the meaning of their separation and my heart froze: two of them were going towards the big room, and Jan accompanied by one accomplice was going up. It was not difficult to guess who the targets were and what their intended fates should be. I turned to Tom and told him quietly: 'Tom. From now on, silence. Communicate with your dad only by text. And send him the security feed as soon as you can'. I turned to the caretaker, a Hispanic middle aged man, visibly scared to death: 'I am going to take care of this. Lock the door behind me. Do not open it under any circumstances. No lights, Tom can work with the illumination of his screen, but make him stay only at the back in total silence. I repeat: No noise, no lights, OK?'.

As he nodded, I rushed out of the room. I heard the lock and I saw the lights go off under the door. I ran through the hallways, as fast as I could. I was barefoot and therefore relatively quiet. I had decided on what I needed to do. I reached the side door through which Jan had come in; it was unlocked.

***

Joao climbed the wall at the same spot from which the intruders had made their entrance. And he found the folding ladder they had used lying in the grass at the base of the wall. The walls were supposed to have sensors built-in, but they had either been disconnected, or this was a blind spot. Either way, the fact was that those people were inside and the occupants were in danger. Joao checked his cell again, but still no service bars icon on the screen. He hoped Zeca had managed to summon help, though he had no choice but to try to mitigate the situation. He started running in a crouched position towards the building, attempting to discern the shapes of the intruders. He thought he saw some movement on the left side of the building, and accelerated in that direction, as low as humanely possible, and using the bushes as cover. As he got closer, he saw that the side door, often used for deliveries, was opened and there was a human form entering. The door was closing behind it, and Joao had no idea if the guy was alone or not. Joao kneeled for an instant to recover his breath and evaluate the situation. He looked around. Suddenly, the silence was broken by two vans coming down the driveway towards the main entrance. What was happening? Things were going from bad to worse. He felt the urge to do something, but what? Joao ran to the side door, and pulled out the gun he carried on his back, held by his belt. He listened carefully in the direction of the door and heard some whispering and shuffling. He decided the best tactic would be to go in behind them and try to get them one by one, guerilla-style. He checked his watch, and just as he was ready to go, the door burst open.

Chapter 40

bxc3 Re2+

The Prometheus Foundation, Washington County, New York State

Jan knew the building well, and he knew most override codes as well as all security protocols. He even had a master key. He sent two of his men to check Olivier's office, as he knew he often worked late and frequently slept on the couch. He actually expected him to sleep in one of the serviced flats on the second floor though, probably with that Laura slut. He would start with the flat Olivier usually settled in, and then the largest one that was used by the woman psychiatrist, or at least had been used while he was still Head of Security at the Fund. Aivars wanted them dead, both of them, and did not care for collateral damage. He had not requested that Jan Thompson do the job, but Jan wanted to lead the men himself; Laura and Olivier were responsible for the obliteration of his most profitable business venture ever, and they had made him lose the complete confidence in which his employer once held him. He would enjoy killing them both. Aivars had insisted that the job be done fast after the Islands fiasco; it was his rule never to appear weak or hesitant. Vengeance and retribution had to be swift, even if reason counseled patience. As an experienced chess player, Aivars knew he should have planned ahead and taken his time. *La vengeance est un plat qui se mange froid.* Vengeance is a dish best *eaten* cold as the French say. But as a mob boss, he had to show all those who knew him that he was ruthless. This was something Jan could easily understand.

Jan was using the back stairs to accede to the second floor. He heard more people walking around than he was expecting, but he kept going, treading as silently as possible. Even if they were discovered, he was intent on completing his mission. At the first floor, he and his accomplice had to cross the width of the entire floor to reach the back stairs to the second floor. They heard doors opening and closing, and more walking-around noises. At the base of the stairs, Jan took out his cell to call the other two, sent to Olivier's office, and check in. He was deeply troubled as he noticed the strangest thing: There was no reception. None at all. No emergency service, nothing. He put the phone back in his pocket, irritated. Technology always betrayed you when you needed it the most, though he began to feel, in the back of his mind, the tingling of something more sinister taking place. He signaled his acolyte and they started climbing the stairs to the second floor. The hallway was empty, and they went directly for Olivier's usual flat. The door was locked, but Jan had a master key from his old days. He opened the door slowly, hoping it would not creak, and entered the dark room with his silenced pistol held forward. This flat was a one-room version, except for the bathroom. Olivier's bags were there, so it was definitely occupied by him; but there was nobody in the bed. Jan checked the bathroom, it was empty too. It suggested Olivier was either in his office or in Laura's room. Jan checked the cell phone again, still no service. OK, Laura's room then.

He signaled, and they both exited the room silently, locking it back behind them. The apartment which Laura had obtained when he was still in charge was at the end of the hallway. It was the largest and best-appointed. Jan heard some muffled noise, again; he even imagined he heard glass breaking somewhere. Something was going on and they had to hurry. They walked faster, but carefully, to the door, and Jan used his master key again to unlock it. Surprisingly, it was unlocked. How could people be so stupid? Jan pushed the door open slowly. Nothing happened. He was looking forward to exact his revenge. He peeked carefully inside: It was all dark and quiet. This was a three-room apartment and the bedroom was at the end. He entered slowly, followed by his accomplice who closed the door behind them. This apartment was definitely occupied. The first room was an entrance lobby coupled with a kitchenette, and it was clearly in use. Jan steered the way through the opening leading to the lounge and eating corner, his gun extended forward, in anticipation of the sweet dispatching of his enemies. He was wolfishly smiling in the dark.

Chapter 41

Kh1 Be4

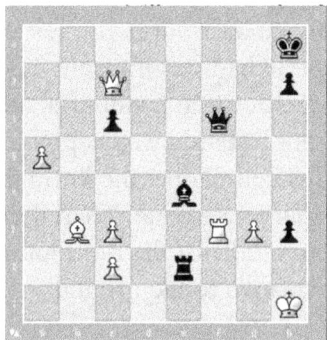

The Prometheus Foundation, Washington County, New York State

Jan's other two thugs had already checked the big room and were now climbing the stairs to the mezzanine gallery. From there they would go across the hall and to the aisle with Olivier's office. Both had their handguns out. Both were ex-Fund employees, recruited by Jan for both Fund work and outside tasks. One of them, named Eduards, was of Latvian heritage, thrust upon Jan by one of Aivars' lieutenants. The other one, blue-blooded American, was an enforcer named Matthew.

The door to the gallery suddenly opened and they found themselves face-to-face with two men, fully clad in black, with balaclavas, and holding pistols with suppressors. Matthew was in front and lifted his Colt 45 in reflex, but before he could point the weapon towards the unknown newcomers, he was shot twice in the head. The suppressed double tap was even more frightening because of the lack of noise. Eduards saw the back of his friend's head explode. He lifted his hands in surrender as Matthew was falling back on him, and that is probably what saved him. As he fell down the stairs under his friend's body, he let go of the gun. The two attackers were running down the stairs just behind them, and kept their guns aimed at him.

Eduards did not feel the pain of the tumble on the metal stairs; he was shrieking: 'I surrender, I surrender' in badly-accented English. One of the intruders pulled Matthew's body from him, while the other was holding the silenced Glock 17 to his face. Eduards was turned over on his belly, and, irrationally, felt good about it: it was concealing the fact that he had wet himself. They tied his hands behind his back with plastic strap handcuffs, and tightened them hard. It hurt like hell, but Eduards was happy to be alive. They frisked him and took his cell phone, the knife that was strapped to his lower leg and his spare magazine. Then they lifted him to his feet, leading him to the middle of the big room, towards Number 3's lounge, where he was thrown to the ground.

Eduards was lying on his belly on the carpet, scared like never before in his life. He was a bully who enjoyed terrorizing ordinary people, but he had never been on the other side of the equation. He heard a commotion upstairs and lifted his cranked neck to see three or four people with their hands in the air, being led down quietly by another two men in black. What was going on here?

**

I pushed the side door of the building and ran outside; there was no time to spare. But someone kicked my rear foot as I stepped out and I crashed on the floor. I rolled immediately sideways into ground guard, but the silhouette rushing me stopped in his tracks.

'Olivier, is it you?'

I recognized Joao. As he helped me onto my feet, I told him: 'No time to lose. Jan is on his way to kill Laura. Do you have a gun?'

'Yes. Take it'. He handed me his Beretta.

'Joshua is on his way. He has the feed from the security cameras'. I waved at the camera, just to make sure Tom and his dad would see us. 'Stay here and wait for them here. There are thirteen armed bad guys inside; no way you can fight them alone. But first come with me, I need you to help me jump up'.

I led Joao further away along the side of the building where there were metal fire escape stairs, which last leg was reeled up to the first floor. I placed Joao under the closest first floor balcony, and had him place his interlocked fingers in front of him, his cupped hands at groin level. This is the typical position of what in French is called *la courte echelle,* the short ladder. I told him: 'As I put my foot in your hands, push up. Then wait for us'. I took a few steps back for greater impetus, ran towards him and stepped into his cupped hands. From this position and with his help I jumped up, used my other foot on his shoulder for more power and took off. I caught the side of the balcony, pulled myself up on the stone banister, and used the momentum to jump towards the metal emergency stairs. I climbed them three by three and, once the second floor was reached, I kept climbing the metal construction holding the ladder up to get to the roof top. For an experienced *parkour* practitioner, this was a piece of cake. The cornice of the roof was ornate and wide, as was the common architectural design of the previous century; so I ran fast towards the front of the building, until I was above the balcony of Laura's flat. An easy jump, I remarked as I was looking into her lounge through the open curtains. I was making good time, but I was not there yet. Without hesitation, I used Joao's gun to break a window pane and clean the edges, then I opened the large window using the inside lever. I heard Laura getting up, and whispered as loud as I thought was safe: 'It's me, Olivier. Do not be scared. But we are in danger'.

We met at the bedroom door. 'Take the gun and stay behind the open door until someone comes in. It is Jan, and he is not alone. I'll take out the second guy as he enters the room. Shoot if you have to'. She was now fully awake and looked more pissed than scared. She was an FBI agent after all. She did as I said and flattened herself behind the door. I took the baseball bat near the bed and went to do as Laura, but besides the opening leading from the kitchen to the lounge. A minute or two later, I heard shuffling near the door, then tiny lock noises, until they realized the door was not locked. I heard the moving sound of the door handle being pressed, and finally of the door opening slowly. I tensed and waited. They took their time, closed the door and advanced carefully. I slowed my breathing as I have done countless times during the meditation sessions that concluded many martial art classes, and I tried to enter the *zone*, as fighters do before a fight to let their body switch to autopilot mode. A form passed in front of me, gun pointed forward. I flattened myself even more onto the wall, if it was at all possible. I recognized Jan's silhouette, and I felt he was so malevolently intent on the bedroom door that he could not have noticed me, even if I had stood in the middle of the room. As he came close to the bedroom's open door, the second assailant came in view. He also had his gun-holding hand extended forward. Bad idea. I exploded into action, putting all my power into a downward strike to his wrist. I was holding the baseball bat with two hands and had lifted it as high as possible. The power of a strike being the mass times *the square* of the acceleration, this meant it was a crippling blow. I heard the bones crack, and the gun fall to the floor. However, that was not all I had in store for him. I kept the momentum of the strike uninterrupted after it had gone literally through his wrist, and I started doing a full turn on myself, adding the muscles of my waist into a follow-up strike. I lifted the bat as I pivoted and struck the back of his head horizontally. You cannot pack much more power than with a spin-back like this, and the resounding thud of his skull was sickening. I did not know at the time, but it came very close to a killing blow. I did not care: they were here to murder us. Jan Thompson was at the bedroom door when he heard the commotion and started turning around, waving his gun. But he felt the cold steel of Laura's gun on his neck before he could react and heard her shouting: 'Drop it. NOW!'. I had already dived below the line of fire. Jan was so frustrated that he hesitated a second, but a thrusting hit of Laura's gun to the back of his skull reminded him of the odds. He dropped the gun and lifted his hands above his head. I came forward; carefully circling around, as Laura ordered him: 'On your knees, hands on your head'. Jan went down on one knee, and then stumbled as he went down on the second, losing some balance and leaning forward. But he was not, as we would have wanted us to believe, clumsy or scared to death. Jan was a highly trained mercenary, and, as he straightened up to compensate, he pivoted while hitting the much-too-extended hand which Laura was using to hold the gun. He immediately followed by rolling forward and diving through the wall opening. Laura's weapon discharged loudly, shaking us both. I bent to recover Jan's gun, but before we could both react, Jan had run out through the door. I rushed in pursuit, holding his gun I had collected from the floor. He turned left at the door, in the direction of the back stairs. As I got to the door, I saw him come to a halt at the end of the hallway, and then suddenly crumble to the floor. I looked on, struck in place by surprise, and saw one of the men in ninja-like outfits come around the corner, and shoot Jan in the head from close up. A *coup de grace,* making sure he was dead. There was no noise, as the weapon was silenced. Soon a second man in black appeared, and I took this as my cue to scuttle. I retreated to the doorway, deeply shaken. What was happening? I had previously surmised those were all working together. I withdrew further and closed the door quietly, locking it. I had no idea what was going on, but we had to get the hell out of Dodge, fast. They certainly had heard the gun shot and were bound to come in and check. I ran to Laura, and whispered: 'More killers. Follow me. Quickly'.

I took her by the hand and ran to the balcony. I climbed on the banister and it took me only a few seconds to climb back on the roof. I told Laura to climb on the banister and to wait for me to pull her up, which I did lying on the roof cornice.

Once we were both standing on the roof, I told her intently: 'Do not look down. Look at my back and follow. The cornice is as wide as a regular pavement'. She did not answer, gritted her teeth and came after me. I stopped over the emergency stairs and started climbing down. 'That is easy. Just do as I do, carefully'. It was quite easy, very much like ladder climbing, and much less scary. A minute later, we were on the second floor platform and started climbing down the stairs. At the first floor platform, it was just a question of unlocking the last flight of stairs to the ground, as one would in an emergency. In fact, it strangely crossed my mind that it really was an emergency. Joao was waiting for us on the ground, masked in the shadows.

I told him: 'Protect Laura, please. She has your gun. Wait for Joshua, and Rui, in the bushes near the side entrance. I am going back in'

'What? Are you crazy?' Laura exclaimed

'Tom is inside. As well as all the staff. These people are cold-blooded killers. I have to do something. I'll check with Tom the situation on the security cameras and he'll text Joshua. I'll be very careful. But I have to do something'. And I had promised Joshua to take care of Tom.

I swiftly ran away before she could retort. I approached the side door carefully, but there appeared to be no movement outside. They were probably all inside, trusting the locked-up gates to contain any intrusion. I opened the door slowly and took a peek inside. All was clear and so I ran inside. I stopped at the corner, peeked carefully around and jogged towards the utility room door. I knocked lightly and was surprised to see the door open nearly at once. The caretaker closed and locked it behind me, and whispered: 'Tom saw you coming on the camera'.

I nodded and asked him in the same whispering voice: 'Did they check around here'

'Yes. They opened every room and took out everybody at gun point. This room was locked and marked with a 'high voltage danger' icon so they assumed it is not occupied. Anyway, come look at the laptop, they are rounding people up like cattle'.

I went over to Tom and had a look over his shoulder at the screens. They had gathered all the staff in the center of the big room, most of them wearing their night clothes and all of them with their wrists tied with plastic handcuff wires, usually bound at the front of their bodies. Not that they were flight risks: Those people were regular workers, scared to death, and surrounded by six armed terrorists, for any better qualification. I counted in my head: nine bad guys minus six makes three, still roaming around. Jan and his accomplice were dead or as good as dead, so maybe another two. I asked Tom, who did not look worried at all: 'Have you heard from your dad?'

'Yes'

I forgot you have to be very specific when questioning Tom. 'Did he tell you how far he is?'

'Five minutes'

'Did he see the camera feed?'

'Yes'

I was watching the video stream from the big room, and asked Tom to zoom on the crumpled form at the bottom of the stairs. No doubt that the body was that of another one of Jan's acolytes. One more down. I checked around the room but saw no more bodies. I screened the prisoners slowly, about thirty people, and found the fourth member of Jan's team, with his hands tied behind the back. OK, this team of bad guys was out. But what were those other guys all about? Could Aivars have sent two competing teams? And for what purpose? It didn't make sense for him to do that. Is it part of a strategy I am still failing to understand?

One of the ninja look-alikes was stuttering in front of the prisoners, as if giving a speech. I asked Tom if he could hack into the microphone system we had in the big room, designed to listen to the patients from Jack's and Laura's offices. As usual, Tom did not reply, he simply clicked away. It took him several minutes, but suddenly we were hearing what was going on in the *big room*. The sound was not very good, muffled and resonating, but I was able to make sense of most of it.

Chapter 42

Qc8+ Kg7

The Prometheus Foundation, Washington County, New York State

Joshua had conducted a rapid drive around the property and detected Jan's car parked on the side of road. After seeing the four flat tires, he was sure it was the place from which the intruders had breached the perimeter. Joshua was in a hurry. He had called Rui for reinforcements, but it was a much longer journey to get here from New York City. He parked a few yards away on the side of the road, took out his big haversack from the back of the SUV and ran to the wall. He had no time for niceties; Tom was somewhere in there with very dangerous people. He threw his bag over the wall and simply climbed it, hoping the sensors were not active; which was probable, given the other intruders had used the area too. Joshua had been looking at the feed from the security cameras on his way over here, and he had gathered the general information from Tom. But he was now going in blind; the cell phone jammer was cutting his lines of communication. Joshua jumped in from the top of the wall, rolled to break the fall, retrieved his bag and started running towards the side door where he knew Laura and Joao were waiting. As he got close to the door, but still in the garden, Joao stood up to signal him. They kneeled and Laura joined them. Joshua zipped the haversack open and showed them a full armory.

'Take what you feel most comfortable with'. There were three handguns, one shotgun and two rifles. Joshua had also packed a truncheon, a telescopic stick and a knife. Laura had handed Joao his gun back, so she took a small Beretta 22, with a full magazine of those small caliber bullets. She also went for the telescopic baton. Joao took the shotgun and a box of cartridges. Joshua picked up the Magnum 357 revolver, for its stopping power.

'I have no silencers, so we must try to first neutralize as many as possible quietly', Joshua whispered. 'I'll try to get Tom and Olivier out'. He ran, crouching, to the side door and made "come out"-gestures to the security cam, hoping that Tom and Olivier would see him.

***

The man in black speaking was obviously the leader. He had a silenced pistol in a black shoulder holster, and was addressing the cluster of frightened Foundation employees, concentrated in the big room. The cooks, caretakers, technicians, cleaners and patients were sitting on the carpet in the lounge area of Number 3. They all had their hands tied in front of them with plastic straps. Patient Number 1 was shaking and rolling his eyes, and his caretaker, sitting beside him was trying to soothe him in a low voice. Patient Number 3 was crying and mumbling, alone; his designated caretaker was sitting a few places away and too scared to do anything about it. The other two patients were impassible, as if unmoved and uninterested. The four guards around them were indifferent to the signs of distress.

The leader was speaking in a clear voice to the group; he had lifted the bottom of his balaclava to free his mouth from being muffled by the fabric: 'Nothing will happen to you if you cooperate. Relax and answer my questions, and no harm will come to you. A computer in this building has activated some kind of software a week ago. It has now been disconnected from the internet and is not to be found here. We need to find this computer and the person that activated it. Who knows something about it? Speak up now if you have information about either'. The leader was speaking in perfect American English with no foreign accent.

There was no answer. The prisoners were all cowed, and only a few looked around to see if anybody had anything to say. The upset patients kept crying. The leader waited patiently and surveyed the group slowly and intently, for any reactions or expressions that would lead to the information he needed.

'You must know something about it. Just let us know, and we'll be on our way. You will be safe. If you co-operate, you will not be harmed. This is extremely important. OK, who knows something?'

Again silence, disturbed solely by the muffled cries of patient Number 3.

The leader went to Eduards, the last member of Jan Thompson's team, who was the only hostage with his hands tied behind his back. He was lying on his belly, on the outskirts of the group's circle. The leader took him by the arm and helped him to his feet. He then asked him, loudly enough for all to hear: 'What do you know about this special computer? Tell me now'.

Eduards started lamenting, his foreign accent making his cries nearly unintelligible: 'I do not work here. I do not know. I have nothing to do with this'. He was scared because, being an enforcer, he knew a heartless man like himself, when he saw one.

The leader took out his silenced Glock, and, in a smooth sweep, without hesitation, he shot him in the left knee. After a second or two of surprise, Eduards screamed in agony and collapsed. Most of the hostages were struck silent; a few shouted in shock but closed their mouths immediately to avoid being singled out. Number 3, Tim, started wailing.

'Does this refresh your memory?'. The leader was addressing Eduards.

'I do not know anything. Please. Have pity. I do not work here'. Eduards was screaming and contorting himself on the floor in a pool of blood. The leader looked at him blankly and simply shot him in the head, sending pieces of flesh around in with a gory splash. The room became instantly eerily silent, except for Number 3. One of the guards came behind him and hit him on the head with his gun, but to no avail. He hit him again, harder. With blood starting to flow on his face and neck, Number 3 slid from his wheelchair and started wailing even more. The assailant pushed him to the floor with his foot and aimed the gun to his face. The caretaker for patient Number 3, a young African American who had been working there only for several months, pleaded, in a neutral voice, deliberately unaggressive: 'Please leave him alone. He is sick and does not understand. Please'. The thug looked up, uncertain, and looked at the leader for guidance. The leader said something in a foreign language and signaled with his hand to leave the patient alone. He then signaled the young orderly to stand up.

'What is your name, young man?'

'Rishad Jackson'

'Do you know anything about the computer story I talked about?'. Rishad threw a fleeting look at the body of Eduard in its ever expanding pool of blood, and did not hesitate: 'There was a fuss about a computer here in this room last week. I am only a caretaker, but I heard that they found something wrong with it that scared the patients. There were outside technicians working here last Monday, and they took the computer away. It is all I know, I swear'.

'Where was the computer taken? Who was in charge and who knows where it is now?'

'Management. We have no idea down here. I swear'

'Where are the management offices? Come with me and show me'

Rishad pointed at the offices on the gallery above: 'Maybe there are papers in Dr. Wheelan's office'

The leader of the gang pushed Rishad towards the stairs: 'Show me'. He turned to his accomplices and barked something in the same foreign language as before; it sounded like Chinese. Two of his helpers climbed the stairs behind him and disappeared through the mezzanine door, as the leader and Rishad entered Laura's office.

***

I strained to listen to the leader's tirade, and I had managed to understand most of it. So it was, after all, something to do with the computer virus. And against all odds, this intrusion just happened to take place as Jan Thompson was trying to exact his revenge. The situation was distressing because of the personnel taken prisoner. Calling the authorities would turn this into a hostage situation and the potential of a catastrophe. I spoke fluent Cantonese from my mother's side of the family, but I also understood enough Mandarin Chinese from my school days in Hong Kong, to have gathered the general meaning of the orders shouted: 'Prepare to burn down the place, with everybody in it'. They intended to kill everybody and burn the place down, evidently to cover their tracks. That sent a shudder through my spine.

Tom tapped on the screen to show me the image of his father jumping up and down by the side door, calling us out. There was a thin smile on Tom's face, probably the apex of exuberance for him. I checked the hallways around us on the screen, and ran outside quietly. Joshua was waiting with his gun pointed. I pulled him to the shadows and tried to give him the short version.

'Jan and his group are all dead. There are nine armed terrorists inside, Chinese probably. It is all about the computer virus. Their leader is in Laura's office looking for Steve Gold's address, and they intend to kill everyone inside. Two of the guys are preparing to burn the place down, probably pouring gasoline on every floor as we speak'.

As I talked, Laura and Joao had approached. Laura heard the last sentence and cut in: 'Two guys went to the cars in front and pulled out gallons. They went back inside, but they left a few gallons near the car. They are certainly due to come back for them'.

Joshua was decisive as ever: 'No way can we get the cops to solve this; no time and too dangerous. We'll have to do it ourselves. Laura and Joao, go to the entrance and try to neutralize the two guys when they come back. Quietly if possible, but do not take any risks'

I added: 'There is one of their guys in the lobby. He is our own externally-hired security guard but he is working with them. Be careful and take him out too if necessary'

Joshua continued: 'Remember these are killers. You have no choice, but to kill if your life is in danger. Do not hesitate. I'll go in with Olivier, and we'll try to dilute their ranks quietly. If you hear shots, all hell breaks loose and you take out anybody coming out or getting close. OK. Olivier, take me to Tom'.

I opened the door and we ran quietly through the hallway, stopping at corners. Laura and Joao were going through the vegetation towards the main entrance.

I knocked quietly on Tom's hideout door, and the caretaker opened it at once. Joshua went to his son, and caressed his head while looking at the screen. 'Hey Tom. Great work'. There was so much love in this scene that it was heartwarming, in spite of the circumstances.

I looked over both men's shoulders and saw that there was light in Laura's office. There were only two guards left in the big room. We had to hope three could be neutralized by Laura and Joao; and overall, it meant that there were another three roaming around the building.

Joshua explained his plan: 'We have to save the employees first. Give me the silenced gun from Jan's. I'll sneak downstairs, but I'll need a diversion, so that I can shoot the two guards before they can harm anyone. Can you get to the mezzanine door and come in from the outside? That would have them lift their heads'

I thought for a second: 'The only way would be coming from my office, crossing the first floor platform without being seen by the guy in the lobby'

'OK. Do it. And remember, you'll have to beware of the guy in Laura's office'

'OK. It will take me three minutes'

I took Joshua's S&W Magnum 357 and it felt heavy tucked to my belt at the back. I exited the utility room and ran to the side door. I ran in *parkour* mode, climbed the emergency stairs to the roof, and crossed the roof diagonally. I jumped on to the second floor balcony and from there to my office's balcony on the first floor. This had been an exhilarating run; I was totally in the zone. I stopped for a moment to look through the glass. Nothing. I broke a window pane with the big gun, cleaned the shards and opened the French window. I ran lightly to the door, opened carefully and checked the office suite.

I heard the noise of a door opening in the distance. From the slit of the opened door to my office, I could see one of the intruders in black coming in at a leisurely pace, checking around. He was on track to check the office too. I flattened myself on the wall, near the door and waited. He pushed the door open and his hand looked for the light switch. I hit him on the head with my gun, as hard as possible. He fell to his knees with a grunt. We still needed silence and I had no choice but to hit him again, brutally. I hit him twice more on the head with the gun, and I was sickened by the noise. But, sadly, I was becoming used to violence. I grabbed his silenced gun; It was much lighter than the huge cannon Joshua had given me. I frisked him and was glad to find plastic straps to handcuff his hands behind his back. I had no time to gag him; I hoped he would be out long enough. But then I suddenly had a great idea and took out the downed and obviously Asian intruder's balaclava. Of course, I was still barefoot and in my boxers, but my tee-shirt was black. Maybe it could fool the guard downstairs, if he could not see my lower body which view should remain blocked by the banister.

So, I crossed the first floor platform without running, as if I belonged there. Just as I was in the middle of the platform, I looked down discreetly to see if the guard at the reception desk was noticing anything strange. But what I saw, surprisingly, was Joao pointing a gun at me.

***

Joao and Laura had been observing the cars and the main entrance to the building from the closest bush. The fuel jerry cans that had been taken out of the back of the black SUV's were in plain sight beside the cars. Joao told Laura, lying beside him on the grass: 'Give me the stick and cover me in case of trouble. I'll wait for them under the car'. Laura gave him the telescopic baton and took the shotgun. Joao ran for the closest car, and slipped underneath it.

It only took two or three minutes and the two intruders came back with empty gallons. They set them on the floor near the waiting full ones. Joao crawled slowly from under the car on the hidden side, and waited, kneeling. The two men exchanged a few words in Chinese, and one of them took two jerry cans and lifted them with a groan. Joao was taken aback by the harsh smell of gas emanating from those two; they had definitely been pouring it around. As the second man lifted his two full gallons, Joao pounced. He jumped up from behind the car and used the telescopic baton to hit the intruder's head at full power and extension. The telescopic baton is an extremely effective weapon because of the extra energy provided by its extension and its flexibility during the strike. The man came down at once without a word. The first man heard the sound generated by the impact, and started to look back while lowering his cans, but Joao was already on him with his baton. The second would-be pyromaniac was also out cold. Joao gave them both another heavy-handed strike, on the knee this time, to prevent them from moving at all in the coming hours. He then took away their handguns and frisked them. One of them had a stun-gun, and they both carried plastic handcuffs. Joao signaled Laura to come and asked her to handcuff them. He gave her one of the silenced Glocks which he had relieved them from, and kept the other. He ran up the stairs of the main entrance and sprung in with his newly acquired gun extended in front of him. Neither time nor inclination for sophisticated niceties any more. The security guard in league with the bad guys was standing beside the desk, and was caught unawares,- he had thought the place secure. He still went for his gun. 'Hands up. Now!'. But the traitorous guard was either stupid or high on adrenalin: He took out his gun and started to lift it. Joao did not hesitate. He was only a few paces away and fired twice. The guard collapsed from the hit to the chest. Joao caught his collar in stride and pulled him behind his desk to keep him out of sight. He took the guard's gun too to keep it away just in case. He was now carrying three guns.

Joao decided to move back outside, but suddenly heard a door upstairs. He saw a masked figure traversing the first floor platform. He lifted his gun, as the intruder looked down and saw him. This guy was wiser; he lifted his hands in the air at once, surrendering. He then used his right hand to slowly and deliberately pull his ski mask up. It was Olivier!

Chapter 43

Qg4+ Qg6

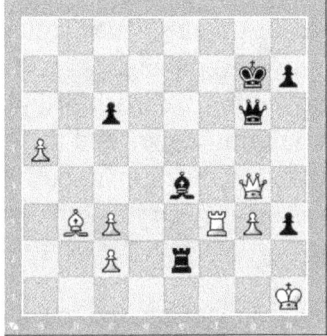

The Prometheus Foundation, Washington County, New York State

That had been a close one! Joao looked up at me with an "I am sorry"- hand gesture, and then signaled that he had neutralized three intruders: he showed me three fingers, and then allowed his index finger to pass in front of his throat in a slicing motion. That was pretty gruesome, but clear. He jogged out of the building as I was putting my ski mask back on. I took a deep breath in and pulled the door open. I went in on the gangway and looked down: I could see the two armed men in black looking up. My heart was beating fast and I was praying that Joshua was in position. And that he would not miss. I had become, unwillingly, a regular hero. Both men were staring up. In spite of my mask, something was bothering their unconscious mind, though they had not identified the problem yet. I lifted my hand in a recognition signal to confuse them a little more, and they were suddenly falling back, hit by Joshua's bullets. I was again surprised by the lack of noise of suppressed handguns: loud pops that are just discernible, but not frightening. With the elimination of the guards, the former prisoners did not stay quiet. Shocked by the surprise and the violence, and seeing Joshua advancing into the room with his gun, some of them started to shout, some in surprise, some others with relief.

I was pulling off my balaclava, again, to make sure Joshua would not shoot me by mistake. He was not yet in my field of vision, when the leader of the attacking party, alerted by the commotion downstairs, stormed out of Laura's office at the end of the gangway with his gun pointing down to the big room. He saw me, and as I had unfortunately removed my ski mask off, turned his gun towards me. My own gun was pointing down, and there was no way I was going to beat this. I started to dive down, but I knew in those microseconds that I was an easy target, and that I had no chance to get out of this alive.

As the leader of the men in black started to squeeze the trigger, I saw from the corner of my eye someone bursting out of Laura's office like a steam-roller crashing into the would-be shooter. It was Rishad, the huge African-American caretaker, pushing the assailant over the banister, as if at football practice. A shot was fired from the man's gun, but it went haywire, as he fell from the gangway on to the concrete floor below. I did not see the impact, but heard it. It was quite a nauseating sound, when you thought it was a human being landing. I was on my belly and looked up at Rishad, with gratitude in my eyes. He nodded and went for the banister, visibly shaken. He was after all, in the healing profession, and not used to throwing people overboard. I got up and went to him, grabbing his shoulder in a thank you gesture and looked down with him. Our aggressor had landed badly, on his belly. He was out, definitely, and Joshua was already over him, kicking his weapon away and checking his pulse. 'He is alive. Quick, guys. We need to take these people out'.

I ran down the stairs, followed by Rishad. Joshua was already addressing the employees: 'You need to be disciplined. Follow this man', he was pointing at me, 'quietly and in an orderly line. Walk fast and in silence. I will be closing the line. We are going out'.

I started walking fast to the quarters' door, my gun pointing forward, and the employees made a queue behind me. I checked the hallway and started leading the way towards the side door. There were still two bad guys around, and we needed to be careful. We reached the side door in a minute, and Joao was waiting outside. Laura was a few yards away, with a shotgun, no less, watching out for surprises. Joao led the gush of employees into the grounds, away from the building.

Joshua shouted: 'Laura, Joao. Stay with them until the authorities get here. Stand guard and protect them. There are two more armed hostiles around. We are going back in'. He signaled me with a head nod.

I followed him back in. He was very careful now, kneeling at each corner and peeping carefully from very low. It would have been stupid to get hurt now, after all that we had been through. We reached Tom's hideout without encountering anyone; the caretaker was waiting for us at the door. He opened even before we knocked, and asked immediately as we were coming in: 'You are taking us out too, -right?'

'In a minute. Do not worry', Joshua answered.

He went to his son at the back of the room and asked him: 'Where are the last two bad guys, Tom?'

Tom did not answer, as usual, but he pointed at the screen to the picture showing the hall of the second floor. There was nobody there, but they could be in the flats lining the hallway. As if on cue, they suddenly appeared on the screen: the last two, unaware of what had befallen their accomplices. They were checking the flats one by one, undoubtedly in search of any remaining witnesses in the house, from top to bottom.

'We need to neutralize them too. They are too dangerous to be left alone. And I would rather take them alive. Any ideas?' Joshua asked me.

'They are a few minutes away from finishing the floor. We could ambush them as they descend the stairs'

'No time to place ourselves. And if they get to the first floor, they'll notice the bodies in the big room'

'And what will they do? If they run away, we could get them at the main door?'

'They look like professionals. They could stick to help the other members of the team… No. We need to take them as they enter the big room. Good for us that they have blacked out cell signals: They are as deaf as we are. Let us get to the room, fast'.

As the caretaker opened the door for us, I told him: 'After this, there will be no more danger, we'll take you out. In the meantime, no noise and keep the door locked'. He nodded gravely, though he looked more confident than at the beginning of the incident. Regular decent people become heroes if needed.

Joshua ran in front of me; there was not much time, but we knew where they were. We entered the big room. The restrained intruders were still at the same spots. One of them was moaning. Joshua hit him on the head and lifted him in a fireman carry. The man was full of blood and it was gruesome. Joshua climbed the stairs, carrying the limp would-be terrorist. He threw him in the middle of the gangway, and then made me lie down on my belly at the end of the hallway, where it was darker. He told me: 'Wait for me to start and just cover me'. Then he ran to Jack's office at the beginning of the gangway. He opened the door, slipped inside and left the door ajar, kneeling in the dark.

We waited patiently. After four or five minutes of silence and immobility, the door opened and the two men accessed the gangway. They immediately noticed the form lying down and ran toward it. As they passed Jack's office door, Joshua stood up and shot the last of the two from close range in the right shoulder. He immediately took another step forward and pointed the gun at the head of the first man in, as he was turning back. I shouted "stop" in Mandarin Chinese to confuse him further. *'Zhe'*. This was a wise man and hence he let the gun fall to the floor as he lifted his hands in the air, surrendering. I was already up and went to take the weapons of both men. The wounded one was writhing on the floor, holding his bloody shoulder and groaning in pain. It is funny how cold-hearted killers do not like pain when it is inflicted back upon them.

'Check them for other weapons and see if they have something we can use to restrain them'. They had no other weapons but, they both had plastic straps. I bound the hands of the first guy behind his back, and of the second one in front. He was shrieking as I was manipulating his wounded arm, and I told him in English: 'Sorry mate. But you came here to kill me, not the other way around'.

Joshua asked me: 'Do you speak Chinese?'

'They speak Mandarin, which I have learned at school. So yes, but pretty basic'

'Can you ask him where the cell phone jammer is?'

I did break my teeth in my attempt to structure the question, but it came back to me surprisingly fast. The prisoner looked at me disdainfully and did not answer. I did not really know if it was because of my poor language skills or because I was the enemy. I was very upset about all that had happened, and in no mood for any more bovine excrement. I put the gun to his head, and told him that we were not the police and would kill him if necessary. One can usually determine from another person's eyes whether he is really mad or just faking it. I do not know if I would have pulled the trigger. Probably not. It was either that, or my Mandarin was improving fast. But he rapidly informed me that the jammer was in one of the cars out front. As I was warming up, I asked him what was it all about and who had sent him?

The first step is always the most difficult. He had already told us about the jammer, so the gates were open and he did not need too much encouragement. He started blabbering so fast that I lost him and I had to tell him to slow down.

After a few moments, I looked at Joshua: 'The jammer is in one of their cars outside. He also told me that they were sent to kill anyone who could have discovered anything about the computers and burn up any evidence related. What we have stumbled upon is top secret and undeniably a spy thing, a foreign military plot. It has nothing to do with the Foundation. I suppose the autistic patients have stumbled on it and triggered it by accident'

'This could be very big. The Feds or the CIA will sort it out. Let us call them up'

'Just a moment, Joshua. I think I have got the full picture and I have an idea. Bear with me for a moment, please'

'I am listening, but hurry. We are in a house full of cadavers and we have to call that in. And we do not know for sure, whether there are any more hostiles around'.

'Just give me five minutes with you and Tom, and then we go out and call the authorities'.

Chapter 44

Qd7+ Kh6

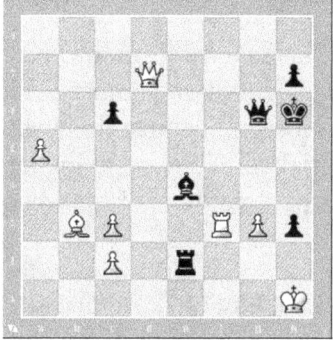

Riga Suburbs, Latvia

Aivars Bartulis had been snappy all morning. He was sitting in his home office, waiting for a call. The call had not been forthcoming, yet, and this was obviously trying his patience. The maid was surprised that the huge breakfast she brought on a tray had been left virtually untouched. That never happened with her boss. Aivars had barked at her when she enquired whether he had finished.

Aivars had tried to take his mind off things with a game of chess against his computer. Even that did not work. He, who during his incarceration in a soviet prison, had played-out entire games in his mind taking the role of both black and white, could not concentrate on the game in front of him. Of course, the game reminded him of Van Dijk and the severe loss of face suffered because of him. Hopefully, his honor would be avenged and restored soon; Jan's phone call should come in any minute.

Aivars stood up, incapable of sitting idly. He should get something to eat anyway. As he reached the door, he heard a ping from his desktop computer. Curious, he came back to the desk. That could not be Jan; Jan was supposed to call. He checked the screen: It was an email to his private account. Strangely, it was from himself. Having the best of firewalls and virus detection software, he was not worried and, his curiosity aroused, he clicked the message open. It read: ' Qg2# , CHECKMATE! Olivier Van Dijk'.

Aivars could not unglue his eyes from the screen. He was reddening with rage, fulminating. He took the empty Rosenthal tea cup from his desk and threw it violently against the wall. "Pis sudoo",- *fuck shit* in Latvian-, he shrieked. He was having an apoplexy. He had to sit down; his rage, coupled with his obesity had him feel nauseous. His breath became labored.

Aivars thought that the failure of Jan's mission and Olivier's taunting were his biggest problems right now. How wrong was he! That assertion was soon to be proven quite false.

***

Colonel Jeung was still in his small office despite the late hour, under the white light of old fashioned fluorescents. There was so much to do in the new field of cyber warfare, and so many things to coordinate around the super-secret *Peng* project. The phone rang. At this hour, it could only mean bad news. It was Corporal Ma, again the bearer of bad news: 'Colonel, we had another spontaneous activation of a *Peng* unit, this time in Riga, Latvia'.

Jeung swore quietly. Not again. He did not need this problem, on top of everything else. The mole in the US was yet to report, and now they already received another case? He hoped there was nothing wrong with the design that could be causing this. All the re-testing done since the first instance pointed at an all-clear and that the design was in fact operating properly as planned. Of course, as Jeung knew too well, some of the best engineers on this project had been brutally and needlessly murdered...

'Do we have an asset available in Latvia, Ma?'

'No, Colonel. I already checked. We have only the cultural attaché at the consulate'

'We have to send a team then, fast. Where is the closest'

'It would be from Ukraine I suppose, Colonel. But I'll have to check'

'Do it. This is the highest priority, on my authority. No inquiries this time. In, out destroy computers and any evidence, and terminate anyone in the vicinity'

'And General Wong, Colonel?'. Ma wanted as much access to the General as possible, obviously to advance his career. He had no idea this could actually work against him.

'I'll inform him myself. Go now and set it up. I want everything done by tomorrow night'.

Then Jeung put the receiver down abruptly. He was not really relishing the thought of telling Wong. He was praying that this all-important project he had based his career on was not spinning out of control.

***

I was sitting in the big room on one of the couches, with my arm around Laura's shoulders. I was still in my dirty and bloody night clothes. Joshua had taken me to Tom after hearing my plan, and we asked Tom to remotely activate the hardware virus in by Aivars' computer by using a simple email. Joshua was amused by the cunningness of my idea. I had in my memory the email address from George's bank data, which Aivars provided himself. It had taken silent Tom the whole of seven minutes, but seemingly no undue hardship, to adapt the activation key and send it out. I could not resist the chance to finish my chess match with Aivars and rub his nose in it. It was stupid of me to tease the lion, but I expected him to be out of commission very soon, by a team like the one who had just visited the Foundation.

Having completed that, we had taken Tom and his caretaker outside and looked for the cell phone jammer in the cars. Once switched off, Laura called the Feds, and Joshua called his friend David Gold for his CIA contacts, and to make sure the computer parts were secure. We led all the employees back inside, to rest in the big room. Rishad came to help me group the wounded and to gather the neutralized intruders in the far corner of the room. It had been hard work. We left the corpses in place for the feds to sort out. Joao was not helping us; he went to look for Zeca on the entrance's look-out. He met Rui at the gate, who had just arrived from Manhattan with two more students of his, and they went out to look for Zeca together. When they found his lifeless body near his motorcycle, they were first crushed, and then quickly thirsty for vengeance. Luckily for the surviving intruders, the local police showed up at the right time and prevented what would have been a vicious lynching, which I do not think I could have prevented. The scene was heartbreaking, and I was crying with them as I was helping the cops to restrain them.

That was three hours ago, and everything had calmed down since. Everyone was exhausted, and the FBI agents, who had arrived *en masse*, were interviewing, cataloging and photographing to their hearts' content. It was already daylight, and all signs were pointing to another long day. Too many weapons and corpses. Laura had used her FBI connections to smoothen things out, and then had fallen asleep on my shoulder, as I was caressing her matted hair.

I am not a religious man, at least not in the context of organized religion, but I was praying really hard that this was the end of all the turmoil my life had been thrown into of late. No more embezzlement, no more mafia bosses, no more Chinese spies. I wanted to rebuild my life, mourn my friends, enjoy my new found love and repair the trouble my carelessness had caused as best as I could.

Chapter 45

Bf7 Bxf3

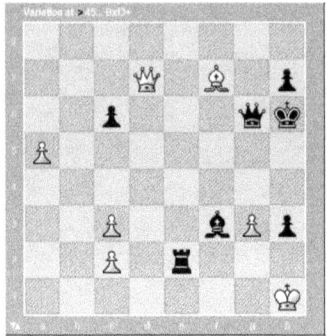

The Baltic Times

Leading businessman Aivars Bartulis and six household members die in fire that completely destroys the tycoon's luxury villa outside Riga

Aivars Bertulis was a well-known businessman with close political ties to the Popular Front party, the second biggest in the Saiema. He was close to oligarch Valdis Berzins and rumored to be a heavy contributor to his political movement, while staying behind the scenes. Having been in Soviet jails at a young age for his nationalistic leanings, he was rumored to have met there members of the Haritonov gangs and kept some underworld connections. But the fire that killed him, his wife of thirty five years and another five employees, has been ruled as the result of an accidental nocturnal electric failure. The palatial villa was burnt to the ground and there were no survivors. It took the fire department six hours to control the remaining blaze.

The Catholic funeral of Mr. and Mrs. Bartulis will take place in St Catherine Church, next Friday, in a private ceremony. They left no children behind.

Chapter 46

Kg1 Qxg3+

The White House, Washington D.C.

Four months have elapsed since the fateful night of the attack on the Foundation. What ensued proved to be rough and uncertain times. Weeks of investigations had finally cleared the entangled picture of two gangs attacking us at the same time. All people involved were asked to sign National Security confidentiality papers for the Chinese angle, as soon as the scope of the conspiracy became clear. Tom, chaperoned by his fantastic dad, had been helping the cyber warfare experts to sort out the triggering and neutralizing of the Chinese-implanted hardware virus. He was clearly enjoying his genius status and the acknowledgement of his talents.

After recovering from our wounds, Laura and I started to work on setting up our new hedge fund/care facility. My deal with the authorities was progressing slowly through the layers of bureaucracy, helped by all kinds of Feds and spooks who felt they owed us some kind of gratitude.

I was sitting, with Laura at my side, in a small room on the ground floor of the White House, in Washington DC. Yes, this White House! I had dressed up for the occasion, of course, black tie and all. I was especially proud, though, of conservatively dressed up, yet fabulous Laura, at my arm. There were about thirty people sitting with us on the red velvet chairs in front of the podium, and it had taken us the better part of an hour to go through security and reach our seats. We did not know most of the people sitting with us, all working in different areas of Homeland Security.

The President was announced by the MC, and we all promptly stood up for the most powerful man in the world. The president was a busy man, but he knew how to make you feel as though he was there just for you. From the podium, he made a short speech about the silent warriors of America who must stay in the shadows and whose contribution to America's security cannot be made public. It was a pity that in the difficult world we lived in, such an award ceremony had to be kept secret and the three recipients of the Presidential Medal of Freedom could not tell the world of their exceptional contribution to Peace, Freedom and Security.

I have always been very skeptic of politician's blabber and use of clichés, but there is something to be said about the pomp and décor. I really felt awed by the occasion and part of something bigger than myself, at this particular moment in time.

After his short speech, the President pinned in turn the most prestigious of all American Medals on the lapel of two middle-aged men from the CIA for undisclosed contributions to the safeguard of our way of life.

The President then turned to Tom, nearly unrecognizable in his suit and tie. Joshua was standing beside him, his eyes wet with emotion. Tom was aloof, like always, as if uninterested, but standing straight as a rod and doing exactly as told during the rehearsals of the ceremony. I looked at them and felt very emotional. Turning my head to check on Laura, I saw tears on her cheeks. The president's address sounded even more personal and from the heart than before. Of course, this was a politician's dream, to be able to talk about a special needs-person, son of a distinguished soldier, having done such great service to his country. Tom was really a very special boy, and Joshua a very special father and a righteous human being. I knew he had invited Tom's mother, who had abandoned them when Tom was very young, to the ceremony. She was sitting a few chairs away from us, but kept to herself, probably eaten away by shame. But to her credit, she still had turned up.

When the President pinned the medal on Tom's lapel, I could swear that I saw a tiny smile on his Tom's lips. I looked at Joshua to check if he had seen it. He probably had not, his vision blurred by the tears of joy and pride flowing down to his cheeks.

Epilogue

Kf1 Qg2#

Military Intelligence HQ, Guangzhou, People's Republic of China

Colonel Jeung knocked on the door, and waited for an answer, before coming in. He signaled the two soldiers accompanying him to stay outside, and closed the door.

He stood before General Wong's desk silently, staring at him intently.

'Yes, Colonel. Do what you have to do'

'I will have to ask you to come with me, General. But, before, I want to tell you how much I respect you and your work. I did not always agree with all your methods, but I think you are a real patriot driven by his principles'

'So you think it is about my methods, Colonel? You are still that naïve? It is all about plausible deniability. It is about a scapegoat to appease the Americans. Do you understand? The leaders of this country are still apologetic to the Americans. The US can sell arms to Taiwan, but we have to deny trying to prepare our own defense?'

'General, the rightful leaders of this country may have long-term strategic objectives that are served by acknowledging *'Peng'* as a rogue operation of reactionary elements in our Defense Establishment. *'Peng'* is dead either way, so they have to make the best possible use of the situation'

'This is no strategy, Colonel. They want more iPhones and Hollywood movies to appease the people, more Gucci stores in Beijing and Shanghai to flaunt the country's riches. They have lost their sense of purpose. Sun-Tzu once wrote: -Strategy without tactics is the slowest route to victory. Tactics without strategy is the noise before defeat-'.

The ever-quoting Wong.

'I am sorry it must end this way, Sir, but I need you to come with me. I also need your side arm please'

'You are afraid that I'll commit suicide? Do not worry Jeung; that is the way of the cowards. I know they are going to execute me anyway. And then run to the Americans'

General Wong stood up, and grimaced at his bad back. He took out his side arm, a vintage TT33 from Norinco. Jeung was slightly apprehensive until Wong laid it on the desk. He then looked straight at Jeung, with a thin and bitter smile. 'I have been on the phone with the Vice-Premier a few minutes ago. We served together a long time ago. He was a better politician than me. Do you know what he told me at the end of this conversation?'

Jeung shook his head to indicate he did not.

'That three people can keep a secret if two are dead. Isn't it ironic?'

Epilogue 2

"Laura dear, I'll be staying at my flat tonight. Too late for the drive up. See you tomorrow. Love you."

His message recorded, Olivier exited his 4x4, and collected his gym bag from the back. He strolled, whistling, towards the parking elevator. He had a spring in his step, in spite of his pulled calf muscle. Love had that effect, and his life had definitely taken a turn to the better. He was still playing stupid young men sports, but he had matured a lot. He was even considering proposing to Laura. In fact, it was more the how and when already. Life was good. What could go wrong?

As the elevator door closed behind him, a parking attendant with an out-of-place cap came out of the shadows. His eyes fixed on the elevator door, the attendant took out a deck of playing cards and started to shuffle. He stopped, took the uppermost card and turned it up.

THE END